FISTFUL OF DYNAMITE

The ranger felt a chill run up his back, and he dropped flat. "Cover up!"

He heard a sharp metallic click . . . *Oh, God!*

The explosion ripped high and wide.

Sam felt the flat earth beneath his chest rumble and jar, as it seemed to rise for a moment, then crash down hard. He shot a glance up and saw parts of a man, rock, and earth swirl upward in the air and fall toward him. Sam covered his head with his forearms.

Even in the cloud of dust and debris as the explosion still resounded, Ernesto called out, "When *I* set a trap, it lasts forever."

The Ranger coughed and fanned the dust with his sombrero. Now, this he hadn't counted on.

BADLANDS

‹———◄❖►———›

Ralph Cotton

Ⓢ
A SIGNET BOOK

Signet
Published by the Penguin Group
Penguin Putnam Inc., 375 Hudson Street,
New York, New York 10014, U.S.A.
Penguin Books Ltd, 27 Wrights Lane,
London W8 5TZ, England
Penguin Books Australia Ltd,
Ringwood, Victoria, Australia
Penguin Books Canada Ltd, 10 Alcorn Avenue,
Toronto, Ontario, Canada M4V 3B2
Penguin Books (N.Z.) Ltd, 182–190 Wairau Road,
Auckland 10, New Zealand

Penguin Books Ltd, Registered Offices:
Harmondsworth, Middlesex, England

First published by Signet, an imprint of Dutton NAL,
a member of Penguin Putnam Inc.

First Printing, October, 1998
10 9 8 7 6 5 4 3 2 1

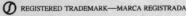

Printed in the United States of America

For Mary Lynn . . . *of course*

Part 1

Chapter 1

The ranger stood in the doorway of the long stone building and looked out across the prison yard. Outside, the weather lay dry-hot with no breeze stirring. Scorched brown dust stood in the air. He could smell the heat, the smell of heated wood and heated metal and oil, the arid smell of adobe blocks, and above all else the smell of man.

The smell of man was most distinctive. . . .

His Christian name was Sam Burrack, but everybody called him "the ranger." Over the years his reputation as a ranger had far overshadowed all other aspects and possibilities of his life. Somewhere along the way, his badge and title had moved in between him and the world around him, like an eclipse, gradually, until Sam Burrack the man had all but disappeared. In his place stood the badge—behind the badge stood the ranger.

Well, so be it . . .

He ran a hand across his wet forehead beneath the brim of his gray sombrero, then wiped sweat on his trouser leg. In an uncertain world, not many men could say they'd found their life's work early on, as he had. To him, law work was more than a job, it was a calling. As surely as a man of high spiritual conviction felt called to the pulpit, he, like any lawman of any moral substance was *called* to deliver the law . . . chapter and verse.

In most cases he was called upon to deliver it without benefit of judge or jury. So he did, to the best of his ability.

It must've been a hundred and ten degrees inside the stone walls of the prison, and he'd been waiting over an hour for a guard to come and escort him back to the holding cells. While the ranger waited, he leaned against the door frame, watching three men work on the big wooden gallows across the dusty prison yard. Their shadows lay long and thin behind them in the evening sun. The longer shadow of the gallows mantled their every move.

The workers' shirts clung to their backs, streaked dark with sweat. He noticed when one of them picked up the coiled rope and climbed the steps with it; instead of hefting the entire rope up on his shoulder, he held the noose out arm's length from himself as if to keep death from rubbing off on him.

Did he think hanging was a disease he might catch? The ranger broke into a thin smile. On his way into the prison he had passed through a small gathering of people who'd come to protest the brutality of hanging a man. An old priest he'd seen many times in his travels across the badlands stood holding a placard sign that read: HANGING IS NOT THE CURE. Yet in reading the sign, the ranger had noted that nowhere on it had there been any mention of what that cure might be. Behind the old priest, a young priest had stood leading the people in prayer.

Thinking about it now, maybe crime was a disease . . . maybe someday there would be a serum to burn the evil out of man. But until that time . . .

He adjusted the big pistol on his hip, watching one of the workmen move across the scaffold, stepping wide of the trapdoor, although the door was firmly secured with no chance of falling open. Most people were superstitious about death, and the ranger found that interesting. But he knew there were no dark spirits lurking within the fibers of the rope or the grain of the wood.

Rope and board had started out as a product of the earth, a product further hewed and cultivated by the initiative of man, whereas a rope might be cut from a longer stock and much of it going to the purpose of staying a dragline or lifting a load. The scaffold boards came from timber, cut and milled for many purposes. Only by circumstance had it come to its present use.

The ranger ran a hand across the deep scar on his weathered cheek and pressed his bandanna against the sweat running down his neck. Neither rope nor wooden plank wished man harm, he thought, yet on the coming morning these things would interact one within the other in the manner of man's fashion; and with the law of gravity and the weight of flesh and bone turned to it, these things would snap a life from the face of this earth in far less time than it took God to create it. He was not superstitious.

There were no dark mysteries of mind or spirit to which he lent his thoughts. He accepted that man was free to choose, and should wrong choices someday lead a man to stare his last through a hangman's noose . . . so be it. Man had no right to blame God or the devil—it was all man's doing.

He had no sympathy for Ernesto Caslado, and gave no thought to what might have brought the man here. How the man might've been treated as a child, how badly life had treated him since, or what particulars might have come about and brought him to becoming such a foul piece of work. These things made no difference to the ranger.

At one time Ernesto Caslado had been a leader of his people, a man to whom the peasants looked for justice and hope. But that had been a long time ago. Now Caslado was nothing more than a bandit in the guise of a revolutionist, a murderer in the pretense of a freedom fighter, a taker of things, a robber of banks, and a killer of man, and a . . .

Well, he thought, if there was anything low and evil that Caslado hadn't done, he didn't want to imagine what it might be. Come tomorrow morning when the first thin reef of sunlight sparkled on the horizon, Ernest Caslado was going to swing . . . from rope and wood. Good enough.

When the guard came, with a flat expression he'd asked the ranger if it was hot enough for him. But the ranger only looked at him through narrowed eyes until the man turned his head and motioned for the ranger to follow him back through a long, dark corridor. They walked along the corridor, where a row of hands lay out through steel-barred doors like small sprouts of human flesh grown from within the stone itself, until they passed each cell in turn and saw above the hands the caged and hollow eyes staring out at them.

"It's that ranger," one voice said as they passed, and the ranger heard a spitting sound, but did not look around. A hand reached out and swiped at his arm, but he walked past it.

Nearing another cell, a face pressed against the steel bars and said in a growl, "Let *me* have at him."

"Get back, Hawk," the guard said, banging his bat against the bars as he passed. He chuckled under his breath and said to the ranger, "Hawkins would love to kill you. Said you bent an iron skillet across his face." As the guard looked back over his shoulder at the ranger, the ranger noticed the dark pits in his sweaty face, as if the man had slept face-down in a pile of gravel. "How many more of these bummers are waiting to hang because they met up with you, ranger?"

"If they meet up with *me*, they usually don't end up *here*," the ranger said. "I ruined a good skillet on Hawkins to keep from wasting a bullet. My mistake."

"I bet." They'd stopped outside the second to the last cell

in the corridor, and the ranger saw a small, faded tattoo of a blue star on the guard's neck as the guard turned to him. The guard looked him up and down with a dark smile, his swarthy face damp, oily, and shiny with sweat. "You get ten minutes, ranger. Stay back from them bars," he added; and he turned and walked away, his shirt clinging wet across his broad shoulders.

The ranger gazed into the far corner of the cell and saw the narrowed eyes lift out of the darkness toward him. "Ernie Caslado, I came to talk to you. Come on out here where I can see your face."

"Go to hell, ranger." The voice came low and level, the eyes staying steady on him. "Tomorrow I hang. I will answer to God. But today I answer to no one. Especially to a *pig* like you."

The ranger heard a spitting sound. He pushed his gray sombrero up with a tip of his finger, let out a breath, and ran his fingers down into his shirt pocket. "You can't blame me for where you're at, Ernie. You know if I'd run into you first, I'd have shot you down and saved you six months of living in this sweatbox."

"What? You would not have hit me with a skillet?"

"Naw, skillets cost too much, as it turns out." He paused, then added, "What do you say, Ernie? Gonna come over here and talk like a man? What have you got to lose?"

A low laugh came from the darkness, and the ranger heard a chain clink as the man stood up from against the wall and moved forward. "My name is not Ernie, it is *Ernesto* . . . at least show that much respect."

"I've got no respect for ya, *Ernie*. But I have got some tobacco here." He pulled out a bag of fixings and held them close to the bars.

Ernesto Caslado stopped a few inches from the bars and fixed his dark eyes on the ranger's. The ranger jiggled the bag until Caslado reached out the length of his chains, snatched it, and pulled it back, his eyes never wavering from the ranger's.

"Late tonight while the others sleep," Caslado said, as he loosened the drawstring on the bag, "they will take me to the bathhouse and let me take a bath." He glanced down, struck out a leaf of paper, and began tapping tobacco into it. "So tomorrow I will be clean and cool when they hang me."

The ranger smiled slightly. "Always something to be thankful for, I reckon."

Caslado just stared at him, rolled the paper, licked it, ran it in and out of his mouth, and let it hang from his lips beneath his thick dark mustache. "You did not come to bring me tobacco, ranger." He leaned close to the bars. "Like all the others, you come to find out about the money, eh?" He gave a tight smile, looked at the bag of tobacco in his hand, squeezed it, then looked back at the ranger. "I hate you, as I hate all lawmen . . . but I do not hate you enough to tell you where the money is hidden."

What a strange thing to say. . . . The ranger looked at him for a moment, then said, "I don't care about the train money, Ernie." He struck a match, held it between the bars, and watched it glow on the hard lines of the condemned man's face. "Money comes and goes. I reckon the railroad can stand the loss." Then he shook out the match and dropped it to the floor.

"Oh?" The question still stood in Caslado's eyes as he blew a gray stream of smoke. "You are not interested in finding what so many others have failed to find?"

"No, not in the least. I came to ask you about the killing at Cold Creek. I figure you were innocent of those two, and I need to get it clear in my mind, before you take the big drop in the morning."

Caslado took a deep draw and blew it out, studying the ranger's eyes. "*Sí*, you are right, ranger. I am innocent of those two. But the timing was right . . . so I must carry the blame." He shrugged and let go a breath of smoke. "What is the difference?"

"The difference is, if you didn't do it, somebody's getting away with murdering that poor girl and her father. I owe them the decency of setting things right."

"You knew these people?" Caslado's eyes searched his through the bars, behind a long stream of smoke.

"No." The ranger shook his head. "But something tells me you did. Something tells me there were things you knew and wouldn't tell. I want to know why you confessed so quick, didn't try to deny it like you did everything else."

The ranger watched something stir across Caslado's dark eyes for a second; but in another second it was gone, and the man drew deep and let the smoke go as he glanced away. "No. There is nothing to tell you. She is dead. I will hang. There is nothing more to say."

The ranger noted that he had said "she"—not her and her father—only "she." He started to make mention of it, but decided to wait, see what else might slip out without Caslado noticing it. He took a broken rowel of a spur from his shirt pocket and held it closed in his hand for a moment as he said, "It was a shame about that young woman." His eyes watched Caslado's. "She was with child, you know."

The ranger saw a tendon tighten in Caslado's throat, saw him almost sway and swallow hard. But then he caught himself, and looking away, he said in words as hard as stone, "So? These are the way things go for everyone on this earth. Everybody dies."

Even in the harshness of his words, the ranger caught the slightest tremble in Caslado's voice, and he moved to one side to see his eyes, not letting him look away. "But still, Ernie . . . a little baby?" His voice dropped low and soft. "Just think, some small innocent thing that never got the chance to breathe a breath of air, never got to taste its mama's milk, never got to—"

"What do you want from me?" Caslado hissed, spinning back to him, grasping the bars, the fire falling from the cigarette. "I told you I did not kill them! I will die for it! What more do you want? How do I know who killed her? What can I tell you?"

Again he only mentioned "her," the ranger thought, seeing the fleck of spit on his lips, his knuckles tight around the bars, his eyes tortured and wide. *It's time* . . . He brought his hand up and opened it and let the broken rowel lay on his palm only inches from Caslado's face. "You can tell me who wore this spur, Ernie. Tell me *this,* and I'll be on my way."

There was no breath in the man for a moment, and the ranger stood in silence, watching dark recognition move in his eyes. Then Ernesto gathered himself and swallowed again and said, "This . . . this thing. How did you come upon it?"

"Well, Ernie," the ranger said, bouncing the broken rowel on his palm as he talked, still watching those dark eyes, knowing he was touching raw nerves in there somewhere. "I had an old undertaker dig it out of the woman's face before he cleaned her up to bury her. You see—" He bounced the rowel some more, turning it over and over on his palm. "Whoever killed her, didn't just shoot her right away. No, sir. He took his time . . . tortured her, stomped her face in, gashed her with his spurs. Just imagine—her pleading, begging for her life."

He snapped his hand shut over the rowel, Caslado still staring at it. "Now, Ernie, whatever we might both think of one another, I know we both agree that whoever did this has no right to go on living. And since you're gonna be busy dancing with the angels come morning, I figure the only way to set things right for that poor woman and her baby is to tell me who this belonged to."

He opened his hand again, slowly, knowing he'd get what he came for, knowing that what he'd thought was right—

Caslado knew something—and knowing what he'd just told Caslado was true—the ranger was the only one who could set things right. Now all he needed was a name, and that name was coming. He knew it.

But Caslado whispered under his tight breath. "I will kill—" Then he stopped short, caught himself, and turned his wrath on the ranger. *"—You! I will kill you!"* He snatched at the ranger through the bars, his hands stopping against the bite of steel around his wrists.

The ranger stepped back and just stared at him. He wasn't buying it . . . whatever Caslado was trying to pull. Something had almost slipped out . . . a name? Maybe. But now Caslado was turning the heat on him, trying to get past something that raged in his mind, trying not to give it up. From the end of the corridor the big sweaty guard came running.

"Tell me, Ernie, quick!" The ranger pushed hard now, wanting to squeeze it out of him, choke it out of him if he had to. "It's the only way! Can't you see that, Ernie? Who wore this spur?"

"Here now! That's enough!" The guard ran in between the ranger and the bars, his keys and billy bat hanging within inches of Caslado's hands. The ranger saw it, and started to say something; but before he could, the guard turned, facing Caslado. "Get back now, before I beat your teeth in."

Caslado hesitated for a second, staring past the guard into the ranger's eyes. The guard's hand went to the billy bat at his waist, but stopped there, no tension there, no whitened knuckles. "Get back, *now*!" the guard shouted, his hand still not drawing the bat.

"*Sí*, I will move back." Ernesto Caslado moved back an inch, then another, then he took a deep breath and pitched the tobacco bag through the bars to the ranger. "But soon, ranger, someday—"

"I mean *shut up*, Caslado!" Now the guard drew the bat

and banged it against the bars, drowning out Caslado until he moved back into the darkness and out of sight.

"Come on, ranger," the guard said, turning to him, gesturing the billy bat toward the corridor. Voices jeered and shouted, and he banged his bat against the bars, barely missing the dirty clawing hands that reached toward them as the two of them walked along.

"You said ten minutes," the ranger said above the hoots and curses from within the cells.

"Well, it turned out to be a short ten minutes," the guard called back over his shoulder. "I've got better things to do than fool with you all evening."

When they stepped through the steel door and the guard swung it shut behind them, the ranger said, "Caslado has information I need."

"Then you'll just have to whistle for it. You're through here, ranger."

The ranger started to say something else, but thought better of it, took a deep breath, and let it out. "All right then. I'm through . . . there's no point in arguing with you. It's your job, right?" He offered a thin smile.

"That's right." The guard also let out a tight breath and ran his fingers back through his sweaty hair. "Didn't mean to get sharp with you, ranger. Seems like everybody gets a little loco the night before a hanging. Tension, I guess."

"Yeah, I know." The ranger lifted his sombrero, ran a hand back across his hair, and put the hat back on. "I suppose you've taken precautions against his men coming and busting him out?"

"Aw yeah." The guard swung a hand toward the front of the prison. "We've got crack troops out there . . . not that we'll need them though. These convicts are all the same before they die. They make threats . . . their gang's always on its way . . . you'll never hang *them*."

The ranger smiled. "Is that right?"

"Yep, they all do it."

"That's funny," the ranger said, still smiling. "Ernie Caslado never said a thing like that."

"Oh?" The guard shrugged. "Well, maybe he's got it all out of his system."

"Yeah, maybe that's it." The ranger bounced the bag of tobacco on his palm, looking at it, wondering why that small bag felt so strange to him now. Then he shoved it down in his shirt pocket, tipped his hat, and walked out into the evening heat. When he'd ridden his white Spanish barb horse through the front gates and heard the big gates swing shut behind him, he rode past four young soldiers who lounged against a wagon out of the heat.

He looked down at the soldiers, shook his head, and rode over to the old priest who came walking toward him. The younger priest stood back, the hood of his faded brown frock partially covering his somber face.

"I know you are not here to support us, ranger," the old priest said, "but all the same, it is good to see you."

The ranger smiled down into the weathered face. "It's good to see you too, padre. Even under the circumstances." He nodded toward the young priest and the small gathering of people near the prison gate. "Looks like you've gained some followers. Think they'd be here if it was one of their loved ones Ernesto Caslado killed?"

"No, I don't think so," the priest said, "but we must take whatever kindness of spirit is at hand, and hope that someday it reaches all our hearts."

The ranger tipped his gray sombrero. "I certainly can't argue that." He then rode on through the small community of weather-bleached shacks and adobes that stood like supplicants before the stone prison walls. He rode on, southward, until the looming prison with its smell of sweat and its clinking of metal lay a few miles behind him.

He thought of Caslado and of the look on the man's face

when he'd seen the broken rowel. He thought of the brutal-
ized bodies he'd seen at Cold Creek—the young woman, her
father. The woman may or may not have known that her father earned his living dealing guns back and forth across the
border. But that didn't matter. She hadn't deserved to die
that way, nor had the unborn child inside her.

As he rode and thought about these things, at the end of
each thought he pictured the bag of loose tobacco, the way
Caslado had pitched it back to him through the steel bars.
Something wasn't right about that . . . what was it? Something he'd seen? Something he'd felt? It gnawed at him.

At a point where the trail forked upward into a stretch of
buttes on his left, the ranger stopped his white barb horse,
turned it around on the trail, and looked back, as if being
summoned to do so by some dreaded voice in the still air behind him. In the far distance, beyond the prison, dwarfing
the stone walls and all lesser things beneath it, he saw the
broken rise of the badlands stretched east to west, upward on
the roll of the earth to the far end of vision.

He settled his horse and sat there, his riding duster wet
with sweat and heavy across his shoulders. And he let go of
a long breath, feeling small as he looked back. He ran a
gloved hand along the barb's damp withers—man and horse
alone there, in the face of this harsh and desolate land.

Something *had* spoken to him from within the upreach of
that distant rocky land and wavering heat. It was the silent,
familiar ring of the badlands, a voice heard only by his
peaked senses. But he listened closely to that silence, scanning those purple faraway ridges. If he'd learned one thing
and nothing more about the badlands, he'd learned to pay attention when something about it stirred inside him.

What he felt now, gazing deep through the distant sheen
of dust, into that lofty netherworld, was a promise of unrest—a break in the natural rhythm of the land and in the ca-
dence of all its creatures, large and small. Were it not for the

clearness of the evening sky he would have guessed that a storm swirled and boiled, up there somewhere above the scalloped ridges to the north. But in the absence of any dark, looming clouds, he could suppose only one other thing. *Trouble*—trouble now, or trouble soon to come. Beneath him, the white barb turned restless and stepped high-hoofed, circling and pitching its head.

"Easy now, Black-eye." He checked the horse down and studied once more the distant upthrust of endless rock, where within its craggy breastwork dark slices of evening shadow stood slantwise against falling light like black holes in the sky. Along the rims of deep, winding canyons where shadows reached but had not yet touched, sunlight glistened the color of blue silk and fire.

He raised a hand to the scar on his cheek, shook his head, and turned the horse forward again, riding on, restless now himself from whatever he'd just heard and felt in the sweep of silence. What was it? He did not know.

But he knew it was trouble, and he knew this restlessness would stay with him. The badlands had just spoken. He was forewarned. It was now up to him, to wait, to watch, to be prepared—to keep his restlessness in check until the trouble came and passed. "Take us up, Black-eye," he said, stepping the horse upward, quarterwise onto the loose sandy trail.

His partner, Maria, stood watching as he rode into their camp, and when she'd spoken to him and asked how things had gone for him at the prison, he'd only nodded and raised a hand in reply. *So* . . . It hadn't gone well for him, she'd thought, moving back to the low fire where she stirred the small pot of beans, busying herself until whatever was on his mind had settled itself into place.

He had stepped down from his stirrups, then loosened the cinch, lifted the saddle, and laid it on the ground. Maria watched him as he looked the horse over. The big white horse with its black-circled eye shifted its weight as the ranger moved from leg to leg, lifting each hoof in turn, picking them, inspecting them.

There was urgency in the ranger's touch. Maria saw it; the horse felt it. When the animal sawed its head up and down and shook out its damp mane, the ranger said, "Be still, Black-eye," and kept about his task until his hands and mind established the horse's fitness. Then he stepped forward, lifted the bridle, and dropped the bit from the horse's mouth. Cupping its chin in his hand, he raised its lip and leaned closer, looking across its teeth and gums.

"Has the horse faltered? Is he ill?" Maria called out to him from beside the fire as he wiped his hands together and leaned down to his saddlebags on the ground.

"No . . . just checking him out," he said. He tossed a nod toward the distant badlands. "Living up there, a man's only as fit as the horse beneath him."

Living out here . . . ? She cocked her head slightly, watching him go through his saddlebags, taking note, she thought, of his ammunition, his personal supplies. "But we do not *live* up there anymore," she said. She paused for a second, then added, "Do we?"

"You never know," he said, without looking up.

"Oh, I see." She folded her arms across her breast and nodded to herself. *Trouble? Yes . : .* Was it something he'd learned at the prison? No, she didn't think so, or at least this was not the feeling she got from him. Had he learned anything at all regarding the killings at Cold Creek, he would have spoken of it as soon as he rode in. She looked around at the camp they'd set up the day before—a long way back from the prison, "away from the smell of it," he'd said.

She sighed, moved near her horse, picked up a small bag, and walked over to him with it hanging from her hand. "Here," she said, dropping the feed bag beside him as he took stock of his trappings, "you will feed him a little extra tonight?"

He looked up at her, but only for a second. "I think so," he said.

And that night at the campsite atop the sandstone butte overlooking the dark desert floor, she watched him sip a cup of Duttwieller's tea beside the low fire, restless, ill at ease, still bouncing the small bag of loose tobacco in the palm of his hand. Beside him, she dropped her saddle on the ground and rolled out her blanket. "Why don't you open the bag and roll yourself one? Perhaps it will calm your mind . . . or at least loosen your tongue." In the past year since she'd been with him, she'd never seen him this pensive.

He glanced at her, then back into the fire. "I am calm," he said, "calm enough anyway."

"*Sí*, of course you are." She'd settled down onto her blanket, took off her boots, then reached over and caught the pouch of tobacco as he bounced it and studied it in the glow of firelight. "Do you want to talk about this now?"

"There's nothing to talk about . . . just a feeling I got, riding back here."

"Not something to do with Ernesto Caslado?" She watched his eyes reflect the low dancing flames.

"Maybe, maybe not. Could be something brewing in the badlands. I can't say yet." He ran a hand down the long scar on his cheek, then around beneath his shirt collar. He rubbed his neck. "Things didn't go the way I thought they would with Caslado. He should have told me what I wanted to know."

"So, you were wrong. You tried. It didn't work." She shrugged and looked at the bag of tobacco. "Tomorrow he will hang. Now you must forget about it. Come morning, we will ride out of here, back to the ranger station where the weather is cooler."

"He should've told me something," the ranger said; and he reached over and took the bag back from her and turned it in his hand, studying it once more. "It doesn't add up. He knows who killed that woman and her father, and I can tell it's eating him up. Why wouldn't he tell me?"

She shrugged. "He is covering for someone?"

"Naw, that ain't what I was reading from him." He looked at the bag, then looked into the fire, then back to her. "He's as interested as I am in seeing that person dead—but he wouldn't budge—wouldn't give the person up."

They sat in silence, and when Maria sighed and turned over and lay the corner of her blanket over her, he still sat studying the bag of tobacco. Whatever was on his mind would have to work itself out in the flicker of firelight.

It was deep in the night when she woke up with his hand on her arm. "Maria, wake up," he said, "we've got to get going."

"What is it?" She leaned up on one elbow and rubbed her eyes. "I hope you are never wrong again, if it means I must be up all night long while you—"

"Listen to me." He cut her off, jiggling the bag of tobacco in his hand. "We've got to get up and get ready to make a move. Caslado ain't going to *hang* in the morning. He's busting out *tonight!*"

"But the soldiers . . . you said there are—"

"They're kids, Maria, babies with rifles. Caslado's men will ride right through them. He's coming out. He had it planned already, but now that he's seen that broken rowel, I've got a feeling he'll be changing his plans and going after the man who wore it . . . don't you see?"

She shook her head. "No, I do not. I think you have stared too long in the fire, and you cannot stand being wrong. He is going to hang. Why would you think otherwise . . . because the badlands have *spoken* to you?" She shook her head again. "Sometimes I think perhaps—"

"No." He cut her off. "Because of this." He shook the bag of tobacco.

"Oh? You have read all of this in a bag of tobacco?"

Even as she spoke, she rolled up onto her feet with her low-crowned Stetson in her hand and brought up her holster belt on her forearm. She dusted the hat against her leg, and she grumbled under her breath until he cut her off, saying, "Listen, there it is." His eyes went off into the darkness in the direction of the distant prison.

She stopped and listened, then looked at him as the faint sound of distant rifle fire drifted in across the desert basin below them. "Sante Madre," she said in a hushed tone, reaching down for her boots. She rocked on one foot, then the other, stepping into the dusty boots and righting them on her feet.

"Hurry! It's begun," he said, turning to their horses. Her hand caught his arm, and as he turned to her, he saw the question in her dark eyes. He was moving quick, but calm now, she noticed, as if the sound of trouble demanded it of him. "The tobacco," he said, shaking the bag in his gloved hand. "What condemned man gives you back a bag of smoking tobacco the night before he's going to hang?"

She stopped short. "This? This is what you spent half the night coming up with? Tobacco? Not some dark warning— some *premonition* from the badlands?" He offered a tight smile, the two of them moving toward the horses, his white barb raising a low nicker at the faint sound of rifles in the night.

"You know better than that," he said. "I'm not a superstitious man."

Chapter 2

Ernesto Caslado lay on his thin pallet against the stone wall of his cell in the sweltering heat until the cool of the desert moved in with the darkness. Even then, with the heat of the day trapped inside the stone and steel, the coolness when it came was clammy and stale and brought no comfort.

But tonight he did not feel the clamminess of night pressing his dirty, ragged clothes to his skin. Neither did he hear the gnawing rats, or the soft scrape and brush of lizards and snakes as they made their way through the corridors and along the ledge outside his barred window.

Tonight he felt only rage, hearing inside him the brutal force of hard boots against tender flesh, the snip of spur against frail precious bone. This he felt in his heart and soul; and although it had been over a year since these things had happened, he saw the scene play itself out in his mind, as real as if it now happened before him. He heard the woman plead and scream until her screams died in her throat. She was *his* woman, and the child who died in her womb was *his child*.

Their deaths were brought about by the coarse stuff of which his life was made. She had died instead of giving him up to those who'd came looking for him, he'd thought. But now he knew he had been wrong. It was not a posse who'd shed her innocent blood, who'd tortured and killed her. It was not the ones it *should* have been who'd done these terrible things.

Had this been done by his enemies, he could at least accept it as one more casualty of war, for in war a man asks for no mercy from his enemies nor shows any in return. But this was *not* done by the enemy, as he had long reconciled himself to believing.

Seeing these things, he felt warm blood run down from his wrists where he'd strained so hard against his chains—against these thoughts, these thoughts that he had managed to choke down and swallow for a time because he was a man who knew that such things happened on this earth. Unless a man knew where to go to bring about his vengeance, his vengeance was best swallowed and forgotten, or it would drive him mad.

But now that he'd seen the broken rowel of the spur, and with it the face of the man who owned it, vengeance raged hot and sharp inside him. He could not *swallow* it, and if he could, he could not keep it down. Vengeance now had a face, and that face smiled in his mind the way it smiled the last time he'd seen it.

When the first rifle shots came out of the night, he did manage to force the smiling face back into a darkened recess of his mind. He stood up from the floor and waited, hearing the other prisoners shouting, and the sounds of the guards running along the corridor.

"I'm not taking the blame for any of this," one guard yelled as he fumbled with the key in the lock. The other two guards fidgeted in place, and one shouted that he'd better hurry up. The guard with the blue star tattoo shot a glance along the corridor and stood back as the other two rushed into Caslado's cell. Then he stepped in behind them with the rifle hanging from his hand, telling them to hurry up or it wouldn't matter who was to blame, they would all be dead here.

Outside the main wall a small field cannon exploded in the night. Men screamed above the sound of rifle fire. "I'm just saying," the nervous guard hissed as he jerked Caslado's wrists up and snapped a longer chain to the shorter one already there, "is that somebody'll catch hell—only twenty men guarding this place with a man like Caslado in here! The warden's plain stupid!"

"Yeah, well, you be sure to tell him that when you see him. Now hurry up," the other guard said, holding up a lantern in one hand while the other checked Caslado's wrists.

Caslado stared past them with a flat expression at the guard with the star tattoo. "Is it now time for my *bath*?" The guard who'd kneeled down and unlocked the shackle on Caslado's ankles stood back up and said, "This is no joking matter. We're gonna move ya, Caslado. You won't give us no trouble will ya? I've got a wife and family. I don't want to die here—"

"Get the hell out of the way, Dubbs, before you start soiling yourself," said the other guard, shoving him to the side. He reached in and grabbed the long chain, wrapped it a turn around his hand, and added to Caslado, "If your men shoot at us, just remember you're going down first!" He nodded back toward the rifle in the hands of the guard with the blue star tattoo. "Keep that rifle ready, JC," he said.

"It's ready," the man replied, his eyes staring into Caslado's. Ernesto Caslado only smiled, a dark guarded smile.

"Good." The guard started to jerk the chain and pull Caslado forward when a streak of fire from JC's rifle flashed in the small cell.

"Oh, Lord!" the other guard cried out as his fellow guard's blood splattered hot on his face. Seeing what was happening, he turned and bolted toward the open cell door. But the next shot from JC's rifle sent him spinning against the stone wall where he sank down, leaving a smear of blood behind him.

"Get these cuffs off of me, JC," Caslado said, holding up his wrists, stepping over the first guard's body.

JC swung the rifle up under his arm, snatched the key from the dead guard's hand, and in seconds let the cuffs and chains fall to the floor. "Horses are waiting out back," he said. "All the guards are covering the front wall. Let's go!"

"Wait." Caslado grabbed his arm and snatched the rifle from under it. He looked down at the dead guard nearest him. "I need his boots and trousers. Go let Hawk and Kreeger and the other prisoners out."

JC looked at him, hesitated for a second, and said, "All of them?"

"*Sí*, all of them," Caslado said.

"Even Crazy Gravy?"

Caslado grinned as he leaned down and wrestled the dead guard's boots off his feet. "Especially Crazy Gravy—but see to it he gets no weapon in his hands while we're here."

JC ran a hand across the blue star on his neck. "Are you sure you want to—"

"Hey! Open this damn door," a voice called out from down the row. The voice belonged to Levon Hawkins, and as he called out, he shook the steel-barred door to his cell.

"He's coming, Hawk," Caslado called back to him. Then to JC, "Go! Set them free!" Caslado shoved him. "You want to ride with me? You do as I say!" Outside a cannon shot slammed the front wall. An orange glow of fire licked the barred window and glittered in Caslado's dark eyes.

While he stripped off the dead guard's trousers, he heard the clinking of steel doors, the hushed voices, and the scurrying of bare feet along the corridor. He closed the trousers around his waist, pulled on the boots, and stamped them on the floor, righting them on his feet. Then he snatched the faded striped blanket from his pallet against the wall, ripped a hole in the center of it, and pulled it down over his head, making himself a poncho.

Taking one last glance around the tight stone walls, he spit and stepped out into the corridor, where JC stood checking a pistol he'd carried with him under his shirt. Beside JC stood two other ragged convicts, Levon Hawkins and Al Kreeger. They both leaned forward and grasped Caslado's forearm. "We won't forget this, *amigo*," Hawkins said. "We'll meet you out back."

Caslado flashed a smile, nodding, nudging them away. "Good. Now get moving." As they moved off along the dark corridor, Caslado turned to JC. "Where is Crazy Gravy?" He looked all around at the ragged, scurrying prisoners. "Did you open his cell?"

"Yeah, but he ain't budged. He's still in there," JC said, nodding toward the last cell in the row. "Acts like he ain't in no hurry to leave here."

"Oh?" Caslado stepped over and looked into the darkness, seeing malevolent eyes gazing back at him—the eyes of some dark and terrible creature of the wilds, he thought; and although Caslado was a man with no fear in him, something about those eyes caused his skin to crawl. "You are free to go," Caslado said, testing the tone and sound of his own voice there in the darkness as screams and gunfire split the night.

"I know," said the voice from beneath the eyes, a voice as soft as mud, yet within it something as fertile with evil as the low hiss of a rattlesnake.

Caslado stood for a second longer, but the voice said nothing more; and he moved away when JC called out to him from the steel door at the far end of the corridor. "Come on, before they get regrouped on us."

"Remember me as the one who set you free," Caslado said into the darkness before moving away.

"But of course," the voice said, hollow and flat. "I'll remember you."

Caslado joined JC beyond the steel door. They left the door standing open and crept out front into the flickering light of rifle fire and the rise of flame and smoke. From the front wall of the row of holding cells, they moved low and swift, through the scurrying prisoners and the guards running in all directions firing their rifles.

"JC!" a guard called out, running up alongside them. "Thank God you're—" His words stopped as he saw Caslado, and before he realized what was going on, Caslado shot him in the forehead. He motioned JC forward, and the two of them moved on, around the corner of the building as a cannon shot tore chunks of stone and wood from the lower half of a guard tower. Sparks spun upward in the darkness. Flames spewed from windows and licked up from the roof of the administration building and the cell-block building behind it. Trapped prisoners screamed.

"Stay close to me," Caslado called out to JC. "They will think I am your prisoner."

"Hell, they ain't thinking about nothing right now," JC called out, "except how to stay alive." They moved on.

At the rear of the long stone building they unhitched three frightened horses, and had to check them down, mounting as the animals nickered and bolted and drew away from them. The horses' eyes lit wide with fear, glistening in the glow of fire. Caslado's horse bolted forward, and he ran beside it, a few quick steps, then swung himself upward on its back. Once on the fleeing horse, he only had to rein it toward the small delivery gate at the back wall. Three guards ran chasing and firing on the ragged screaming prisoners. The horses shot forward, JC close behind Caslado, leading the third horse by its reins.

When they were only a few yards from the small steel gate, a young guard stepped out, threw it open, and waved them on. "Hurry!" he shouted, flagging his arms up and down. He had just jumped forward and snatched the reins to the third horse from JC's hand when a rifle shot knocked the horse down on its front knees. "Oh, no!" The young guard looked up at JC while Caslado sailed forward into the night.

JC's horse stepped back and forth, high-hoofed and terrified, and JC held the pistol up, looking down at the young guard. "Sorry, Sammy-boy, there went your ride."

"No! Wait!" The young guard looked all around in panic. "Don't leave me here! Please! No!" At his feet, the downed horse thrashed on its side in a spreading pool of blood. "Help me, JC! We're partners!" As he shouted, Levon Hawkins and Al Kreeger sped past him and through the gate, on two horses they'd pulled from the burning livery barn. Rifle fire rang out behind them.

JC ducked and shook his head. "Got to go, Sammy-boy! You wouldn't have liked this life much anyway." He jerked the horse around, nailed his heels to its side, and let it shoot out through the open rear gate in a flurry of dust.

"I'll catch up," the young guard called out, watching JC fade into the darkness. *Jesus!* What had he just done? But young Samuel Burns knew he had gone too far into this nightmare to turn back. He was as guilty as JC and the others. There could be no stopping now. He glanced around wild-eyed for a horse, saw none, then ducked and covered his head beneath a heavy volley of rifle fire. *Damn JC!* Leaving him like this . . .

When the volley lifted, he lunged forward and sped across the hard ground toward the livery barn, where flames licked upward above the screams of trapped horses. His heart pounded in his chest.

Outside on the narrow trail, Ernesto Caslado looked back toward the open rear gate, lying low on the horse while it fled the fire and explosions. Behind him, JC's horse leaped over the body of a young soldier lying in the middle of the trail; and as Caslado slowed his horse, he saw dark figures on horseback creep out of the shadows of broken boulders and scrub brush and swing in around him.

"Ernesto!" a voice called out to him. He turned amid the gathering horsemen, sliding his horse down and circling it in the dirt trail. Hands reached out, slapping his back, his face, and arms.

"Aw, *mi amigos, mi compadres*!" He laughed with tears in his eyes and slapped back at them. "I am free! Free!"

Behind the tightened circle of riders, JC held his horse in check, and in the light of a half-moon saw Caslado sweep a tall sombrero from a man's head and shove it down on his own. Behind them, a hundred yards away, the battle raged. But here they milled and laughed and called out each other's names. *Greasers* . . . JC spit and ran a hand across his mouth. Well, at least he wouldn't have to put up with them for long.

Some of these were men from Caslado's old ranks, who had fought as soldiers with Ernesto and his brother Ramon. Others were young men with little or no experience who'd left their homes and families to come join Caslado's revolutionist army. *Viva revolucion* . . . ! JC smiled to himself. He looked at all of them in the same light. There wasn't a man there he wouldn't kill if that man stood between him and the money Caslado had promised him.

A rider drew his horse back beside JC's and said to him, "It is a great thing you do here, *mi amigo*. Now you can be proud. You are one with us! *Su amigos,* eh?"

"Yeah," JC said in a lowered tone, heeling his horse forward into the gathered riders. "Just like musketeers, ain't we."

"*Sí,* musketeers . . . that is us." The young Mexican grinned and heeled his horse forward into the throng of raised rifles, dusty sombreros, and glistening bandoleers. Amid the riders sat Levon Hawkins and Al Kreeger. Their eyes searched back and forth among the Mexicans until JC rode in beside them.

One of the Mexicans spoke to Caslado as Caslado slipped a bandoleer of ammunition up across his chest. "But we must hurry, back across the border, as we planned, Ernesto. This is a bad country, with a strong army, *sí*?"

"*Sí*, Carlos," Caslado said to the swarthy older man beside him. "But I will worry about the American army. You must take the rest of the force back across the border. These new men will ride with me and the gringos. We will rob the bank in Three Rivers and meet you across the border." He took a brace of holstered pistols from an extended hand and swung the belt over his shoulder.

"But it was agreed that we would all go together. I do not understand—"

"You do not *need* to understand, Carlos. I am back in charge now." Caslado snapped a pistol from one of the holsters, checked it, and spun the cylinder. "Something more important has come up." His eyes swept across JC and the two convicts and across four men JC had recruited for the escape. These four men looked at him with eyes like ravaging wolves. Unlike the young Mexicans and their cause, these men were killers and border thugs.

Caslado said to the young Mexicans, "Give them your guns, quickly. We must get away from here."

Carlos pointed at JC as the Mexicans passed rifles and pistols to the two convicts and the other new men. "But Ernesto . . . this one, he wears the uniform of a prison guard."

"So he does." Caslado grinned. "But now he wishes to rob banks with us, and be a desperado." He grinned at JC and added, "Tell them why you wish to be a desperado, *mi amigo*."

JC smiled a flat smile. He looked at Hawkins and Kreeger, then around at the others. "Because I just spent seven years of my life sweating behind bars, just like a desperado. If I got to live like one, I might as well get paid like one." He spit and ran a hand across his mouth. "Now, let's all get ta raising some hell . . . making some damn money!"

The four new men laughed and hooted and slapped at him the way they had slapped at Caslado. One of them took off his sombrero and shoved it down on JC's head. But Carlos and the young Mexicans only starred at Caslado until the others settled. "We are not desperados, Ernesto. We are revolutionists. I do not like bringing in all these outsiders, especially these gringos." He spit. "And I do not like changing our plans at the last minute. This is not how your brother, Ramon, would do things."

"My *brother*? Oh, I see." Caslado smiled and shrugged. "Well then." He raised the pistol and shot him in the forehead. Then he shrugged again. "Poor Carlos," he said as the older man flipped backward from his saddle and landed amid scurrying hooves. "He never understood anything."

Horses nickered and shied, and the Mexicans starred at Caslado while they drew their reins taut to check the animals down. The new men stared through caged eyes. "Well now, looky here," Al Kreeger whispered.

Levon Hawkins chuckled under his breath. "Shot that sucker dead," he whispered back.

"Miguel Torin . . . are you here?" Caslado called out, his eyes searching across the group.

"*Sí*, Ernesto." A stocky young man who'd ridden with Caslado for years stepped his horse out from behind the pack. Eyes flashed as he moved forward, cutting his horse around the body in the dirt.

Caslado stared at him. "Will you go and take the main force back with you . . . do for me what Carlos would *not*?" The pistol hung loose in his hand, still smoking, his thumb lying at ease across the cocked hammer.

"*Sí*, of course." The man shrugged.

"Good!" Caslado jerked the pistol up, uncocked it, and cut his horse back and forth in front of the group. "If there is no more to say, let us be gone from this hellhole and tend to our business. Draw our men from the front wall and lead them home. Tell them we will meet again soon, in *Mejico*."

As Miguel Torin and three others turned their horses and headed away into the darkness around the far wall of the prison, Levon Hawkins checked his newly acquired pistol and spun it on his finger. "This oughta be a hoot," he said to Al Kreeger in a lowered voice.

"Yeah," Kreeger said, flashing a glance across the others, "so far it has." He'd stepped down and picked up Carlos's rifle and hat from the dirt. Now he swung back up in his saddle, dusted the hat against his leg and pulled it low on his forehead. "I'd shoot any of these greasers, right here, right now, for one good bottle of whiskey."

"Me too." Hawkins grinned. "It wouldn't have to be a good bottle at that."

Ahead of the pack, Caslado swung his arm in a circle and snapped it toward the endless stretch of darkness to the north. JC sidled his horse up close to Hawkins and Kreeger and said just above a whisper, "Keep your comments to yourselves. We can go along with anything for three hundred thousand dollars, can't we?"

"You got it, JC," Kreeger said, gigging his horse forward.

"That's right, JC, *mi amigo*." Hawkins chuckled. "You got it all."

Moving as one, the body of men rode forward, a dozen horsemen strong, riding two and three abreast into the desert night, while behind them the rest of the rebel force pounded the front gates with cannon fire, amid the cries of dying men and horses.

Chapter 3

In the dark distance before them, the ranger and Maria saw the orange glowing reef of fire above the burning prison. They'd rode at a safe but steady pace across the first stretch of sand flats, careful to not push the horses too hard, or to wear out the pack mule that struggled along behind the ranger at the end of a lead rope. When the ground beneath the horses' hooves turned rocky and the horses slowed down on their own, Maria stopped her big roan in front of the ranger and swung the horse back beside him.

"Did you hear something up there?" She nodded toward the stretch of harsh, rocky land before them, at black upthrusts of broken boulders standing against the purple night.

"Yeah, I heard it," he said in a hushed tone. "Sounded like wagon wheels."

They moved forward more slowly now, then stopped beside the trail winding into the rocks. There they sat their horses in silence, listening for any sound akin to the motion of man. After a moment when no sound came, the ranger handed Maria the lead rope to the pack mule, then looked around in the darkness and heeled his white barb forward at a cautious walk.

"It's a good place for an ambush," he said in a whisper, "but we can't sit here all night." He slipped his big pistol from his holster and let it hang down his side in his right hand. "Give me a ten-yard start."

She counted seconds to herself, watching him slip out of sight into the black shadows of broken boulders. She eased the rifle from her saddle scabbard, nudged her roan forward leading the mule, and scanned the darkness around her. Only once did she hear the scraping sound of the ranger's horse as its hooves sought purchase on the rocky terrain. When she heard it, her breath stopped in her throat for a second. She stopped her horse and stilled it, waiting for a tense second until she heeled forward once more.

No sooner had she started forward when a voice called out in the darkness ahead, "Hold it right there! You're covered! Don't make a move!"

"Don't shoot, you've got me," she heard the ranger call back to the voice. Hearing the ranger's voice, she dropped silently from her saddle, pulling the reins and the lead rope, and faded off to the side into the cover of rock with the animals beside her.

"There's five of us here! We're armed! We better hear a gun hit the ground *real quick*, or we'll start shooting."

A silence passed, and the voice added, "Hear me there? Throw down all your weapons! If ya want to live!"

Another silence passed as she waited, tensed, with her rifle poised above a low broken boulder. *Where was he . . . ?*

Her question was answered by the sound of the ranger's pistol firing rapidly, three times, the flash of it revealing his white barb horse in the middle of the thin trail, its saddle empty. In the orange-white explosion, three figures stood crouched, ten feet ahead of the ranger's horse.

"*Jesus!*" On the second shot, one figure fell to the side, screaming. On the third shot, one had turned; but now Maria saw his shoulders snap back as he crumbled to the ground. The last dark figure had spun toward the muzzle flash in the rocks beside him. A shotgun was up, ready. But she snatched a quick aim along her rifle sights and shot him just as the shotgun blasted.

A silence settled over the dark trail. Smoke drifted on the night. A voice moaned low and tortured, and the ranger's white barb answered in a low nicker, and blew out a breath.

"Coming out, Maria," the ranger said.

"No, wait! That was only three! Where are the other two?"

"He lied," the ranger called out to her. "There's only three of them."

She let go of a tense breath and stood up. Ahead in the darkness, she heard the ranger say to one of the downed men. "You miscounted, didn't you?"

"Yeah . . . just three of us," a pained voice replied. "But five sounded better . . . don't ya think?" His words sounded clipped and strained.

"Ordinarily it might've," the ranger said. "Convicts, are you? From the prison?"

"Yep . . . that's us. Figured we'd . . . go on a spree. Damn shame though. I only had . . . four months left."

Maria shook her head, stepping forward, leading the animals. A match flared in the darkness; then the light widened as the ranger stuck it to a candle lantern and leaned down over the dark figure on the ground.

"I'm gut-shot bad, ain't I?" The dark figure grunted and struggled upward as the ranger raised him slightly and rested his head against a small rock. "Guess I'll be feeding some buzzards come daylight."

"Afraid so," the ranger said. He set the candle lantern on a rock and leaned back down over the man. "You could've stood on your head for four more months, couldn't you?"

"Yeah, you'd think so. But I already had . . . nine years behind me."

"I understand." The ranger laid open the dirty gray prison shirt, looked at the gaping rifle shot wound, then sat back and sighed and pushed up the brim of his sombrero. Maria stepped into the small circle of candlelight and looked around at the other two bodies on the rocky ground.

The man lifted his eyes to her and said, "You— You're the one what shot me?"

"Yes, I shot you," she said, avoiding his face. She picked up the shotgun, swung it up under her arm, stepped over and nudged each body in turn with her rifle barrel.

"Dang it all. Ain't even seen . . . a woman's face in nine long years . . . now I'm kilt . . . by one." The man tried to laugh, but it turned into a deep racking cough. When he'd settled, he added in a weaker voice, "It just goes . . . to show ya, don't it."

"Shows what?" the ranger asked, taking out cartridges and reloading his big pistol.

"I don't know . . . but *something* I reckon. Can I . . . have some water before I die?"

The ranger stood up, stepped over, and took a canteen from the pack mule. When he'd uncapped the canteen and started to lean back down with it, the man asked, "Can . . . the woman give it to me? Please?"

"Here, I will give it to him," Maria said in a soft tone before the ranger could answer for her. She took the canteen from the ranger's hand and stooped down. The ranger took a step back and holstered his big pistol.

When the man had taken a sip and coughed it back up, he looked at the badge on the ranger's vest and said, "You're . . . that ranger, ain't you?"

"I am," the ranger said, looking down at him.

"I might . . . have known you was. You kilt my . . . cousin, Donald Kurtz."

"What's your name?" The ranger watched as Maria poured water into her cupped hand and swabbed it across his dirty brow.

"Amil . . . Sweeny," he said. "If they ask . . . tell 'em I gave ya a good fight, will ya?"

"If they ask, I will," the ranger said. "Who are these other two?"

"Them two is Tommy Bass . . . and Jake something-or-other. Never knew him much . . . before today. We grabbed . . . a wagon. It's broke down back there. Mule's dead." He coughed, then added, "Thought we'd follow . . . Caslado. But we saw him head north. Most of . . . his men went south."

The ranger studied his eyes. "Are you sure it was Caslado, headed north?"

"I orta be sure. Been seeing his . . . ugly face every day for a year."

Maria tipped the canteen against his lips. His eyes went from the ranger back to Maria. He swallowed and coughed, but this time managed to keep the water down. "You . . . You sure are . . . a pretty thing," he said to her, trying to smile. A trickle of blood spread across his lower lip and spilled down.

She lowered her eyes and started to draw back from him. But he raised a weak hand and laid it on her forearm. "No. Please, don't go. Just sit here . . . for a minute or two?"

She lifted a glance to the ranger, then sat back down near Amil Sweeny. With the edge of his dirty shirt collar, she wiped the blood from his lips. His eyes began to cloud over; his breath fell shallow. "*Sí*," she whispered in a soft tone, taking his dirty hand in hers. "I am here. We will sit here for a minute or two."

When the ranger had taken a shirt from one of the bodies and laid a rock on it to mark the spot, they dragged the dead men into the cover of broken boulders, laid them close together, and spread a blanket over them. They covered the bodies with small stones and left as the first thin streak of gray drew along the eastern horizon.

"It will not keep the coyotes out for long," Maria said as they heeled their horses back onto the thin trail.

"No . . . the buzzards either, if they're hungry enough.

But it's all these boys get until the prison sends somebody out here for them. We've got to keep moving."

They rode on in a steady pace and swung wide of the prison, three miles out, knowing that Caslado and his men would be miles away by the time they got there. At a rail crossing they stopped; and the ranger stepped down and dusted his hands together, gazing out through the first light of dawn, his eyes following the hoofprints of many horses leading northeast toward the prison. Then his eyes moved back in, down to the broken rails at his feet.

Maria had moved forward on her big roan. She pointed down with her rifle barrel at the spot where horses had dragged away more sections of loosened rail and left the spikes laying scattered on the ground.

"Caslado's no fool," the ranger said, standing up from beside the long gap in the steel rails reaching off to the west. "I'll give him that."

"Many of them have separated here and rode south, with their field cannon," she said, letting the rifle barrel follow the set of hoofprints until they faded in the dim light. "The others have headed . . . *north*. Just as Sweeny said."

"That's what it looks like all right." The ranger gazed back and forth across the ground.

"But why would Caslado be with those headed north?" Maria asked, puzzled, "when he has all the men and protection he needs down across the border? It makes no sense."

"It must to him," the ranger said without looking up. "I've got a feeling Caslado needs to take care of some business up in the badlands."

"The railroad money?" She stepped her horse over to him and stopped with her rifle propped up from her hip.

"Maybe for the money . . . or maybe for something more important to him." The ranger looked at her, then trailed his eyes northward and up as if reading something in the morning air. She gazed off with him, until the ranger nodded.

"Yep. I think ole Sweeny was telling the truth. I'll follow these tracks north and see what I come up with. They'll wear their horses out across the sand flats. San Paulo will be their last chance to take on fresh animals before crossing the badlands."

"There are a dozen horses headed north," Maria said, gesturing toward the ground. "When we catch them, we will have our hands full."

He looked at her and shook his head. "Uh-uh. *I* will have *my* hands full. You're riding back, as soon as we get to the prison and see what kind of shape they're in."

"No," she said. "I ride with you, as always."

"It's too dangerous, Maria. I'm afraid you'll have to sit this one out."

She put her free hand on her hip, and swung the rifle up on her shoulder. "Oh? In that case, I will stay behind and wonder if you will ever come back, or if you lay dead in the desert with the vultures picking your bones—"

"That's enough. I'm going alone this time, and that's final." He sliced a gloved hand through the air and walked off to his horse.

She called after him. "You say that this Ernesto Caslado is not a fool. Then why are you being one? You cannot possibly think that you and your big pistol will stand a chance against this many men. They will not let you simply walk in and kill Caslado."

He stopped and turned to her as she walked toward him. "I'm not going to go after Caslado head to head. I plan on staying back from him, just track him. I'm after whoever killed the girl and her father over at Cold Creek. My hunch is, if I follow Caslado, he'll lead me there."

"Then where is this danger that is too much for me? Is this Caslado any worse than the monster, Montana Red? Did I not do my part in killing him?"

He raised a hand. "I couldn't have taken him without you. But that's not the point—"

"Have I not done my part in bringing down a dozen others in the past year?"

"I'm not saying you haven't done your part—"

"Do I not handle a pistol as well as any man?"

"That's got nothing to do with it—"

"A rifle? Can I not shoot as well as you with a rifle? Can I not ride as well?"

He gazed away for a moment, then back at her. "You've always done your part. I'm not saying otherwise. But something could go wrong tracking this many men. I don't want to see you hurt."

She shook her head, passing him in a huff, stepping up on her big roan, and jerking the reins. "I do not believe you sometimes." She turned the horse back onto the trail and kicked it out at a fast trot. Dust rose in her wake. He shook his head, stepped up in his saddle, and caught up to her a mile from the prison, where she'd stopped her horse and sat staring ahead, to where black smoke curled up in a steady stream and drifted on the morning air.

"They sure took a beating," he said, gazing across the battered front wall of the prison, pieces of broken timber and stone littering the perimeter. "I'd like to get my hands around the neck of whoever sold the rebels that field cannon." He sat quietly for a second, judging her mood, hoping she'd settled a bit.

After a pause, she let go of a tight breath. "*Sí*," she said in a softer tone, sitting her horse with her wrists crossed on the saddle horn. "But how do you know someone sold it to them? Don't men like Caslado's rebels take what they want?"

"Men like Caslado's rebels always get what they want. Buy it . . . take it, as long as there's killing to be done, men get the tools to do it, some way."

He heeled his white barb forward, and they rode the last hundred yards past small adobes, where in the yard gray mesquite smoke rose from the *chimnea* of brick ovens left unattended while the people who lived there stood about in front of the prison and looked on at the aftermath of battle.

Two guards with faces smudged by black smoke walked in from the west carrying a dead prisoner tied to a pole between their shoulders, like fresh game they'd taken in a hunt.

As he and Maria stepped down from their horses to walk them the rest of the way in, the ranger said, "Can't spend much time here if I'm going to stay on Caslado's trail while it's warm."

A stoop-shouldered man wearing a ragged straw sombrero heard the ranger's words, and he glanced at him, then turned from among the onlookers, shaking his head slowly. "*Terriblemente,*" he said under his breath, crossing himself. His bare feet padded away across the sand and back toward the adobes. He did not look back as the ranger and the woman stepped through the debris into the prison yard.

Ahead of him, the man in the straw sombrero saw an old woman walking across the dirt street with a bundle of mesquite brush on her shoulder. He raised a hand to her and called out in Spanish, asking her if the guards had checked her adobe for any escaped prisoners who might have slipped in and hidden there.

She nodded and walked on toward her adobe, saying that yes, this had been done earlier, before daylight, so she had nothing to fear. He ran a hand across his brow in relief and stepped closer to her, saying that this was good, because you could never be too careful in times such as these. And he followed her on into the front yard and talked to her as she dropped the bundle of kindling near her small oven. Then with his hand going inside his faded striped serape, he wrapped his fingers around the handle of his butcher knife and followed her into her adobe.

Chapter 4

A harried young guard with a smudged face came running up to the ranger and the woman with his rifle at port arms as they walked through the rubble toward the gathering of men near the burned-out administration building. The ranger spread his riding duster open and gave the young guard a good look at the badge on his chest, saying, "We're here to see the warden."

"Thank goodness you showed up," the guard said, letting out a breath. "I'll take you right over to him." He eyed Maria up and down, then added, "Is she with you?"

"What does it look like?" Maria glared at him.

"Sorry, ma'am."

The guard rattled on about what had happened as they walked along between two rows of bodies. In one row lay the dead guards, in the other the blackened remains of prisoners who'd died in their cells. The old priest looked up at the ranger from where he kneeled among the burnt remains. Near him, his small gathering of followers stood with their heads bowed, their signs hanging at their sides. The old priest's tired eyes seemed to form a question; but the ranger only shook his head and looked away.

A line of ragged, smoke-blackened convicts sat in the dirt, chained one to another, guarded by a steely-eyed Indian who stood over them with a shotgun. The convicts only stared through hollow eyes as if having long divested themselves of any blame or guilt or feeling whatsoever for anything that had happened out here in this larger world.

"I don't give a blue-tinker's-damn what anybody may or may not have promised you, Mr. Plum!" a big man in a black linen suit raged. "You have a contract! Read the blasted thing! Can't you see what's happened here? I don't have time for your petty, ridiculous accusations."

"He's the warden," the guard whispered, leaning near the ranger's ear. The ranger and Maria stepped behind the man, and looked past him at Rance Plum, the bounty hunter, who stood facing the warden with his thumbs hooked in his holster belt.

"Accusations?" Plum raged. "It is not an accusation, sir, it's a *fact*! We've been screwed, sir!" He raised a gloved finger for emphasis. A few feet behind Rance Plum stood Jack the Spider, his partner. The Spider stood with his good eye cocked toward the warden. His other eye, blind and clouded over by a white film, seemed to swim about on its own. His gloved fingertips tapped out a nervous rhythm on the butt of the pistol holstered across his stomach.

Rance Plum's forehead drew tight with rage. A blue vein stood out beneath his level hat brim. He shot a glance past the warden to the ranger and the woman, then back to the warden as he snapped his hand inside his black riding duster and pulled out a folded piece of paper. He shook it at the warden.

"I *have* read my contract, sir! It says two thousand upon delivery and three thousand more upon the man's death! It doesn't specify hanging, it only says death!" He swung a finger toward the row of dead, charred prisoners. "I submit to you that one of those burnt-up son of a bitches lying there is Ernesto Caslado—and unless you can prove otherwise, I demand our money, sir!"

"Caslado is gone, you fool!" The warden swung a thick arm toward the charred cells where Caslado had been held.

"His cell is empty, nothing but two dead guards in it. A third guard has obviously thrown in with him. I refuse to stand here and argue with you over something this obvious. Anyone with half a mind can see—"

"It doesn't say the contract becomes void if you and your yard screws let the man get away!" Plum stepped forward shaking the contract in the warden's face. The ranger glanced at the woman, shook his head with a slight smile, and looked back at Plum.

The warden snatched the contract from Plum's hand, opened it, ran a finger across line after line, then said, "According to this, you would have received the full five thousand for bringing in Caslado's head . . . but no, you had to bring him in alive! Right here on line seven, 'Should the said felon be apprehended and taken into custody alive, a reward of two thousand shall be paid at that time, and an additional three thousand upon the said felon's execution.' So there, Mr. Plum! Take your stupid contract and shove—"

"You low, rotten snake, you!" Plum lunged forward, but Jack the Spider grabbed him and held him back. "So help me, I'll kill you, sir!" Plum raged.

"Take it easy, Plum," the ranger said, stepping around between the two of them and spreading an arm to keep the warden from lunging forward.

"And who are you?" the warden bellowed.

The ranger turned facing him and let him see the badge on his chest. "We came to see if we could help. Shot three of your escapees earlier on our way here. Their names are Sweeny, Bass, and one called Jake. You'll find their bodies along the trail through the rock lands."

"Well, thank heavens someone is doing something," the warden said, shooting Rance Plum a dark scowl. "That's three less we have to worry about." He settled down and wiped a hand across his sweaty, soot-streaked face. "You certainly got here pretty quick, ranger. I take it our telegraph must've gone through after all?"

"No, afraid not, warden. I was by here yesterday evening, and camped out last night on the buttes. Your wires have been cut, a mile out. We saw them on our way here. As far as I know, we're the only help coming, for now anyway."

The warden pinched the bridge of his thick nose and shook his head. "We still have our engine here. We can send it out to the army post near the border and bring in some troops."

"Afraid not, warden," the ranger said. "The boys who planned all this knew what they were doing. They ripped out three sections of track. We just came from there."

"We?" The warden glanced around, took note of the woman, and let out a breath. "Thank heaven for you too, madam," he said. "Do you suppose you could be a dear? Go find us a pot and some coffee and get us some nice hot—"

"Warden." The ranger cut him off, seeing the dark fire in Maria's eyes as she took a step toward the warden. The ranger stopped her with a hand on her forearm. "We didn't come here to make coffee," he added. "We just wanted to see what kind of shape you were in before we get on Caslado's trail."

"Oh." The warden's red face reddened more. "Well, as you can see, we've rounded up most of the others—what the fire didn't get—and the few that are still loose will become the government's responsibility. I still have a prison to run, such as it is." He swung an arm, taking in the burnt rubble. "We'll have to sort through and identify as best we can who's here and who's not."

"Right there lies Ernesto Caslado!" Rance Plum cut in, pointing at a large lump of burnt flesh still smoldering in the line of bodies. "I'll sign a paper identifying him if that's what it takes to get my money. I defy anyone to say otherwise—"

"Shut up, Plum," the ranger said, cutting him off. "Caslado's gone. We saw where his men's tracks broke up. The rebels are halfway to Mexico by now."

The warden's eyes shot back and forth between Plum and the ranger. "You men know one another?"

"Yeah," the ranger breathed. "We've known one another for a while. He used to be a ranger himself. But the hours didn't suit him."

"The hours had nothing to do with it," Plum snapped. "But it's true I used to be a ranger, warden," he added, again pointing to the smoldering lump of flesh. "And unless you're questioning my honor as a former law enforcement officer, I insist you allow me to identify Caslado lying there and collect my reward!"

"He's right," Jack the Spider said, stepping forward, pointing at the smoldering pile of burnt, twisted flesh. "If that ain't exactly what Ernesto Caslado would look like burnt to a crisp, I'll eat my damn hat."

"See what I'm trying to deal with here, sir?" The warden shrugged toward the ranger and dropped his arms, ignoring Plum and the Spider. "Perhaps you'll explain to these two bounty hunters—"

"I can't explain nothing to Plum." The ranger shook his head, cutting the warden off. "If there's nothing we can do for you here," he said, "we'll be on our way while Caslado's trail is still fresh."

The warden looked at the badge on his chest. "But . . . But, you said he's heading to Mexico. You have no jurisdiction across the border."

The ranger smiled tightly. "I said most of his rebels are halfway to Mexico by now. I didn't say Caslado went with them."

"But where else would he possibly go?" The warden spread his arms, taking in all of the land around them.

The ranger glanced at Plum and Jack the Spider and decided to keep his hunch to himself. Their eyes perked toward him. "I have no idea, warden. That's why I want to get under way. Maybe I'll figure something out as I go."

"Oh, I see." The warden looked all around. "In that case, no, I suppose there's nothing you can do for us here. We'll send one of the soldiers to the army post by horseback straightaway. He'll bring back some help . . . a cleanup crew I suppose." He rubbed his chin. "As far as prisoners missing, they'll start making their presence felt here and there before long, I'm afraid. One of them is Crayton Gravely. He might be quite a problem." The warden shook his head, adding, "I'll have a month's worth of paper work explaining all this."

The ranger and the woman had started to turn away, but at the warden's words they stopped and turned back to him. "Who did you say?" the ranger asked, catching a glimpse of Rance Plum's eyes as he and the Spider also snapped toward the warden.

The warden looked cornered and confused.

"Did you say 'Crayton Gravely'?" The ranger stepped toward him and the warden took a step back. "You mean Crazy Gravy? He was here? He's one of the missing convicts?"

The warden tried to compose himself as all four stepped near him. "Well . . . as I say, we won't know for certain who is or isn't here until we've sorted through all the remains." His hand gestured once more toward the long row of smoldering bodies. "He may very well be among those bodies."

"And so might Ernesto Caslado," Plum said, cutting him off with a raised finger.

"Lord have mercy." The ranger slumped a bit and pushed up the brim of his sombrero.

Maria turned and looked all about the prison yard, her dark eyes searching. "Do you realize what kind of devil you've let escape, warden?" she asked.

"See here, young lady," the warden said, trying to add an air of authority to his voice. "I didn't simply let this happen. And yes, I'm fully aware of what Crayton Gravely is . . . I've had charge of him for the past two years."

The ranger shook his head, looking all around. "So this is where the government's kept him hidden—playing it down real quiet like hoping everybody would forget about him." His eyes narrowed back onto the warden. "I suppose there's been a little something extra in the budget for you here . . . for going along with it?"

"Everything we've done here is completely aboveboard, sir," the warden said, tilting his chin a bit. "The government wanted to study Crayton Gravely. There is much to be learned from someone like him. His mental depravity might well be correlated to the shape of his skull, you see."

"Horseshit." Jack the Spider spit and rolled his good eye upward. His free hand went up behind his hat brim and absently felt the base of his skull.

"Gravely is a raving madman," Rance Plum cut in.

"Exactly, sir!" The warden shot him a cold stare. "What better place to study madness than in a mind such as his?"

"You don't study something like Crazy Gravy," the ranger said in a low tone, leaning his face within inches of the warden's. "What you do is kill it . . . hang it, shoot it, bury it in a deep hole somewhere and pile heavy rocks over it. Once you've captured it, you don't keep it alive. Not if you care at all about what it'll do if it ever gets loose."

The warden tried to offer a tight, nervous smile, running a hand across his brow. "I'm sure we're getting a bit carried away here, gentlemen. I mean . . . We don't know yet if he has escaped, and if he has, let's have faith that our government will soon be stepping in here and taking this matter in hand."

"Ha." The ranger turned, and he and Maria started walking away.

"Well, ranger," the warden called out, "if you're so concerned, perhaps you should stay and help us determine whether or not he's actually escaped."

"You'll know soon enough," the ranger called back without stopping. "And he won't be hard to track at first . . . just follow his trail of bodies."

The warden swallowed and turned back to Rance Plum and Jack the Spider. "What about you gentlemen? If he has escaped, I'm certain we can come up with some sort of reward for his return. Isn't that your job?"

Jack the Spider mumbled something under his breath, spit, and ran a hand across his mouth. Rance Plum hooked his thumbs back in his holster belt, smiled, and said to the warden: "You have some gall, sir. We're still waiting for our pay on the last job we did for the government."

The warden tossed his hands in the air. "But, Mr. Plum! You can't possibly blame me . . ."

The ranger and the woman heard Plum and the warden bicker back and forth as he and she walked their horses back through the rubble toward the main gate. "If Crazy Gravy is alive and running loose, this changes everything, yes?"

"Nope," the ranger said, gazing straight ahead. "I've got to get on Caslado's trail while it's fresh. I owe it to the dead girl and her father. Somebody else will have to deal with Crayton Gravely."

"Then it is more important what we owe the dead than what we owe the living?"

"Don't start on me," he said. "I've got too much on my mind right now."

"And I do not? Then perhaps I should stay here and find the coffeepot for the nice warden . . . and fix him a good fresh pot of coffee."

"You know what I mean," he said. "Besides, if I know Rance Plum, him and the Spider are cutting some kind of deal right now to hunt down Crayton Gravely and the others. So let them have at it. I can't catch every madman in the world. I learned that a long time ago."

"But Rance Plum always trips over his own feet. You've seen it many times."

"But he'll keep Crayton Gravely on the dodge at least . . . until somebody with better sense comes along and catches him. Who knows, Plum might get lucky. He did manage to capture Ernesto Caslado the last time. Maybe he'll stumble onto Crayton Gravely and kill him by accident."

"So, you are certain that Crazy Gravy is alive, and that he has escaped?"

"Didn't want to say a lot in front of Plum, but yep, I'd bet Graveley's on the loose. I'd also bet that Ernie Caslado set him loose, just to keep everybody busy back here instead of following him. If I stay here looking for Gravely, it's just what Caslado wanted."

"I am impressed." She smiled slightly, watching his face as he stared ahead. "Then we must take on supplies and get under way. It will be hard tracking these men in the badlands."

He stopped at the broken main gates and looked at her. "It's not *we* this time. I already told you, I'm going alone." He shook his head and walked on, leading his horse until he passed through the onlookers. When he stopped again and stepped up into his stirrups, she did the same and swung her roan over near him.

"Perhaps you are right. You go on alone this time, and I will stay back here."

He looked at her and saw the trace of a determined smile as she gazed ahead. "I see what you're doing," he said. "But it ain't gonna work. You're not going to push me into taking you along just to keep you from staying here and looking for Gravely . . . so forget it."

"I am free to come and go as I choose, and I have no fear of Crazy Gravy," Maria said as they rode slowly along the dusty trail past the small adobes and stopped their horses while an old woman ambled across in front of them with her faded serape hooded over her head. Rawhide kindling straps swayed back and forth in her hand. The ranger took note of her aged, sun-weathered hand beneath the edge of the serape, and of the kindling straps swaying back and forth in it as she gazed away from them and off toward the mesquite brush in the near distance.

After a quiet moment as they heeled their horses on, Maria added, "They say Crazy Gravy dried the hearts of his victims and kept them on a string for many years."

"I heard that one myself," the ranger said.

"And that his prey are mostly women," she added. "It is said that no one has any idea how many women he has tortured and butchered over the years. And that he has a face that no one remembers for long after they see it. He is like a lizard that blends into all around him . . . that no one knows he is there until he strikes. And that once after he had killed a young woman, he cut her body into pieces no larger than your hand and scattered them—"

"All right. That's enough. You're going with me, okay?" The ranger reined his horse sharp and spun it toward her. "We're going to be covering a lot of hard ground and going through some dangerous places." He glanced around the barren land. "Looks like we won't be taking on supplies until we get to the old relay station. We'll have to move on nonstop until then."

"Of course." She smiled. "I still have some tea and jerked beef in my saddlebags. We will make do."

As they heeled their horses forward, out in the sand among the scrub pinyon and mesquite brush, the edge of the faded striped serape lifted slightly, and Crayton Gravely raised his eyes toward the ranger and the woman who moved away along the trail in a low wake of fine brown dust. He smiled, and with his pale white fingers he opened the old woman's severed hand, took the kindling straps from it, and dropped the weathered hand to the ground. Working the rawhide kindling straps between his bloody fingers, he drew them tight, liking the dull pain it caused as his fingers pulsed against them.

What a splendid young woman, he thought, seeing them grow smaller along the trail, and still recalling the scent of her, and the fire it had sparked in him when he'd brushed past her outside the prison walls. It had taken all of his self-restraint to keep from hurling himself on her then and there.

He smiled, picturing his face on her warm throat, picturing it so clearly he could feel it, could taste it. He could not remember ever wanting anything as badly as he wanted this woman. He would have moved on her like a panther, so quickly no one could have stopped him. A moment was all he needed . . . to taste her, to do what he would have done to her before the ranger killed him. He could do a lot in one swift brutal moment.

But enough of that. There was plenty of time. She would keep until later. He shook his head and gazed out across the sand flats where the young priest had kneeled down beside a body on the ground. Beside the priest stood the horse. *Ah-yes, a big, strong horse complete with an army saddle . . .*

He now had in his possession a butcher knife, the rawhide straps, a bag of food he'd taken from the old woman's adobe, and under his faded serape the battered straw sombrero he'd found blowing across the ground just before daylight. Next he would have a horse, and the robe and mantle of a holy man. His eyes moved from the kneeling priest to the young soldier who searched the brush in the sand flats three hundred yards away. Soon he would have a pistol, and a rifle perhaps. He could even have a soldier's uniform if he wanted it. But he found the clothing of a priest more promising. *Aw, the possibilities . . .*

Acquiring things was not hard for him. It never had been.

Things had always come to him as he needed them, it seemed; and he always took what was needed from these blessed, mindless creatures who roamed the earth. He smiled down at the weathered hand lying at his feet, ducked his head, and moved toward the priest, the kindling straps between his hands, his hands folded beneath the serape.

He knew the priest would see what he wanted to see coming toward him across the sand flats . . . an old woman gathering brush for her *chimnea* because in spite of all that had happened in the night an old peasant woman would know that life must go on . . . and so she went about her daily task. Crayton Gravely growled low under his breath and lapped his tongue out and across his lips. His head bowed as he moved forward, his feet taking halting steps, the way an old peasant woman would.

The priest would have no idea that what was coming upon him was not an old peasant woman at all—not even a man in fact. What came upon him, Gravely knew, was a half-man, half-panther . . . something out of the nightmare of a sick and frightened child; yet something real, alive and well, and still killing after all these many years.

Chapter 5

Rance Plum and Jack the Spider rode out through the broken main gates of the prison, Plum seething and the Spider mumbling and cursing under his breath. They rode along the dusty trail where some of the onlookers returning to their adobes had to jump to one side and fan their way through the dust when the horses rumbled past them. At the far end of the adobes the sand flats opened wide before them, and they reined down and sat staring for a moment until Plum said, "I should've shot that peckerwood and left him lying in the dirt."

"Yeah, shoot the warden. That would've solved everything," said the Spider, "except getting our money. Caslado is the one we should've shot, back when we caught up with him. Bringing him in alive was your idea, not mine."

Plum glared at him. "You have a lot to learn, Mr. Spider. A man cannot make a good, solid name for himself by simply shooting everyone he comes across. Have you forgotten how dashing we looked the day we threw Caslado down from his horse in chains? Remember how the newspapermen all gathered around us? How they hung on our every word?"

"Dashing, your arse." The Spider spit. "I'd druther remember how we got all our money like we would've if we'd gone on and shot him. Now we're broke, hunting escaped convicts for ten dollars a head. By the time you figure grain for the horses, our cost for supplies, we won't make squat on this deal . . . can't afford to shoot one of them convicts over once or twice or we'll go in the hole paying for our bullets."

Plum slumped and glared at the Spider with a disgusted expression. In Rance Plum's boot he had five hundred dollars folded and stuffed inside his sock—something he wasn't about to mention to Jack the Spider. "Do you honestly think I intend to hunt convicts for ten dollars a head, when I still have a contract here worth three thousand more dollars once we kill Caslado? I only agreed to round up convicts in order to keep our hand in the game. We're going after Ernesto Caslado, rest assured."

"I don't know," the Spider said in a hesitant tone. "That means we'll be crossing paths with that ranger and his woman. I don't like fooling with them. Don't forget, he once broke a board over my head."

"Then you do propose to stay here and work for ten dollars a head?"

The Spider squinted, running it all through his mind. "What about Crazy Gravy? The warden said two *hundred* for him. Maybe we'd be better off just staying around here close and tracking him down."

"For crying out loud," Plum shouted. "Look around you." He swung an arm, taking in the sand flats. A hundred yards away they caught a glimpse of a priest riding off on a big army horse. "How can we track a man on foot when every convict who escaped is on foot. Can you distinguish Crazy Gravy's footprint? Of course you can't."

The Spider spit and ran a hand over his mouth. "Unless the sumbitch is invisible, there has to be some way to identify him."

"No, Mr. Spider. On the contrary. Nobody seems to be able to identify this lunatic—even the warden's description is vague, and he's had the man in custody the past two years."

"Horseshit! You mean to tell me they been squeezing his ears, measuring his head, and God knows what all else for two years, and they've got no damn notion at all what the sumbitch looks like? And they call *him* a lunatic?" He cocked his head toward Rance Plum. Sunlight glistened on his clouded eye.

"All I'm simply saying is—"

"Alls you're saying is, we're gonna get screwed out of more money if we don't play this right. I ain't afraid of no rat-eating lunatic. I'll sink his head on a fence post."

"Oh, you will?" Now Plum lifted a brow. "And what if we should happen upon him, not knowing it's him? Have you heard what Crazy Gravy does to his victims?"

The Spider let out a tight breath and watched the priest ride out of sight over a low rise of sand. "All right then, how do *you* want to play it? It'll be hard tracking Caslado across the border, you know."

"Of course it would, if we were going across the border. Didn't you hear what the ranger said? Caslado isn't headed for the border; he's headed for the badlands . . . right back to where we caught him the first time."

"Do you . . . Do you think he's going back for the train money? Nobody ever found it. He had to hide it somewhere up there."

Plum rolled his eyes upward. "Spider, Spider. If ignorance is truly bliss, you must be the happiest man on earth. Of course, he's going after the money, you idiot! What else would keep him from running south?"

"You don't have to be insulting." The Spider huffed.

"Yes, well, be that as it may . . ." Plum tossed a gloved hand. "We'll simply let the ranger and the woman lead us to Caslado. We'll stay back and follow them. Once they take us close enough, we'll get in first, kill Caslado, and come back, the conquering heroes as it were." He grinned, again cocking his head to one side.

"What about the money? If we find it, we'll have to give it back. I mean, it wouldn't be right to keep it, huh?"

Plum didn't answer, but only sucked his teeth and gazed off with a tight expression.

"And what about all of Caslado's men? How we going to handle that many armed gunmen?"

"We'll think of something as we go, Mr. Spider." Plum tapped a gloved finger to his head and heeled his horse forward. "Not everything falls in your lap. Sometimes you have to keep your eyes open and use your head."

As they rode away in a swirl of dust, behind them the people returned to their adobes and talked back and forth from their yards about all that had happened the night before. After a while when the heat of midmorning began to press down and waver beneath the sun's harsh white glare, they withdrew indoors; and a young woman asked her husband if he had seen the old woman since daylight.

He shrugged and told her that he hadn't seen her, nor had he noticed a cook fire in her *chimnea* come to think of it. Then he went on to say, "She is old and growing more foolish every day."

The woman considered things for a moment and said, "You don't suppose she was come upon by one of the prisoners?"

"I wouldn't think so," he said. "The soldiers and the guards searched everything."

"Perhaps you should go see if she has wandered off in search of kindling."

He gazed out across the wavering sand flats, across mesquite and scrub pinyon. Then with a sigh he said that he would go search for her, but first he would go to her adobe. An old woman like her might well have gone back to bed after all the commotion and was now fast asleep while they stood here worrying about her.

"I am sure you are right," his wife said as he turned and

took his battered hat from a peg on the wall and slipped out into the sunlight.

While he was gone, she stepped out back beneath the canvas overhang where their mule looked at her with a strand of dried grass hanging from its turning jaws. She gathered her husband's hammer and trowel and stone-working tools and shook the dust from them and put them in his wooden toolbox. There would be much work for him now at the prison. She smiled to herself, leaning over the toolbox. There was much irony in this world where even in the smoke that rose from an act of man's violence came promise of substance for man's future.

In a moment she heard the back door creak open, and without looking around, she said, "Was she all right? Did you find her?"

When a silence passed and her husband did not answer, she heard the heavy, rasping breathing behind her. She turned toward it, then gasped and threw a hand to her mouth. She stood and took a step back to escape what came slowly toward her. But then she stopped, realizing she could not escape.

She crossed herself and stared in horror as her husband moved forward, his breath rasping in his chest, dark blood running down the front of his trousers. Cradled in his arms was what might have been the remains of an elk set upon by a pack of wolves. Yet she knew this naked mutilated thing was no elk, as her husband bent down and laid it in the dirt at her feet.

It was afternoon by the time the ranger and the woman drew nearer and nearer to the old relay station on the far side of the sand flats. The hoofprints led them wide of the low foothills to the west and higher up toward the tall, jagged rocks that stood like grim sentinels along the edge of the badlands. It would take a rider two days to reach the border army post south of the prison, and another two days to bring back any help.

Meanwhile, the ranger knew that he and Maria were the only ones following a warm trail. Rather than have that trail grow cold on them, they pressed on with wary eyes on the hoofprints, ever mindful of the possibility of coming upon escaped prisoners.

The ranger always kept a list of names of the wanted men he hunted inside his faded tan riding duster, and now as they rode along, he took out the list and a pencil stub, and across the very top he wrote the name Ernie Caslado, and beside it he drew a question mark. This he did to remind himself that he was out to do more than catch Ernesto Caslado. If he was any judge of men, the ranger knew Caslado was out to settle a score. Caslado would lead him to a killer. He was sure of it.

Ahead of him ten yards, leading their pack mule, Maria looked back and saw him fold the list and put it away. Seeing it, she shook her head and turned around. He smiled to himself, watching her ride on, sitting tall in her saddle with her rifle propped up from her thigh. Her long dark hair swayed back and forth with the slow rhythm of the horse. She was a beautiful young woman, and it had taken him a while to get used to her, to accept her into this harsh life he led.

He'd met her over a year ago while he searched for the killer, Montana Red Hollis, and although he had taken her prisoner after one of the desert *comadreja* she rode with had wounded him with a poison arrow, she had later saved his life. She'd also been there when at last he'd faced off with Montana Red, and had it not been for her that day . . .

Well, he didn't like to think about what might have happened. Montana Red was dead now, and that was all that mattered.

Maria had been with him ever since. She rode, and

fought, and read sign as well if not better than any man he'd ever known. Now he watched her stop her big roan and lean slightly and study the prints on the ground. If he dared think there was such a thing as decency left in this dark, violent world of his, it was because he'd seen a spark of it in this woman's eyes. She'd shown him something within himself he'd long denied, a caring of sorts, for himself, for others.

He watched her now as she raised her eyes back to him and said, "We have something new here." She swung her rifle over and pointed it down at the ground.

He heeled his white barb forward and stopped beside her, then looked down at where two sets of barefoot prints cut across the horse's hoofprints. "Yep, a couple more escapees no doubt," he said. "Looks like we'll be dealing with convicts this whole trip." His eyes followed the footprints across the sand, then he straightened and gazed all around the wavering flatlands. "They won't get far on foot. We'll find them hiding somewhere around the old relay station, most likely."

"If the old man still tends goats there, I will ride in and bring us back supplies," she said, turning her roan away from the trail they'd followed and heeling it out in the crooked path of the two footprints. "I'll meet you along the trail."

"Wait up," he said. "I'll ride with you. These prints will still be here an hour from now, I reckon." He heeled his white barb beside her, the barb puffing and slinging froth from its muzzle.

She smiled slightly, looking away from him. He was worried about her. She knew it. But she didn't mind. She liked it, in fact, to a certain extent, although she'd never admit it. Before him, it had been a long time since anybody had worried about her, or cared one way or the other if she lived or died. "*Sí*," she said, "we can both ride in."

When they stopped at the top of a low rise looking down

on the old crumbling adobe coach station a hundred yards below, the ranger squinted and said under his breath, "Looks like they've been here and done their worst." From the bough of a stark cottonwood tree, they saw the body turn slowly in the air, hanging from a rope around both wrists.

"But that is not the old man who tends goats," Maria said; and they put their horses forward into a trot down the slope of sand and onto the valley of rock and space clumps of juniper and gramma grass.

Nearing the station, they heard a sharp yelp, followed by harsh laughter. Then the old man's voice rose like gravel rattling in a bucket. "Steal my goats, eh?" They saw his hands raise a wooden rifle stock above a crumbled adobe wall, then fall with a solid thud. Behind the wall the voice of another man cried out.

"Easy there," the ranger said, sliding his horse down near the cottonwood tree. He glanced up at the body hanging there and saw the ragged prison-issue trousers as he moved quickly over to the crumbled wall. "What's going on here, old-timer? Are you all right?"

"Ha! I'm fine!" The old goat tender straightened up on the other side of the short crumbled wall and spit down at the bloody man on the ground. "I've got me a couple of goat-killing horse thieves here," he said. "Gonna do them both in." He raised the rifle stock for another swing, but the ranger caught his forearm. The old man shot him a hard glare, then spit down on the battered man moaning at his feet. "I'll finish him off later then."

Maria had stopped her horse beside the man hanging in the tree. He moaned across bloody swollen lips and tried to focus on her as she stepped up on her saddle and cut him free with a small pocketknife.

"Here! What are you doing, little lady?" The old goat tender scrambled over the short wall and started toward her swinging the rifle stock over his head. "Don't cut that rascal down! I liked to never got him up there!"

"Take it easy," the ranger said, stopping the old man, taking the rifle stock from his hand. "Don't you realize what you've got here? These men escaped from the prison last night. There could be some reward money for you capturing them."

The old man stopped short. "Ranger, are you serious? I've caught me some hardened criminals here?"

"That's right." The ranger glanced at Maria, who'd stepped down from her horse and now helped the man to his feet and against the cottonwood tree. "But whatever reward they pay will be for returning them alive," he added.

"Aw, hell. They don't look very hardened to me." The old man rubbed his scraggly beard and squinted toward the man against the tree. "Are you real sure about that alive part? They kilt a fine goat of mine and was making off with it." He thumbed toward a spindly-legged dun horse that stood beyond the crumbling adobe wall. "Fixing to take my only horse too."

"Yep, I'm pretty sure there's a reward," the ranger said. The man on the ground dragged himself up and held onto the crumbled wall. The ranger reached out, and with the old man's help pulled the prisoner across the wall and leaned him against it. "It'd be easier on you if you march them back on foot instead of hauling their bodies in."

The old man grunted, rubbed his jaw, and said, "I suppose you're right. If they're dead, they get to ride, and *I* have to walk."

"That's right," the ranger said. "This way, you ride, let them walk."

The old man laughed with a wheeze. "Glad ya came along when ya did, ranger. I'm so tore up over that goat, I ain't thinking straight right now."

Maria walked over with a gourd dipper full of water, and

before the ranger could stop her, she'd handed it to the prisoner. He took it and drank, then splashed some of it into his parched face and looked around through swollen eyes. "We're so hungry we . . . we would've et anything."

"Not my goats though! You dirty rotten—" The old man drew back the rifle stock, but the ranger held him back with a raised arm.

"The trail you and your friend crossed back there, was it Caslado's?"

"I ain't . . . saying nothing," the prisoner replied. "If he gets away . . . more power to him."

The ranger snatched the water gourd from his hands and shot Maria a glance. "I knew we shoulda questioned ya first," he said to the prisoner.

The other prisoner staggered forward from against the cottonwood tree. "I don't owe Caslado nothing," he said. "Yeah, we saw him and his men leave . . . on horseback when we snuck out the back gates. We followed their . . . tracks most of the night. Better than getting turned around in the dark." His breath still heaved in his chest as he reached out for the water gourd. The ranger gave it to him. "We lost them for a while . . . then found them again out there." He pointed his free hand toward the sand flats. "Couldn't believe they're headed into the badlands."

The other prisoner said to him as he drank from the gourd, "You jack-potting rat, you. I hope Caslado finds out who told on him—"

"Yeah? Well, I'll jack-pot him all right." The prisoner splashed water on his face and wiped it around with his hand. "If Caslado was . . . any kind of friend, he'd let us know first . . . so we could've planned something ourselves."

"So nobody knew about it but Caslado, huh?" The ranger watched his eyes.

"And JC, the guard," the prisoner said, his breath coming

back stronger. "He was in on it. He's an outlaw in the making."

"The guard with the star tattoo on his neck?" the ranger asked, still watching his eyes.

"Yeah, he's the one. JC McLawry. Hawkins and Kreeger probably knew about it too. We saw them leave together." He handed the water gourd back to Maria, shot a defiant glance at his partner, then looked back at the ranger. "Anything else you want to know?"

"Yep. What about Crayton Gravely? Did he get away?"

"I don't know about Crazy Gravy." The prisoner shook his wet, dirty head. "He was still in his cell when we left. Wouldn't come out. The building was flaming high when we looked back on it. I hope he never made it. That's one man oughta be put in the ground. You hear what he done back in Illinois? They say he—"

"*Wouldn't* come out, huh?" the ranger asked, cutting him off.

The prisoner nodded. "That's right. I can't see anybody living through that fire, the way it was blowing. Shows you right there how crazy he is."

The ranger looked at Maria. Their eyes met in question for a moment, then he turned and looked back in the direction of the prison, now miles behind, beyond the wavering heat of the sand flats. "Sounds pretty crazy to me," the ranger said. He looked back at the prisoner. "Who opened the rear gates?"

"The what?" The prisoner only stared.

"Somebody had to unlock the rear gates, didn't they?"

"I guess so . . . but I have no idea." He scratched his dirty head. "They only used that gate now and then, for hauling out garbage mostly."

"Who kept the key to it?" The ranger still watched his eyes.

The prisoner shrugged. "A guard, you figure?"

The ranger didn't answer. Instead, he turned to the old man and said, "Since one of your goats is dead anyway, let's skewer it up and cook it. I'll pay you for it."

"Naw." The old man waved him off with a rough hand. "Your money ain't no good here, ranger. This goat's on the house."

The old man chuckled and walked off, and Maria turned to the ranger and said, "So, we will not be leaving in an hour as you said?"

"Naw. We'll spend the night here, keep an eye on things. Strike out for San Paulo at first light. We know where to pick up Caslado's trail." He glanced at the two prisoners, then back to her. "He'll get an early start back to the prison with these boys. Meanwhile, let's keep him company."

The old goat tender came back with the slaughtered milk goat under his arm as Maria and the ranger led their horses to a trough beside the well, loosened their cinches, and let them draw water. In moments a fire licked and crackled of mesquite brush, and the skinned goat stood skewered on a turning rack above it.

The ranger and the woman watered their horses and rubbed them down with a handful of dried gramma grass before resting them beneath the thin shade of the cottonwood tree. While the old man turned the skewered goat above a bed of hot coals, the prisoners sat watching with their hands tied in front of them, a few yards away under a lean-to tarpaulin, out of the afternoon sun.

"Keep an eye on him tonight while I'm gone," the ranger said in a low tone, nodding toward the two prisoners. "That one will make a break for it if he can."

"You mean the surly one?" Maria asked as she dropped her saddle against the cottonwood tree.

"No. I mean the talker. The surly one's done in and he knows it. That's why he's got nothing to say. The talker figures he's still got some play left in him. That's why he's being so helpful. Wants to get our guard down."

She nodded. "How long will you be gone?"

"Not long, a couple of hours. I just want to see what the smell of cooked meat brings in off the sand flats tonight. This could turn into a busy spot. I want to get far enough out to see whatever moves between me and the firelight."

Evening shadows grew long and thin until the fiery red reef on the western horizon smoldered down like spent candle wax. The old goat tender talked on and on above a tin plate full of steaming goat meat, recalling how once this crumbling relay station had stood strong and sparkling behind new corral railing, and had served sometimes as many as ten or fifteen travelers a day back when the stagecoaches still ran. And he picked a fleck of blackened meat from between his long teeth, spit it away, and said that soon the stage business would return once people came to their senses, once they realized that no rails could last in this blasted country.

The ranger and Maria listened to him and passed a guarded smile back and forth. Then the ranger moved his empty tin plate back and forth through the low flames, then sat it on the ground, and stood up, dusting the seat of his trousers. He ran a glance across the prisoners. The surly one lay collapsed back in the dirt with his shirt open and his full belly swollen. He snored with his hands tied and a forearm thrown over his face.

The other prisoner, the talker, had sat staring for the past hour, at first into the crackling coals, then at the ranger and the rifle across his lap, then at the horses, then off across the darkness past the circling glow of firelight. Maria caught the slightest turn of the ranger's eyes as he gestured them toward the horses; and without another word he walked out of the firelight, bridled his white barb, and walked away south, leading the horse bare-backed into the night.

"He's not leaving, is he?" the prisoner asked, looking concerned.

"No," she answered and offered no more.

A few moments passed, and the prisoner squirmed and looked uncomfortable, then said, looking embarrassed, "Ma'am, I hate to mention this, but I got to go something awful. All that water on top of the goat meat, I suppose." He looked from her to the old man, then back. "Any chance he might walk me over somewhere?"

She gave a thin, tight smile. "No, not at all."

"But, ma'am." He squirmed some more, looking distressed. "This is serious. Can't he just keep an eye on me?"

She stood up, dusted her trousers, and let the tip of her rifle go forward. "Come on then. *I* will keep an eye on you."

The old man chuckled and wheezed under his breath. The prisoner stared at her for a second, then looked away. "Maybe I can wait a few more minutes."

"I'm certain you can." She sat back down, jacked a cartridge up into the chamber of her rifle, and laid it across her lap, her gloved finger wrapped around the trigger, her dark eyes fixed on his until he at length broke their gaze and lowered his face. Then she looked up past the golden glow of firelight and into the dome of darkness above them. She almost smiled to herself. The ranger was right about the prisoners. This one still had some play left in him.

Chapter 6

The ranger had lingered nearby, outside the circle of fire-light, listening to the prisoner and Maria bicker back and forth until he'd heard the metallic click of Maria's rifle lever. Then he smiled and moved away as quiet as a spirit, leading his horse, hearing Maria's words fade behind him amid the low crackling of mesquite embers.

He knew she would resent his staying close by the way he had, long enough to see how she handled herself. But his nature demanded that he watch all things. Quiet vigil was part of the stuff he was made of—his instincts. His nature took nothing for granted, not of himself, nor of those who rode with him. To deny his nature would be to deny the nature of all things that were a part of this harsh and deadly world. Like all creatures who survived the badlands, his ways were ingrained in him.

When he'd moved thirty yards out, he walked the horse in a broad circle until he stood north of the campfire near the trail they'd followed in from the prison. There he found a low scrub pinyon, hitched his horse to it, walked away a few feet, and rested in the sand with his duster wrapped around him. He leveled his breathing to the pulse of the desert and the silence of night until the land and its darkness and all things they held became a part of him. An hour would pass before the first soft brush of padded paws moved across the sand.

Above the whisper of panting breath, two red eyes glowed toward him in the darkness of a quarter moon. *Coyotes* . . . He sat still as stone. In a moment the pair of eyes were joined by another, and both pair blinked and stared, and slunk forward, low to the ground. When they drew close enough for him to hear one of them whine low under its breath, he made a sharp hiss toward them and saw them spin in a black flurry and race away.

In a moment something big and dark swept down from the sky in a powerful batting of wings and settled itself atop the scrub pinyon. And the ranger settled in with it, akin to it now, his eyes training to the darkness with it, scanning and sifting through the black essence for another half hour before hearing the faint flat sound of hooves, moving forward from a long way off.

He knew he would never have discerned the foreign sound of man and horse had his senses not been tuned to the still rhythm of the desert floor. This too was a part of the stuff he was made of. This was a part of him he could not explain, neither to Maria nor to anyone else, although there was nothing magical or mystical about it. He simply read the land through the senses of those things around him, and acted on instinct, theirs as well as his own.

In a while, behind him, above the pinyon, the wings of the large bird stirred restlessly at the distant sound. *Got it* . . . He shifted slightly toward the sound, waited as it drew nearer, then as the bird thrashed and rose up from the pinyon in a heavy thrust of wing, the ranger moved forward and stopped in the darkness where his boot heels felt the edge of the narrow trail beneath them.

In moments, another pair of coyotes moved closer and blinked their red eyes at him, but this time he did not make a sound to shoo them away. He waited until the sound of the single horse and rider drew within a few yards. Then the red eyes flashed toward the sound and moved away across the sand. The ranger crouched lower, downwind of the horse whose labored breath he now heard as it struggled nearer. A frightened voice goaded the animal in a harsh whisper. "Come on, damn your hide!"

The tired animal let go a tight cry beneath the sound of reins slapping its side; and in another second the ranger laid his rifle on the ground and swept up and forward, a dark figure coming out of nowhere. Before man or horse could detect him, he grabbed the animal by its wet bridle and jerked it sideways to a halt.

"What the——" The rider tried to call out as he yanked against the reins, but the ranger's free hand slipped the stirrup from his boot and pitched him up out of the saddle.

"Don't shoot! Please! Don't shoot!" The man thrashed in the sand with an arm thrown up to protect his face. "Take the horse! It's yours! Please don't kill me! I'm one of you . . . one of——"

"Shut up," the ranger said. He scanned the darkness along the trail, then turned his eyes back to the dark figure on the ground. "How many more are behind you?" Beside him the tired horse swayed and nearly fell.

"No . . . Nobody. Just me. I'm trying to get away, the same as you."

The ranger listened to him, but with his hearing partly tuned to the dark trail behind them. He heard nothing along the trail, yet his senses felt something out there, something silent and unseen, something lurking. "Don't lie to me," he said.

"I'm not lying. It's just me. We're both in the same shape here, on the run."

The ranger moved closer, but stopping a few feet back in the darkness. "Oh? A convict, huh?"

"Yeah, yeah, that's right!" The man squinted, trying to see the trigger more clearly in the thin moonlight. "Can't we work together here? Team up? Two heads are better than one, right? We can share the horse till we get to the old relay station up ahead—there, you can see the fire from here." He pointed a finger toward the glow on the horizon.

"You've done this poor animal in." The ranger moved even closer, bending down over him, swinging his duster open and lifting his pistol from his holster.

"That's all right. We'll get another. We'll take what we want once we—" His words stopped short as he caught sight of the badge on the ranger's vest through the open duster. "You're . . . a lawman?" His voice lowered.

"Yep, a ranger. Makes you feel foolish, don't it?" He reached out with his free hand, took the man by the shoulder, and raised him to his feet. Once more he sensed something out in the darkness, but he shook off the feeling.

The man dusted his face with a dirty hand, hesitated for a second, then let out a breath and said, "No, not at all. The fact is, I thank God you found me. I'm a lawman myself."

"You don't say?" The ranger reached out a gloved hand and patted the man down for weapons. "Are you packing anything I need to know about?" When the man tried to take a step back, the ranger grabbed him by the shirt and jerked him forward.

"Take it easy! I told you, I'm a lawman myself—a guard from the prison."

"You sure reformed real quick," the ranger said. "Now keep both hands up where I can see them, till we both decide whether you're a good guy or a bad guy." He let go of the man's shirt, but kept him covered with his pistol.

"Oh. But I just said all that convict stuff in case you was one of them. My name's Samuel Burns . . . I really am a prison guard, honest I am."

"I believe you," the ranger said.

"You . . . you do?"

"Yep." The ranger glanced at the tired horse where it stood swaying, its breath pounding, its legs going limp. "But

I also believe you're trying just as hard as them convicts to get away from something." The horse staggered, went down on its front knees, and collapsed over on its side. "If you're not, you've sure killed a horse for no good reason."

"No. I'm not running from anything." Burns fidgeted in place, his hands chest high. "I'm just out here tracking, the same as you, seeing if I can round up any convicts before they hurt somebody. It's my job, ranger; surely you understand."

"Sure, I understand." The ranger looked out across the darkness at the red eyes of coyotes staring back at them from a safe distance. "I understand who you are and what you've done."

"What I've done? What do you mean?"

The ranger didn't answer, but instead stepped over to the downed horse and leaned near it, drawing his knife from his boot. Burns winced, turning his face away in the darkness at the low gasping sound of the horse. In a second, when the horse fell silent, he turned back to the ranger when the ranger stepped over to him with the bloody knife hanging from his hand.

"Look, ranger, maybe you and I have gotten off on the wrong foot here." He gave a stiff smile in the darkness, letting his raised hands drift down a bit. But his hands stopped and came back up when the ranger leveled the big pistol close to his chest.

"Who paid you to do it?" The ranger's eyes searched his in the thin moonlight.

"What? I don't know what you're talking about—"

"I'm talking about opening the back gate. Who paid you? Where'd you get the key? Did the other guard give it to you? The one called JC? The one with the star tattoo?"

"You're out of your mind, ranger."

"Naw, I'm not." The ranger shook his head, then bluffing,

he added, "The warden already knows about it. He told me all about you."

"He . . . He did?" Burns swallowed a hard knot in his throat, hesitated for a second, then recovered. "Well, he's wrong! Dead wrong!"

"All right then." The ranger shrugged. "I won't waste no time on you. I'll shoot you, leave you here with the horse. Let the coyotes have at you." He cocked the pistol with a flick of his thumb.

"Wait! My God! You'd just shoot me? What kind of lawman would do a thing like that?"

"What kind of prison guard would unlock a gate and let prisoners escape?" The ranger poised the pistol an inch from Burns's heart. "Killing you right here doesn't mean a lot to me. Start talking."

A nerve twitched in Burns's jaw. He glanced all around in the darkness. "What's the use?" His shoulders slumped, and he shook his head. "Lord, what have I done? It was all JC's idea. He brought me in on it. Said we could make more money riding with Caslado than we'd ever make as prison screws. We were supposed to rob some banks and have a gay ole time."

"Did you always carry a key to the back gate, or did JC give it to you?"

"Neither." He shook his head. "Nobody but the warden ever carried *that* key. He gave it to me that afternoon."

"Is that right?" The ranger lowered the pistol an inch.

"Yeah. Just a stroke of luck, I guess. We'd figured on having to shoot our way out through the front. It woulda been a mess with those cannon firing and all."

Stroke of luck? The ranger considered it for a second. "And where were Caslado's getaway men waiting? Out front?"

"No. Some of them was waiting out back for us. But I never made it. Had to get out on my own after my horse went down. Found me another one and thought I could catch up to them along the trail. Never figured them to head north into the badlands though."

"I think they might have had a change of plans." The ranger lowered the pistol some more. "You don't do well with horses, do you?"

"I never did," the young guard said. After a second of silence, he asked, "What do you think they'll do to me? Hang me?"

"Naw. I doubt if they'll hang you. But it might be best if they did. How you figure the other prisoners are going to treat you once you're in there with them, pulling your time?"

"I . . . I didn't consider it at the time." Burns looked down. "It just got so danged terrible working there, day in, day out. I had to do something, or else go crazy. It was no better than being a prisoner if you think about it."

"I reckon you'll have plenty of time to think about it, once they slam the cell door behind you," the ranger said. Even in the darkness he could see that he was not much more than a child. He shook his head, "Come on, Burns, let's go." Taking Samuel Burns by the shoulder, he shoved him forward, ahead of him toward the pinyon tree where the white barb stood scraping a hoof in the sand. "Act like you've got some sense, and you'll get something to eat. But make one cross move and you'll be feeding the buzzards, fair enough?"

Samuel Burns swallowed a dry knot in his throat. "Yes, sir. I'll do the best I can."

Thirty yards behind them, Crayton Gravely sat on his haunches against a cusp of sandy soil with his horse's reins hanging from his hand. He listened to the sound of their words drift to him on the night air. They had moved farther away now and stopped for a moment. A metallic sound clicked in the darkness, then they moved away again. This would be the ranger snapping handcuffs on Sammy-boy

Burns, he thought; and he smiled, glad that he hadn't killed the young guard earlier, glad that he had simply stayed back, waited, bided his time, and followed him.

He was good at waiting. Two years within the confines of his steel-and-stone framework had taught him to hold his senses and impulses in check. He'd learned to set quietly over the past two years, and had swallowed the white rage that hummed inside his brain, as the doctors shaved his head and measured and drew sketches of his skull. The wild creature within had learned to subdue itself, to draw back from the urge to cast itself forward and feel their warm throats break against the crush of its jaws.

Now the creature clawed and screamed out from inside him. But he could hold it back a while longer. He could gaze out through the patient eyes and pretense of the holy man whose spirit he'd devoured, while inside him his hunger pitched and boiled. The warm scent of Sammy-boy, the guard, had drifted back to him along the trail, so strong that at times he'd been able to follow him by scent alone, yet he'd managed to be patient. *Patience, my son . . .*

He lifted the broad, flat-brimmed hat from his head and fanned it back and forth in front of his face, stirring the aroma of the desert and the feeling it left in his nostrils. His senses were charged and keen. The musty smell of coyote wafted in the air, with it the scent of reptile and rodent. These scents aroused his hunger, and he looked up at the dark silhouette of the horse beside him. The horse shifted back and forth on its hooves, sawing its head against the reins and casting a dark wide-eyed gaze down at him.

Crayton Gravely barred his teeth upward toward the nervous animal, and felt the horse shy back against the reins. Then, laughing under his breath, he stood up, jerked the animal over close to him, and slipped up into the army saddle. This dumb brute had nothing to fear. Not for now anyway. He needed this horse, this warm, pulsing, blood-filled thing beneath him. Better prey lay ahead, across the rise and fall of sand. Somewhere out there at the glowing dome of light would be the woman. He knew it. He could feel it. He could sense the warm blood coursing through her veins, her flesh warming perhaps at that very moment before the distant firelight. He would have her. Soon . . . he would have her.

On the first upward plateau beyond the tall, jagged walls of the badlands, the rickety freight wagon sped through the purple night, bucking, swaying, leaning dangerously far to one side, then to the other, across the rocky ground. Dust billowed and spun from its spokes. The wheels left the ground and slammed back down, hard, pitching the shotgun rider over the wooden seat and onto the canvas-wrapped cargo. He scrambled up onto his knees, swaying, his floppy hat flying off his head. His shotgun exploded in the darkness, its flash revealing the terror in his red-rimmed eyes. His white beard stood sideways in the onrush of desert air.

"Lord God, Victor! Did you hit anything?" the driver yelled over his shoulder, slapping the long reins hard against the mules' sweaty backs. Behind the wagon, rifle and pistol fire blossomed and exploded. Caslado and his men drew nearer, their horses tired, but still overcoming the four-mule team.

"Not a thing!" the shotgun rider yelled in reply. His long gray hair swept across his dirty face. He shoved it aside and fired back into the darkness. "We're done in for sure!"

The driver slapped the reins. The four mules brayed loud and pounded on. "Take my pistol," the driver called back. "Get as many as ya can!"

The shotgun rider rocked forward, snatched the pistol from the driver's holster, and said, "It's been good knowing you, Tack! Reckon we'll cash in here!" He turned, pitching back and forth, and fired back as the shots from the riders slapped into the cargo bundles and whistled past his bearded face. An edge of the cargo canvas pulled loose and flapped in the air. Books and bags of coffee beans spilled out and blew upward in the wake of dust.

"Brace up, Victor," the driver yelled. "I'll run us off an edge before I let them bastards take it!"

"Do it then!" the shotgun rider yelled, still firing back.

But as Caslado's men drew up flanking them, the wagon threw a rear wheel and slid sideways, pulling the mules off balance and off their hooves. For a moment the pulse of the world seemed to slow down as a rolling ball of cargo, wood, man, and mules tossed forward above the ground in a blast of dust, then spread itself out in a long, dark streak and settled on the desert floor.

"Hot-dang," Al Kreeger said to Levon Hawkins, fanning dust with his hand as he and the others stepped their horses in among the strewn debris. "Now this is my kind of hoe-down!"

One of the young Mexicans crossed himself and whispered the name of the Blessed Virgin under his breath. "Is this what we have come here to do?" he whispered to the other young Mexican beside him.

"Be quiet," the other man said, nudging his horse forward. "You saw what old Carlos got . . . and he has been with Caslado a lot longer than us."

"Yee-hiii," Al Kreeger shouted, "got me some boots here! Some gloves too!" He sprang out of his saddle and over to one of the old teamsters lying on the ground. The old teamster groaned, and Kreeger snatched the pistol from his waist and cocked it down in the man's face.

"Don't shoot him," the young Mexican called out. "Save your ammunition."

"Yeah? Well, you can kiss my see-through, boy!" Kreeger laughed and started to fire.

"He's right, Al," JC said, stopping him. "We need what bullets we've got. The old man's as good as dead anyway."

Levon Hawkins stepped in and started pulling the old teamster's boots from his feet. Al Kreeger shoved him away, laughing. "Get your own boots and gloves, Hawk, these babies are all mine."

"Then you better put your pistol away and get ta taking them," Hawkins said. He turned and walked over to the other teamster twenty feet away. The man had stirred and started crawling inch by inch across the rocky ground. Hawkins sat his foot down on the man's back. "Where you think you're going, this time of night, huh?"

The injured mules lay braying and thrashing in pain until shots rang out, and one by one their tortured voices stopped short. In moments the wrecked freight wagon was set ablaze. Flames licked high into the night. Gathered back from the fire, and half circling it, the dusty men sat on their haunches with their horses's reins hanging from their hands. They swished warm water in their mouths from gourds and canteens and spit it into their cupped hands and rubbed it on their necks and faces.

They'd watched with eyes like ravaging wolves while three of their compadres chopped a slaughtered mule into quarters and staked the raw meat in the outer reaches of fire. Now the meat began to blacken and broil in its juices, rendering long streams of grease that ran down, flaring and sizzling on glowing oak embers. Within the fire, nail heads and metal rivets from the wagon hull grew white hot and popped like pistol shots.

A torn and battered book lay near Al Kreeger, and he reached out with the toe of his newly acquired boot and kicked it away. "What good's books anyway. Ain't nobody gonna read 'em. You'd think in a whole wagon load of goods there'd be one damn bottle of rye, at least." Then he spit and ran the back of his hand across his parched lips.

"Yeah, you'd think," Hawkins said, staring above the flames into the curling rise of black smoke and within it the spinning fiery ashes. "Suppose some of them greasers mighta found some whiskey and ain't telling us?" His eyes moved across the backs of the Mexicans haunched nearer to the fire and over to the two teamsters lying in the dirt. Firelight flickered on their bloody faces. One of them moaned, then fell silent. Flies glistened and swirled above them.

"I better not find out they did," Kreeger said. The three Americans sat back a few yards behind the Mexicans, the Mexicans themselves divided into two groups—the new men JC had brought in and the ones who'd ridden with Caslado in the past. Kreeger nodded toward all of the others and added, "Look at 'em. Ain't a damned blasted one of 'em wouldn't cut our throat for a broken belt buckle—uncivilized bunch of bean suckers."

JC McLawry stood up beside Hawkins, dusted the seat of his trousers, and said. "We'll be in San Paulo come morning. There'll be whiskey there."

"That's tomorrow," said Kreeger. "I'm thirsty now. Can't see what it'd hurt if I just eased around a little . . . maybe see if I can smell any on their breath. If they're lying about it, I'll find out—"

"Don't go messing around," JC said, cutting him off. "I been a year setting this thing up. Ruin it, and you'll have me down your shirt with both feet." He walked away, leading his horse. Kreeger and Hawkins watched him move deeper into the glow of firelight until he stopped beside Ernesto Caslado twenty yards away.

"Shiiiit," Kreeger growled under his breath. "He won't want down my shirt. That boy don't know it, but he never showed me much as a guard. He damn sure ain't showing me nothing now—kissing that greaser's arse like it's a cone of honey."

Hawkins gave a dark, thin smile. "Ain't you beholding to ole JC for cutting us loose? I'm surprised at you, Al."

Kreeger spit, glared at the backs of the Mexicans, then at

the blackening quarters of sizzling mule meat, then into the billowing fire. "Ain't nobody owes nobody nothing in this world, the way I see it."

Hawkins looked him up and down, eyed the butt of the pistol sticking up from Kreeger's waist and the belt of ammunition hanging from his shoulder. "Yeah, same here." He stood up, stretched, and jerked his horse forward. "Come on, Al, looks like that meat's about right, don't it?"

Near the fire, Caslado took a sizzling slab of blackened meat on the point of his knife blade, blew on it, and bit off a mouthful. Beside him, JC drew a knife from his boot and stepped in between two of the Mexicans. He cut a slice of dripping mule meat and stepped back with it on his blade. "Things are looking up, Ernesto," he said.

"Aw, *sí*," Caslado said through a working jaw of gristly meat. "Tomorrow we hit San Paulo, take whatever we need and head on north." Hot pink juice ran down his stubbled chin. He wiped it on his dirty finger, then stuck his finger in his mouth.

"North?" JC took a bite and chewed it as he spoke. "Thought you said the money was *east* of San Paulo, up in the high canyons?"

Ernesto shrugged. "It is. But *we* go north. There is something I must take care of first. A personal matter—then on to the money."

JC hesitated for a second, watching Caslado's hard-lined face in the flicker of firelight. "Our deal was to get the money first, remember?"

"Things change, *mi amigo*." Caslado bent his head sideways and took on another mouthful of meat. He chewed and wagged his gloved finger. "Patience. I am a man of my word, no? You will get what is coming to you. I will see to it. First we ride to the top of the badlands." He shrugged. "Two days—three at the most. Are you with me?"

JC wanted to push the matter, but recalled how quickly

Caslado had killed the Mexican the night before. He nodded, then said in an easy tone, "Sure, I'm with you. Does this have anything to do with that old ranger coming to see you? He had you pretty riled up, didn't he?"

Caslado stopped chewing for a second and shot him a somber glance. "No! He has nothing to do with this. He is a fool, like all gringo lawmen. He came to me with his questions and his tobacco. But I gave him back his tobacco and sent him away with *nothing.*"

"I know," JC said. "But from what I've heard about that ole buzzard, he always finds out something, whether you mean to tell him or not. I figure it's best we hurry and do what we came to do."

"Ha! You must not worry about the ranger. He is old and stupid. And he is on his way home now, thinking I have gone to my grave."

JC took another bite of meat and chewed as he spoke. "I hope you're right."

"What? You are afraid of him?"

"No. But he *is* the one who killed Bent Jackson, Montana Red Hollis, and a dozen others. He's no fool. He brought ole Hawk in, *alive,* and Levon Hawkins is one of the slickest gunmen ever came out of Kansas."

Caslado swallowed, and considered it, then said, "This is true. But the ranger did not face Hawkins in a gun duel."

"No. Instead, he rang his head with an iron skillet. Said he didn't want to waste a bullet on him. Hawk couldn't tell daylight from dark for nearly a week—spent a month in his cell before he knew he'd been convicted."

Caslado worked a piece of gristle from between his teeth and blew it out. "If the ranger comes looking for us with a skillet, I will worry. Until then, forget about him. He is gone home. Besides, if he did stay around, like all the other lawmen, he will be hunting for Crazy Gravy." He tapped a finger to his temple. "This was part of my plan."

JC chewed his hot mule meat and shook his head slowly. "Like I said, I hope you're right."

At the fire, Al Kreeger and Levon Hawkins shouldered their way between the Mexicans and wrenched meat off the charred mule carcass with their gloved hands. The Mexicans stared at them. One of them bristled and drew away as Kreeger leaned near him and sniffed close to his face, like a dog. Then Kreeger gave a nasty grin. "Just checking, boy," he said. And as he and Hawkins moved away, chewing on the hot meat, the Mexicans stepped back in with their knives and murmured curses under their breath.

"They are *peegs*, these gringos," said the one whose face Kreeger had sniffed. "When Ernesto is finished with them . . . I want *that* one. I will cut his sniffing nose from his face." He slashed the blade of his knife down the slab of meat and watched it spread open before him. Outside the circle of fire, coyotes moved in, closer to the smell of blood. They lowered on their haunches and sat still as stone, staring in at the raging fire and at the dark figures of man who milled before it.

Chapter 7

Rance Plum lowered the field lens from his face as the priest rode out of sight over a rise of sand in the distance. "Drat it all!" He rubbed the glare of sun from his eyes, collapsed the brass field lens, and shoved it down into his waist belt. A fiery reef of thin sunlight glittered on the eastern horizon. He spit the taste of dust from his lips and looked down at Jack the Spider, sitting below the edge of the dry wash where they'd spent the night.

"Nothing out there, huh?" The Spider turned up a drink of tepid water from his canteen, then capped it and laid it in the sand beside him. Across the narrow dry wash from him sat an old convict who'd turned himself in to them the night before. He stared at the canteen through glazed eyes and licked his parched lips.

"Nothing indeed," said Plum, "save for that idiot priest!" He kicked idly at a rock and stirred a drift of dust. "For two cents I'd shoot that confounded bead-counting peckerwood and turn him in as a convict."

He stepped down into the dry wash and picked up the canteen from beside Jack the Spider. "What on earth is he doing out here anyway? He certainly can't plan on saving any souls out in the badlands." He swished the water in the canteen, uncapped it, and threw back a short drink. When he lowered it, the old convict leaned slightly forward and raised his bony fingers toward it.

Plum slumped, shook his head, reached out, and placed the canteen into the trembling fingertips. "I've never seen a human being require as much food and water as this old buzzard."

"I say we don't give him any more," the Spider said, staring hard at the old convict's gaunt, drawn face. "Never should have let him turn himself in to us. We've got no time for all this."

The old convict lowered his white-bearded face and wiped a hand across his lips as the Spider spoke. "If he's the only one we catch, it ain't worth riding back to prison. Not for ten damn dollars." Spider spit and stood up, dusting the seat of his trousers.

"Don't forget, I turned *myself* in," the old man said, squinting and wagging a bony finger at the Spider. "I'm entitled to food and water . . . it says so clearly in the Constitution of the United States of America."

"Does it, Plum?" Jack the Spider turned his good eye to Rance Plum, looking uncertain.

"No, for heaven sakes." Plum shook his head.

"The hell it don't!" The old convict rose halfway to his feet, his bushy brows narrowed. "I know my rights here, by thunder. You fellers are responsible for my well-being, whether you like it or not. When they wrote that Constitution, it was done for people like me, who might—"

"That's it. I've had it with him!" Plum jerked his pistol from his holster and cocked it in the old man's face. But before he could fire a shot, something moved around a turn in the dry wash. Plum and Jack the Spider spun toward it. The Spider's pistol came up from his holster in a slick blur of steel and cocked.

"Don't shoot!" Four convicts cowered together in the center of the dry wash with their hands raised. "We're giving up! You got us. Take us into custody."

"How the—?" Plum and the Spider glanced at one another, then back to the four ragged, dirty men. "You were supposed to be watching," Plum hissed at the Spider. "Must I do everything around here myself?"

"Don't blame me!" the Spider said to Plum, but kept his eye on the convicts.

"We been waiting right around the turn here all night long," the convict in front said. "Couldn't risk coming in while it was still dark—afraid you might shoot us. But we're surrendering here, see?" He wiggled his raised hands, stepping forward, adding, "Ole Scratch there is right . . . you got to take care of us till we get back to the yard. It's the law."

"Law, your filthy arse!" Plum fanned them toward the side of the wash with his pistol barrel. "All of you spread out along there. Keep your hands up and drop down to your knees." He tossed a glance to Jack the Spider. "Keep them covered. Can you at least do that?"

"Don't start on me, Plum," the Spider sneered, stepping forward a step.

The old convict chuckled under his breath and said to the newcomers in a raspy voice, "Boys, you just missed one hell of a good breakfast here."

"We did?" a convict answered as he and the others lowered down on the ground with their hands raised. "We're hungry enough to eat a full-grown—"

"Shut up!" Rance Plum shouted, his face gone red and his pistol swinging from one to the other. "You're our prisoners! We're not here to cook and fetch for you! Next one opens his mouth, I'll put a bullet in it! So help me!"

The convicts fell silent, staring up at Plum and the Spider, until the Spider nudged Plum and said in a quiet voice near his ear, "How are we going to feed them?"

Plum fumed. "We're *not* going to feed them, Mr. Spider. Isn't that what you just said a moment ago?"

"Yeah, but I didn't know we'd be breaking the law. I don't want to go to jail. If we've got to feed them—"

"It's not a law, you imbecile. Trust me!" Plum's face swelled red. "You can't listen to these jail-house rats! If they knew anything at all, about *anything,* they wouldn't be here. Now would they?"

The Spider scratched his head up under his hat brim. "Still, it'll take two days to walk them back to prison. We can't just let them starve—"

"Hell no, ya can't," the old convict chimed in. "They'll have you in jail quicker than a cat can scratch—"

"Shut up!" the Spider raged at the old man. Then he calmed himself and glanced at Plum for an answer.

"I know we can't let them starve, Mr. Spider! We simply have to figure out a plan here." Plum shot the Spider an irritated scowl and turned back to the convicts. "Are there any more escapees lurking nearby?"

The convicts looked at one another. "No," said the one nearest him, "the ones who was really serious about getting away, already have." He shrugged. "We only ran because everybody else did. We couldn't just stay there and burn up, could we?"

Plum looked at Jack the Spider. "Perhaps this works out well for us. Instead of searching the entire countryside, we'll take these five back, get our fifty dollars, and get right back on the ranger's trail straightaway. Perhaps he'll even have Caslado in his sights by then."

The Spider squinted. "But our deal with the warden is only for the prisoners we capture, not for the ones who turn themselves in. How's this gonna work?"

"It will be our word against this band of yard-birds." Plum ran a tense hand across his forehead, getting more and more put out with his young partner. "For crying out loud, Mr. Spider. Must I do *all* the thinking here?"

"Aw, yeah?" The Spider sneered and took a step toward Plum with his shoulders leveled. "If you're ever going to do any thinking at all, I wish you'd get started on it."

"Oh?" Plum cocked his head to one side, wiggling his pistol back and forth in his hand. "Well, let me tell you something . . . !"

While Plum and the Spider argued back and forth, the old convict glanced at the newcomers. They stared back at him through caged and hollow eyes. He winked beneath a bushy eyebrow and chuckled under his breath. "It's good to get out and stretch our legs now and then, ain't it, boys?"

Eleven miles ahead of Plum, the Spider, and their ragged dirty prisoners, the ranger tightened the cinch on the white barb, dropped the stirrup, and turned to the old goat tender. "You sure you'll be all right? What about leaving your goats here alone?"

The goat tender stood beside the pack mule the ranger had traded him for his spindly-legged dun horse. A gourd full of water hung from his shoulder by a strip of rawhide. The shotgun hung from his hand. "I'll be fine, so will the goats. They're used to me being gone a couple days at a time. And don't you worry about me handling these yard-birds." He gestured toward the two convicts, who stood with a rope lead drooping between them, the end of the rope wrapped around the mule's saddle horn. "Either one of them gives me any trouble, I'll shoot them both in the leg . . . let them limp their way back to prison."

The convicts looked at one another, the surly one whispering a warning under his breath.

The ranger smiled and lifted the brim of his sombrero. "Yep, you'll be all right. Be sure and tell the warden I'm keeping Samuel Burns with me for a while, just for some questioning. Tell him there's some things I want to get straightened out when I bring him in."

The goat tender chuckled. "I'll sure tell him, ranger. Hope he don't give me any guff about paying the reward money. I caught these two fair and square, didn't I?"

"That you certainly did," the ranger said as the old man stepped up into his stirrup and swung over into the saddle. The mule brayed once, let go a short kick, then settled and swished its short tail. "Tell him Maria and I are your witnesses if you need any." The old man reached out a gloved hand and slapped the mule on the rump. The animal moved forward in short, choppy steps, causing the two convicts to move forward ahead of him.

"Take it easy," the surly prisoner said over his shoulder. He hurried ahead in a quick shuffle, to keep the mule from butting him.

The old man tipped his hat to Maria and the ranger and patted the shotgun across his lap. "You know, I'm kinda taking a shine to this law work. Seems easy enough, so far."

"We knew you would," the ranger said as the mule moved along. He and Maria watched them ride away. By the time they'd attended to their horses and prepared to ride north toward the badlands, they could see only the wake of dust rising up behind the mule, as it lifted high and drifted on the morning breeze.

"All right now, *Sammy-boy*," the ranger said, using the name one of the prisoners had called Burns last night when the ranger brought him in. "Are we going to have any trouble out of you?" He dusted his gloved hands together.

Samuel Burns stood beside the spindly-legged dun horse, staring down at the ground. He'd never liked being called Sammy-boy, but this was not the time to mention it. At the sound of the ranger's voice he raised his face and said, shaking his head slowly, "No, sir. I'll do as I'm told." The morning breeze lifted a strand of his hair, and he moved it from his face with a dirty hand. "I just wished I'd never done any of this."

He had no idea why the ranger decided not to send him back to the prison with the others, and he wasn't about to ask. Soon enough he would feel the heat of the stone cell and hear the sound of steel bars slam shut behind him. He would try to not think about it. For now, each passing hour of freedom was all that mattered to him. Before stepping up into the stirrup, he gazed up and away across the deep morning sky, as if within the endlessness of it lay some reprieve from the dark future that stood before him.

The ranger looked from Samuel Burns to Maria. "Let's ride," he said.

Maria cut her gaze from Burns to the ranger, shook her head, and stepped up atop her horse. With her teeth, she tightened her glove down onto her wrist. "*Sí*, let's ride." She kicked her horse forward of them, the ranger drawing his white barb back a step and motioning for Samuel Burns to fall the dun in between them.

In moments they'd turned into three dark specks, ahead of a drifting sheet of dust; and at the crumbling adobe wall, three goats moved forward and stared at the distant emptiness until the lead goat bumped and nudged and pushed them back into the small herd at the center of the corral.

No sooner had the dust from the three riders settled when a new speck rose up and came forward from the other direction on the sand flats, growing larger and larger through the swirl of wavering heat. Seeing it, the lead goat let out a long, stuttering bleat, tossed his knobby rack back and forth, and scraped his narrow hoof in the sand—his instincts taking a fighting stance against some ancient enemy.

The bell on the goat's neck clanked, then settled in silence amid the stillness of the desert floor. He stood with his nostrils flared and his eyes shining until Crazy Gravy brought his horse forward from the wavering heat and reined it down near the crumbling adobe wall. The herd bleated and milled, then cowered closer together in the small corral.

Rance Plum and Jack the Spider had pushed their prisoners forward across the sand for well over an hour when they came upon the goat tender and his two ragged prisoners. Plum had gigged his horse upward ahead of the others, and there atop a low rise of sand, he rode straight into the glistening bores of the goat tender's shotgun.

"Keep your hands up where they are," the goat tender said, almost smiling at the way he'd gotten the drop on the man. He sat atop the mule with a ten-gauge up and cocked.

Startled, Plum reined down hard, his horse twisting sideways in a spray of sand when it halted. He kept his hands chest high and steady, glancing at the old man, then at the two prisoners sitting in the sand in front of the mule. *Jesus!* He let out a tight breath, collected himself, and said in a clipped tone, "Kindly turn that *barn-blaster* away from me, sir!"

But the old goat tender only grinned at Plum. "Got ya good, didn't I." He fanned the others out in a line as they topped the rise.

Plum spoke back over his shoulder to the Spider without taking his eyes off the cocked shotgun. "Mr. Spider, we have a situation up here. This gentleman has a shotgun pointed at me. *Please!* Don't do anything stupid."

"I won't if he won't," the Spider said from below the rise. In a second his horse topped the rise by itself, the empty stirrups swaying against its sides. Plum tensed, catching a glimpse of the old goat tender's hand tighten on the shotgun. The convicts stared back and forth, their hands up in a cautious show of surrender.

"Now drop that shotgun, old man," Spider's voice called from out of sight.

"For God sakes! Spider! Are you daft! I'm covered here!" Plum pleaded in a shaky voice.

"But I'm not," the Spider said, his voice coming from a few yards away and beneath the edge of the rise. "Now, do like I said, old man, or I'll empty this pistol in ya."

"I'll blast your friend here, *high wide and away,*" the goat tender said to the Spider in a firm voice, staring hard into Rance Plum's eyes from ten feet away.

"Go ahead . . . but I'll still empty this pistol in you," said the Spider, his voice sounding equally determined.

"Spider! Damn, it, all! Have you gone completely insane?" Plum's eyes widened; spit flew from his trembling lips. He cut his eyes back to the goat tender. Sweat beaded on his brow. "Pay no attention to him, sir! We're bounty hunters, same as you! Surely we're all reasonable men here!"

On the ground beside Plum's horse, the old convict glanced along the line at the others and nodded. He smiled across stained and broken teeth and said, "I had a similar thing like this happen the last time I broke out of a prison." The others only stared, blank-faced.

"Bounty hunters, huh?" The goat tender eased a bit, but kept his hand tight on the shotgun.

"Yes! Goodness, yes! Why on earth would we be traveling with this ragged-arse crew if—"

The goat tender cut him off. "I'll lower this shooter once your skittish friend steps into sight and does likewise."

"Hear that, Mr. Spider? All's well here. Just do as the gentleman tells you."

"Uh-uh," the Spider said. "How do I know *he's* a bounty hunter. This could be a trick or something."

"A *trick*—?" Cold sweat broke free on Plum's forehead and ran down the side of his nose. "It's no trick! If you have *any* spark of intelligence left, please use it!"

"Damn it to thunder," the old convict said, stepping out of line, moving along the edge toward the sound of Spider's voice. "I ain't standing here all day, starving to death, whilst you fools figure out who ya are." He stopped and turned his back to the Spider, who stood crouched below the edge of the rise. "Get up here behind me, sonny boy. I ain't got nothing to lose." He shook his dirty head and added, "Damned if you ain't the *puniest* bunch of lawmen I ever seen."

"Watch your mouth, *convict*." When Jack the Spider moved up behind the old convict and lowered his pistol and let down the hammer, the goat tender eased the hammer down on his shotgun and lowered it as well. Plum slumped a bit in his saddle, raised a hand, took off his hat, and ran a shaky hand back along his sweaty forehead.

"There now, all settled," Plum said. He lowered his hat back on his head and added, "I trust you are on your way back to the prison with these two?" He nodded toward the two dirty men sitting in front of the goat tender's mule.

"Yep," the goat tender said. "Two's all I got, unless I happen to catch a few more on the way in." He cut a glance to Jack the Spider, standing tense, with one arm looped around the old convict's neck in front of him. "I'll swing this shotgun over my lap if you'll holster that weapon. You strike me as a really nervous young man."

"That he is," Rance Plum said, shooting the Spider an impatient scowl. "I'm afraid his inexperience still gets the best of him at times."

"Yeah?" Spider returned the scowl, easing his pistol down in his holster. "Nobody got the drop on me like I'm some kind of newcomer, now did they?"

Plum ignored him, his face reddening a bit, and he said to the goat tender, "Speaking of newcomers, I must suppose you've only recently taken up the trade of bounty hunting?" He eyed the goat tender's clothes and the mule beneath him.

The goat tender grinned. "True. But once I take to something, I go at it whole hog." He gestured down at the convicts in front of him. "Every knot on their heads belongs to me. Hadn't been for a ranger stopping me, I would've hung 'em out to dry on a cottonwood tree."

Plum's eyes perked at the mention of the ranger. "Do tell." He cut a glance to the Spider, then back to the goat tender. "This *ranger* who stopped you . . . how far ahead might we find him? It's important we keep in close touch with him."

The goat tender considered it for a second, seeing a chance to better his reward money. Then he lied, saying, "Oh, he's way on ahead by now, I reckon. Him and his woman left last night, right after supper."

On the ground his two prisoners looked at one another. One scratched his dirty head.

"Last night, eh?" Plum fidgeted in his saddle. "Headed up into the badlands, no doubt?"

"Yep." The goat tender pushed up the brim of his dusty hat and let out a breath. "Talked like he had a pretty tight bead drawn on running down that Ernesto Caslado feller." He looked along the line of prisoners standing beside Plum. "By the time you two drop these birds at the prison and get back on the trail, it'll all be over, I expect."

Plum cursed under his breath, gazing away along the trail toward the border. Then he snapped his gaze back to the goat tender, having come to a quick decision. "Listen, sir. We both seem to be in a position to help one another here. What say you pay us *forty* dollars for these five prisoners and take them on from here? You'll collect *fifty* when you turn them in." He smiled. "Not a bad profit for a day's work, eh?"

"That'd be a good deal all right." The goat tender spit and chuckled. "But I ain't got forty dollars. Ain't seen forty dollars all at once since the summer of—"

"I understand." Plum cut him off with the toss of a hand. "How much *do* you have on you?"

"Not a dime," the old man said. "Best I could do is take them off your hands, I reckon. But even that would create a hardship for me, feeding them, watering them and all. Plus it would be three times as much trouble keeping an eye on them." He turned and spit again, then shook his head. "Naw, I'm sorry. Looks like you'll have to take them in yourself."

"Speaking of food and water," said the old convict, still standing in front of Jack the Spider as a shield, "when *are* we gonna eat?"

Rance Plum winced, rubbed his damp neck, and shot an impatient glance at the Spider. The Spider stared back at him through his one good eye with a look of uncertainty. "Uh-uh, Plum," the Spider said. "Surely you're not thinking what I *think* you're thinking."

Plum snapped, "Shut up, Spider! Can't you see what's at stake here? We can't quibble over *pennies* here while the *dollars* fly away, now can we?" He turned back to the goat tender. "Take these prisoners in for us, sir. The reward is all yours."

"Like hell it is!" Jack the Spider shoved the old convict away and stepped toward Plum. "I've got a say in this!"

"Boys, boys." The goat tender shook his head again, raising a hand. "Maybe you didn't hear me clearly. I can't take them in for you . . . no way. Not for free anyways." He turned his head slightly and sat staring at Plum.

A silence passed until the old convict stepped back in front of Jack the Spider and shrugged. "When in the *blue-hell* are we gonna get something to eat?"

The Spider shoved him back, then looked up at Plum. "I don't like doing this. We're losing money at every turn here."

Plum gritted his teeth and gazed out along the trail. He cursed, seeing the dark speck of a rider skylighted on a rise of sand in the distance—that confounded priest, he supposed. Then he collected himself and reached inside his shirt for the leather wallet where he carried his loose money, not about to pull the five hundred dollars from inside his boot. The goat tender gave a thin smile. *This bounty-hunting business might be worth considering full-time.*

Part 2

Chapter 8

At the end of the day when the animals had been attended to and enough scrub brush had been gathered to raise a fire, Samuel Burns collapsed beside the small campfire beneath the sandstone overhang. He'd ridden all day without gloves. They hadn't traveled fast, but they had traveled steady, non-stop, except during the hottest part of the day. Then they'd been out of their saddles only long enough to rest the horses—to let them blow and draw water from a thin stream amid a sparse stretch of cottonwoods.

Burns's hands were stiff, raw, and blistered from handling the reins beneath a merciless sun. Ten hours in the saddle had left his back, legs, shoulders, and crotch throbbing equally in pain. But it was a pain wrapped in a bone-weary numbness, an aching deep down and throughout him, like nothing he'd ever felt.

He hadn't even bothered batting the thick dust from his trouser legs or sitting up long enough to eat or drink a cup of tea. No sooner had he felt the solid earth beneath him when he'd fallen fast asleep.

With a blanket under his arm, the ranger stepped around the fire from beside Maria to where Burns lay flat on his back in the dirt. He stooped down beside him, raised each of his dirty wrists across his chest, and snapped on the hand-cuffs. Burns did not stir. The ranger shook the blanket out and let it settle over the young man. Then he stood up and shook his head. "He should've moved around some more and walked it off," he said in a low tone, knowing that Burns's pain wouldn't hit him with full impact until the morning. "This boy is about as green and foolish as any I've ever seen."

"*Sí,*" Maria said from across the low flames, keeping her voice quiet in the night. "He may think he wants to be a desperado, but his first crime in life was simply being young and foolish."

"Yep. That's how it starts with most people." The ranger nodded, gazing down for a second and thinking what life would be like for Burns once they took him back to the world of steel and stone. "If crime is a disease, Sammy-boy has sure been exposed to it, working around the likes of JC, Caslado, and the rest." He gazed down another second at the sleeping young man before turning and stepping back around the low fire.

"A disease?" Maria lifted her eyes to his and watched him settle beside her and pick up his tin cup of hot tea from the ground.

He smiled tiredly, gazing into the low flames as they danced and flickered beneath a pale golden glow. "It's just something I thought about the other day," he said quietly. Far off in the night, a coyote wailed long and lonesome. "Saw a man handle a hanging rope like he was afraid something bad might rub off on him. It seemed foolish at the time." He stopped for a second, gazed across the fire at Burns lying in the dirt, then let out a breath and added, "But maybe there's more to it than I realized."

She studied his weathered face in the flicker of low flames, seeing his eyes probe deeper and deeper into the glowing embers as his thoughts drew away to some distant place. Earlier that day he'd told her everything about Samuel Burns—about the key, the way the warden had just handed it to him the day of the prison break, about the way

JC had won him over with talk about big money and adventure.

He'd also gone on to tell her how Burns had killed his horse, running it to death crossing the sand flats; and when he'd told her this, his eyes had taken on a strange mix of rage and pity toward the young man, and he'd asked her what kind of desperate force must be at work to cause a man to kill the one thing that could have saved him. She'd only replied, "Who knows?" But now, watching his face in the glow of light, she realized that deeper questions had been at work in his mind.

"So," she asked after a pause, "do you think this young man is not responsible for his actions simply because he was led astray by those who saw his weakness and took advantage of him? That they passed this disease on to him? That he was powerless to resist them, and therefore should not be held accountable?"

Without facing her, the ranger lifted a brow slightly and said in the low, dancing flames, "I've never thought any man shouldn't be held accountable for himself, young or old . . . foolish or wise." A silence passed beneath the soft crackle of mesquite embers. Then he added, "All men get used and misled, one by another, to whatever purpose the world sees fit. It just leaves a bitter taste, knowing that in Sammy-boy's situation he had the criminals on one side and the authorities on the other . . . both sides using him, neither side caring what it done to him."

Maria nodded. "This is true. But I have heard you say many times that every man starts out equal, on new legs. If he doesn't prove strong enough to stay his own course, there is always somebody ready to take charge of him . . . someone who will use that part of him that he leaves unattended."

He shrugged, reached up, took the faded bandanna from around his neck, and spread it flat on the ground beside his tin cup. "Yeah, that's what I always say, all right." As he spoke, he lifted the big pistol from his holster, unloaded it, broke it apart on the bandanna, and laid each piece separate. "It's always been a dog-eat-dog world, I reckon."

He picked up the long barrel and rolled it back and forth between his palms, inspecting it, looking through it into the fire, seeing the groves glisten, spiraling round and downward with each turn of his hands. "But now and then, it'd be nice to see somebody get themselves straightened out, without benefit of a hangman's noose or a .45 slug."

As he spoke Maria had lain back on one side of her blanket and flipped the other side over herself. She adjusted the saddle beneath hear head, smiled up at him, and said, "Oh? Can I believe my ears? Are you feeling sorry for Samuel Burns?"

"Watch your language." He glanced at her and smiled. Then he blew a breath through the barrel, laid it down, and picked up the cylinder. "We've got a hard ride come morning if we plan on catching up to Ernie Caslado and his bunch. Reckon we both better get some sleep." He looked across the fire toward Samuel Burns, then up across the endless sky lying north above the badlands. Starlight glittered like diamonds on dark velvet.

In a moment, he'd cleaned the pistol, reassembled it in a series of clicks and turns, loaded it, and laid it on his blanket beside him. Out in the broad desert night the lonesome sound of the coyote lingered and drifted above the silence. He lay back on his saddle, tucked his pistol up under his arm, and wrapped his blanket around himself. Asleep beside him, Maria breathed peacefully and quietly—the soft whisper of a child; and he lay listening.

Sleep should have come upon him right away, yet it didn't. Somewhere out on the desert floor between himself and the call of the lone coyote, there lurked a presence of some sort. He felt it. It was not something he heard, unless he heard it in some manner through the coyote's voice—

some scent that lingered in those keen nostrils and called out in warning to all other creatures of the night.

He listened longer, then decided that whatever was out there was not man. The presence of man was something different, something distinctive and of its own; and man brought in his presence a foreboding that in some way stilled even further the already quiet voice of the desert. It was something he could not explain—perhaps something that could only be experienced. But when man was near, his presence was felt . . . by anyone or anything attuned to the pulse and balance of the land.

Then it's not man . . .

With that thought he relaxed. A large cat? Perhaps. He listened for a moment longer until the coyote ceased its cry. A big cat prowling out there somewhere? He supposed so. Yet, if it was a cat, why hadn't it called out? He closed his eyes now and let himself drift. No predator would venture in close to the fire. If it did, he or Maria would hear it. As long as whatever stirred about out there wasn't man, there was no real cause for concern. It had been a long day. . . .

But at first light, the ranger had been wide awake for over an hour. As bone tired as he'd been, sleep only came and went, but would not stay with him throughout the night. Whatever he felt out there in the night had kept him restless, disturbed, and he woke up every few minutes, feeling as if something sat near, something dark and lurking, watching him in the low flicker of firelight.

At one point, he'd awakened with a jolt and sprang up from his blanket, feeling as if something quiet and deadly had just brushed past him. *The breath on the devil,* he'd heard old Mexicans call it. But he'd always considered that to be their way of putting a face on something they simply could not otherwise identify. *Devil's breath* . . . Superstition, he thought. Yet wasn't the very thing that unsettled him most about whatever he'd felt, the fact that he couldn't name it?

Had something actually passed by him in his sleep? Of course not. Then what bothered him? He'd even checked his blanket and saddle for a rattlesnake. He would have taken a certain amount of relief in finding one.

Maria lay on her side, drawn up in a ball against the chill of night with her blanket off and gathered beside her. He spread it back over her. Then, running his fingers back through his hair, through the thin, cold sheen of sweat on his forehead, he spent the rest of the night close to the fire, just listening—for what, he had no idea.

This was foolishness . . .

His senses had been drawn tight. He'd stoked up the fire, boiled tea, and sat sipping from a steaming tin cup when Maria sat up on her blanket and rubbed sleep from her eyes. She looked over at him, and before she got a chance to read the look on his face, he said to distract her, "Tea's up. Better have some. We'll be pushing on without breakfast."

She shook her head to clear it, then looked back at him. "What is wrong? You look as if you haven't had a wink of sleep."

"No. Just wanting an early start is all. We need to stay on Caslado's trail as close as we can," he said.

She flipped her blanket from across her, stood up, and reached down for her boots. "So, the best way to get an early start is to stay up all night? Ride all morning on an empty stomach?"

"It's one way," he said, and rounding his finger inside a tin cup, he filled it from the steaming pot and sat it near her. He caught himself scanning the land around them more than he ordinarily would have. Grainy light cast a dark haze over upthrusts of rock and low-standing brush; and in the shadows of quiet dawn, he felt once more the strangeness that had been with him throughout the night.

"Nonsense." She nodded across the fire to where Samuel Burns lay sleeping. "He will be hungry . . . as hungry as we are. I will get some jerked meat from my saddlebags." Maria pulled back her long hair, checked it in place with a strip of rawhide, and reached down and picked up the cup of tea.

"Then we'll eat it in our saddles," the ranger said, standing and lifting his blanket from beneath him. He shook out the blanket, rolled it up, and swung it up under his arm. "We're clearing out of here."

She just stared at him, puzzled, as he walked over to the horses and led them back. Before she could comment, he said, "It'll probably take both of us to get Sammy-boy up and on his horse."

"I know," she said. She sipped her tea and watched him, feeling some strange, dark caution in his every move . . . his every word and manner. Only when they'd broken camp and rode out in the morning light did the ranger seem to let up and release whatever tightly drawn cords had wrapped around him in the night. *What was it?* She'd never seen him like this. *A bad dream? Some dark premonition?* No, she thought. He never concerned himself with such things. Or did he? He'd been hesitant to have her along on this trip from the start. . . .

Above them, on the edge of the sandstone overhang, Crazy Gravy watched as they rode away. He opened his mouth in the snarl of a panther, but made no sound . . . only the gesture, and swiped a hand through the air as a big cat might do. He rolled over on his back as they rode out of sight around a turn in the rocky trail. The sandstone felt good beneath him, and he wallowed back and forth, one side to the other, while the horse watched him through frightened eyes and drew against its reins wrapped tight around a stand of jagged rock.

Crazy Gravy's nostrils probed the air for any lingering scent of the woman. He reached inside his holy man's frock and took out the long strand of glistening black hair he'd braided during the night, while he'd stared down into the glow of fire. Toying with it now as he studied it closely, he wrapped it around his hand and pressed it to his face, breathing through it. She was there, against his skin—the essence and smell of her, the *feel* of her.

This felt good, he thought, the way he was playing it, brushing it back and forth his palm, the way a big cat might play with some object of its attention. He could take his time with her. She was his now. He knew it. He had a piece of her. Soon he would have more.

Somewhere in the passage of this hateful night his old friend Victor had died in his arms. Tack had crawled to him while the gunmen filled themselves on mule meat and coffee before the raging fire. It seemed fitting that even in death, the mules had once more saved the old teamsters' lives—even if only for a short time. Victor would have appreciated that.

Lying there with an arm thrown over his partner, Tack stared at the glistening rib cage of one of their fine animals pinned to the licking flames. The men laughed and cursed, tearing at the carcass, gorging on the red meat like ravaging wolves.

Beneath his arm, he had felt the shallow rise and fall of Victor's breath, and summoning up what failing strength was left within himself, Tack had managed to get an arm around his friend's shoulders and drag him off to the shelter of tangled brush outside the circle of firelight. There they'd lain throughout the hours of darkness. He'd felt Victor's breath grow more and more faint until finally it had ceased altogether, while before them death moved back and forth in the harsh golden glow.

At some point death had moved over near them and relieved itself, spilling its sour, putrid smell in a short blast on earth-bare roots and sand. Then death had grunted and blown its nose against its thumb, and hiked its trousers up and moved back into the firelight. "Where's them old geezers?" A voice had asked in a hollow tone amid the crackle of fiery embers. Another voice had answered, "They're around somewhere. We'll cut their throats come morning."

At the sound of the harsh words, Tack had hugged Victor's body close to him and tried to will them both invisible to these men and their dark intent.

It didn't seem right, Victor dying on him this way—leaving him alone, arm's length from death—not after all the scrapes, the close calls, and the hard times they'd faced together over the years. *Dang your hide, Victor.* Tack shook his friend's body lying limp across his lap and swiped a strand of bloody hair from Victor's face. *First the mules, then you . . .*

But now night had passed, and when death wagged a thumb toward him in his tangled brush in the cool gray morning light, Tack swallowed a dry knot in his throat and hugged Victor's cold still body against himself. Death looked toward him and grinned, a dark, cruel grin. Standing beside death, a young Mexican drew a long dagger from his boot and walked toward Tack, a fixed grim expression on his face. At the brush, Tack raised a trembling hand and saw the blade reach in for him.

"*Quieto,*" the young Mexican whispered. "Lie still." The blade pressed down on its flat side into the dark blood on Tack's shirt, then moved back out of the brush. Tack stared, breathless, as the Mexican turned and walked away, wiping the blade against his trouser leg. At the horses someone asked, "Did you cut 'em both good, Homer?"

"*Sí,*" the young Mexican said, "both of them, good." Taking his saddle horn and swinging up, the young Mexican shot a glance toward the tangle of brush in the grainy light; and Tack whispered something akin to a prayer under his trembling breath and ran a hand across Victor's dead face. Warm tears fell on the back of his bloodstained hand as death gathered and collected itself and rode away through the strewn debris, through dead mules, mule bones, and entrails, in a low rumble of hooves onto the thin upward trail of the badlands.

Chapter 9

By noon Maria had led the ranger and Burns up through the narrow rock pass onto the first level of the badlands. They'd followed the day-old tracks of a dozen riders who'd pressed hard and fast on tired horses into the upward slope of rocky soil and sage grass. The ranger had been right about Samuel Burns—it had taken both of them to get him on his feet and into the saddle. But once under way, the young man soon loosened up and kept pace with them. It was Burns who caught the first glimpse of thin blue smoke spiraling up from the burnt freight wagon.

They found wagon ruts and followed them, through spilled cargo for a hundred yards or more until they stood amid dead mules and mule bones near the pile of charred wood and iron wagon bracing. Two buzzards had batted up and away at their arrival. Now the big, dark birds circled and swayed above them. "Caslado and his men," Maria remarked in a low tone.

"You can bet on it," the ranger said. Beside them, Samuel Burns stared at the wreckage. "At least this might have let off some of their steam before they hit San Paulo," the ranger added, looking at Samuel Burns through accusing eyes. Burns looked away, avoiding his gaze.

They heard a groan and turned toward it. Over in a tangle of dried brush, a man raised a trembling hand. "Help us . . . ?" His voice trailed; his hand fell. Above the tangle of brush, flies spun and snarled in a dark cloud.

Behind them two hundred yards, Crazy Gravy lay flat on the rocky land at the upper crest of a swell of sand, his flat-brimmed hat on the ground beside him. He watched the ranger and Samuel Burns carry the first man out from the mesquite brush and lay him on a blanket the woman had spread beside the thin trail. In a moment the two of them returned to the brush while the woman lifted the man's head and gave him water from a canteen.

Crazy Gravy smiled, watching. In another moment the ranger and Samuel Burns carried a second man from the brush and laid him down. He'd been so near them last night, he could have killed them in their sleep—this ranger everybody talked about would have been powerless against him.

The young prison guard with his hands cuffed across his chest would have given in to death without a struggle. Then he could have done as he pleased with the woman. But he liked the feel of this, liked the sweet pain and pleasure of watching her—her with no idea he was near. Now it was time to move closer.

He scooted back from the edge, pushed himself up from the ground, and dusted his frock and hat on the way back to his horse. The horse shied back a step from him, but settled as Crazy Gravy loosened the cinch, dropped the saddle, rifle, and scabbard, and left the saddle blanket on the horse's back. He pitched the army revolver on the ground. Guns were not his style—not suited to his taste in killing. Firearms were not personal enough. There was not that feel of a heart making its last beat on the end of a blade.

It was time to divest himself of all outward trappings not a part of a holy man's image. He closed his eyes for a moment and searched his mind for the proper voice and gestures to use. He needed to be disarming, vulnerable, a poor clergyman at odds with this brutal land and its inhabitants. He could do that.

Beneath his frock, he kept the butcher knife and the braided strand of the woman's hair. When he'd poured all but a few drops of water from his water gourd, he'd started to slip atop the nervous horse. But then he stopped, looked at the revolver lying on the ground, and on second thought decided that perhaps he could use it. It might be the perfect prop for his little show. With it, he could raise a slight doubt for just a second. When he removed that doubt, with it would go all other doubts the ranger and woman might have about him.

At the blanket on the ground, Maria held Tack's head on her lap and wiped his face with the wet bandanna. "I . . . I never thought anybody would come along here," he said, his old eyes cloudy and swimming slowly back and forth, from one to the other of the three shadows above him. Maria looked up at the ranger and shook her head slowly. The dying man had managed to tell them what had happened, and how the young Mexican had spared his life at the last minute.

"We'll make them pay," the ranger said, looking down at the old man. When he raised his eyes, he caught sight of the rider coming toward them across the rocky stretch of land. The flat-brimmed hat of a priest, with its short rounded crown, bobbed in the wavering sunlight as the horse drew nearer.

"We've got company," the ranger said to Maria without taking his eyes from the lone rider. Then he said to Burns in the same manner, "Sammy-boy, take the reins to the horse. Don't try nothing stupid."

"I won't," said Burns, lifting the reins from the ranger's gun hand. "I've learnt my lesson."

"Yeah?" The ranger whispered, more to himself than to Burns, "We'll see." Still he kept his eyes on the rider; and when Maria started to stand up, he said to her, "Just do what you've been doing. I've got this one covered."

The rider stopped his horse at the place where the long stretch of debris began amid the wagon tracks. Broken books lay with their pages swaying in a warm, stirring breeze. As the hat turned down and the rider gazed back and forth among the dead mules and the charred wagon remains, the ranger called out, "Over here," and stood watching from thirty yards away with his right hand resting on the butt of his big pistol.

The rider bolted upright, startled at the sound of the ranger's voice. The horse nearly reared and spun, but the rider checked it down. "Stay where you are," the rider called out. His hand fumbled with the pistol in the waist of his faded brown frock and drew it, almost letting it slip through his unsteady fingers. "I'm armed . . . I'm . . . I'm warning you."

"Well, I'll be darned," Samuel Burns said. "It's one of those priests from the prison. I saw them there."

"So did I," the ranger said, his eyes still watching the rider, his pistol butt still beneath his hand.

Maria looked over at the rider, saw the pistol in his shaking hand, and said, "What kind of priest carries a weapon?"

"Out here . . . a *smart* one." The ranger almost smiled as the rider fumbled with the hammer on the pistol. "Take it easy, Padre," he called out. "We're peaceable folks. Put that gun away before you shoot yourself." He stepped forward, but kept his hand on his pistol butt. "We could use your help here, holy man. There's an old fellow dying."

The priest's hand shook as the ranger came closer, the revolver looking ridiculous in his pale fingers. "I'm warning you . . . stay back!"

The ranger stopped, raised his free hand chest high, and opened his duster, showing his badge. "It's no trick," he said. "One man's dead and the other one's dying. If souls are your calling, you couldn't come at a better time . . . he's about gone."

The priest hesitated, craning his neck and looking past the ranger to where Maria sat with the old man. "Perhaps you're not really a lawman . . . ?" He stared skeptically at the ranger, squinting against the sun's glare.

"Perhaps you're not really a priest," the ranger said; and with that his hand rested more firmly on the pistol butt.

The priest let out a sigh, lowered the shaky revolver, and pitched it near the ranger's feet. "I am so ashamed," he said, slipping down from the horse. The horse shied until he turned his face back to the ranger. "And you are right, of course . . . I'm no holy man."

"Oh?" The ranger stepped over, picking up the revolver.

The priest added in a tired voice, "I'm a fraud, nothing more." He rubbed the glare of sunlight from his caged eyes and looked closer at the ranger. "I know you. Yes, I saw you at the prison before the—" He crossed himself, shook his head, and let go a short scornful laugh at himself. "Forgive me, ranger . . . But after what I witnessed at the prison, my faith has been staggered. I've become a frightened fool."

"We all have our off days, I reckon, Padre." As he spoke, the ranger broke open the revolver, saw it was empty, and said in a quiet tone, "This could be a dangerous habit for a man to get into, Padre . . . carrying an *unloaded* pistol."

"Oh, but, I could never shoot anyone. I still have at least that much divine spirit in me." His hand went inside the frock and came out with five bullets and handed them to the ranger. "I only carried this to scare away anyone on the badlands whose intentions might be to—"

"You don't scare anybody off in the badlands, Padre," the ranger said, cutting him off. "All that'll stop them out here is to put a bullet in them. This is a land of serious killing. Living and dying is no game."

"You are right, of course, although by the nature of what

I am, I must think otherwise and pray it is so." He bowed his head slightly and folded his hands over the reins. This ranger knew nothing of games and who did or did not play them. Of course killing was a game—the only game of any interest or consequence. But serious, no, Crazy Gravy didn't think so, not for something like himself, something that people could not even identify, let alone understand.

"Now take me to this poor soul, ranger," the priest said. "Pitiful though I am, I'm all the salvation he'll find on this terrible day."

"Where are you headed, Padre?" the ranger asked as they walked toward Maria and Burns.

The priest turned his hat brim slightly, but not enough to let the ranger get a full look at his face. "After the escape the warden asked for someone to ride in each direction and warn everyone. I chose to ride north."

The ranger eyed him closely as he asked, "How close have you been following us?"

"Very close," the priest said. "I've traveled in your dust since the relay station . . . camped within shouting distance from you last evening. I should have had more faith and ridden into your camp, but I was afraid. I had no idea who you people were. This morning I ran out of water and had to come forward and take a chance."

"I understand," the ranger said, dropping back a step as the priest stooped beside the wounded teamster. Hearing that the priest had been camped close by throughout the night partly explained why the ranger had felt so strange. Had this been the presence he'd felt near him? While it hadn't been an animal, in a way it had not been a man, at least not in the ordinary sense. The presence had been that of a priest. Perhaps that explained his failure to identify it.

For the next half hour Maria and the priest sat working with old Tack, the priest on one side, Maria on the other. They cleaned his wounds and gave him water; and in the shade of the people gathered over him, the old teamster seemed to revive a little. Tack lay watching as the priest's hands tore strips from a faded bandanna and applied them to the wound in his chest.

"I'm . . . going to make it, ain't I, Father?" Hope had come back to him slowly, and now, in each passing moment, he began to believe that he might actually live to see another day. The priest only patted his shoulder and kept about his work.

Maria saw the change in the old teamster, as if the arrival of the priest had brought about some sort of miracle. She glanced up at the ranger and nodded. The ranger offered a thin smile in return, then turned and gazed upward across the badlands in the direction of San Paulo. By now Caslado and his men would be heading into that small, helpless town. The ranger couldn't wait. He looked down at the old teamster, then at the priest.

"I have to push on," the ranger said. "Will you stay here with him, Padre? We can leave you some water and jerked beef."

"We'll see," the priest said, flashing the ranger a glance, but keeping his face partially hidden by the brim of his hat. Samuel Burns had caught only a glimpse. The face looked familiar, yet under the circumstances, he recognized him only as one of the faded brown figures who'd stood outside the prison gates. Knowing this, Crazy Gravy only smiled to himself, and making the sign of the cross, began to whisper some sort of prayer over the teamster.

Maria glanced up at the ranger, and seeing the look in his eyes, she stood up beside him and wiped her bloodstained hands on the wet bandanna, and asked quietly, "Will he live? He seems stronger now."

But the ranger shook his head slowly with a grim expression. "No. He won't last until sundown. Meanwhile, we need to get on ahead to San Paulo. That place won't stand a chance against the likes of Caslado's bunch."

"But we cannot leave him," she said softly.

"The padre will sit with him."

"No," Maria said. "I will sit with him. It is only right."

The priest heard their words and turned his shadowed eyes up to them. "Then both of us will stay with him." He looked at the woman. "You can be of much help to me . . . and much comfort to him." He nodded at the old teamster, who'd closed his eyes.

"I don't like it," the ranger said in a lowered voice between Maria and himself.

"I know . . . nor do I," she whispered, "but it is the only right thing to do. Go now. I'll be all right here."

When the ranger left, with Burns riding in front of him on a thin trail, Maria had stepped away, staring at them until they rode out of sight. Behind her, Crazy Gravy leaned over close to the old teamster's face and looked down into his eyes. The old teamster had faded once more, and Crazy Gravy leaned in close, shaking him, and whispered, "Don't die too quick on me, old man. Let them get a good distance away first." He grinned and patted the man's bloody chest.

The old teamster stared at him through weak and fading eyes, but as he heard the words and saw the expression on Crazy Gravy's face, his failing eyes filled with terror. "You're . . . You're no *preacher*, you . . ." His voice trailed, weak, exhausted.

Crazy Gravy smiled down at him, his hand moving up from his chest and gently stroking his bearded cheek, while the old man gasped, but could say no more.

"What did he say?" Maria asked, stepping back over to them. "Did he say that you are not a preacher?" She leaned, looked at the old teamster, then at Crazy Gravy's bemused expression.

Crazy Gravy lifted his eyes to her with a sad, tired smile. "Yes, that's what he said." He looked back into the old man's eyes and said to him in a comforting tone, "But do not worry, my son. We do not have to be of the same faith at a time like this. God will understand."

"Oh. I see. What can I do to help, Padre?" Maria asked.

"He is of a far different faith than ours." The priest shook his head. "He said there is a Bible of his somewhere in the wreckage. Perhaps having it would bring him comfort." He gestured his sad eyes toward the strewn debris.

Of course," Maria said. "I will go look for it." The old teamster groaned and tried to speak before she left. He wanted to stop her, to warn her. But his words were lost beneath a racking cough as Maria looked again into his pleading eyes. "Don't be afraid," she said, soothing him. "I will find your Bible for you."

As she turned and walked away, the teamster raised a weak hand toward her, again trying to speak. This time Crazy Gravy shoved his arm down and pressed down on his chest with both hands, cutting off his words. He turned with his hands pushed down tight, and waited and watched until Maria was up among the wagon ruts among the wreckage and dead mules. Then he turned back, moved his hand from the man's chest, and up across his gaping mouth and his flared nostrils.

He tightened his hand, looking into the fading eyes, eyes that showed terror, no less than they'd shown the night before when the gunmen converged on the small wagon. "Rest, my son," the priest said, smiling down at him. He leaned close to Tack's face, smiling, his breath caressing the old man's ear. The breath felt cool and stale, like an updraft of air from an open grave. "You must rest and sleep. Sleep . . . and let the darkness of sleep be your salvation."

The teamster tried to struggle against him, but Crazy

Gravy grinned, staying close to the old man's ear. "You wouldn't have lived long anyway," he whispered.

Casting a glance over his shoulder to where Maria stood watching a drifting stir of dust settle along the trail, Crazy Gravy clamped down harder, until he felt last nerves twitch and quiver in the old man's legs. Then he ran his palm gently from the parted lips and once again across the bearded cheek. For the next twenty or so minutes he sat there, staring down into the blank hollow eyes with dark, cruel fascination.

"I can't find it," Maria called down to him from thirty yards away among the wagon ruts. He looked at her and saw her raise her hands and drop them.

Without changing his expression, Crazy Gravy chuckled low under his breath and waved her back to him. He had her now . . . just the two of them out here alone; and he stared closely, watching each sway of her body as she came back toward him. He reached his hand down and had just closed the man's eyes when she stooped beside him.

"I'm afraid it is no use," he said in a soft tone, patting the old man's chest. "He has just this moment slipped away from us."

Maria looked at the old teamster and crossed herself. She closed her eyes and bowed her head for a moment, and Crazy Gravy watched her lips part slightly as she muttered a prayer. When she finished her prayer and opened her eyes once more, he'd turned his head and pretended to have just done the same. Maria sighed and said as he turned facing her, "Now we must bury him, Padre, and be on our way."

"Of course," he said, watching her as they both stood up. She brushed aside a wisp of loose dark hair and pushed it up under her hat brim. His hand went inside his faded brown frock and wrapped tightly around the handle of the butcher knife. Blood pulsed and pounded in his forehead. She'd turned and stepped away, he right behind, only inches from her, when the sound of a horse somewhere up among the wagon wreckage caused her to spin with her pistol coming up out of her holster.

Crazy Gravy jumped aside, turning, and saw the two riders sitting atop their horses beyond the dead mules. "Hello, the camp," Rance Plum called out, raising his rifle and waving it back and forth in a slow sweep above his head.

"Oh, no," Maria said under her breath, "not *these* two."

Crazy Gravy cursed in silence and brought his hand from inside the frock. "Does this mean trouble?"

"No." She waved Plum and Jack the Spider in. "This only means we will be stuck with them. They have a way of spoiling everyone's plans."

Indeed, they had . . . Crazy Gravy nodded, and watched them move closer and stop near the burnt wagon and the dead mules.

"I don't like fooling with her and that ranger," the Spider said just between himself and Rance Plum. "Still say we're better off on our own."

"Nonsense, Mr. Spider. Simply follow my lead," Plum said to him, but smiling toward Maria, keeping his eyes on her as he swung down off his horse with his rifle in his hand.

"Careful," the Spider said, his voice still low. "You're gonna step into something you shouldn't."

"For heaven sakes, Spider, must you always be so negative—" His words stopped short as a tangle of flies spun around him. "Oh, God," he said, looking down at the slick black pile of mule intestines beneath his boots. He yanked off his hat and fanned at the flies, but his horse mistook his actions. It jumped sidewise a step with Plum's hand on the reins. Plum lost his balance.

"*Whooooooa!*" he yelled just as his boots slipped in the putrid mess, and he went down into it on one knee before he caught hold of a stirrup.

"I tried telling ya," said Jack the Spider, shaking his head and nudging his horse forward.

"Damn it all! Mr. Spider! Give me a hand here!"

"You got yourself in, get yourself out. I ain't getting it all over me."

"Whooa boy!" Plum pleaded with the horse, pulling on the stirrup, spitting away flies from his lips as he struggled back up onto both feet. He gagged at the smell around him until he stepped free of it and came forward. He stopped, leaned down, and rubbed his boot and trouser leg back and forth across the dirt. Flies sought him out. He yelled and cursed, slapping at them with his hat.

"I see you have found us," Maria said, her hand on her hip, speaking up to Jack the Spider while behind him Rance Plum continued shouting and slapping his hat back and forth like a wild man.

"Oh, found you?" The Spider looked down at her. "What makes you think we've been looking for you?"

She shrugged. "All right then, let's just say that once more our paths have crossed."

The Spider smiled and gestured with his good eye toward the priest. "I see you've gotten religious since last we met." Before she could respond, he asked the priest, "Are you the same holy man we've been seeing every time we look around? If you are, you've been getting on our nerves something awful."

Crazy Gravy stared at him a second—this man had no idea what he'd just interrupted. "If you've been seeing a priest between here and the prison, then yes, I must be the one."

Jack the Spider gave him a sharp glance, then said to Maria, "How far ahead is the ranger?"

Maria ignored his question, looked over at Plum as he came forward cursing, and said to both of them, "Shouldn't you two be collecting prisoners or something?"

Plum looked down at his wet boot and trouser leg, then snapped his eyes back up to her. "We go where we're most needed. How far ahead is your friend, the ranger? I know he can't be far. He wouldn't leave you alone—"

"I am not alone, as you see." She swept a hand toward the priest.

"I'm afraid I didn't come here to socialize. I simply haven't the time right now. I do need, however, to catch up to the ranger. I'm afraid this is one time we simply must force ourselves to work together."

She just stared at him for a second, then letting out a breath, said, "All right. We can start right here. We must bury these men. You can help us."

"Ha, not likely, my dear Maria. It doesn't take four people to dig two graves."

"It will today, unless you want to sit here while the ranger captures Ernesto Caslado before you get to him." She folded her arms and stared at him with a determined expression. Crazy Gravy looked back and forth between the two men and thought of how much pleasure he would take in choking them with his bare hands.

Chapter 10

In the hot afternoon sunlight the riders swooped down from the high ridges surrounding the dusty little town of San Paulo. Their horses crowded and shoved one another on the narrow trail, until at length they abandoned the trail altogether. They spilled over the edges of the switchbacks and back-stepped down the steep, sandy slope. Rearing on their haunches, the worn animals slid downward through loose rock and sand, neighing and thrashing, their nostrils flared beneath wide, frightened eyes.

The riders spurred them on, shouting, cursing, leather-riding quirts rising and falling against sweaty horseflesh. Some riders drew rifles and used them as clubs to force the horses onward. Strings of white froth spewed from the horses' muzzles. Pistols rose up and fired into the air, streaming gray smoke behind them in the rising dust.

At the bottom of the slope the tired horses steadied themselves on the stretch of flatland and rumbled forward like a dark storm. Caslado led the pack, his sombrero brim standing high in front against the onrush of air. From the dirt street of San Paulo, eyes turned toward the billowing dust in fear, then turned away at the sound of pistol fire and searched for places to hide.

An old Mexican woman who'd lost her daughter and son-in-law to such a band of madmen ten years earlier pushed her granddaughter toward an ancient adobe hovel as she prayed under her breath. The young girl hesitated for a moment in shock, stunned at the spectacle coming across the stretch of flat lands. "Run, child," the old woman cried out. "You must run and hide! Stay hidden until they are gone!"

The girl hurried away, but then stopped and looked back at the old woman standing against the coming riders. "Grandmother! Come with me!"

"No, I stay here . . . you go!"

On the edge of a boardwalk a big woman looked down at the old Mexican woman in the street. "Go, take care of little Connie," she said. "I'll handle these birds." The big woman's shoulders were as broad as any man's, and her face bore the scars, the lines, and the rough edges of her past life as a whore's madam.

"No, Miss Fannie," the old Mexican woman called out to her. "I no longer run from such monsters as these."

"Suit yourself then, but stay out of my way," said Miss Fannie, folding her big hands and popping her thick knuckles as she stepped down into the dusty street.

The old Mexican woman turned to the young girl and shooed her away. "You go now, quickly! Do not let them see you." The young girl turned and ran to the adobe hovel.

Few people still lived in the town of San Paulo, a small collection of old men and women, prospectors and misfits whose trail had stopped here and whose aged and brittle legs would lead them no farther. A blind Southerner who'd come up to San Paulo after the war between the states stood at the edge of a sun-bleached boardwalk. He raised his face in his private darkness toward the sound of pounding hooves, and the sound of townspeople scurrying away.

"What have we here, Miss Fannie?" he asked, feeling his way down into the street beside her. "Are you able to handle it?"

"Go on away, Colonel," Miss Fannie said. "I'll handle it all right." She raised her dusty black dress hem, swished it back and forth, and took a firm stand in the dust. "They'll likely be no more than a bunch of hell-raisers looking for liquor and horses. I'll keep them in check."

An old Indian who cleaned the colonel's small cantina came out carrying a wooden bucket and stood down beside him. He said nothing; yet as the riders broke their horses down sidewise in the dust, he stepped forward, dropped the bucket, and raised his weathered hands up as if to stop them.

"What's this shit?" Al Kreeger said, staring down at the old Indian. He'd ridden in up front with Caslado, Hawkins, and JC. As the old Indian took another step and started to speak, Kreeger brought up his pistol, cocked it, and shot the Indian twice in the chest. "No stinkin' Injun raises a hand to me."

Caslado shot him a glance, then turned to the big woman whose eyes fixed on him in a cold, level stare. "You low, murdering bastards," she hissed. "Get out of this town!"

The blind colonel stepped forward, his hands shaking, probing the air. "Yano? Say something, Yano!" Miss Fannie swung an arm sideways and halted the colonel.

"Stay back, Colonel. Yano's dead." Miss Fannie's words were harsh, and her eyes stayed fixed on Caslado's. The old Mexican woman had gasped at the sight of the shooting. She cowered, but stood her ground beside Miss Fannie. "We've got nothing you murdering trash want here," Miss Fannie said, "so keep right on riding."

"Be still, old *puta*," Caslado said. "We come for horses and ammunition . . . for food and water. Give us these things most *pronto* and no one else will die. Resist us and we will kill everybody."

Beside Caslado, Hawkins chuckled under his breath, drew his pistol, and let it lay across his lap. On the ground the blind colonel had managed to move past Miss Fannie and stumble onto the body of the Indian. He fell to the body and searched the bloody chest with his fingertips. "Oh, Yano . . . no. *No!*"

Miss Fannie fixed her broad hands on her thick hips and squinted at Caslado in the sun's glare. "I know you . . . you and your rotten brother, Ramon. You're *Ernesto*. Both of you shoulda had your heads mashed the day you were born. Now turn this ragged mess of trash around and light out of here. You'll get nothing from San Paulo but my foot up your behind!"

The rest of the riders had settled their horses and now cast glances back and forth among themselves. The new men smiled at one another; but the young Mexican, Homer, looked at the men he'd ridden with the past few years and saw the stunned looks on their faces. He turned and stared down at the dead Indian, then at Al Kreeger's back. He sliced a curse under his breath. This was not the way revolutionists conducted themselves. This was the way only wild and heartless animals conducted themselves.

"Oh?" Caslado smiled down at the big woman. "You know me and my brother, Ramon? He lives near here, *sí?*" He glanced back at the others. "Hear that? She knows me!" Then he turned a harsh stare back at her. "Then you know I was supposed to hang . . . then you know I will think nothing of killing you where you stand!"

"Ha. Is that supposed to turn me to jelly? In my own town?" As she spoke, Miss Fannie stepped forward and raised the colonel from the Indian's body and shoved him back toward the boardwalk. She added, "There's not a half dozen horses in San Paulo. Whatever ammunition we've got has turned green. Take what you feel you're big enough to take . . . but we're not bringing it to you."

"She's got too much mouth to suit me," Kreeger said, jiggling the pistol in his hand.

"Shut up, Al," Hawkins said, grinning, reaching over, and shoving Kreeger's pistol aside. "That's the first damn woman I've seen in the longest time. You ain't about to shoot her . . . not yet." He slipped down from his saddle and let the reins fall to the ground.

JC saw what was about to happen with the woman, and he said to Caslado, "We need to get on. This ain't making us a thing."

"But if there are no fresh horses here, we must rest these animals, or we will never make our way across these badlands."

"Across?" JC looked at him. "You mean all the way?"

Caslado didn't answer him, but instead turned his horse toward a dusty, sun-bleached livery barn. He raised a hand back to the others and said, "Take this worthless place apart. Find what we need."

The Mexicans hesitated for a second, looking at one another.

"I need whiskey," Kreeger called out. He heeled his horse forward up onto the boardwalk, knocked the blind colonel to the side, and rode in through the open door. Three riders gigged forward and followed him, laughing over their shoulders.

Some of the Mexicans followed Caslado; others rode off along the street. Four of the new men sprang forward and joined Hawkins as he advanced on Miss Fannie. "Let's have us some fun, boys," Hawkins called out.

Young Homer Corona shook his head and stayed atop his horse, turning it from the others, looking back at them in disgust as they circled Miss Fannie like a pack of stalking dogs. He reined his horse toward a cracked and dusty window where above it hung a faded green sign that read: WEAPONRY & AMMUNITION. He was a serious young man who had joined Caslado's rebel forces at the age of fifteen, having seen his mother and sister killed by drunken *federales*—men who had acted like wild beasts, men no different than these new men he now rode with. He would have none of this.

The men drew closer around Miss Fannie, snickering and whispering dark threats. "Oh, yeah?" She stood her ground like a large bear set upon by wolves, stooped, and picked up the wooden bucket the Indian had dropped. She tightened her grip on the handhold of the bucket and swung it side to side. "Come on then, you gobs of slop . . . you've never paid more than what this'll cost yas."

Through a crack in the hovel door, the young girl gasped and watched one of the Mexicans jump in at Miss Fannie, then fall back and to the side as the swinging bucket clipped across his forehead with a loud *thunk*. The men laughed, turning it into sport, reaching in and picking at the big woman, then jumping back as the bucket swished past them. From the small cantina, pistol shots rose above dark laughter and cursing.

The old Mexican grandmother had moved away when the men circled Miss Fannie. Now she came back, as if from out of nowhere, carrying a broken shovel handle. She shouted as she swung it, and one of the men, who'd drawn a knife from his boot and began poking at Miss Fannie, caught the shovel blow on the back of his head and sank sideways to his knees. The knife flew from his hand. Other men hooted and jeered. But when the old Mexican woman swung the handle again and clipped Hawkins on his forearm, he punched her in her face, hard, and she crumbled backward on the ground and didn't move.

"Grandmother!" The young girl sprang from the door of the hovel and ran to the old woman.

"Looky-here, looky-here!" Hawkins snatched at the girl, but missed as she sped past him.

"Aw! *Mas fina!*" One of the new men, a big Mexican known only as Big Roedor, the rodent, hooked his arm around the girl and swung her up off the ground. She screamed, and Miss Fannie moved toward Roedor, still swinging the bucket as the other men punched at her and laughed.

One of them had snatched the knife off the ground and slipped in low behind Miss Fannie and sliced her long dress open. She spun and struck him with the bucket, but as she did, one of the others grabbed the dusty flapping dress and ripped it free.

In the dusty gun shop, Homer Corona found an old man huddled behind a counter, and pulled him to his feet. Outside the hoots and jeers resounded, but when the old man looked toward the dirty window, Homer shoved him over to a gun case and made him open it.

"This is all the guns you have here?" Homer looked at a few battered old pistols laid out on a canvas-covered shelf. He shook his head.

"That's all," the old man said, his voice trembling. "Ain't nobody needs much weaponry around here." He flinched at the sound of pistol fire from the cantina.

"Out of my way!" Homer brushed him aside with his forearm, swept up the pistols, sticking each of them into his waist belt. He stooped, opened a door beneath the counter, and took out box after box of cartridges.

"I . . . I wouldn't count on none of that." The old man shook a trembling finger at the cartridge boxes. "It's been laying around a long time."

"So it has." Homer looked at the boxes in disgust, but gathered them anyway. He glanced around inside the lower counter shelves, shaking his head. "All of this ammunition, and nothing to shoot it with . . ."

Inside the cantina, Al Kreeger had stabbed a long knife into the bar top and tied his horse's reins to the handle. He swilled back a long gurgling drink and let some of it run down his chin. The others with him had dismounted. They tumbled over the bar and began tossing back long drinks and gathering dusty bottles under their arms.

Their loose horses milled and blew and coughed up dust in long strings of saliva. Al Kreeger let out a long whiskey hiss and shouted, "Give these horses some beer. When I drink, everybody drinks!"

The blind colonel had felt his way inside and along the front wall, where he cowered down in the corner and flashed his dead eyes back and forth at the sound of pounding boots, breaking glass, and milling horses.

At the sound of a shotgun blast followed by three pistol shots, Kreeger spun and stomped over to the open door. In the street lay an old Mexican in a spreading pool of blood. At his hand lay a shotgun with smoke curling from the barrel.

"Ha! Looks like some do-gooder just got done good," Kreeger said. In the street he saw Hawkins and Roedor arguing, Hawkins shoving the big man back a step, Roedor lunging back at him, holding the kicking screaming young girl over his shoulder. "Boys, bring some of that whiskey . . . see if we can't help our *amigos* out a little."

Miss Fannie still swung the wooden bucket, her high, pinned hair loose now and swinging back and forth in her battered face. But her arms had grown tired, and now she swung only in short swipes as the men stepped in and out, punching her, kicking her, and laughing as they tormented her.

Her black dress was gone. Her dusty pantaloons were smeared with blood where some of the men had taken out knives and stuck her thick legs with short, stinging jabs. One of her large breasts had spilled out. It shone pale white and trembling in the harsh sunlight. "You . . . bunch of swine," she rasped.

Al Kreeger swung two dusty bottles up under his arm and stepped outside when the two others joined him at the door. "Now this is my kinda town," he said.

In the livery barn Caslado stood up from running his hand

down the leg of the tall chestnut gelding. He looked at the horse and the two others beside it and dusted his hands together. "If this is all we get, we have a big problem," he said to JC, who stood near him. "There must be others around somewhere." He turned to the Mexican beside him and spun a finger. "You, go search the town for horses. *Apresurar!* Round up the people and ask where their horses are. If they say there are no more, shoot one of them, then ask again."

The Mexican hurried away, and Caslado turned to JC. "You must stay here at the front door and keep watch on these three. If there are no more, you and I must keep these three for ourselves."

JC nodded toward the rear of the barn, where the timber had been framed against a steep rock slope. The only way out the back was through a trapdoor in the roof. "I can watch the front door from across the street," JC said. "Can't nobody take horses up a ladder and across the roof, can they?" He looked back at Caslado, saw the dark hot eyes bore into his, and he shied back and said, "All right, I'll be here. Just have somebody bring me food and water . . . some whiskey wouldn't hurt."

Outside in the dirt street, Homer Corona stood with a double-barrel shotgun in one hand and a cocked pistol in the other. The shotgun he'd picked up from near the dead man's hand in the pool of blood. It had one shot left in it, and that one shot was pointed at Roedor's big belly from two feet away. "Turn her loose," Homer said, "or by all the saints, I will kill you."

Beside Roedor, Hawkins ran a hand across the bloody welt Homer's pistol barrel had left on his cheek. Hawkins's hand had gone to the butt of the pistol in his waist. But his hand stopped there, with Homer's pistol covering him.

The new men had turned to Homer, backing Roedor. The young Mexicans fixed their eyes on the new men in a cold stare, ready to back Homer Corona.

Caslado stepped forward from the livery barn. "*Facil, mi amigos,*" he called out, slowing a step as he drew nearer. "Take it easy! What is going on here?" The men had ceased all sport with Miss Fannie. They stood in tense silence. Miss Fannie had gone down on one knee, the bucket hanging from her hand. One eye had swollen and closed. With her free hand she cupped her large naked breast. Beside her the old grandmother lay still in the dirt.

"I told this rodent to give me the little girl," Homer said, his voice a low hiss. "If he does not, I will—"

"Aw, the girl." Caslado cut him off, chuckling. "It is for your own pleasure that you will kill your *compadre*?"

Homer considered it for a second, then let go of a tight breath and said, "*Sí*, I want her first. I saw her first."

"Lower the shotgun, Homer," Caslado said in a calm voice. "We must all share what we have."

Homer not only kept the shotgun poised and ready, he even moved it slightly toward Caslado. "I will take the girl one way or the other," he said.

Caslado glanced across the other faces, then back to Homer Corona. He knew Homer Corona to be a high-strung and serious young man. He had no doubt this young man would pull the trigger. If he did, Caslado also had no doubt that the shot would take out Roedor and himself as well.

After a tense second of pause, Caslado chuckled under his breath, then let the chuckle turn into a laugh. "Look at our *compadre*," he said to the men. "He has fallen in love, I think." He said to Roedor. "Go on, give him the skinny little girl. He has been with me longer than you. You can have her later. Homer is afraid you will flatten her if you take her first. Isn't that so, *mi amigo*?" He smiled at Homer, reaching over and lifting the girl from Roedor's shoulder as she kicked and scratched at him.

Homer forced a tight smile himself. "Yes . . . that is what I feared."

"See, there is no harm in Homer taking her first. We spend the night here. There is plenty of time for everyone to make themselves happy." Caslado passed the young girl on to Homer, who caught an arm around her throat without lowering the shotgun.

"I ain't forgetting what you done, greaser," Hawkins said, glaring at Homer with his hand against the bloody welt on his face.

"Who you are calling greaser, gringo?" a voice called out from the other men. They moved away from Miss Fannie and closer to Hawkins.

"Ever damned one of yas," Hawkins said as Al Kreeger moved over beside him and handed him a dusty bottle of whiskey. "Now who wants to *what* about it?" He laughed, threw back a long drink, and ran his bloody hand across his mouth. "Damned bunch of beans suckers!" He pitched the bottle to one of the Mexicans, and the man caught it and called back to him, saying that the only good gringo was dead gringo. And Hawkins said, "Yeah? There aren't enough hammer-headed chili-poppers to make that dream come true."

As the men spoke back and forth, first cursing, then laughing as they tossed insults and bottles from hand to hand, Caslado watched Homer slip back with the girl until he'd circled them in the street and took her off toward the livery barn, her screams muffled by his sweaty arm around her face.

"There he goes, Ernesto," Al Kreeger said in a slurred voice, raising a pistol toward Homer Corona. "I'll drop him for ya right now."

"No!" Caslado reached out and shoved his pistol aside. "Homer is a good soldier, with much hot anger inside himself." He shrugged. "Let him go cool himself out with the little girl." He gestured down to where Miss Fannie struggled in the dirt. "There is enough woman to go around."

Kreeger laughed. "You call that a woman? I'd sooner pick lice off a she baboon!"

"Then go search for a baboon," Caslado said. "The rest of us must take care of our horses and gather what we need for ourselves. Tomorrow we ride on. Let our horses rest today."

"Rest these nags?" Al Kreeger gazed at Caslado through bleary eyes. "These horses won't be up and worth nothing for the next week. Mine's in there right now, getting drunker than a damned dog."

"Go get your horse watered and fed, and out of the sun," Caslado said. "Or he will be of no good to you."

"He don't need rest. He ain't that kind of horse. He druther drink beer and raise hell with us ole boys!" Kreeger laughed and spun in the dirt street, a bottle hanging from his hand. Caslado laughed with him, but only a short laugh in pretense. *This ignorant pig of a man . . .* Then he turned to where one of the men came walking forward, leading an old goat and carrying three thrashing chickens by their legs.

In the doorway of the cantina the blind colonel stood turning his face back and forth. "Are they through? Are they leaving now?" he called out from within his darkness.

Al Kreeger laughed hysterically and shouted, "No, you blind-eyed peckerwood! But *you* are." And he raised the pistol and shot the blind colonel in the face.

"Looks like drinks are on the house," Hawkins cried out. In a surge of dust and boot heels, the men swept up onto the boardwalk and into the cantina. Hawkins grinned down at Miss Fannie and raised her to her feet. She'd dropped the wooden bucket, but swung an exhausted arm at him. He ducked and shook her roughly as she staggered against him. "Come on, big ole darling. You belong to me now."

He struggled with her to the doorway of the cantina, where shots rang out, and two horses spilled out onto the boardwalk and down into the street to where the other horses stood winded and blowing. Two of the Mexicans ran out and caught their horses. Then they gathered the others by their reins and led all of them toward the town well.

"You get out of here, too," Kreeger shouted. In a second his horse bolted through the door and into the street. The animal milled for a second, as if lost, then followed the others, staggering from heat and exhaustion.

Inside the cantina Hawkins dragged Miss Fannie across the floor and stood her against the bar. He snatched a bottle of whiskey and splashed some in her face. "Wake up, darling, and stand real still. I ain't shot a bottle off a whore's head for the longest time."

At the livery barn Homer swung the door open, stopped, and faced JC while the young girl struggled against his chest. "The hell's going on over there?" JC craned his neck toward the cantina. Sweat streamed down his face. "Somebody was supposed to bring me food and water."

"Go get it yourself," Homer said. "I will need the barn for a while."

"Can't leave," JC said. "He's got me standing guard here like some danged flunky."

"Guarding what?" Homer pushed past him with the girl under his sweaty arm.

"Never you mind what." JC turned with him, following inside.

Homer stopped at the sight of the three horses shying close together in a rear stall. "Oh, I see what. He has found some horses . . . for *himself*, and for *you*, no doubt."

"What of it? He's the leader."

"You are right." He struggled with the girl in his arms. "I will say nothing about it to the others. Now go stand outside and leave us alone," Homer snapped.

JC tipped his dusty hat and smiled, chuckling. "Sure. Take it easy, *amigo*. I'd never be one to stand in the way of passionate romance."

When the door swung shut, Homer carried the crying girl

back to the rear of the barn, where a pile of gramma hay lay in an empty stall. She saw the piled hay and pleaded, then kicked at his shins as he turned her around toward him and held her out at arm's length. "No, no! *Por favor!* No! I am yet a—"

"Shut up, little girl." He shook her. Her loose thin serape came down off one shoulder. Her tiny dark breast quivered. She snatched his forearm and kicked harder. "You are a wild little *animalia,* you are."

He held her out from him with his right hand and with his free hand slapped her across the face. She nearly crumpled, but he shook her again, soundly, and said close to her face, "Listen to me, child! You are leaving this place." He straightened her serape up onto her shoulder and dragged her over to the ladder leading up to the trapdoor in the roof. "You must run as fast and as far as you can from here. Do you hear me?"

"But . . . but my grandmother. She is out there . . ." Her voice trailed. She stared in his dark eyes, stunned, a thin trickle of blood running from her mouth.

He settled himself, wiped away the blood with his thumb, saying in a whisper, "I know, I know. But she is dead, and you cannot change that. Please forgive me, little one . . . and find a way to someday forgive those others. They are crude, simple men who are being misled. Do not spend your life hating us."

He hugged her against his sweaty chest and felt her frailty. Then he shoved her back toward the rickety ladder. "Now, go . . . I will wait for one hour, but no longer . . . until you are away from here."

She stepped up the ladder to the trapdoor, then hesitated, and asked, "Will you see that my grandmother is blessed and buried?"

"There are no blessings here for her, little *muchacha* . . .

none for any of us in this terrible land. Go . . . get out of here!"

She lifted the trapdoor, stepped up onto the hot roof, and, staying low, moved back to the rock slope and up it hand over hand. Five feet up, she slipped into a black shadowed crevice and followed it upward. At the top of the slope she broke forward and ran, out across sandy soil full of broken bottles, half sunken and sticking up like some dark, sharp growth spawned from a lower region beneath the earth.

She did not look back, but sped through hot sand and up-reaching spiny cactus until she circled above the town and reached the trail into the switchbacks leading up to the long stretch of flatland.

At the top of the switchbacks, she stopped long enough to catch her breath and let her heart stop pounding. Then she slowed to a walk in the cover of rocks along the rim of the high ridges, while evening shadows stretched long from the west. That night she slept a thin, tortured sleep of exhaustion, hungry and thirsty, her arms drawn up around her knees against the chill of the desert, and the cruel laughter and gunfire that sang back and forth in her mind.

When silver-gray morning seeped upward on the horizon, she moved from beneath the sandstone shelf, away from the dank coppery smell of the snakes and lizards that would soon come forth and lay glistening in sunlight. She crept close to the edge of a flat rock and gazed out and down at San Paulo. The town lay peaceful and quiet beneath a gray morning haze, as if all that had happened the evening before might have been a bad dream. She lay there feeling warm tears run down her face until behind her a quiet voice said, "Careful, little lady . . . that's a long drop."

She spun, startled, and saw a man standing back on the far edge of the flat rock twenty feet away, with a long rifle over his shoulder. His weathered face smiled at her, a warm gentle smile; yet her heart pounded, and she glanced back and forth like a trapped and frightened fawn.

"Easy now," the quiet voice said to her. "No harm's going to come to you. I'm a lawman." He let her see the badge on his chest, and pushed up the battered brim of his gray sombrero. "Bet you could drink a hot cup of tea, couldn't you? We're getting ready to make some."

Behind him she saw a younger man, this one holding the reins to two sweat-streaked horses. The ranger stood still, waiting for her fear to settle. She didn't answer, but she didn't bolt and run as he thought she might. She was from San Paulo; he knew it. And he knew in finding her up here, that Caslado and his men would be in the town below them. "Well . . . it's mighty fine tea," he said, "if you decide to join us." Then he backed off a step, down to the edge of the rock and waited.

After a moment she stepped down and saw the other man gathering a small pile of brush for a fire. "They . . . they killed my grandmother," the girl said, turning to the ranger. He swung the big rifle from his shoulder, leaned it against a rock, and caught her in his arms when she fell against him. She sobbed, low and quiet, her shoulders trembling.

"I understand," he said, stroking the back of her head. He looked over at Samuel Burns with a hollow stare, and Burns, feeling the accusation, turned his eyes away and down to the teapot beside the pile of dried brush kindling.

Chapter 11

Rance Plum walked back from the scattered debris, still swatting flies and cursing under his breath at the sight of bloated mule carcasses and the glistening black pile of entrails—the smell of them no different from the smell coming from his boot and trouser leg. He wiped his boots and trousers in the sand some more, then poured water on them. But it helped very little. Flies still sought him out and circled near his leg. He couldn't risk taking his boot off and washing it, fearing that Jack the Spider might see the folded money inside his sock.

He joined the others and dropped a dusty shovel on the ground near the priest. "Since you'd like to stick around and pine a few holy words over our dearly departed, Padre, you can dig a couple of holes for them." He swatted a fly from his cheek and added, "Although if you would simply leave them where they lay, I'm certain these damnable insects will have them picked clean in a day."

"You are a crude pig," Maria said to Plum. "We cannot leave these bodies lying here. And we cannot leave a priest out here alone. We must stay and help him bury the dead."

"Suit yourself," Plum said. "But the Spider and I are riding on, with or without you. We have clear enough tracks to follow." He gestured toward the trail. "This is one time when you and the ranger are going to have to include us in your plans. Right, Mr. Spider?" But the Spider didn't answer.

Plum turned and saw Jack the Spider thumbing through a dusty book. "If you can pull yourself from your current literary pursuits, I suggest we get started now."

"Uh, yeah—" Jack the Spider's face reddened. He tossed the battered book aside. "Nothing wrong with looking through a book, is there? It ain't like I was going to read the thing."

"Indeed," said Plum, his hand resting on the pistol butt across his stomach. "Perhaps when this is over, we'll find you a nice one with many pictures in it."

Crazy Gravy looked from one to the other and thought about the rifle he'd discarded back on the ground. He wished he had it now. For a second he'd thought of springing on them with his butcher knife, but that would be risking everything he'd gained, possibly even his life. These two were idiots beyond reason, but even idiots could pull a trigger. For now, he'd have to resolve himself to waiting a while longer—let the woman go, but stay close. He let out a tense breath. *Patience, my son . . .*

He managed a weary smile and said to the woman, "You have much to do, so go, please. I'll be fine. I have plenty of water now. Once I finish here, we will meet again along the trail."

"Are you certain, *Padre*?" she asked. "If you need our help, we will stay."

He reached out and patted her forearm. "Don't worry. God is with me always, and with you as well." Just the feel of her skin against his hand caused his blood to quicken. He smiled and drew it away.

Maria bit her lip and looked at Plum and the Spider. She couldn't possibly let them go alone and catch up to the ranger at San Paulo. These two were good men with a gun, but they had a way of bungling everything they touched. At least if she rode with them, she could see to it they didn't move right in and wreck whatever plans the ranger had made.

She turned to the priest and said, "I know you cannot leave these men lying here, Padre. We will be expecting you soon."

"Of course, my child." Crazy Gravy had picked up the shovel and now folded his hands on the handle. Plum and Jack the Spider had stepped up on their horses. Maria turned and did the same. As they left, Crazy Gravy stood watching until they dropped out of sight over the rise of land.

His hands tightened on the shovel handle, and his eyes turned dark and tense with rage. He'd had her right where he wanted her, but now she was gone . . . gone because of those two fools. He swung around, yelling, lifting the shovel, and brought it down in a solid blow on old Tack's cold dead face.

Bury the dead? Let them bury themselves, he thought. He calmed himself and ran a hand over his face. Above him, three buzzards swung in a slow circle, and he shook his head and set about dragging the bodies out of sight, back into the tangle of brush, where the two men had spent their last night on earth. When he'd finished, he stood near his horse and drank from the water gourd.

A hot breeze rose up from the west, and he let it caress his face for a few minutes as he drank. He would need to wait a full hour at least, just to make it look good. Then he would ride on.

Along the trail Maria, Plum, and Jack the Spider rode at a steady pace, keeping their horses fresh. They stopped only once at dusk to rest the animals, and let them draw water from a rock basin. Then, with the light of a three-quarter moon above them, they pushed on through the night toward San Paulo, at times walking, leading the horses across the sand and sparse clumps of grass, until the first light of dawn stood thin and grainy in the east.

A morning breeze swept in from the north, and Maria stopped on the narrow trail. She sniffed the air, then raised a hand to Plum and the Spider. "Do you smell something?" She gave a thin smile and sniffed again.

Plum sniffed as well. "No, I smell nothing. But then, I may never smell anything, ever again after this putrid stench of mule guts."

"Why don't you put it out of your mind, Plum," said Jack the Spider, "so the rest of us can." He turned to Maria. "I smelled something . . . but I don't know what."

"It is Duttwieler tea boiling," she said, reaching around to her saddle horn and stepping into the stirrup. "Come on. He is close by."

The ranger had gone to the edge of the flat rock and set up a small shooting stand made of three short branches tied together into a tripod, then checked the big Swiss rifle and laid it there. Beside it he'd unrolled the canvas cartridge belt and checked the big brass bullets. He took three of them out, wiped them with his bandanna, pressed each one into the rifle chamber with his thumb, and closed the bolt behind them.

He racked the bolt back and forward, raising the first cartridge, and snapped the bolt down in place. Then he kneeled down behind the rifle, raised the stock to his shoulder, and sighted down the long brass scope into the distant street of San Paulo.

"Someone's coming," Samuel Burns said in a lowered voice from the other edge of the rock. "It's the woman . . . and two others."

The ranger turned and looked back over his shoulder, recognizing Maria as she came forward in the gray dawn light. He'd started to smile, but his smile faded as he caught sight of Rance Plum and Jack the Spider riding beside her. *Those two* . . . He shook his head and looked back down through the scope. Well, they were here now. He might as well accept it, and give them something to do.

Scanning the street through the scope in the gray light, he saw the smoldering remains of last night's fire in the middle of the street. A skinny dog stood chewing on the leg bone of a goat amid littered whiskey bottles, chicken feathers, and bones.

Near the fire sat a brass bed. In it lay three sleeping men, tangled in a dirty quilt with their mouths thrown open toward the sky. A horse stood on the boardwalk out front of the small cantina. A high, plumed lady's hat had been sat on its head and tied there with a long red ribbon. A man's striped necktie swung from its neck. Along the street doors swung open and broken half off their hinges, their contents spilling out across the boardwalk and into the dirt, like disemboweled carcasses sat upon by wolves.

"Hello the camp," Maria said behind the ranger, in a quiet voice.

The ranger answered, then stood up, dusted his knees, and walked across the flat rock as the three of them moved in close and got down from their horses. Samuel Burns took their reins. Plum and the Spider eyed him closely, taking note of his striped guard's trousers. During the night, the ranger had taken the cuffs from Burns's wrists.

The young girl sat wrapped in a blanket near the low fire. Maria saw her and stepped over to her. "We found her earlier," the ranger said. "She got away from Caslado's men and spent the night up here. Says they've torn the town apart—killed her grandmother and some others." As he spoke, he had taken out the big pistol, checked it, and dropped it back in his holster.

"There, ranger, you see?" Rance Plum stepped toward him, raising a gloved finger for emphasis. "Had we been working together from the start, we might have prevented this from ever happening."

"I can't see how," the ranger said. He sniffed and looked Plum up and down. "What's that smell, Plum?" Behind Plum, the Spider stifled a short laugh, and Plum swung around, glaring at him.

"I inadvertently stepped in something," Plum snapped.

"I'll say you did." The ranger moved away, and when Plum turned back toward him to say something else, the ranger had stepped over to Maria and the young girl by the fire. "Where's the priest?" he asked, stooping beside Maria.

She explained what had happened, how the old teamster had died just before Plum and the Spider came along, and how the priest had stayed behind to bury the dead. When she'd finished, she nodded toward the far edge of the flat rock and asked, "How far will you be shooting?"

"Too far to talk about," the ranger said. "They'll be up and stirring any time now." He stood and gazed out across the rock at the rifle stand.

"You can't hit anything from *this* distance," Plum said. "I suggest Spider and I move down and set up a line of defense just outside of—"

"See why we never get along, Plum?" The ranger glared at him. "You haven't been here ten full minutes and you're already trying to run the show." He sniffed toward Plum again and shook his head. "What in the world did you step in anyway?" Again, the Spider stifled a laugh.

Plum's face swelled red. "Never mind what I stepped in! If you're wise—if you care anything at all about those poor townspeople, you'll allow us to work with you here. This is not the time to try to be a one-man show, for God's sake!"

"I couldn't agree more," the ranger said, turning as he spoke and stepping up onto the flat rock.

Rance Plum was taken aback by the ranger's words. He batted his eyes. "You . . . you couldn't?"

"That's right," the ranger said. "It's a good thing you came along when you did. The way I figure it, the more guns they hear along this ridge, the better. A force that size could easily decide to circle up around me if they think there's only one man with a rifle up here."

"Oh?" Plum tossed a smug glance at the Spider, then looked back at the ranger. "Well then . . . let me make it clear. Mr. Spider and I will be glad to lend our services and expertise. But once Ernesto Caslado is in hand, we're claiming the bounty owed to us. We will *not* share it with you."

"You oughta know I've got no interest in the reward money," the ranger said. "I'm just here trying to do the job. Whatever you and the Spider make off Caslado is between you and the warden. Fair enough?"

"Absolutely then." Plum nodded, patting the pistol on his stomach. "You won't regret this, ranger." He looked over at Samuel Burns, again taking note of the stripe down his trousers. "Who might you be, young man?"

"He's Sammy Burns," the ranger said, speaking up before Burns got the chance to answer. "He's one of the prison guards . . . threw in with us near the old relay station." Burns was glad to hear the ranger drop the Sammy-boy, and just call him Sammy.

"Oh?" Plum cocked an eye, feeling there was more to it than the ranger was telling. "There were two guards involved with Caslado, according to the warden. This wouldn't happen to be one of them, would it?"

"Yep." The ranger looked down at them from where he stood atop the flat rock. "But don't go getting no ideas. He's with me, under my protection till I find out just who all was involved in this thing."

"*Ideas?*" Plum and the Spider took a step toward Burns. Plum's hand went tight around his pistol butt. "This little snake has cost me money . . . letting Caslado get away!"

"Easy, Plum," the ranger said in a low tone. "If you want in this game, you're going to play it my way. Burns is with me, until I say otherwise."

Plum seethed, but lowered his hand from his pistol, still glaring at Samuel Burns. "Very well, for now, sir. But this young man will answer to me when this is all settled. That I promise you."

"Meanwhile"—the ranger reached behind his back, took out a pistol, and pitched it to Samuel Burns—"this young man is working for me." Burns caught the pistol, fumbling it, almost dropping it.

Plum's eyes widened. He pointed a finger at Burns and said to the ranger, "You can't be serious! Give this man a gun and we'll be lucky if he doesn't back-shoot us!"

The ranger looked at Burns as the young man stared at the pistol in his hand. "Are you going to back-shoot us, Sammy?"

"No." Burns raised the pistol, turning it in his hand. "You have my word. Tell me what to do and I'll do it."

"There, Plum, you see." The ranger smiled, turning to the big rifle. "He gave me his word. Now, if you and Spider want something to do, spread out around this ridge and get your rifles ready. Once I wake this bunch up, I want them to think they've got a full posse down their shirts."

Throughout the night, Homer Corona had slept very little. He'd waited an hour before coming back from the livery barn, and was prepared for whatever happened once Roedor went for the girl and found out she was missing. But when Roedor had started toward the barn, Caslado had shoved him aside, told him he was too drunk, and had insisted that he himself be the next one to have the young girl. Roedor had grumbled about it, but given in, the way any lesser dog gives in to the leader of a pack.

For the next half hour, Homer had sat tense in a chair inside the cantina with his pistol across his lap while the others drank and cursed and fought back and forth among themselves. He would deny turning the girl loose. Perhaps his denial would be enough. Perhaps Caslado would believe that she had slipped out and away on her own. If Caslado pushed it, Homer was prepared to raise his pistol and blow Caslado's brains out. *This* he'd resolved himself to do.

Yet, when Caslado had not come back after a half hour, Homer had stepped out onto the boardwalk and looked toward the barn. JC was not there by the door, and that made Homer realize why Caslado had insisted on going to the barn next. He and JC were gone on the fresh horses. There wasn't a doubt in Homer's mind, but he'd walked over to the barn anyway, just to ascertain it for himself. And he'd been right.

When he'd gone back to the cantina, three of the men came running past him along the street, carrying the brass bed toward the raging fire. And he walked on, past the raging fire, where a goat had been skewered whole and now turned slowly with flames licking and blackening it. The men were too out of control to talk to right then, and he'd spent the rest of the night deciding what to do once morning came and the men found themselves abandoned by their leader.

It would have been simple for him to take two or three of the best horses and slip away himself. Nobody would have noticed. But he had not come all this way to free Ernesto Caslado, just to be left in a one-horse town. With or without Caslado, there was still a revolution to be won south of the border. He'd spent the night questioning himself as to whether or not he, Homer Corona, could lead them. Along with Roedor, there were four other new men the gringo, JC, had recruited—along with the two convicts. These new men were animals, but perhaps they could be taught. From what he'd seen of the two gringo convicts, they were low men . . . men with no heart or decency left in them.

Then, at first light as his decision had been made, he'd closed his eyes to sleep for the next couple of hours, when a man screamed out in the street, his voice followed by the echoing sound of a rifle shot from a long ways off. Other shots resounded as Homer rolled from the chair, slinging off his blanket, but these shots sounded small, like play toys, compared to the first one.

"Ernesto! Ernesto! Come quick!" a man yelled, running from the smoldering fire toward the cantina, where Homer had crouched down in the doorway. But as the man ran, he broke into a forward roll in a spray of blood; and in the second following, the big sound exploded again.

Homer's eyes fixed on the high ridge in the distance, at a point where the loud shot came from. On either side came other shots, but they fell short, too short to be of concern. Behind Homer, Al Kreeger ran from the small room behind the bar with a holster belt swung over his shoulder. Behind him came others, their shirts open and hanging from their chests, their hair wild, their eyes red-rimmed and full of drunken sleep. "The hell's going on?" Kreeger slid down behind Homer Corona and peeped around him into the street.

"Be still," Homer snapped, his eyes still fixed on the high ridge, waiting for the next big rifle shot. In the street two of the new men lay dead, one sprawled out facedown in a pool of blood, the other draped sideways off the brass bed. Al Kreeger's horse had bolted off the boardwalk with the woman's hat hanging down the side of its head. It ran in panic back and forth in front of the smoldering fire.

"Cover me," Kreeger shouted. "I've got to get my horse!" He started forward around Homer, but Homer grabbed his arm and pulled him back.

"Cover you how? You imbecile! With this?" He shook the pistol in his hand. "Can't you see what we have here? We are pinned down like rats."

"I got ta have my horse," Kreeger said. He started forward again. This time Homer jammed his pistol barrel into Kreeger's ribs.

"You should have put your horse in the barn last night and cared for it. Stay put, before you cause the others to make a run for it."

The other two men who'd been in the brass bed had rolled out and scurried beneath it. Now one of them saw Kreeger almost run from the cantina, and he scooted out and rose up into a running crouch toward them. "No! Get back," Homer called out to him—but too late. Halfway to the boardwalk, the man's forehead blew out in a long spinning ribbon of blood, and he flattened forward in the dirt. Then the big sound came again, echoing out from the high ridge and across the sky above them.

"Holy Madre," the other man said from beneath the bed. He crossed himself and called out to Homer and Kreeger, "Where is Ernesto? He will know what to do!"

"Yeah, come to think of it," Kreeger said, glancing around the dark cantina at the other faces, "where is our fearless leader?"

Chapter 12

All night they'd ridden hard, eastward, pushing their new horses until the animals were blown and frothed and making little headway. They'd stopped for over an hour after midnight, long enough to rest the horses, without water. Then they'd pushed on. When JC had asked where they were headed, Caslado hadn't answered. Instead, he'd only pointed up eastward toward the high grasslands and spurred the big chestnut horse forward, leading the spare horse behind him. At dawn they'd stopped at a place where a thin stream of water ran out from beneath a stand of rock.

When they'd watered the worn-out horses and filled their empty canteens, JC had gotten ready to step up into his stirrup when his horse swayed sideways and nearly fell. Caslado saw it, and he'd spoke for the first time since they'd fled San Paulo, saying, "No. We will wait here for a while, until after daylight. Let the sun get above us, out of our eyes. My brother's rancho is somewhere ten or so miles ahead. He will take us in. He is a good man, my brother. We will be welcome there."

JC saw something dark in Caslado's eyes as he spoke, but he didn't question him about it. "Good enough," he replied; and he stepped back from his horse and let out a breath. "This horse is about dead anyway."

"*Sí*." Caslado stepped back and ran his hand along the spare horse's flank. "You take this one."

"But you brought it for yourself."

"So I did. But you need it more than I. We are *compadres* eh? What is mine is yours." He slapped a gloved hand on JC's back. Dust billowed. "This is how it must be among friends. Now change your saddle over."

"All right then." JC smiled. *Dumb Mexican bean sucker* . . . Caslado didn't know it, but as soon as they got to Ramon's rancho, then got their hands on the railroad money, this friendship was over. Nobody in his right mind would trust Ernesto Caslado. He sure didn't—never had. But it didn't matter. JC had better plans already made. All he had to do was play along a while longer.

He stripped off the damp sweaty saddle and blanket and swapped them over to the fresh horse. He would have felt better with Kreeger and Hawkins alongside him. But it looked like for now anyway, Caslado was staying true to his word. *Who knows?* Maybe Caslado meant it when he said he'd get all that was coming to him. After all, JC thought, hadn't he risked his neck, breaking him out of prison, one step ahead of a hangman's knot?

Caslado squatted against the trunk of a cottonwood tree and watched him swap the saddle and bridle. "By now, the young one, Homer Corona, will see what we have done," he said. "If he is wise he will take the men back to *Mejico*. They will continue on with the revolution. Ah, that *revolucion* . . . It is always there, like the wind and the sky. It changes its colors and its strength. But always it is there."

JC finished saddling the horse and walked over near the edge of the stream and relieved himself. "Not having second thoughts about leaving them, are you?" he asked over his shoulder.

"No," Caslado said. "In the prison I came to realize that no man is ever free. What a man wants for others he must first take for himself."

"Yeah? Well—" JC attended to himself and chuckled

under his breath. "—I decided, all I want is money. And I don't mind taking it a bit. Them that can't take what they want in life, better learn to live without it. That's how I see it." He turned facing Caslado and froze when he saw the cocked pistol in Caslado's hands.

Caslado smiled, shaking his head back and forth slowly. "Aw, it is true what you say about money. To have it you must take it from another, eh? You must use others to get it . . . and once you have used them until there is nothing left, you must leave them behind and go on."

"We . . . we have a deal here." JC's voice trembled. "We're partners, Ernesto! Remember?"

Ernesto shrugged. "Of course, I remember." He turned his pistol toward the staggering horse and shot it. It sank down on its front knees, then fell over on its side with a low groan. Caslado smiled, turning back to JC. "The animal gave us all it had to give. Now it is of no more use . . . and so it dies." He slipped his pistol back into the holster hanging from his shoulder and stood up.

JC stared at him and swallowed a dry lump in his throat as Caslado walked over, picked up his reins, and walked his horse toward a stand of sparse juniper twenty feet away. *What was that all about?* Caslado sending him a message of some sort? He knew a little about how this man's mind worked. Caslado might have drawn his pistol to shoot the horse, but the pistol had first been pointed at *him*. There was no mistaking that. Yep, JC thought, he was glad he had other plans already made. To hell with Ernesto.

A half hour had passed, and still nothing moved in the streets of San Paulo except the dazed horse. Had this been a horse that was up and fresh, the ranger would have shot it, to put it out of use. That would leave one man without a way out of town. But this animal wasn't going anywhere for a while. He watched it move back and forth on unsteady legs, looking gaunt in the flanks, streaked with dried white sweat.

With the plumed hat swinging from the side of its face, the animal looked like something cast aside by a traveling show, a sad and worn-out clown horse.

He scanned the street once more. Nothing. The last shot he'd made had been through the thin feather mattress of the bed when he noticed the bed had moved inch by inch closer to the boardwalk. He couldn't afford to waste the big cartridges, but this shot he'd allowed himself. After he had made the shot, the bed had jerked to a halt, and in a moment a man had crawled out slowly from beneath it and stopped. Dark blood circled his hip. He lay spread-eagle in the dirt, and now and then raised a weak hand toward the boardwalk, as if pleading for help. The clown horse milled near, swinging its head and scraping the dirt.

"What now?" Rance Plum called over to the ranger from his spot along the ridge. "We can't lie here all day, can we?"

The ranger didn't answer. Instead, he kept his eye against the long scope, concentrating on the slice of shade lying black in the morning sunlight alongside the livery barn. They had made it to there, he knew. He'd watched them one by one jump across the back of a narrow alley behind the cantina. It was no more than a flash as each of them spanned the five-foot stretch of dirt—not worth risking a shot.

What the gunmen didn't realize was that the ranger wanted them out of San Paulo, away from innocent people. Once out in the open land, he wanted them to stay a good distance away, where he knew their firepower would be useless against the big Swiss rifle. He would fall back onto their trail and take his time with them.

Now they had moved along behind the adobe and frame buildings and made it to the blind side of the barn. They were huddled back there, deciding which of them would make a run across the twenty-foot stretch of ground across the front of the barn. Their horses stood in the open corral, shied against the east side of the barn. The ranger caught glimpses of the animals as they milled in and out of sight.

In the black slice of shade, Roedor turned to Homer Corona and said, "If I thought you knew Caslado was leaving us here, I would kill you."

All the men stood pressed and huddled against the west side of the barn. Homer glared at Roedor and said, "If you think I would do such a thing to my *compadres*, then you better kill me, right now!" He stepped back from the wall of the barn and faced Roedor with his pistol hanging from his hand.

"Jesus!" Hawkins said, snatching Homer by his shirt and pulling him back against the wall. "Can't you greasers go a minute without wanting to fight each other?" Hawkins had Miss Fannie pressed to him with his arm around her throat, his gun hanging from his hand and down her naked breasts. Her face was puffed and swollen; she stood naked, save for the blanket she'd grabbed when Hawkins had slung her from the cot and kicked her before him through the back door of the cantina.

Homer glared at Hawkins and said, "Call any of us greasers once more, and you will see your tongue on the ground beside you." He turned to the others as they cursed and grumbled and tried craning their necks for a peep around the barn. "Listen to me, all of you. Find something to loosen these nails." He pounded a hand on the wall of the barn.

"We ain't a bunch of carpenters! Who put you in charge?" Al Kreeger asked, then spit in the dirt, glaring at him. The others only stared. Homer stepped back and along the shadow to where a steel pry-bar stood against the side of the barn. He picked it up, came back with it, and pitched it in the dirt at Roedor's feet. Roedor looked down at it, then back up at Homer.

"Whoever can lead, must lead," Homer said, looking from one to the other. "If Ernesto were here, he would send one of you out there in the open and get you killed. I say we must take boards from the wall and go through it. Do you agree?"

A dark smile stirred on Roedor's face. He reached down and picked up the pry-bar and shook it in his hand. "I cannot forgive you for stealing the little girl from me," he said; and turning to the others, he added, "But he is one smart *hombre*, eh?"

They fell onto the wall, Roedor with the pry-bar, others with their long knives. Two of the men moved along the shadow and returned with a pick head they'd found near the rear of the barn where the ground slope met the metal roof. In moments boards came free with a ripping sound and fell to the ground at Homer's feet.

"Weaseling your way right in and taking over, ain't ya?" Al Kreeger said, standing now, facing Homer with a bottle of whiskey hanging from his dirty hand. "Well . . . I ain't taking no orders from ya. I'll leave here when I'm damned good and ready—go my own way! So will he." He spit, thumbing toward Hawkins, and threw back a long swallow of whiskey. He passed the bottle on to Hawkins, who took it with his free hand.

"It is true, you will not be leaving with the rest of us," Homer said, glaring at Kreeger, his pistol hanging from his hand. "You have been a fool and left your horse to die in the street."

"That horse is fine. You best not concern yourself with what I do, or how I do it!"

Homer looked at Hawkins. "You are free to ride with us. But you must turn the woman loose. Do you understand? I am not Caslado. I will not stand for such things."

"Whoa now." Hawkins laughed. "You've gone an' grown a big head on us." He shook Miss Fannie against his chest.

"So happens, me and my big darling don't do nothing 'less we do it together." He raised the bottle, drank from it, then held it to Miss Fannie's tender, swollen lips. She resisted and tried to turn her face away, but he jammed the bottle against her teeth until at last she sipped from it. She convulsed it back up, coughing and gagging as it ran down her chin.

"There now, hon." Hawkins squeezed her hard against him, his sweaty beard stubble pressing her swollen eye. He grinned cruelly at Homer. "Ain't we just the latest thing, me and her?"

Homer Corona clenched his teeth against the pulsing rage in his forehead. *This pig . . . this stinking, rotten,* animalia! He'd started to raise his pistol and put a bullet in Hawkins's face when Roedor shook his arm from behind him and said, "We are through the wall, Homer! We are through the wall."

Homer forced himself to turn away from Hawkins, toward the open hole where the men scrambled into the dark barn. "To hell with them all," he heard Al Kreeger say behind him.

Inside the barn Homer pointed at the other wall. "Now, open it quickly . . . bring the horses through here, and let's be off, away from this place of shame."

The men started in on the wall. Horses nickered on the other side. "But, Homer," Roedor said, "there are too many rifles up there. They will shoot us to pieces when we hit the street and get farther away."

"No, *amigo*," Homer replied. "There may be many rifles, but there is only one that is doing the killing. The others are out of range." He laid a hand on Roedor's thick shoulder as the men ripped boards from the wall. "Trust what I tell you," he added. "We must find cover along the trail, but we do not want to get too far ahead. We must stay in range in order to defend ourselves. Whoever is shooting the big rifle *wants* us far ahead . . . where he *knows* we are powerless against him."

Roedor's eyes widened as if a light had snapped on in his broad forehead. "Ah, yes . . . you are right." He beamed and turned to the others as they pried and pulled on the long rough boards. "You heard Homer! Let's get this wall open, *pronto*!"

Up on the ridge, the ranger had heard the distant banging and the creaking sound of wood being pulled loose. Dust billowed and drifted along the edge of the barn. He relaxed for a moment behind the rifle stock. *Pretty smart of Caslado . . .*

The ranger wondered what else Caslado might have in mind. Would he know enough to stay in close among the cover of rock and brush, and fight back against the long range of the big rifle? Or, would he make a run across the easier flatland above the town—risking his men's lives while he stayed out front and kept them between himself and the rifle fire?

The ranger turned and looked back at Samuel Burns, who stood holding the reins to the horses. The young man looked over at him with the pistol hanging from his hand. "Ready when you are," Burns called over to him. He stood like a soldier awaiting his next order. The ranger swung his arm up on his left, motioning for Plum and the Spider to fall back to the horses. When he turned to the right, he saw Maria and the young girl already moving back.

Jack the Spider grumbled as he and Rance Plum moved along the ridge. "I hate being told what to do by *him*."

"Certainly you do, Mr. Spider," Plum replied, speaking back over his shoulder. "But you must admit . . . he is good at what he does. Not saying that *I* wouldn't do better of course. But after all, he isn't interested in getting his fingers in our pie once we have Caslado where we want him." Plum smiled. "You see . . . fortunate for you, I have this all worked out up here." He tapped a gloved finger to his fore-head.

"Shiiiit," the Spider said. He spit and ran his hand across his mouth. "You better figure out how to rid yourself of that god-awful smell, before buzzards start nesting in your drawers."

In the dark barn Homer and the others checked their horses, saddled them, and gathered near the broken wall. "These horses are still spent," one of the Mexicans said. "I don't think we can outrun anyone on them."

"Shut up," Roedor said to him. "Homer knows what he is doing. We follow him now."

Outside along the blind side of the barn, Kreeger and Hawkins stood watching, passing the bottle back and forth as the riders came out single-file and eased their horses along the wall in the shadow. Hawkins looked up, holding Miss Fannie in front of him with both arms around her below her breasts, his pistol still in his hand and pressed against the blanket around her. "Five'll get you ten, none of you makes it to the back trail," he said.

Homer started to turn his horse toward him, but Roedor said under his breath, "Let the gringos be. They will die here, eh?"

"*Sí*," Homer said in a hiss, "and good riddance to them." He raised a hand and looked along the line of riders. "All right, *mi compadres* . . . stay close behind the buildings. Ride like the devil, and do not stop until you are up in the rocks on the trail!"

"And theeeey're off!" Al Kreeger laughed and staggered with the bottle in one hand and the pistol in the other as the riders bolted away in a rise of dust. Hawkins watched with a thin smile, bracing himself against the wall, expecting the sound of more rifle fire from the high ridge. In a second when no shots came and the last of the riders had climbed upward onto the steep rocky trail northwest of town, he leaned slightly forward with Miss Fannie pinned against him. "The hell happened, Al? Reckon they ran out of bullets up there?"

"Danged if I know," Kreeger said with a drunken smile. "If it's that easy, I might as well ride out myself."

"Not me," Hawkins said in a whiskey slur. He nuzzled his rough face against the side of Miss Fannie's bruised throat. "We like it here, don't we, darling?"

Chapter 13

The ranger stood watching as the riders gigged their horses along behind the buildings and up onto the narrow rocky trail leading north out of San Paulo. He could see their horses were gaunt and tired, not acting in quick response, even to the sharp spurs against their tired flesh. No sooner had the last rider faded upward onto the trail before their dust settled when a stocky man ran from beside the barn to the horse in the street. The ranger watched him snatch the plumed hat from the horse's head and throw himself up into the saddle.

The horse buckled down in its haunches for a second, then sprang forward at the feel of Kreeger's boot heels against its ribs. But the animal was too worn out to collect its weight just right. It ran unsteady along the dirt street. Kreeger had just glanced along the ridge and caught sight of a dark speck up in the morning sunlight, when he felt the horse's front legs falter and go down.

The ranger watched, shaking his head, as man and horse became one in a rolling cloud of dust, hooves, and boot heels. He raised his big pistol, pointed it out at arm's length, and sighted it down on Al Kreeger as the man struggled to his feet in a staggering run. The horse rose up brokenly from the dirt and shook itself off. The ranger's pistol barrel followed Kreeger a few yards along the dirt street.

"Bang," the ranger said under his breath. He lowered the

pistol, smiled, and holstered it. Down in the street, Kreeger ran up onto the boardwalk and through the open door of a pillaged mercantile store. Inside, he hung onto the dusty counter, his whiskey-coated breath heaving in his chest. When he'd caught his breath, he pushed away from the counter, ran through the store, and out the back door toward the livery barn.

Above, on the ridge line, Plum stood back by the horses, watching the ranger, an annoyed expression on his face. "I can't believe you, ranger," he called out. "We should be after these scoundrels right this instant! Yet, you're fooling around! While they ride away!"

While he'd watched the riders make their break, the ranger took note that Caslado was not among them—something he wasn't about to mention to Plum and the Spider just yet. He picked up the big rifle, kicked the makeshift tripod away, and walked back to the others slowly, glancing up at the sun. "Trouble with you, Plum, is you must've got kicked away from your mama's tit too early. It's made you a bit skiddish and ill-at-ease."

"How dare—!" Plum bit his words short and seethed in silence as the ranger stepped past him, faced Samuel Burns, and said, "There's one shot left in that pistol. If I let you hang onto it, will you promise not to shoot one of us, Sammy-boy?"

Sammy-boy . . . ? There it was again. Burns hated that name. It made him feel like a weak simpering fool. He looked down at the gun in his hand. "I . . . I know I didn't do us any good with it."

"You made a noise with it . . . that's all I wanted." The ranger turned and took the reins to his white barb.

They mounted and rode down the switchback single file, the ranger in the lead, followed by Burns, then Maria riding double with the young girl, and Plum and the Spider bringing up the rear. When they reached the flatland below and started across it, Plum and the Spider started to kick their horses into a run, but the ranger held up a hand, stopping them. "What the—?" Plum reined down, jerked his horse over near the ranger, and glared at him. "This is insane, sir! Are we *trying* to let them get away?"

The ranger gazed ahead toward San Paulo as he spoke. "They're lagging up along that trail right now, wanting us to get within range." He spit and wiped a gloved hand across his mouth. "I won't do it though. They're going to have to play the game *my* way. Their horses are too worn out to shake us off their trail. They have to get us closer to them before they can put up any kind of fight." He grinned at Plum. "Pay attention here . . . you might learn something."

Plum seethed, but kept silent, and fell his horse over beside the Spider. "If he thinks we're going to dawdle around in San Paulo and let Caslado slip away, he has another thing coming!" He relayed what the ranger had said, and when he'd finished, Jack the Spider only shook his head and looked him up and down with his one good eye.

"Don't let this give you hives, Plum, but I think he's right," the Spider said. He nudged his horse forward. Plum sat staring for a second, clenching his teeth, then cursed under his breath and moved forward.

From the open door of the livery barn, Levon Hawkins stood with an arm around Miss Fannie, holding her against him. He squinted against the morning sun's glare and watched the ranger and the others move across the flatlands. *Yep. Should've known it would be him* . . . He'd recognize the ranger anywhere. He gave a dark smile. "All right now . . ." he said in a low tone, "come and get it, ranger."

Miss Fannie raised her swollen face at the sound of Hawkins's words against her cheek. "I . . . hope he . . . kills you," she said.

"What?" Hawkins laughed and shook her hard. "After all

we've meant to each other? I can't believe you'd say a thing like that!"

He chuckled and leaned forward, looking along the dirt street to where Al Kreeger's horse stood spread-legged, its saddle hanging down its side, the necktie still hanging from its throat. "Looks like Al's in a world of trouble." He drew back inside the barn and glanced out through the hole in the wall, toward his own horse as it milled alone in the corral. "Come on, darling, we got to get prepared for company here."

On his way to the livery barn, Al Kreeger had gone into the Weaponry & Ammunition store and rummaged through the shelves beneath the counter. Nothing. *Them damned greasers* . . . He had five shots left in his revolver, and that was it. On the floor lay a disassembled double-barrel shotgun. He snatched it up in three parts, fitted it together with sweaty hands, and snapped both hammers to make sure it worked.

His whiskey was wearing off. *Damn that whiskey!* He needed a drink. Rummaging in the debris on the floor, three loads rolled out from within a wadded-up blanket. He snatched them up, loaded the shotgun, and headed out through the back door. There was one horse left. It belonged to Hawkins . . . but Kreeger would take it, one way or another.

He slipped through the alley to the street and looked out at the riders coming in across the flatlands. *Damn it all!* Why hadn't he left the booze alone long enough to tend to his horse last night? All his life his pa had told him he was a raving idiot . . . Maybe he'd been right. *Well, too late now* . . . Kreeger wiped a shaky hand across his sweaty face. *Man!* He needed a drink, bad. Just one bottle from the cantina, he thought—if there was still a bottle left. *Them damned greasers* . . . He licked his fevered lips and moved up onto the boardwalk to the cantina.

Hawkins had brought his horse into the barn and stood in the middle bay. He'd found a rope and, with the horse pulling it, had raised Miss Fannie up by one ankle and had her hanging upside down from a rafter, four feet off the dirt floor. "There now, that'll keep you out of trouble," he said, tying the rope off to an upright timber. He chuckled and swung her back and forth. Then he searched through the barn, found a sharp sickle, walked over to the horse, and felled the animal with one swift slash across its throat.

When Al Kreeger stepped through the hole in the barn wall, he froze at the sight of Hawkins standing near the downed horse, the horse rasping, making its death throes in a dark pool of blood. Kreeger only glanced at Miss Fannie swaying and turning on the end of the rope. "Godamighty! Hawk! You've kilt the only horse left in town!"

"Yeah, I know." Hawkins stood smiling at him, taking note of the bottle of whiskey hanging from his left hand, but taking more note of the cocked shotgun in his right. "Didn't want these folks to arrive and find the two of us bickering over a horse." He stepped over, shoved the shotgun barrel aside, and took the bottle from Kreeger's hand. Kreeger stared in disbelief at the dying horse.

"Buck up, Al." Hawkins laughed, threw back a drink, and ran a hand across his mouth. "There's *five* horses riding in here. I'd hate to think we ain't able to take them, wouldn't you?"

"Damn it all, Hawk." Kreeger let down the hammers on the shotgun. "First JC let me down, and now you. At least *one* of us could have got away."

"We'll be all right. Just kill them peckerwoods with me." He raised his pistol from his waist and twirled it.

"Face-to-face?" He swallowed hard, watching Hawkins's pistol spin on his finger. Kreeger's eyes were bloodshot, bulged, and watery. He added in a low tone, "I've been a straight-up back-shooter all my life . . . and damn proud of it. But fighting armed men ain't never been my style." He took the bottle back, drank from it, and let out a whiskey hiss. He shrugged. "Sure, I shot that old blind fool . . . and that Indian, but they wasn't shooting back, don't forget. I always said, if you make a practice of shooting at armed men, there's a good chance you'll get yourself killed. If you can't kill a person without them knowing about it, you shouldn't even be carrying a—"

"Don't go soiling yourself, Al," Hawkins said, cutting him off. "You've been acting tough ever since I've known ya. Now it's payoff time." He stopped twirling the pistol and pointed it off toward the flatlands. "Out there's the dirty bastard that rang my head with a skillet—my nose ain't been right ever since. When they get here, you either kill them, or they'll kill you. That's how it stacks up . . . so drink up and put it out of your mind till they get here."

Hawkins turned, chuckling, and gave Miss Fannie a spin on her rope. She growled and clawed out at him as she spun, but he stepped back. "Besides, Al, what can go wrong? We've got my darling here, praying with our best interests at heart."

Nearing the town, the ranger stopped his white barb and said to the others, pointing ahead at the mercantile store, "I saw one run into the store. There could be others. Let's spread out and make a sweep."

Maria reached around, helped the young girl down from behind her saddle, and said, "Go—stay hidden until I come back for you." The girl touched ground and ran off to the cover of an upreaching cactus. Burns stared warily at the town. "Stay close to me, Sammy-boy," the ranger said. "You're gonna hold our horses. These animals might be real important to whoever's left in San Paulo."

"Are you out of your mind, sir?" Plum's eyes widened.

"You cannot leave your horses with this man. He should be in chains as it is!"

"Plum, don't you ever let up?" The ranger shook his head. "I told you Sammy's with me. Now let's cut the fal-da-ral and go to work."

Now it was Sammy once again. One minute Sammy, the next, Sammy-boy. Burns wondered why the ranger kept doing that.

Plum swung his eyes to San Paulo, then back to the ranger. "How do we know this is not a trap?" He glared. "Perhaps they left some men to hold us up here while the rest of them got away. I think we should swing around town and get after them on the high trail."

The ranger took out his big pistol, checked it, and laid it across his lap. "Oh? Then go ahead, Plum. But how do you know the man I saw wasn't Caslado himself?"

Plum cocked an eye. "Was it? Was it Caslado?"

"Can't say . . . the sun got in my eyes." The ranger smiled and moved his horse forward.

"Confound you, ranger!" Plum jerked his reins hard and away, gigging his horse. "Come on, Mr. Spider. Let's get this over with." Jack the Spider fell in behind him, and the two rode off across the sand.

Maria pulled the glove from her right hand and folded it down in her waist. They watched as Plum and the Spider circled wide in a wake of dust and closed in on the far end of San Paulo. "You should not torment him so," she said to the ranger.

"Ah— He expects it," the ranger replied. He looked over at her as she drew her pistol and turned it in her hand. "Don't suppose it would do any good to ask you to stay back here with the girl?"

"None at all," Maria said; and she checked her pistol, kept it in her hand, and nudged her horse forward.

"All right." The ranger tapped his reins to the white barb

and nodded for Burns to follow him. "I'll take the north side of the street, by the barn. Give me a twenty-foot head start and take the south side."

They rode forward to the edge of town and stopped behind the sun-bleached trunk of a downed cottonwood tree. "This is as far as you go, Sammy." The three of them stepped down, and Maria and the ranger handed Burns their reins. "Now, you've got one bullet and three horses, Sammy," the ranger said, staring into Burn's eyes. "Are you gonna be here when we get back?"

"Don't worry," Burns said, feeling better now that the ranger had dropped the Sammy-boy and started calling him Sammy again. "I'll be right here. You have my word."

They moved forward on foot, the ranger and Maria, into the dirt street of San Paulo. Before they spread out and moved away from one another, Maria said in a low tone, "You think someone is in the barn, *sí*? That is why you wanted me on the *other* side of the street, isn't it?"

"I wish we could do this without a lot of discourse." The ranger let out a breath and moved forward, slowly, a bit sideways, and closer to the barn, the big pistol hanging in his hand.

Inside the barn Hawkins stood to one side of the open door. There came the man who had caused him to spend the last two years of his life behind bars. This was the man who had ruined his nose with the skillet—the man who only days ago had stood outside Caslado's cell and made the remark . . . that Hawkins was not worth the price of a bullet. *All right, now we'll see.* He opened and closed his hand on the butt of his pistol. *That's it, ranger. Just a little bit closer. . . .*

Behind him he heard boots pounding away across the dirt floor, and he turned just in time to see Kreeger disappear through the hole in the wall. *Kreeger . . . you bastard!* Miss Fannie had stopped swaying on her rope. She stared at him through swollen eyes, her face turning blue, her matted hair hanging loose toward the dirt floor. "I changed . . . my mind. I hope . . . he *doesn't* kill you. I'd rather—"

"Shhhh." Hawkins cut her off with a finger raised to his lips, grinning. "Be real still, darling, so I don't have to do you like I done the horse."

He turned and peeped back out to the street. *What the—?* The ranger had vanished. Across the street he saw the woman moving from storefront to storefront—but no sign of the ranger! *Now what?* He leaned out just a fraction and looked west at the far end of the street. Two men spread out, moving forward cautiously, their guns drawn—but no sign of the ranger. Hawkins ducked back into the barn. His eyes darted back to the rear of the barn and up to the trapdoor. Had he just heard something up there? Footsteps?

Hawkins crouched, watching the trapdoor. He raised his pistol toward it, knowing that at any second it would open, and there would be the ranger. He had him! He couldn't miss from here! The ranger was as good as dead—*What*? He saw the look in Miss Fannie's swollen eyes staring at him, a strange, satisfied expression. "Hawkins!" The voice yelled behind him, and he swung back toward the door.

Oh-no! He caught a glimpse of the big pistol barrel, saw a flash of metal, and felt the hard blast against his face. Shot in the face! O God! Then the ground came up in his face, fast, too fast for him to close his gaping mouth or his widened eyes.

Outside, Maria spotted Kreeger as he slipped across the barn roof and up into the rocks. "Got one," she shouted. She moved from the boardwalk into the street, her eyes following Kreeger as he stumbled and slid with the shotgun in his hand. He moved east and down, sliding and tumbling down the rocky slope in a flurry of dust until he hit the flat ground and took off through sand and mesquite brush toward the downed cottonwood tree. "He's going for the horses!" she shouted and took off after him. "Burns! Look out!"

Horses? Burns? Kreeger didn't look back, but no sooner had he heard her voice when he saw them there beyond the downed tree—the young prison guard, Sammy Burns, and three big, beautiful horses? He batted on through the sand, faster, cocking the hammers on the shotgun, the whiskey bottle falling from his waist down the inside of his trouser leg and bouncing off his boot. He stumbled once, and a blast from the shotgun spit up a spray of dirt and rock.

O Lord—! Samuel Burns froze for a second, seeing Al Kreeger bounding toward him, seeing the shotgun explode, then raise up toward him from thirty yards away, coming fast.

"Shoot him, Burns!"

Beyond Kreeger, Burns caught a glimpse of the woman, running too, her pistol up. *Jesus!* He raised his pistol and fired his only bullet at Kreeger. It missed! Kreeger let out a terrible war cry, coming on. Burns heard the blast of the shotgun, felt the buckshot nip his arm as the load whizzed past him. Kreeger came on fast, ten yards, nine, eight, the shotgun swinging back above his head. A club coming at Burns in the hands of a killer—seven yards, six . . .

Burns crouched, too scared to run, the empty pistol coming up and cocked, pointed at arm's length. "Drop it," Burns shouted. Kreeger slid to a halt less than six feet from him, the shotgun drawn back like a ball bat. His breath heaved in his chest.

"You ain't got the guts, Sammy-boy!" Kreeger's mouth spread in a nasty grin. "Now get away from them horses!" He took a step forward; Burns stood fast, his hand tightening on the pistol.

"I'll kill you, Kreeger, so help me." There was nothing Burns would have liked better than to turn and run, let him have a horse—all the horses! But the man was too close.

One swing of the shotgun was all it would take from here, and Burns knew it. "Drop it, *now*!"

Maria ran, her pistol raised, but she wouldn't risk a shot, not as close as the man stood to Burns.

Kreeger slumped and let the shotgun down. "Come on, Sammy-boy, let me go." His bloodshot eyes pleaded. "Huh? What do you say, ole buddy?"

"Pitch it away, Kreeger, *right now*," Burns shouted.

Kreeger let the shotgun fall from his hands and glanced around at the woman running toward him. "Ain't this some shit." He sighed and raised his hands as she slid to a halt.

Chapter 14

Along the rocky trail, Homer circled his horse in the dust and waved back for the men to move out of the rocks and come forward. There had been shooting back in San Paulo. He figured the two gringos were now lying dead in the street. Maybe they'd at least managed to take a couple of the posse with them, but he doubted it. They were drunks and madmen, those gringos. He sat his horse still until the last of his men had moved forward and gathered near him.

A young Mexican sidled his horse beside him and said, "Homer, if we wait for the posse, we end up dead. I think maybe we head straight for the border now. All the men agree, this is no place for us."

"No," Homer said. "We do as I said. We move forward in two groups, one group must cover the other while we rest these animals. If all of us get too far ahead at once, they will pick us off with the big rifle. We will be helpless."

The young Mexican shrugged. "One big rifle, or many small rifles, what is the difference? Dead is still dead, no?"

Roedor crowded his horse between them. "Listen to him, *hombre*. Homer knows what he is doing! If our horses give out on us, we will die here—you shut up and let Homer think for you." He swung off his sombrero as he spoke and slapped the young Mexican with it.

"*Facil*, Roedor," Homer said, raising a hand. "Easy, my friends. We all must work as one if we are to ever see *Mejico* again." He turned from one to the other of the men. "Ernesto has used us and betrayed us . . . but now we must keep our heads and pull together." He pointed east across the ridges where beyond lay the higher grasslands. "We rest our horses here, then we ride east to the grasslands."

The men stood down from their horses, and Homer reined over to a higher bluff alongside the trail. Roedor rode up beside him and after a moment asked, "Homer, why do we ride east?"

Homer looked at him. "Because Ramon Caslado has a large rancho east of here, with many horses. I think it is where Ernesto headed."

"Then it is revenge you want?" Roedor crossed his thick hands on his saddle horn and shook his head.

"No, my friend. I do not want revenge. I want to get all of us back to *Mejico* . . . but to do it we must have horses and supplies. Where else will this many men find those things?"

"But if we come across other horses and supplies along the way, we will take them, eh?"

"No, Roedor. That was Ernesto's way of doing things, not mine. If we must become pigs ourselves in order to fight for our cause, are we then any different from those we fight?"

"It is going to take some time to get used to you, Homer," Roedor said. "You are not easy to understand." He smiled, raised a hand, and pounded himself on the chest. "But you have my loyalty, *mi amigo*, in spite of taking the little girl from me."

Homer returned his smile. "I let her go, you know."

"You—? You let her go?"

"*Sí*, I turned her loose."

"But first, you . . . ?"

"No, Roedor, I did not touch her. I let her go because she was just a child, and she did not deserve for such a terrible thing to happen to her. She deserves the same peace and freedom that our families deserve. We are soldiers, not *desperados* and rapists as Caslado said we were."

Roedor hung his head. "But, I was going to take her. I was drunk. It seemed all right . . . now you make me ashamed."

"Caslado brought the bad blood out of us. We followed his example. He was a good leader when I joined his forces. But he went to the prison as a man, and came back as an *animalia*. It is good that you feel shame . . . but more important that you feel repentant. That you have learned something from it." He backed his horse, turned it toward the resting men and horses, and said, "Come, let us go rest ourselves with our soldiers, where we belong."

"*Our* soldiers, you say?" Roedor heeled his tired horse along with him.

"*Sí*, our soldiers. You and me. You were the first to trust me as our leader. So, we are in command together now. Set a good example with me, so we can someday look back and be proud of what we do."

Levon Hawkins had thought he was dead, he still wasn't completely sure one way or the other. His head had exploded and he'd left for a while, but now he drifted back in from some peaceful, faraway place. His hands were cuffed underneath him. He batted his eyes and looked up the ranger's leg. On his chest stood the ranger's boot, and for just a second he thought he had awakened somewhere back in time. It looked like the same boot that had stood on his chest the time the ranger had bent the iron skillet across his face.

Halfway up the ranger's dusty trouser leg, Hawkins saw the open barrel of the big pistol gaping down at him. Up beyond the pistol he saw the ranger staring down at him with a tight, thin smile.

"See, Hawk," the ranger said, "you still ain't worth wasting a bullet." He gestured the pistol barrel toward Miss Fannie, who was now down from her rope, wrapped in the ranger's riding duster, and standing with Maria supporting her. "You ought to be ashamed of yourself. Every time I look at this poor woman, I want to crack this barrel over your face again." He tensed the barrel sideways; Hawkins winced and tried to turn his face away.

Rance Plum stepped into the barn, followed by Jack the Spider, who stood holding a wet rag against a red welt on his jaw. "Are you all right now?" Maria asked the Spider, and saw Plum turn his head slightly away and grin, finding a little humor in his friend's misfortune.

"Yeah, I'll do," said the Spider. "No thanks to that ole geezer." He nodded toward the old gun shop owner, who stood to the side with a broken pick handle hanging from his hand. As Plum and the Spider had been checking door to door along the street, the old man had hidden in the doorway, and thought Jack the Spider was one of the gunmen coming back to kill him. He'd swung the pick handle with all his strength. . . .

"I'm as sorry as I can be," the old man said, shrugging.

Plum stopped grinning. "Yes, well—" He collected himself, cleared his throat, and said to the ranger, "Now that we've cleared this town, may I suggest we get right onto Caslado's trail?"

While he'd slipped up on Hawkins and waited outside the barn door, the ranger had taken notice of three sets of horses' hooves leading away from the barn, headed east. Two sets of prints were deeper than the other. Two riders had left, leading a spare horse behind them. *Caslado?* He'd bet it was. He figured Caslado and another rider—JC, if he had to guess, since he hadn't seen JC leave town with the others.

Now the ranger looked at Plum and said, "We can't leave for a while. We've got prisoners to attend to and we've got this town to look after." He shook his head slowly. "Naw, we better stay here until we get things squared away some."

"This is madness, ranger," Plum raged, and swung his gloved finger from Hawkins beneath the ranger's foot to Kreeger, who lay against a stall door in handcuffs. "Shoot these two vermin in the head . . . let the town take care of itself!"

"It ain't my way," the ranger said.

"Gads, sir!" Plum rubbed his face in frustration. "Then Spider and I are riding on, with or without you . . . while the trail's fresh and their horses are worn out. Certainly you can understand that."

"I understand," the ranger said. "You two go on if you want to. We'll catch up."

Plum searched the ranger's eyes for a second, looking for any sign that the ranger might be playing him off. Then, seeing none, he sucked at his teeth and turned to Jack the Spider. "Very well. Let's be off, Mr. Spider."

The Spider hesitated. "I think we ought to stay, Plum. So far this thing is going our way here. No point in—"

Plum snatched his arm, cutting him off, and shoved him toward the barn door. He said over his shoulder to the ranger, "We'll keep our eyes peeled for you, of course."

The ranger smiled and raised a hand. "Don't press them too hard, not that many all at once."

Plum spun around at the door. "Don't presume to tell me how to hunt down thugs, sir, if you please!" In a second the two were outside, leading their horses across the dirt street at a fast clip, Plum's face red and tight. Jack the Spider scowled at him and said, "Don't you ever grab my arm again, Plum. We ain't *that* close, you and me."

"Move along, Mr. Spider; can't you see what's going on here? We've outlasted that ole ranger, by thunder. Haven't you figured that out?"

"No," the Spider said, looking puzzled, "Can't say that I have."

"Well, luckily I see it. Think how this will sound once the

word gets out—the ranger unable to keep up with us, the two of us bringing in Caslado, on our own."

"That's not the way I took it," said the Spider.

"Trust me, that's how it will be told." Plum's red face settled, and he smiled, tapping a finger to his forehead. "Once I find the way to put the proper slant on it."

Inside the barn the ranger turned to Kreeger with his boot still pressed on Hawkins's chest. "So, Al, you let my friend, *Samuel,* take you down with an unloaded gun?" He shook his head, cutting a glance to Samuel Burns. Burns took note of what the ranger had just called him—no more Sammy-boy. Now it was Samuel. Much better, he thought.

"He got lucky," Kreeger said. "I been drunk all night."

"He's a back-shooting, chickenshit coward," Hawkins said from under the ranger's boot. "Give me two minutes alone with him, and I'll roll his eyes across the dirt like marbles—"

Hawkins's voice cut short with a grunt as the ranger raised his boot heel and dropped it on his chest. "Be still, Hawk, or I'll give you over to Miss Fannie right here and now, and I'll go find her a gelding blade."

"Yes, please," Miss Fannie said through swollen lips. "Please give him to me right now."

"Maria," the ranger asked, "why don't you take Miss Fannie to her place . . . help her settle down and get doctored up a little. Samuel will stay with me here." He nodded to the old shop owner and the young girl. "Why don't you two go see if you find the child's grandmother, if she's still alive. And put the word around that it's safe for folks to come out now."

As the others left, the ranger reached out and took the broken pick handle from the old man's hand. "Let me borrow that a while."

"Sure." The old man handed it to the ranger with a gleam in his eyes. "There's lots of good left in it yet."

Once they were gone, the ranger rolled Hawkins over, lifted him by his handcuffs, and pitched him over beside Kreeger. Hawkins landed with a thud and a stir of dust and straw. Burns winced, but watched, holding the reins to the horses. "Now then," the ranger said, looking down at the two men, "I'll ask you some questions, and everytime you're slow in answering, I'll crack your shinbone, like this." He whacked the pick handle a solid blow on Hawkins's shin, then Kreeger's. Burns winced again, watching.

"Jesus, ranger," said Hawkins, "that's cruel and uncalled for!"

"I know," the ranger said. He leaned slightly and asked, looking from one to the other, "Who's running the show now that Caslado's cut out?"

Kreeger let out a breath and said, "Some young peckerwood named Homer something-or-other. Thinks he's Napoleon, I reckon."

"Thank you, Al," the ranger said; and he reached down and cracked Hawkins on the shin.

"Damn it all! What was that for?" Hawkins scooted his leg back and forth and rubbed the calf of his other leg up and down it.

"That's for letting Al here answer before you did," the ranger said. "Makes you want to hurry up and get the next answer out, don't it?"

Samuel Burns stood and watched for over a half hour while the two men talked until their mouths went dry. The ranger walked over, took a canteen down from his saddle, watered them, and started them talking again. They told the ranger about attacking the two teamsters, and how the next morning they had sent Homer over to cut the old men's throats. The ranger just listened and didn't mention that he had found the two old men—that their throats hadn't been cut. They told the ranger how Caslado and JC had taken the only fresh horses and abandoned the men here.

Homer, huh . . . ? The ranger thought about it as they spoke. Homer was the same name the little girl had mentioned—a young Mexican, not a throat-cutter, not a rapist. Now this man was in charge. What would be his plan? How did he think? Would he take his men and ride back to Mexico? If he was any kind of leader, he would.

When the ranger asked if that was all there was to tell, he stood, patting the pick handle against his palm, until Kreeger told him there was one more thing. Then Kreeger went on to say that once when he was a child, he'd robbed an old man who lived down the road from him—had taken his money and set his house on fire.

"I always knew you was born bad, Kreeger," the ranger said; and he cracked his shin one more time. He looked at Hawkins. "What about you? Anything you want to confess to me . . . we're all the way back to childhood now."

"Naw, that's it for me. You can beat me to death . . . I got nothing else for ya." He stared at the ranger for another second, then added, "Except that Caslado has a brother living east of here. Don't know if that means anything or not."

Ramon Caslado . . . Yes, it meant something all right. It might not have, had the ranger not seen the hoofprints headed east. But now? Yes, it meant a great deal. He'd already decided Caslado and JC had headed east. Now he knew why. "How far east is his brother's place?"

Hawkins shrugged. "I've no idea . . . just up on the high grasslands is all I know."

The ranger straightened up and pitched the pick handle away. The two men slumped and let their heads fall to their chests. "Could we get a drink of whiskey?" Al Kreeger asked under his breath. "I'm sicker than a dog."

The ranger turned to Burns and said, "See if you can

round them up a bottle, Samuel. It'll be their last one for a while."

When Burns had tied the reins to a post and left, the ranger leaned down again and asked them, "Young Samuel there . . . what kind of guard was he?"

"Like any other guard," Kreeger said, "he wasn't fit to be shot."

"Just a stupid peckerwood kid," Hawkins added. "Never seen much out of him."

"Did he seem honest enough?" the ranger asked, watching Hawkins's eyes. "Ever seen him do anything dishonest or untoward?"

"Hell," said Hawkins, "how would I know what's dishonest or untoward? I'm a crook, for God's sake." He shrugged. "Never knew of him taking money for anything . . . tobacco or such, like some of them do. Never saw him beat anybody. Like I said, just young and stupid."

"That's all I wanted to know, boys." The ranger straightened up again. "Now sit tight until the sheriff gets squared away and takes you into custody."

"The sheriff," Hawkins said. "Ha! If this town had a sheriff, he couldn't be much. Sure didn't do anything to defend it when we all hit town."

"That's not what I heard," the ranger said. "I heard the sheriff did everything to stop you, but just couldn't."

"That's a damn lie," Kreeger said, "and I'll say it to the sheriff's face. Yeah, leave us in custody here, ranger. This ought to be a hoot."

"Kreeger's right, ranger," Hawkins said. "If there's any sheriff around here, I sure don't know about it."

The ranger smiled and shook his head. "Well, you should. That was *her* you had hanging from the rafter."

"You . . . you mean?" Hawkins's eyes went flat. His face turned the color of a three-day sickness. Kreeger moaned under his breath.

"You can't leave us here with her," Hawkins said, coming around from the shock of the ranger's words. He leaned forward, but the ranger reached out with the toe of his boot and shoved him back.

"It ain't fair," Kreeger said. "She shoulda said something to let us know."

The ranger shrugged. "Didn't she tell you this is her town? Tell you to ride on?" He shook his head. "What did you need, to see something in writing? You boys shoulda been paying more attention. It's always polite to leave when somebody asks you to the first time."

"She wasn't wearing no badge or gun." Hawkins stared up at the ranger.

"The law doesn't have to wear a badge or gun. It's still the law," the ranger said. "I shouldn't have to tell you boys that."

"It ain't fair," Hawkins said. "How was we supposed to know she was somebody important?"

"If you ain't breaking the law, you don't have to know who's who. Nobody has to tell you anything. It's called decency, boys. Can either of ya even spell it?"

"But she looked like some old New Orleans whore to us," Kreeger said.

"I'll tell her you said that." The ranger smiled. "Fact is, she was a professional woman years back. But anybody has a right to change occupations, don't they?" He pushed up the brim of his sombrero.

"You've got to talk to her for us, ranger," Hawkins said. "Tell her I was just kidding. Tell her I meant her no harm."

The ranger just stared at him for a second, then said. "You can tell her yourselves. They won't hang you here, since you're both federal prisoners. They'll hold you until the prison sends a detail out for you. For the next few days you'll have plenty of time to tell Miss Fannie whatever she'll listen to."

Burns came back to the barn, carrying a bottle of whiskey. He handed it to the ranger, and the ranger passed it on. When each man had taken a long drink, the ranger corked the bottle and gave it back to Burns. "Put it in my saddlebags, Samuel. We've got another hard ride ahead of us."

"They found the girl's grandmother," Burns said. "Looks like she'll be all right. She crawled over under a boardwalk. Said Hawkins here was the one who knocked her out."

"Burns, you little snake! Why don't you shut your hole?" Hawkins spit toward him. "You ain't no better than us. Hadn't been for you, we wouldn't been out here in the first place!"

"Yeah, that's right, ranger," Kreeger joined in. "What about this peckerwood? What're you doing about him?"

"Don't worry about Samuel Burns," the ranger said. "He's already on his road to rehabilitation."

Chapter 15

When Maria and Miss Fannie came back to the barn, the cuts and bruises on Miss Fannie's swollen face had been cleaned and tended to. She wore Mexican sandals, and loose-fitting bib overalls with the legs rolled up to her knees, bandages around her thick calves. "I explained to the boys here, who you are, Miss Fannie," the ranger said.

Her eyes gleamed toward Hawkins and Kreeger, full of death threats and dark promises. "Good," she said across swollen lips, "then I don't have to bother. I need my energy for other purposes." She lifted two sets of leg chains from her bib overalls and let them hang from her hand as she turned to the ranger and Maria. "I can't thank you enough, Sam, for all you and your people have done here. I was about done in by these devils."

"Sam? Who's Sam?" Kreeger asked Hawkins in a low tone.

"Sam Burrack's his name," Hawkins answered in a whisper, nodding toward the ranger. "Don't you know nothing?"

"Seeing you on your feet is all the thanks we need, Miss Fannie," the ranger said. Then he gestured a gloved hand toward Kreeger and Hawkins. "We'll help you haul these two over to your jail."

"Don't you dare," Miss Fannie said with a tight turn in her voice. "These birds are all mine. And don't feel like anybody has to be in a hurry getting them back to prison, either. I'll take *good* care of them."

They watched her shake out the leg chains, fasten them on both men, and drag them to the center of the barn. Hawkins looked up at her through wide, pleading eyes. "I just told the ranger before you got here . . . how I was only kidding around with ya."

"You'll think 'kidding,' " Miss Fannie said. She stepped between them, took their leg chains in her big hands, and dragged them away. Their eyes turned back to the ranger as they scraped across the dirt floor, but he only shrugged and spread his hands.

"Let's get our horses quartered and fed," the ranger said to Maria and Samuel Burns once Miss Fannie and her prisoners were gone. "We'll rest them here, out of the sun for the day, then we're headed east, *tonight*." He looked at Maria. "Didn't want to mention it to Plum and Spider, but we're cutting straight up to the grasslands."

"*Sí*," Maria said. "I saw the tracks as well. But we cannot follow tracks at night, even in a waxing moon."

"I saw the tracks too," said Burns.

"You both saw them." The ranger spoke as he loosened the cinch on his white barb and hefted the saddle onto his shoulder. "Plum should've seen them too . . . would have, if he'd taken his nose out of the air long enough to look."

"Still," Burns asked, "how will we follow the tracks at night?"

"We won't. There's only three open passes up to the grasslands, and they're spread out over a thirty-mile stretch. It figures that Caslado would take the nearest one. Come daylight tomorrow we'll pick up their tracks once we've cleared the pass."

What about Plum and Jack the Spider?" Maria loosened her horse's cinch also. "They could be in real danger if they catch up to the Mexicans."

"Those two would be in danger wherever they went," the ranger said. "But I've got a feeling the man leading that bunch is only interested in getting out of here—back to *Mejico*. They've been betrayed by Caslado. They know it was all a big mistake coming up here. They'll be lucky if the army's not on their backs before they reach the border."

"Then we let them go?" Maria's eyes followed him as he took his saddle and draped it over a stall rail.

"Unless they press a fight on us," he said. "And I don't think that's going to happen. I'm learning about this young man, Homer. He didn't kill the two teamsters as he was told to do—didn't do anything to the girl except turn her loose. He's no saddle trash. I think he just got sucked into something." For a moment the ranger stood, thinking about this man, Homer, about how his mind worked, about what to expect from him. In a second he said to Burns, "We know how that can happen, don't we, Samuel?"

Maria said, as Burns lowered his eyes, "Kreeger would have gotten away if not for Samuel. He did well, yes?"

The ranger took the reins to his white barb and led the horse to a stall. He said over his shoulder, "Bet you was wondering what the outcome would be when Kreeger came at you with that shotgun."

Maria and Burns looked at one another, then Burns shrugged and said, "I didn't really have time to wonder about it. To tell you the truth, I was scared senseless."

The ranger came back, carrying a feed bag, and spoke as he filled it from a nearly empty grain bin. "You might have been scared, but you weren't senseless. It's times like that, your mind kicks in and does what's according to your nature whether you intend to or not. You could have run . . . thrown down your pistol." He stopped filling the bag and turned to him. "You could've taken off with him, couldn't you?"

"No. I . . . I wouldn't do that. I gave you my word. Believe it or not, my word's still worth something."

"But if you were senseless, you wouldn't have thought about your word, would you?" He raised a gloved finger. "See, that was you acting from the inside . . . from a part of yourself you might not know is there. When you was offered to throw in with JC and Caslado, you had plenty of time to think about it . . . but you acted under their influence. A while ago, you acted on your own, on your natural instincts. No time to *think* it out—you just *acted*."

"I think what he did took courage," Maria said.

"Did it?" The ranger looked from her to Burns, then he turned, walked back to the stall, strapped the grain bag over the white barb's muzzle, and wiped the horse down with a handful of straw while it crunched grain and swished its damp tail.

Crazy Gravy managed to slip into the pillaged town and make his way to the livery barn, unnoticed, while townsfolk went about the task of cleaning up San Paulo. In the darkness of the livery barn, he found Maria's horse in its stall, and ran his hand along the animal's withers. The horse shied at the touch of his hand and drew its head away from him, its eyes shiny, wide in fear. But he settled it by backing away, slowly, and out of the stall. Horses didn't like him? Well, he had news for them . . .

He smiled, seeing the broken pick handle lying against a stall door, where the ranger had left it.

When he left the livery barn, he heard the animal whimper in a low voice as he walked his sweat-streaked horse up the middle of the dirt street, spreading his arms in amazement at the sight of debris, broken furniture, and dead bodies that had been dragged to the side and propped against the boardwalk. He stopped an old man and asked him what terrible thing had happened here, and what he might do to help.

The old man scratched his head for a second, coming up with nothing, then, looking the priest up and down, said that perhaps the priest just being there was help enough—that the mere sight of someone who came in peace would mean a lot to the people of San Paulo right then. "Bless you," Crazy Gravy said, making the sign of the cross. "I met a ranger and his party along the trail. Tell me, are they in town somewhere?"

"Yep. Over at the cantina," the old man said, pointing a finger as he moved away and back to the task at hand. Crazy Gravy smiled, thanking him, then walked his horse to the town well, dipped up a wooden bucket full of water, and let the animal draw while he gazed around the sacked town. He kept an eye on the cantina until Maria stepped out on the boardwalk, pulling her long hair back and tying a strand of rawhide around it. She had washed her hair when she bathed in Miss Fannie's bathing tub, and now her fingers felt something different back there, a spot where her hair felt shorter than the rest. Just a spot. *Oh well* . . .

She ran her hand down her hair and had placed her battered Stetson on her head when she looked over and saw the priest watering his horse. He happened to look up at the same time and seemed surprised, as she stepped down and walked toward him.

"I have been worried about you, *Padre*," she said when she stopped near him and spread her arms to him.

"Ah, my child . . . and *I* you," he said, embracing her, "you and your ranger, and the young man." The warm, fresh scent of her against him was almost unbearable. He held her back at arm's length and said, "God has been with us . . . as He always is."

She smiled. "Yes, as he always is." She looked at his worn-out horse, its flanks sunken, its neck and withers gaunt and wet with sweat, wet mane clinging to its neck. "Come, Padre, there is some grain left in the barn. Your horse looks terrible."

"Ah, yes . . . and I am so ashamed," he said, nudging the

horse's head away from the bucket and raising it by the reins. "If God judges us harshly, I fear it will be for the suffering we inflict on these poor noble beasts." He was getting good at this, he thought, smiling gently.

She nodded and walked beside him to the livery barn. On the way, while she told him what had happened in San Paulo, he stayed close to her, watching her, seeing each flicker of dark eyelash, each rise and fall of her lips as she spoke, each pulse of soft flesh in her throat as it kept time to the beat of her heart. His blood raced.

Inside the barn she helped him tend to the horse. She dropped the saddle and bridle; and after graining the tired animal and rubbing it down with clean straw, they led it into a large stall where someone had mercifully fed and tended Al Kreeger's worn-out horse. She led the priest's horse inside the stall, closed the stall door behind it, and nodded to the other horse. "This one belonged to one of the prisoners," she said. "Perhaps now someone will put it to better use."

Crazy Gravy only nodded.

When they walked past her horse's stall, she heard the slightest whimper and turned as the big gelding poked its head above the stall door. She rubbed its muzzle and saw pain in its eyes.

"What is wrong with you, my friend?" she asked the horse, as if the horse would answer. And in a way it did, by shifting its weight in an awkward manner and standing wrong and unsteady. "Oh, my goodness," she said softly, swinging the stall door open and stepping inside. Crazy Gravy glanced back once through the open front door and stepped in behind her.

"What is it?" he asked, staring down at her back while she stooped and softly placed her hand on the swollen tendon hoof of the horse's rear leg. She did not notice the difference in the priest's voice—that it had gone flat and smooth, as if there were no breath in it. "Can I do something?"

She did not glance around, but said over her shoulder, "How could this have happened?" She looked across the darkness of the stall for any way the horse might have kicked and injured itself on a protruding board of stall post. *But this horse does not kick its stall . . .* She eyed the straw-covered floor for any sign of a snake or lizard that might have frightened it. *Nothing.*

Behind her, Crazy Gravy hovered nearer. His hand slipped inside his faded brown frock and around the handle of the butcher knife. He almost swooned at the heady scent of her rising up to him. He leaned to the side and down, his hand coming out slowly, his lips parted nearing her throat. *That pulsing warm throat . . .*

The horse shifted restlessly and whimpered, fearing the dark shadow at its side. "Easy," Maria said, shifting with it. Crazy Gravy's hand started out of the frock with the knife . . . one quick plunge was all he needed.

"What's going on, Maria?" the ranger asked, leaning in the open stall door.

Crazy Gravy jerked his empty hand from inside his frock. Maria turned her eyes up to the ranger as the priest stepped back. Even in the darkness, the ranger noted the wild look in his eyes. The priest's breath heaved in his chest. Then he caught himself and raised a trembling hand. "Oh, my! You startled me."

The ranger looked away from him and back down at Maria. She stood up, dusting her hands together. "His tendon is swollen, bad."

"But how?" The ranger glanced around the stall, the same as she had. "He was all right earlier, wasn't he?"

"*Sí.*" She raised her arms and dropped them. "Who knows? Perhaps he hurt himself at the cottonwood tree, but it has taken a while to set in."

"Well, whatever happened, it's sure put us in a bind. We need to be getting on. There's not another horse in town fit for anything right now." The ranger let out a breath, pushed up his sombrero brim, and looked back at the priest. "Glad to see you made it here, Padre. Got the teamsters buried all right, I suppose?"

"Oh, yes, may God have mercy on their souls." Crazy Gravy crossed himself and tossed his eyes upward. This would still go the way he'd planned it. All he had to do was wait, be patient.

The ranger looked back at Maria. "All we can do is leave Burns behind with Miss Fannie. You can take *his* horse."

Oh, no—! Crazy Gravy's eyes flashed back and forth between them in the dark barn. He waited, tensed, for Maria's reply.

A silence passed as she swept a glance around the dark barn as if doing so might make a horse appear. "No," she said. "I will stay behind. Miss Fannie has enough to do already."

Good . . . good. Crazy Gravy almost sighed in relief. "If . . . if I might be so bold," he said. "You're more than welcome to use my horse if it will help." He knew they wouldn't be able to use his spent horse. He had her now. "I mean, after it has rested overnight, of course."

Maria swung her eyes to him. "Thank you, Padre." Then she turned back to the ranger. "We will do that. As soon as his horse is rested, I will find you along the high trail."

"No, I'll be moving fast. It's too risky—you riding up there alone. You could drop right into the middle of something up there."

She had started to protest; the Priest raised a hand. "I know little of such things, but I think he is right. If it will help, I'll ride the prisoner's horse and go with you once both horses are rested."

Maria and the ranger looked at one another. There would be no point in telling her no—she'd come anyway. He let out a breath. "All right. Burns and I will go on. Do what you've got to do here, then come ahead." He raised a gloved finger as he spoke. "But don't take any foolish chances."

She cocked her head slightly. "Oh? When do I *ever* take foolish chances?"

Crazy Gravy smiled, watching, listening, and folded his hands across his waist.

The hottest part of the day had passed when the ranger and Samuel Burns rode their rested horses out across the stretch of flatland toward the upreaching trails leading east from San Paulo. Samuel Burns felt better now that they had bathed, ate, and rested for a while without a hard saddle beneath him. They'd taken on what few supplies the pillaged town could spare them; and from the top of the switchback trail headed east, Burns had looked back down at San Paulo and saw the town through the thin, dusty air.

"Tell me, Samuel," the ranger asked, riding beside him and a couple of feet ahead, "are you a religious man?"

Burns considered the question for a second. "As much as the next, I suppose." He shrugged. "I was raised to it anyway."

The ranger nodded and gazed ahead. "Familiar with the sign of the cross, are you?" Something had him thinking about the priest, something the priest had done. He wasn't sure what it was, but he couldn't shake it from his mind.

"The *sign*?" Burns looked puzzled.

"Yeah, you know?" The ranger raised a gloved finger and circled it about his chest.

"Oh." Burns nodded. "No, I was raised to another religion. Why?"

"Just curious about something." The ranger still gazed ahead, and after a second of silence asked, "What do you think of the padre back there?"

"Haven't given him much thought really. Used to see him come to the prison quite a bit with the old priest. The two of them were in and out—after a while you don't really see them. You just take them for granted, like the desert."

"You *never* take the desert for granted, if you're wise," the ranger said, heeling his white barb a little, testing its stamina. It responded sharp and strong, and he let it back down and ran a hand along its withers. "But you are familiar with this man, this *particular* priest?"

"Sure, his face seemed familiar, sort of. Like I said, he was always around, him and the older priest." They both moved forward with the sun lying low and hot behind them.

Behind them in San Paulo, Maria and the priest had stood watching them until they moved up the switchbacks and disappeared onto the next stretch of flatland, heading east. Crazy Gravy stood close beside her and smiled, watching the calm, steady pulse in her throat. She was his . . . this time there was no doubt about it.

He had her to himself now, and he would keep it that way. Just the two of them. For a moment back there in the barn, his beast had gotten the better of him. He would have killed her for certain had not the ranger came in when he did. But now he was glad it had happened that way. He wanted her alone . . . alone, and with no distractions. Seldom did something like this come along in a man's lifetime. He wanted all the time in the world with her.

"You worry about him, don't you?" he asked, laying a hand on her forearm, then letting it drop.

She nodded, gazing off to the high ridgeline. "We work so well together . . . it is difficult to imagine either of us working apart."

"Then we must not keep you apart for long." Crazy Gravy let his gaze move about the town as he spoke. "Perhaps tomorrow the horses will be up and rested."

"Perhaps, but I doubt it," she said.

"You must have faith," he said. "Now that I'm with you, you will be surprised at how things go." There was a slightly different tone to his voice now, and noticing it caused her to turn to him. *What was it? Stronger? More assertive?*

"Oh?" She stared into his eyes. His eyes looked bolder now for some reason—a man who had just accomplished something. And yet as she looked into them, they seemed to change back, to soften as if into submission.

Crazy Gravy caught himself—just in time—and his character stepped back into that of a priest the way an actor stepped back into the shadow of a stage curtain. "I mean . . . as long as God leads us . . . we must expect good things to come to us."

Was there some characteristic there that hadn't been there before? Something she had overlooked in this man? She wondered, as she watched his eyes for a second longer. She thought about her horse . . . about how it had gone lame for no apparent reason. Something about it bothered her now, as if the horse going lame brought with it some darker promise of things to come. *Good things must be expected . . . ?*

Yet she summoned up her usual pleasant smile and offered it to him, as his eyes seemed to lose their certainty and question her eyes in return. "Yes, you are right, of course, Padre." She ran a hand down her long hair gathered behind. "Things come to us, both good and bad . . . we must always be prepared to act on them."

That night, while Maria slept in a spare room at Miss Fannie's house, a hand reached down and shook her soundly. She turned over and looked up into Miss Fannie's swollen face in the glow of a lantern in the big woman's hand. "Wake up, Maria! They're gone, both of them! Do you hear me?"

"I hear you," Maria said, sitting up on the side of the bed. But it took her a second to comprehend. "Who is gone?" She rubbed her face with both hands and looked back at Miss Fannie. On a bed across the room, lay the little girl and her grandmother. Her grandmother only moaned and laid an arm across her bruised face, but the child sat up and stared through sleep eyes.

"The prisoners are gone!" Miss Fannie shook her once more by the arm.

Maria sprang to her feet, reaching for her trousers and shirt across the foot of the bed. "Gone? How?" She threw on her freshly washed shirt, stepped into her trousers, jerked them up, and reached for her boots beneath the bed.

"I have no idea," Miss Fannie said. "I left only long enough to go to the jake. I came back—their chains were lying on the floor! They're gone!"

"*Sante Madre*," Maria whispered, pulling on her boots. She righted them on her feet, and snatched her gun belt from the top bedpost. She snatched out her revolver, checked it quickly, and shoved it back into the holster. "How long ago was this?" She slung the gun belt up on her shoulder and stuffed her shirt into her trousers.

"Ten minutes, maybe fifteen," Miss Fannie said, out of breath, but her voice settling some. "I couldn't have been gone any longer than that. They must have had it planned, just waiting for me to turn my back on them. I put the key in the desk before I left . . . how in God's name could they have gotten to it? I had them chained to the wall!"

Maria stopped, stared at her for a second, then said, "Someone had to have helped them—some of the others? Have they slipped back here?" But even as she said it, she realized how unlikely that would be. Plum and the Spider were on their trail. They wouldn't risk riding back to San Paulo; and if they had, they would not have slipped in. They would have come in force and taken the men at gunpoint. She had just started to say something more when the priest came running in, his face pale, his hands trembling.

"The convicts have escaped," he said in a rush of breath. "I saw them running out of town!"

"Yes," Maria said, "I just found out. How long ago did you see them?" She spoke as she walked out, snatching her hat from a stand beside the door.

"Only a moment ago," he said. He crossed himself quickly with a shaky hand, following close behind her, Miss Fannie coming along behind him with the lantern raised. "I . . . I was awakened by them as I slept in the barn. When I got up, they saw me and ran. They did not get the horses."

"Then I will catch them . . . even on a tired horse," Maria said, moving down the stairs and to the front door. "They can't get far on foot."

"You can't go out there alone," Miss Fannie said, stopping her at the door, holding the lantern in one hand, her free arm tucked across her stomach. "I'm going with you."

"No." Maria stopped with her hand on the doorknob. "You are in no shape to go out there. I'll be all right alone."

"Forgive me for disagreeing with you," the priest said, "but Miss Fannie is right. It is too dangerous for you to go alone. You must wait until daylight . . . and find some townsmen to go with you."

"No. I'm going right now. Even on foot they can be a good ways off by morning. If they come upon someone on the trail, they will kill them. I cannot take a chance on that happening."

"Then I'm riding with you," the priest said as she swung open the door.

"Padre, what can you do against such men as these?" She gazed into his eyes in the glow of the lantern. "You cannot shoot them."

"No, but I can at least watch out for them up among the rocks and see that they don't take you by surprise."

"Stay here, Padre," she said. "I'll do better on my own."

"No." He shook his head and raised a finger. "I must insist. How could I ever forgive myself if something happened to you?"

"He's right," Miss Fannie said. "Let him go along. He can watch your back."

Maria looked from one to the other and nodded, not wanting to waste time. "Come then, Padre. Let's hurry."

"I'm right behind you," he said; and as Maria moved at a sharp pace off the boardwalk and toward the livery barn, he smiled, ducking his face back into the shadowed darkness of his hooded frock, and followed her along the starlit street.

Above the back of the town, Kreeger and Hawkins scrambled upward across small rocks and broken boulders, their breath heaving, their hands scratching and clawing the ground ahead of them, until at the top of the steep trail they collapsed for a second to catch their breath. "I . . . can't believe we're out . . . and at it again," Hawkins said. "Who was that stupid peckerwood?"

"Don't know, don't care," Kreeger said. "Too dark to see . . . his face." He raised up on his knees, then struggled to his feet, his bare feet cut and bleeding from the climb. "Come on . . . keep moving. We gotta find some guns . . . some horses somewhere. That big woman's nearly beat me to death."

"Me too," said Hawkins. "Think she was really going to do what she said . . . with that hog knife?"

"I don't know . . . don't even want to think about it. She's an animal, that woman! Let's just get out of here."

Part 3

Chapter 16

By midmorning JC McLawry and Ernesto Caslado had come to a fork in the thin trail they'd followed across the high grasslands. One fork led off southeast toward a distant stretch of rising foothills, the other up to the north into a maze of tall standing rock and narrow canyons. They stopped at the fork and stepped down to rest their horses. When Caslado studied both forks of the trail with a troubled expression, JC moved over beside him and asked what was wrong.

"Nothing," Caslado said. He gazed back and forth and raised his sombrero and rubbed his forehead.

JC gave him a skeptical stare. "Are we lost?"

"No, we are not lost." Caslado looked away.

JC asked, "How many times have you been to your brother's place?"

"Never." Caslado's jaw tightened, and he looked back and forth again. "He took the place a short time after I went to prison. But I know we are close to it."

"Close? In this country, 'close' can end us up down in Missouri if we ain't careful." JC spit and ran a hand across his dry lips. "We better come up with something pretty quick. I just figured you knew the way—"

"Be still, so I can think!" Caslado cut him off, and looked back and forth again. "An old man who died last year in prison told me how to get here. He said it is known as the old Royal Spread. My brother bought it from an English cattle company."

JC shook his head, lifted his canteen from his saddle horn, and sat down on his haunches beside his horse. He twisted the top from the canteen, swished a mouthful of water, spit it out, then drew in a long drink and swallowed it. He recapped the canteen and gazed to the north. After a silence while Caslado paced back and forth, staring from fork to fork along the trail, JC stood up and took a coin from his pocket. "Tell you what," he said. "Will you take a toss of the coin?"

"Don't talk foolish." Caslado glared at him.

"Things are feeling a little tight," JC said. "Come evening we'll need to water these horses, or we'll lose them. Whatever you decide is fine by me . . . but you'll have to do it pretty soon."

Caslado let out a breath and reached for his reins. His horse jerked its head up, chewing a mouthful of pale green grass. "We go southeast," he said.

"Are you sure, Ernesto? You said earlier that your brother's place was a few more hours away. Looks like there's nothing that direction but hills—we'll be lucky to reach them before dark."

Caslado cursed under his breath and spit. "Then flip your coin!"

"I'm just saying—"

"I know, I know. Now flip your coin."

JC took the coin back out of his pocket, tossed it two feet in the air, caught it, flattened it on his cuff, and raised his hand, just enough to shield it from the sunlight. He looked under his hand, then shrugged, took the coin off his cuff, and squinted as if questioning the choice. "The coin says north," he said. "But what do you think?"

Caslado looked north and nodded. "If it is the wrong way, we will know soon enough, and turn back, eh?"

"Whatever you say, Ernesto." JC turned to his horse and gathered his reins. "I just figure we've got to do something."

They stepped up on their horses and moved away north along the thin trail until the grass grew thinner, and the ground harder and more rocky beneath the horses' hooves. Inside a narrow canyon they rode upward among spills of small rocks that stretched across the trail, and at times around larger boulders whose presence had redirected the path of elk and coyotes and whatever other creatures came through. There were no signs of man, no hoofprints of horses.

After an hour Caslado lingered behind on his horse as JC topped a rise in the trail. "I think we turn back here," Caslado called to him.

But JC turned, facing him and gesturing forward. "Take a look at this first," he said.

When Caslado reined up beside him and gazed out across the green, rocky valley below, he let out a breath and ran a hand up across his forehead. "It looks like your coin was right, *mi amigo*," he said.

JC gazed ahead, a slight smile on his parched lips. "I've always been lucky."

They sat and gazed across the valley at the sprawling house of log and adobe, at the long wooden fencing surrounding a corral off to the right of the house, and at the long barns and outbuildings around it.

"My brother's *rancho* home . . ." Caslado's words trailed, taking in the welcoming sight below him. Then he added, "My brother has always been the smart one in my *familia*. Had it not been for him, the *revolucion* would have failed long ago. He taught me to cross the border and rob the American banks and railroads, where the money is big and easy."

"Is that a fact?" JC asked without facing him. As far back as JC could remember, there'd always been a revolution going on in Old Mexico. Why should he consider Ernesto Caslado's *revolucion* any different from the rest?

"*Sí*," Caslado said in a hushed tone. "Ramon has always had a head for making money come to him . . . for making things go his way."

JC chuckled. *Money! Soon, his money. Yeah, that's what makes it different . . .* He turned to Caslado, smiling, and nudged his horse toward a steep downward path through the rocks. "Then what say we get down there. Maybe some of it will come to us."

Ramon Caslado took breakfast as he always did, at the battered oak table in the large dining room of his ranch. To himself, he liked to refer to his fine adobe-and-log *hacienda* as Casa Caslado. To others, his sprawling home with its large glass windows and indoor kitchen complete with a stone baking *horno* had been known for years as the Royal Spread. He'd purchased the place when the English cattle company eagerly abandoned their failed investment. Over the two years he'd been here, although he'd raised no more than enough cattle for his own use, Ramon had turned a profit on the old Royal Spread—a large profit.

He looked around the huge room and sipped his rich black coffee. His home was as fine as any he'd seen in the high country of *Mejico* when he and his brother, Ernesto, found work there as children. He smiled to himself. Now his land stretched far beyond the roll of the earth both east and west. But on high grassland such as this, Ramon did not sit at the head of a cattle empire as a person might expect.

He made his fortune in brass, steel, and gold. *Ah, yes . . .* That's what he did. His smile broadened. He tipped his coffee cup as if in salute to himself, then tossed back the last of it. He offered brass and steel in the form of ammunition, rifles, and heavier armament to the highest bidders in Old

Mexico, in exchange for their gold. For Ramon Caslado, life was good.

For a time he'd wished his brother, Ernesto, could share in this good fortune; yet he knew that could never be, not now. His brother would never understand what strange turns of fate had brought Ramon to his present position. Ernesto had never possessed more than the simple mind of a soldier, and later of course, under Ramon's guidance, the mind of a thief.

Ernesto would not be able to comprehend how the very ones they once had fought were now the ones who'd made Ramon a wealthy man. *Poor Ernesto* . . . Ramon sighed, pushed himself up from the oak table, and turned toward Earl Jaffe—one of his gunmen—who stood gazing out the front window toward the west. "Come Jaffe, we have much to do this morning."

"We have two riders coming in with some of the boys, boss. Looks like the boys met them hitting it hard across the badlands."

"Oh?" Ramon stepped over beside him and gazed out. Seeing his brother, Ernesto, and the gringo riding beside him in the group of men, Ramon rubbed his hands together and smiled. "Then yes, you are right . . . we have much to do." He turned, took his sombrero from a rack near the door, and with Earl Jaffe beside him, stepped out on the wide wooden porch.

When the riders brought their horses to a halt, Ramon stepped off the porch with his arms spread and caught Ernesto and hugged him close as the two brothers slapped each other's backs and made their salutations. Dust billowed.

"Touching, ain't it?" JC glanced at the rider nearest him.

The riders only looked him up and down, then turned their eyes back to Ramon and Ernesto. "I've heard a lot about that ole boy," one rider said, nodding down at Ernesto.

"All of you, listen to me," Ramon called out to his men, turning with an arm across Ernesto's shoulder. "This is my brother, Ernesto. Only through a miracle is he alive and here with me. See to it he is treated with the respect and honor he is due. What he says, *I* say." Ramon patted himself on the chest.

"Sure, boss," one of the riders said. He nodded toward JC, asking, "What about this one?"

Ramon looked at Ernesto. "He is my friend," Ernesto said, taking on the authority given him by his brother. "See to it he is treated well."

JC grinned and started to step down from his horse, but Ernesto raised a hand, stopping him. "Go with these men while I speak to my brother, alone."

Ramon nodded for JC to stay mounted and said to his men, "Go ahead, take him with you. He will join us later."

"Come on," one of the men said to JC. Then his voice dropped low, secretive, "You know how these Mexicans like to get their heads together and *discutir* among themselves." He chuckled and the men turned their horses with JC among them, and moved off toward a large, dusty outbuilding.

When the others had moved away, and Ramon had guided Ernesto up onto the porch, Ernesto stopped and turned and spread his arms, taking in the vast land around them. "My brother, you have become a *patron* here in this big country."

Ramon smiled. "The gringos say that in America all men are created equal. But you and me, we know that is a lie, eh? We are equal only if we *create* ourselves." He slapped Ernesto on the back as they walked into the large house. "And even so, who wants to merely be *equal*?"

Ernesto stopped and looked around the large house, at the big oak desk and at the tall silver goblets and fine polished furniture. "Ah, Ramon." He breathed deep and swept a hand about the room. "There was a time when being equal meant a lot."

"*Sí.*" Ramon smiled, moving his brother to the table. "There was a time when a bowl of hot beans meant a lot . . . but that time has passed for us. Now that I know you are alive and back with me, there is no end to what we can do for ourselves." He seated Ernesto and called out through the house to the kitchen, "Jaffe, prepare food for my brother . . . and bring us more coffee."

"And whiskey," Ernesto cut in.

"Bring him whatever he wants." Ramon pushed a coffee cup over in front of Ernesto and filled it from a silver pot. "Now you must tell me, Ernesto, how you managed to save your hide when so many wanted to take it."

Ernesto told him about the prison break while he gulped his coffee. When Earl Jaffe brought a full plate of eggs and beans and steak, Ernesto attacked it like a starving wolf, talking as he ate, and now and then wiping a hand across his mouth. He commented once more on how well Ramon had done since last they'd seen each other, and of how surprised he was to see so many *Americanos* now working for him. Ramon smiled and listened, and watched his brother eat his fill.

When Ernesto pushed back the empty plate and drank the last of his coffee, he swept a whiskey glass aside, took the full bottle of whiskey, and threw back a long drink. Then he relaxed, let out a whiskey hiss, and asked in a matter-of-fact tone, "So, tell me, Ramon, what has become of all the men who came with you to America? Where is Santiago?"

Ramon's expression turned sad, and he shook his head. "Oh, it is too bad about our ole *compadres* . . . but they are all dead."

"All of them? Even Santiago?" Ernesto watched his brother's eyes as he asked.

"*Sí,* poor Santiago. He was like a brother to us both, eh? But yes, he too is dead. He died shortly after you were captured. The gringo soldiers . . . they killed him."

Ernesto shook his head. "Then he died with his boots on, as they say."

"That he did." Ramon looked saddened by his memories.

"I always will remember the big spurs he wore," Ernesto said, picturing the broken rowel the ranger had held up before him in the gray prison light. "What a sound those big spurs made when he walked, eh?" He held up the whiskey bottle as if in a toast.

"It is so," Ramon said with a sad smile. "He loved his big fancy spurs . . . and so was buried with them, I am told."

"Oh? You do not know? You were not around when he died?"

"No." Now Ramon watched Ernesto's eyes as he spoke. "I was back in *Mejico* when he died. Why do you ask this?"

Ernesto shrugged. "I ask only because I know how loyal he was to our cause . . . and how loyal he was to *you*, my brother. How he always followed your orders and no one else's."

"He was always a good soldier," Ramon said, his eyes narrowing as he stared at Ernesto. "But now he is dead. Him and all the others." He waited for a second, then added, "And I must tell you, that for me the *revolucion* is dead as well. I thank God you are alive . . . but if you come here thinking that we will go back and fight the struggle in *Mejico*, you are wrong. I make my living in a different way now. I no longer fight for the freedom of others. I do what I do for myself from now on."

"Oh? For yourself?"

"*Sí*," said Ramon, jutting his chin a bit, "for myself . . . and for you of course, now that you are here. Will you join me?"

Ernesto looked around the large room. "What business are you now in, brother, that allows you to live in such a splendid manner as this?"

Ramon tossed a hand. "We will discuss my business later.

The important thing is, are you with me? Will you join me no matter what?"

A silence passed as they stared at one another, until Ernesto seemed to ease down as if settling something in his mind. "I thought of many things while I sweated in the prison cell, waiting to die. But most of all I thought of all I would have had in life, had I robbed for myself over the years instead of for the *revolucion*. You were always the smart one, Ramon."

Ernesto tapped a finger to the side of his head and smiled. "And on this we are thinking the same thing. If you say we look out only for ourselves from now on . . . then this is how it will be."

Ramon reached over, laid his hand on his brother's shoulder, and said, "Then today I am truly happy for both of us. I cannot tell you how sad it made me, to hear you'd been captured . . . to know you were going to hang . . . to know there was nothing I could do to save you. Did I not send word that I would break you out?"

"Of course, you said you would break me out . . . but I knew it would place you in great danger. Better that the ones I led should come set me free, eh? They owed me that much."

Ramon nodded, then lowered his hand from his brother's shoulder and let it rest on the table. "It is true, they owed you at least that much, after all you suffered for the sake of the *revolucion*. No one gave more than you. You lost the woman you loved and your unborn baby. But now it is time for you to put the past out of your mind and let me make you rich." He raised his hand and patted the tabletop.

His unborn baby . . . ? Ernesto's hand tightened around the whiskey bottle. How did Ramon know? Ernesto didn't let his expression betray his thoughts. He settled himself and threw back another drink. "I am already rich, my brother. Nobody has yet found the money I hid."

"Yes, I heard about the money you took from the train," Ramon said, allowing a faint smile. "I know you hid it before they captured you. Now you are free to go get it . . . to enjoy it, as you should. I will send some of my men with you, to make sure you are safe."

Ernesto cocked his head. "I will be safe *without* anybody's help." His thoughts raced—about the broken spur, the woman he'd loved . . . about his brother sitting before him, and the many gunmen outside the house.

"Of course you will." Ramon looked hurt by his brother's words. "I make the offer only to help you. Do not think that I have any designs on the money. It is yours and yours only."

"No, it is *ours*. If we ride together . . . we share everything as before," Ernesto said. "You must forgive me . . . I have been so long around those I cannot trust, it has made me suspicious, even of my own brother." He let out a breath. "The money is buried beneath a big rock, inside the old Spanish ruins at the top of Diablo Canyon—"

"No," Ramon said, cutting him off. "Do not tell me. No one should know but you, until you get there."

Ernesto shrugged, dismissing Ramon's words. "But you are my brother. *You* I can trust. There are three flat rocks laid out in a row. At the end of the row is a much larger *round* rock. Beneath it is the three hundred thousand dollars." He grinned— "Now there are two of us who know" —and watched a gleam of satisfaction settle in his brother's eyes.

"Oh," Ramon said, leaning closer across the table. "Even your gringo friend does not know? You did not tell him?"

"Ha! Him I tell nothing. He thinks he is a partner, that I am taking him to the money. But I tell him that so he will do as I say. There were two convicts riding with him, and some Mexicans he brought along . . . but I made him slip away with me. He is a greedy fool, nothing more."

"Oh, I see." Ramon smiled and leaned back, pushing his chair away from the table.

From the doorway to the next room, Ernesto heard a board creak and turned toward it. His hand started to jerk for the pistol at his waist, but froze as JC cocked the revolver pointed at him and said, "Now, Ernesto . . . you've gone and hurt my feelings something awful."

What was this? Ernesto's eyes snapped to Ramon, stunned, as Ramon stood up from his chair and stepped around to him. Ramon's hand went down and snatched Ernesto's pistol up from the holster. Ernesto only stared, disbelieving it. "I should have warned you, Ernesto," Ramon said, staring down at him. "JC is one very sensitive man."

Ramon stepped back two feet, Ernesto's pistol in his hand and now cocked. Ernesto's eyes darted back and forth between them, stunned, wild, and wide in disbelief. "My own brother," Ernesto whispered.

"*Sí.*" Ramon shrugged and gestured a hand about the large room. "Do you think I afford this by raising goats and chickens? I deal in arms now, to the *federales*. Something you would not approve of. I need money to purchase American weapons for them. You were going to die anyway. Why should we both do without, when you have so much money hidden?"

Ernesto shook his head. "But, how could you have gotten in business with the *federales*, unless . . . ?" His words trailed off staring into his brother's eyes.

Ramon let it sink in for a moment, then said, "Your woman's father, the gringo weapons dealer? I took his business from him. Only instead of dealing with both sides the way he did, I deal only with the *federales*. I have become their American cousin." Ramon's eyes went flat and dark, and in that second Ernesto felt the pieces fall into place. He saw the killing at Cold Creek as clearly as if he'd been there. And there, near the spot where the woman he loved lay dead on the ground, he saw the face of his brother, Ramon.

Now, seeing the dark realization move across Ernesto's

face, Ramon said, "I could not leave her there alive, to tell you what I did . . . could I?"

A knot drew hot and tight in Ernesto's chest. "*You!*" He sprang forward, but before he left his chair, JC's pistol barrel came down hard on the back of his head, stunning him. Then JC swung an arm around his throat and held him tight.

"There," Ramon said, stepping back, tugging down on his shiny vest, "now the air is clear between us."

Ernesto's eyes swam about the room, hearing his brother, but hearing him from a long way off for a second. He struggled to stay conscious.

"Did you hear where he hid the money, JC?" Ramon asked without taking his eyes off his brother.

"Yeah, some of it," JC said. "He's been just like you said he would ever since I broke him out—all tight-lipped, not wanting to say where we were headed." He grinned. "The fool was about to get us lost. I couldn't just come out and tell him *I knew* the way. Had to get him straightened out with a coin toss."

Ramon smiled. "But you got him here. That is the main thing."

"Yeah, but I had some help on that." JC moved forward, his pistol still pointed at Ernesto Caslado. "Didn't know how I was going to get him pointed in this direction . . . but that old ranger showed up the night of the break. I think it was something he said that got Ernesto all keen to come find you—"

"A ranger?" Ramon cut him off. "What ranger? What are you talking about?"

JC shrugged. "You know . . . the one that rides the badlands? Carries that stupid list of them he's looking for? The one that killed Montana Red and a bunch of others."

"Him? *That* ranger?" Ramon's eyes flashed about the room as if the ranger might appear there. "What does he have to do with this?" Ramon's eyes went to Ernesto's, who stared at him, seething.

"Nothing. Don't worry about it," JC said. "He was there and talked to him some. But he was gone when we made the break."

"You fool," Ramon hissed. "If he knows about the prison break, he is not gone! He is a devil, that one! He will be on your trail right now!"

JC felt pressured and offered a tight smile. "So? If all he wants is Ernesto here, give him up. You two don't seem all that close anymore."

Ramon snapped his eyes back down to his brother. "What did the ranger come to tell you? What did you tell him?"

Ernesto Caslado stared at his brother through caged and smoldering eyes, his mind clearing now, the pain throbbing in the back of his head. "You were always the smart one, Ramon. You have done well in deceiving me, your *own brother*. You decide what he and I talked about. He showed me the broken rowel—decide what he knows or does not know. You bring me here for the money. Now go get the money . . . and may you rot in hell with it." He spit and slumped back in his chair.

Chapter 17

Ramon's men gathered around as he and JC walked Ernesto out of the house at gunpoint and down off the porch. Ramon stood back a step as JC pushed Ernesto forward and stopped among them. The men looked past Ernesto and JC and stared at Ramon in anticipation, until finally Earl Jaffe asked him, "Did you get what you wanted to hear?"

JC spoke up before Ramon could answer. "Yep," JC said, "it was easier than falling off a log."

But the men only stared past him as if he weren't there, still waiting to hear Ramon. Ramon let out a breath and said, "*Sí*, I know where the money is hidden . . . but so does *this* one." He nodded at JC. "Take them *both* to the supply building and tie them up. I will go and prepare for the trail."

"Huh?" JC started to turn to Ramon Caslado, but rough hands grabbed him and thrust him forward.

With his hands raised, Ernesto looked back at his brother and said, slicing his words through clenched teeth. "You are a dead man Ramon—*a dead man*!"

"Look at him," a man said, gesturing at Ernesto seething at his brother behind a dark hot glare. "Why not save yourself some trouble? Shoot them now," the man said. "What're we waiting for?"

"Because I say we wait," Ramon snapped. "We will take care of them both when I say it is time!"

One of the rough hands closed around JC's pistol and

wrenched it from his hand. "But damn it, Ramon! We're supposed to have us a deal here!" JC yelled, trying to look back as the men shoved him forward behind Ernesto. "Don't treat me this way! I did what you asked me to do, didn't I? You gave me your word."

"Hush up now," said the same voice that had spoken quietly to him as he'd ridden away with them earlier. "You oughta know better than to trust either one of these Caslado boys. Now you've gone and got yourself kilt, ain't ya." JC shot the man a glance and saw the strange smile on his face. The man added, "What kind of fool would share three hundred thousand dollars with an idiot like you?"

As the men led Ernesto and JC to the long, dusty outbuilding, Ramon turned to Earl Jaffe, who'd stayed back with him. "We must move quickly, Jaffe, if we are to get our hands on the money. It has not gone as I planned."

"What's the problem, boss?" Jaffe cocked his head. "We got your brother sprung . . . he told you where the money's hidden. You've got the rifle deal going with the *federales*, and the money to finance it. Once we get the guns to sell to them, our troubles are over."

"Yes, but now there is a ranger involved. He came to see my brother the night before he was going to hang."

"So?"

"I'll tell you 'so.' It is the ranger who rides the badlands. The one I have heard you mention many times."

"You mean . . . ?"

"Yes, that is who I mean. The one who has your name on his list." Ramon gazed back across the stretch of flatlands as if expecting to see someone riding in.

"Well, that does make a difference," Jaffe said. "But I'll take care of him." He grinned. "Besides, what are you worried about? There's nine of us. He can't handle these kind of odds."

"I don't like him sticking his nose in," Ramon said. "He

has a way of causing things to happen. He is like having a bad luck charm around your neck."

Jaffe chuckled under his breath. "You ain't superstitious, are you, boss. Hell, I'm the one with my name on his list."

"No, I am not superstitious . . . But this ranger is not a man to take lightly. Do you understand me?" He leaned toward Jaffe with his hands clenched at his sides. "We must get the money and carry out our plans before he comes snooping around."

"All right, I hear ya, boss." He nodded toward the building where JC and Ernesto had been taken. "But why not just kill those two now, just to keep from fooling with them any longer?"

Ramon's lips tightened. "Because it is not an easy thing to do, to kill one's own brother."

"But you knew we'd have to, boss, once this thing got to rolling."

"Yes, I knew . . . and I *will* kill him. I'm just saying, 'it is not an easy thing.' I still see him as we once were . . . young and innocent, and picking beans and cleaning stables, just for a free meal and a place to sleep." He gazed off again, this time to keep Earl Jaffe from seeing his eyes. "I was always much smarter than him—he knows this. The one who is smarter is always the one with power over the other. When I kill him, I know I am killing someone weaker than myself . . . someone who never stood a chance against me."

"And that upsets ya?" Jaffe shook his head. "That oughta make it easy for ya, boss, the way I look at it." He grinned. "You know when it comes to money, you can't let family stand in the way. Be prepared to shoot your own mama in the back if you have to—is what I always say, if you stand to make a few dollars."

Ramon looked at him with a flat expression. "Go. Bring my chaps and spurs. Prepare horses. We must get under way.

Pick a man to stay and watch about those two. The rest will ride with me."

Inside the outbuilding Ramon's men had taken a shackle chain and, raising Ernesto and JC, had cuffed them wrist to wrist over a lifting timber in the center of the building, the two men's toes barely scraping the dirt floor. "Tell my brother, Ramon, that he is a dead man," Ernesto hissed at the men.

"Shut up, *Er-nest-to*. He already heard ya." One of the men stepped in and lifted him with the swipe of a rifle butt to his ribs. The other men laughed and gave the two a spin on their chain. Then, leaving one man with a rifle to guard them, the others turned and walked back to the house. No sooner were they out of sight, Ernesto gulped in air, his free arm clinched across his ribs, and looked around the dusty building. JC stood silent as stone, doing the same.

Wooden rifle crates stood empty here and there against the wall like coffins, their lids open. A stand for a Gatling gun sat off to one side, flies circling the packing grease on its steel legs. Beside it, the gun itself leaned against the wall, partly covered by a dirty quilt. *So this is how he makes his fortune* . . . Ernesto breathed deep. Only the *federales* brought brand-new weapons. No one else could afford them. Ernesto shook his head and spit.

"When this is over, I will kill you, JC," Ernesto said, swinging himself around on the tips of his toes for a better look at JC's face. "On this I give you my word."

"Yeah? So far I ain't seen anybody's word that's worth the breath it took to give it." JC swung slightly on tiptoe and nodded toward the guard who stood at the door with his back turned, rolling a smoke. His voice dropped to a whisper. "If we plan on staying alive, we better pull together here. There's the man you better think about killing somehow."

Hearing them whisper, the guard turned with his twisted

cigarette in his mouth. "Shut up . . . no talking between you two. I am stuck with you all day and night. Don't make me decide to put a bullet in you."

Ernesto stood staring at the man, sizing him up—a young man, this one, but with a high-strung sharpness in him. A man with a hot temper? His dark eyes told Ernesto that he would not be easily tricked. All right, here goes. Ernesto took a deep breath, and just to feel the man out, said, "Go on and shoot us now. What do we care? Whether you kill us now, or later, what does it matter?"

The man chuckled, lit his cigarette, and blew a long stream of smoke. "To me, it matters nothing at all," he said. "I would have shot you both to begin with, instead of hearing your mouth." He shrugged. "But Ramon says guard you . . . so I will. Perhaps he keeps you alive in case you lied about the money, eh?" He gave a thin, tight smile.

"Maybe I *did* lie about it," Ernesto said. He jutted his dark, stubbled chin. "Maybe they make the ride for nothing."

The guard shook his head. "Do not play with me, Ernesto. If you have lied about the money, I will ask Ramon to let me walk around you with my dagger, slowly, until your belly spills into your boots."

Ernesto stared at him. He could get him to talk—that was good. If he could get him to talk, he could get him to do something else. He could get him to come closer after the others rode away. Once he came closer, Ernesto would kill him. He had no doubt. His brother, Ramon, was smart, but he had made a mistake in keeping him alive. Ernesto hadn't lied about the money's location. It was where he said it would be, inside the old Spanish ruins.

But there was more to getting the money than Ernesto had mentioned. As soon as his brother had let it slip—knowing about his unborn baby—Ernesto's mind had gone to work. He had not come this far to die like a fool. Ramon was smarter, but he had never been as ruthless. Ernesto stared at the guard for a moment longer. He almost smiled, thinking about the look on Ramon's face when JC had mentioned the ranger. *The ranger* . . .

How ironic it was, Ernesto thought, that the man who had stood before his cell, looking for answers he didn't get, was now the very force that caused his brother, Ramon, to act in such haste. Ramon was in a hurry now, not taking the time he usually took to think things through. Ramon feared the ranger. *This is good* . . .

Was that stupid old ranger really back there somewhere, tracking them? Of course he wasn't. As fast as they'd traveled, the ranger could never have kept up. But it didn't matter whether or not the ranger was back there. All that mattered was that Ramon thought he might be.

Ernesto knew a little about how the ranger operated—moving slow and steady, always plodding along, never in a hurry, always planning the next step before taking it. An old fool? Of course he was, Ernesto thought. But as it was now turning out, in this harsh land where living had become a deadly game of all things feeding one upon the other . . . the mere threat of the ranger being near had become his ace in the hole.

Above the edge of the rock wall, high above the stretch of grassland leading to Ramon Caslado's ranch, the ranger lay flat on his belly, looking out through the rifle scope. Behind him, Samuel Burns had dropped from his saddle and leaned against a tall rock, his hands on his knees, a canteen hanging from one hand. His legs and back were numb to the bone. "How do you know that's where Caslado's brother lives?" he asked in a weak, failing voice, then hiked a mouthful of brown mucus and spit it out.

"I don't," the ranger said, still scanning the long front porch, where three men stood by their horses. "But I'm betting on it." Across the yard in a corral, two sweat-streaked horses shied away from the other half dozen or so horses gathered there. These two milled and drew water from a water trough, and looked toward the others the way newcomers do. "Whether it is or not, it pays to see what you're riding into, doesn't it?"

Burns sighed and uncapped the canteen. "Yeah, if you say so."

The ranger glanced at him, shook his head, then looked back down into the scope. "Just think, Samuel, if you'd made it as a desperado, this is the kind of life you'd be living from now on out."

Burns threw back a swig of water, swished it around, and spit it out. "I know." He straightened, stretched his tight back, and rocked back and forth on his numb legs. "It's no wonder most outlaws don't care if they live or die. I'm starting to feel that way myself."

The ranger smiled without turning around. "Aw, now, a young man like you? You oughta be able to better handle this rigorous outdoor lifestyle. Have some more water—cool yourself out. Looks like we might pick us up some fresh horses here."

Burns just stared at him, then blew out a tired breath. The past night and day were only blurred memories to him. They hadn't stopped since they'd left San Paulo—or if they had, he was too tired to recall it. He remembered at one point, near dawn, dropping down from his horse to water it at a thin stream. But the ranger had stepped away for a second, found the dead horse, and came back to him, telling him they had to keep moving.

And so they had, at times walking the horses, with the saddles off and slung over their shoulders. Resting the horses as they moved, the ranger was always one step ahead, his pace steady, never faltering, until Samuel Burns felt his tired legs were no longer a part of him. Then they'd mounted once more and moved on, nonstop, Burns's arm quivering, weak and burning, from carrying the saddle— *God only knew how many miles.* This man was not human, he thought, watching the ranger scan the land below them. This man operated on some type of inner force that was completely foreign to Burns.

"Here we go," the ranger said almost to himself. From the dusty outbuilding where a door stood open a foot, he saw a thin wisp of blue cigarette smoke swept out on a breeze. From another building five men came out on horses and rode to the front of the house, joining the other three. "Yep, it's the right place all right. There's Ramon—but where's Ernesto? Where's JC?" He scanned back to the partly opened door. "Are they in there? I bet they are." *But why . . . ?* He scanned from one rider to the next, then back to the dusty outbuilding.

"Thank God," Burns said, pushing himself from the rock and staggering over to the ranger. He let the horse's reins fall to the ground and lay down on the edge near the ranger. "Just . . . just shoot them when they come out. Please, from up here. Let's be done with it."

The ranger glanced at Burns's tired, sweat-streaked face. "I mean it," Burns said. "I can't go another step."

"You're dong fine, Samuel," the ranger said, turning his face and gazing back down the scope. "But we're not going to shoot anybody just yet. We're going to wait until these men leave, and have ourselves a look around. Something ain't right down there—I feel it in my bones."

In the outbuilding Ernesto listened as the sound of hooves drew away into the distance. The guard sat atop a rifle crate, looking down, rolling another smoke. His rifle lay loose across his lap. Ernesto reached over with his boot toe and nudged JC on his foot until JC raised his bowed head. Without a word Ernesto gestured his dark eyes toward the guard.

JC narrowed his brow and nodded slightly, getting the message.

"So, *mi amigo*," Ernesto said, "do you suppose my brother, Ramon, would mind if you gave us some water?"

"I am not your *amigo*." The guard only tossed him a glance, stuck the twisted cigarette in his mouth, and lit it. The match sizzled and flared. Then he shook it out, dropped it, and stood up, crushing it beneath his heavy boot. "You can die of thirst for all I care. It would save me a bullet."

"Then you are right! You are not my *amigo*!" Ernesto hissed at him through clenched teeth. "What you are is a mindless, stinking pig!" He spit toward the guard. "I am glad they ride off and leave you here. You will never see them or the money . . . ever!"

"Oh, I see." The guard grinned and chuckled under his breath, stepping forward with the cigarette in his lips. "This is where you convince me that I have been betrayed, eh?" He stopped eight feet away, the rifle cradled under his arm, and looked Caslado up and down, Caslado's right arm stretched high above his head, the steel cuff tight around his wrist. "What then, Ernesto? You will tell me that if I throw in with you and your gringo friend, together we will go get the money and share it?"

"Don't count me in on this," JC said, hanging beside Ernesto.

"Shut up, JC," Ernesto snapped at him. Then he said to the guard, "No, I say nothing more to you. But when they do not come back, I will only laugh . . . even as you kill me. You big, stupid son of a—"

The guard stepped closer, making a swipe at Ernesto's face with his rifle stock. But Ernesto jerked back, just enough to let the rifle flash past his face, the guard coming with it, off balance. JC pulled his weight down on the chain, giving Ernesto the support he needed to swing both legs up off the ground and wrap them around the guard's neck before the man could right himself.

The rifle went off, the sound raising dust in the rafters. Ernesto squeezed his legs tight, the guard struggling to get a swing at him with the rifle. Now Ernesto swung his legs up, lifting the guard, and giving JC slack on the chain above them. JC braced down, holding both men up as the guard thrashed and jerked until his arms went limp and the rifle fell to the dirt floor.

Ernesto held tight, his ankles locked one over the other, his kneecaps up against the guard's windpipe. The guard made one last, long rasp before his tongue dropped, still and blue from between his parted lips. Ernesto's breath heaved in his chest. He unlocked his ankles and pushed the guard backward with his dusty boot. "I thought this pig would never die!"

"Here, use my shoulder," JC said, hurrying, stooping a bit toward Ernesto. "Get up and over!"

Ernesto climbed up JC's side, stepped up onto his shoulder, and flipped over the lifting beam. No sooner had he hit the ground when both men made a jump for the guard's rifle, the shackle chain still holding them together. JC's free hand reached the rifle first, and had almost closed around it. But Ernesto took purchase in the dirt with both boot heels and yanked back hard on the chain. "Leave it be . . . I'll kill you!" Ernesto raged.

JC made a roundhouse swing with his fist and missed. Ernesto charged into him, wrapping the chain around JC's neck and falling back with him, JC atop him now, his tongue out, his face going blue. "See! Now you are not so smart!" Ernesto had him; JC knew it. "Think you can make a fool of me—"

Ernesto felt him struggle, the same way the guard had just struggled; and he felt him thrash, giving it his last effort at staying alive. "Now die, you low, rotten—!"

"Boys, boys, boys," came a voice behind them. "No wonder you never get anywhere." Ernesto let go of the chain and reached for the rifle with JC still atop him. The ranger looked down at him from behind the big pistol and clamped his boot on the rifle stock.

"Now turn him loose, Ernesto," the ranger said, "or you'll have to drag his stinking carcass all the way across the badlands."

Ernesto unwrapped the chain from JC's throat and shoved him to the side. JC gasped and coughed. Ernesto struggled and rose to his knees, his shackled hand hanging down beside JC. "How . . . how long have you . . . been on my trail?" Ernesto wiped his free hand across his face and tried to catch his breath, staring up at the ranger, seeing Samuel Burns behind him.

The ranger stooped, picked up the rifle from the dirt, jacked it down to one last cartridge, and pitched it to Burns. "Ever since you gave back that full bag of tobacco, Ernesto," the ranger said, although it wasn't completely true. "That was sloppy on your part." He glanced around the outbuilding as he continued. "I figured once I showed you the broken rowel, you'd be eager to get the man who owned it."

Ernesto slumped on the dirt while beside him JC moaned and coughed and began to stir. "The man who once owned those fancy spurs is dead now," Ernesto said. "But it was my brother, Ramon, who gave the orders. He is the killer. He said as much, to my face."

"And now I figure you've told him where your train money's hidden. So they're on their way to get it?"

"*Sí*, they are." Ernesto settled on the ground. "My brother is on his way to get everything that is coming to him." He smiled guardedly. Beside him, JC rose up and sat staring through watery eyes.

The ranger took Ernesto by the shoulder and pulled him

up, JC coming up with him on unsteady legs. "Get yourselves collected," the ranger said to the two of them. "We're
finding Ramon and taking him down for the murders at Cold
Creek."

"Ha!" Ernesto glared at him. "What chance do you have
against him and his men?" He nodded toward Samuel
Burns. "You and this yard-screw. Besides, I have *already*
killed my brother. He just does not know it yet."

JC stood rubbing his throat. Noticing Samuel Burns
through his watery eyes, he said in a gravely voice, "Well
now, Sammy-boy, never thought . . . I'd see you again."

"That's right, you never," Burns said, stepping closer, the
rifle butt cocked for a swipe at JC's face.

"Easy now." The ranger raised a hand. "His name is
Samuel Burns. Calling him Sammy-boy might not be a good
idea. He's grown up some in the past few days." He turned
back to Ernesto and asked, "What do you mean, you've already killed your brother?"

Ernesto Caslado spit at the ranger's feet. "I tell you now
what I told you before . . . nothing! And I will do nothing to
help you track down my brother. He is dead!"

"Speak for yourself, Ernesto," JC said, still rubbing his
throat. He turned his eyes to the ranger. "I've had it with
both of these snaking Caslado bastards. Take this bracelet
off me, and I'm your man . . . you've got my word on it."

The ranger caught the slightest caged glance between
Ernesto and JC. He looked at Samuel Burns and said, "Can
you believe these two?"

The ranger shook his head, looking at the body of the
guard on the dirt floor with his blue tongue sticking out, his
eyes bulged and glazed. Then he looked around the outbuilding and shoved the two men toward the door. "Let's get
us something to eat . . . maybe we'll all feel better." He gave
a tight smile. "We've got some hard traveling ahead of us."

"We cannot travel like this." Ernesto stopped, shook the

chain on his wrist, and nodded at the body of the guard on the floor. "Aren't you going to get the key and cuff us separately?"

"Why?" The ranger shoved them forward again. "There's nothing you boys do that you can't do together."

Chapter 18

"You better think it over real careful like, Sammy-boy," JC said in a lowered voice. He glared at Burns for a second, then glanced over to the corral, where the ranger had gone to inspect the horses. "What's waiting for you back there ain't no better than a bullet in the brain." He glanced at Ernesto, and added, "Am I telling him the truth, Ernesto?" Samuel Burns sat ten feet away, the rifle with one bullet in it across his lap. JC and Ernesto sat on the floor of the front porch. Tin plates with scraps of beef bones sat in front of them. A canteen of water lay near their crossed legs.

"*Sí*, it is true. You better listen to JC. You think you have an idea what it is going to be like in a dark prison cell. But you do not know." He shook his head. "If you think it was hell working there all day as a guard . . . believe me, it is a worse kind of hell being there as a prisoner."

"Listen to this man, Sammy-boy," JC said in a low tone of warning.

Ernesto looked at the resolved expression on Burns's face. Then he closed his eyes and bowed his head. "Do you know what the convicts always dream of doing to a guard if they ever get their hands on one? Now a real live guard is thrown in among them? *Heaven forbid!*" He crossed himself. "Especially a young man like yourself? Do you know what they do to a young man in a place such as that?"

"I've heard," Burns said in a quiet tone. He raised his free hand and chafed the back of his neck.

Ernesto stared at him. *Good* . . . He had Burns talking now. Once he had him talking—and thinking about it—it would be only a matter of time . . .

JC leaned forward on his haunches, the chain hanging between him and Ernesto. "I know you're sore about me leaving ya back at the prison—I can't blame ya. But you've got to understand something, Sammy-boy. We were hard pressed right then. I told Ernesto here, I'd given anything if it hadn't happened. They all had to hold me down . . . to keep me from riding back for ya. Ain't it the truth, Ernesto?"

"It is true," Ernesto said. "JC does not want to admit it, but there were real tears in his eyes—mine too, when we realized what had happened to your horse." Ernesto tapped his cheek, shaking his head slowly, his eyes fixed on Samuel's. "No man wants to leave an *amigo* behind. Yet, what could we do?"

"See, Sammy-boy," JC said, "there's a strong bond between men like us—and you're one of us. We stand up for one another, no matter what." He shrugged. "Sure, Ernesto and I have had our disagreements . . . you've seen that." He ran a hand across the chain marks on his throat. "But when the going's tough, we're right there for one another—side by side. What's that lawman going to do for you, besides slap you in a cell to rot for the rest of your life?" He shot Ernesto a glance. "Or, wait a minute. Will they charge him with *murder* . . . so many dying and all?"

"As surely as if he pulled a trigger," Ernesto said, giving his face a dark, grave expression. "But perhaps you will be lucky," he added to Burns. "Maybe they will hang you quickly when you get back there. Either way, your life is over . . . unless you do something about it right away."

Sammy Burns swallowed a dry knot in his throat and glanced over to where the ranger stood among the horses in the corral. Burns thought back to the other day when he stood watching Al Kreeger race toward him across the sand, his eyes lit in a killing rage, a shotgun raised above his head. He pictured himself standing there, small, frightened, raising the pistol, and holding it firm. *Jesus!* What was he doing here in this land of madmen . . . this hot, violent place where there seemed to be no letup, no end to the treachery.

He slumped with his hand around the rifle stock, his finger loose across the trigger. Sweat ran down the back of his neck; and he turned back to the two men, who sat leaning slightly on their haunches, watching, waiting for his next words.

"I don't want to go to prison," Burns said in a faltering voice.

"Hell, no! And you don't have to," JC said, his voice still low, but getting excited. "Just pitch me a gun and sit tight. It'll all be over in a second. The ranger will be dead, and you'll ride away with us, free and clear. Can't you see that? We are *amigos* here, the three of us! For God's sake, Sammy-boy! Just give me a gun!"

From the corral the ranger ran a hand down the neck of a big buckskin gelding, but catching a glimpse of the men on the porch. He smiled, seeing Ernesto and JC rocking on their haunches, giving it their all. Well, he couldn't blame them. Any man would do the same, he figured, under the circumstances.

He could almost recite word for word what was being said on the porch right then. This was a hard test for Samuel Burns—facing prison, hearing these two tell him how to keep from going there. The ranger sighed, then stooped, running a hand down the horse's front leg, all the way down to the hoof.

On the porch Samuel Burns had his hand on the pistol inside his waistband. "*Amigos*, huh?"

"You know it kid," JC said, rubbing his free hand up and down his trouser leg in anticipation.

Burns felt a heated rush sweep over him. His breath stopped in his throat; and he jerked the pistol up and pitched it over into JC's eager hand. "Now hurry," Burns said, his voice not even sounding like his own.

Ernesto and JC bolted upright from the porch, Ernesto cutting a sharp look toward where the ranger had stood in the corral only a second ago. *Where was he now?* JC had cocked the pistol, and now held it out arm's length, pointing at Samuel Burns's face. "So long, Sammy-boy, sucker!" JC yelled in a laughing rage. Burns sat rigid, staring into the pistol barrel.

"*Wait!*" Ernesto yelled, turning and seeing the cocked hammer on the pistol in JC's hand. But it was too late. Ernesto saw the hammer fall, heard the metallic click, then the loud explosion. Yet something was wrong. Instead of Burns going down, it was JC, his startled face gone stark white for a split second. JC looked stunned, then flipped forward at a sharp angle as his left leg flew out from under him. Both men hit the porch floor in a billow of dust, JC screaming beneath Ernesto as Ernesto thrashed and tried to right himself.

Wise choice, Samuel . . . In the corral, where he had watched the whole play from behind the low cover of the water trough, the ranger stood up, uncocked his big pistol, holstered it, and walked over to the porch, his hand resting on the butt of it. "Bet they heard that rifle shot clear down to Texas," the ranger said, stepping up beside Samuel Burns. The rifle lay across Burns's lap, a sliver of blue smoke still curling from the barrel. Burns stared straight ahead at the two men wallowing on the porch, a stream of blood running down JC's leg.

"You sneaking, rotten, dirty, little—" JC forced his words through clenched teeth, his free hand grasping his wounded leg.

"Don't aggravate him," the ranger said, "or I'll give him another bullet—he's apt to cock up and shoot you again." He stooped and picked up the empty pistol from the porch, looked at it with a thin smile, and pitched it back to Burns. "You can't be shooting our prisoners now, Sam," he said. "We'll be another hour getting his leg bandaged."

"You stupid *bastardo*!" Atop of JC, Ernesto raged, pounding down on JC with his cuffed fist, the chain between them rising and falling like a steel whip. The ranger stepped in, kicked Ernesto once in the chest, and watched him roll into a ball with a loud grunt.

"I got tired of listening to them," Samuel Burns said to the ranger, still staring at the men on the porch floor. "If we're going to be riding with them, I thought it best to shut them up right now." He raised his eyes slowly up to the ranger's, having taken note that the ranger had just now called him Sam . . . no more Sammy-boy . . . not even Samuel. Just Sam now. Wasn't that what Miss Fannie had called the ranger back in San Paulo? So, they shared the same name, him and the ranger. He said the name to himself, liking the sound of it. "You know what they wanted me to do, don't you?"

"I've got a pretty good idea," the ranger said. "But I never doubted you for a minute." He reached around along his holster belt and flipped up bullet after bullet until he'd gathered a handful. Then he reached over and handed them to Burns. "Let me know when you need more."

Another hour had passed by the time they'd dressed JC's leg wound, gathered some supplies, and set out on the trail northwest into the high rock land. As the ranger tended to

JC, he'd noted that the wound was shallow, deep enough to bleed heavily, but more of a cut than a puncture. He wondered if Burns had intended it this way. How good was Burns with a rifle? Had he only clipped JC on purpose, or had he just fired the rifle across his lap, taking potluck on what the bullet hit.

Burns had come a long way in a short time, the ranger thought, but the threat of prison had a strong pull on any man. The ranger thought of a time when he'd come upon a wolf trap in the wilds, and of how a wolf had chewed through its paw and left that severed part of itself behind in order to escape.

Burns had a lot on his mind. The ranger knew it. What remained to be seen was whether or not Burns had the strength to hold himself accountable for what he'd done and face the consequences.

Ahead of him along the narrow trail, the ranger watched Samuel Burns lead the way. Burns carried the rifle across his lap. Two full canteens hung from his saddle horn. Behind Burns, JC and Ernesto rode double on a strong bay gelding. Ernesto sat in front with his left forearm behind his back. JC sat behind, his right forearm across his lap, the chain hanging between them.

At the rear the ranger rode along on a big dun gelding he'd selected from the corral. He led his white barb behind him at the head of a four-horse string. Without telling them, the ranger had gone back to the outbuilding before they left. He'd taken the key from the dead guard's body, and now carried it in his vest pocket.

When they'd ridden upward along the rocky trail for two hours and come to a stretch of flatland, the ranger moved forward, leading the string of horses at a trot. "Hold 'em up here. Let me check their tracks," he said to Burns as he rode past him. He stopped ten yards ahead, studied the ground for a moment, then called back to Burns, "All right, Sam, let's rest these horses a while."

"He's got to be joking," JC said near Caslado's ear. "We ain't gone ten miles yet."

Caslado nodded and answered in a low tone, watching the ranger study the ground as he rode back to them. "He is old and tires easily. Let's remember this, eh?"

Burns looked a bit surprised and said as the ranger stopped the string beside him, "Right here? Don't you want to gain some ground on them? We've got another four hours of daylight."

"I know it," the ranger said. "But we'll have the sun blindsiding us on our left." He moved closer to Burns to keep the other two from hearing him, and continued, "The tracks say Ramon and his men came up here and headed across fast, in the hottest part of the day. They're across by now, but their horses are winded." He pushed the brim of his sombrero up and nodded toward the stretch of flatland. "We've got a traveler's moon tonight. If we cool these horses all the way down and head out at dark, we'll be less than an hour behind them come morning."

Burns gazed away, out through wavering heat, across the ten-mile stretch of flatland. "So," he said, more to himself than to the ranger, "it's all about horses, isn't it?"

The ranger looked at him, but didn't answer.

Burns shook his head slowly, thinking about how he'd grabbed a horse the night of the prison break and rode away, flat-out, not stopping the horse to rest until the horse spent itself beneath him. *Jesus* . . . What a fool he'd been. Had he only thought things out that night, he could have slipped away and never been seen or heard from again.

He turned in his saddle and looked over at JC and Ernesto Caslado, sweaty, dirty, chained together like animals, waiting for a chance to make one last desperate grab for freedom. Then he looked at the string of fresh horses, the big animals stepping back and forth, high-hoofed and ready to go.

The ranger had swung down from the big dun and stood looking up at Burns with his reins in one hand and the lead rope to the string of horses in the other. When their eyes met, Burns felt as if the ranger had read his thoughts—whatever those thoughts were right then. *What were they?* He wasn't sure. In a sudden rush of heat that swept over him, Burns almost swayed. He wasn't sure of anything.

"Why don't you bring our prisoners over this way, Sam," the ranger said, nodding toward a sparse stand of pine along the edge of the flatland. His eyes lingered, searching Burns's for one narrow second before he turned his back to him and led the horses away.

Burns let out a long breath, feeling his wet shirt clinging to his back. "All right, you both heard him," he said to JC and Ernesto. "Climb down and lead your horses over there." Burns swung down from his saddle with the rifle trained toward them.

"How do you expect us to get down on our own, chained together like this?" Ernesto said, glaring at him from twelve feet away.

"It's not my problem," Burns said, jiggling the rifle. "Now get down and let's go."

"No, this ain't your problem," JC said in a quiet, clipped tone as they swung down from the horse's back and led it past him. "Your problem ain't even started yet. Wait till we get back to prison, you little rat. Nobody shoots me and gets by with it."

Samuel Burns stepped in behind them, leading his horse five feet back, the rifle up and cocked toward their backs. "Oh? Maybe you're not going back to prison," he said, his voice low and guarded.

"Don't threaten me," JC hissed over his shoulder. "You don't have the guts to—"

"Shut up, fool!" Ernesto Caslado snapped at him in a whisper, cutting him off. Something in the tone of Burns's voice had caught his ear. Ernesto slowed a step, gazing at the ranger thirty feet ahead. "What do you mean, Burns?"

Burns chuckled behind them. "What do you think I mean? That rifle graze didn't do anything but raise a little blood, did it."

Ernesto shot JC a glance. Their ears pricked. "Talk to me, Burns, quickly," Ernesto said, gazing ahead at the ranger. "You have a plan? What are you saying?"

They slowed a step. "All I'm saying is, I started out the same as you two . . . now I've earned myself a pistol, a rifle, some bullets."

"And you've gained his trust, eh?" Ernesto looked back as they moved closer to the ranger. "Now you only wait for the right time and place to make your move?"

"You tell me," Burns said. "If there *is* a right time, it'll be when I see that train money you've got hidden."

"It's a deal; shoot him now! I promise to take you to it," Ernesto said, whispering.

"Not a chance," Burns whispered in reply. "I know better than to trust you snakes. We all go there together."

JC said in a rushed voice, "Listen, kid, about me pointing that pistol at you back there—I swear to God, I didn't mean it. I just lost my head—"

"Shut your mouth," Ernesto hissed. Then as they drew nearer to the ranger, Ernesto added, "All right . . . we all go there together? At the right moment you will kill him?"

The ranger looked around as they stepped closer and inside the thin shade. Burns did not answer, but Ernesto shot JC another glance, a faint smile of satisfaction on his sweat-streaked face.

"Are they still trying to work on you?" the ranger asked Burns, taking hold of the chain between the two men and leading them into the shade.

"No," Burns said, sliding Ernesto and JC a glance as they plopped down on the ground. "I think they know where I stand now."

"Good." The ranger gathered their horses' reins and led them a few feet away, where the other horses stood in the string, picking at pale clumps of wild grass along the edge of the shade. When he'd tied them into the string, he came back carrying a canteen.

He drank from it, looking back and forth at the three of them, then passed the canteen to Samuel Burns. "Tell me something, Ernie," he said, stooping nearer Ernesto Caslado. "Are you a religious man?"

Ernesto looked puzzled for a second. "You see the kind of man I am. How can you ask such a thing?" He turned his face to one side, spit, grunted, and glanced past each of them as they stared at him. He tried to look away, but the ranger's gaze stayed fixed on him until finally Ernesto shrugged. "All right . . . I was raised in the church. What of it?"

"Show me how you make the sign," the ranger said.

"The what?" Ernesto looked puzzled.

"You know," the ranger said, "the sign of the cross. You remember how it's done, don't you?"

Ernesto tossed his eyes upward, embarrassed. "Of course I remember how it is done."

"Then show me," the ranger said.

Ernesto studied his eyes for a second. "I cannot do it just to show you how it is done."

"Why not?" The ranger leaned closer.

"Because it is bad luck to do it for no reason." Ernesto squirmed, looking into the ranger's steady gaze, feeling a little uneasy all of a sudden.

"Is that a fact?" The ranger shook his head, gazing around at the harsh land, at Ernesto's ragged clothes, his sweaty face, the steel cuff around his dirty wrist, the heavy chain. "Well, I wouldn't want to cause you any bad luck," he said.

"I know how it's done," JC said. "I'll show you."

The ranger watched closely as JC made the sign of the cross on his sweat-soaked shirt. After a second the ranger said, "Do it again, slower."

JC gave Ernesto a concerned look, then slowly repeated the gesture. "This ain't some kind of trick, is it?" he asked.

The ranger looked at Ernesto. "Is that the way it's done?"

"*Sí* . . . why?"

"Does everybody do it the same way, every time? I mean, a priest does it the same way as everybody else?"

"It is the same for everyone . . . of course." Ernesto saw a caged, hollow look move into the ranger's eyes, a grim expression as it moved over his face like a dark shadow. "Why do you ask this thing?"

The ranger didn't answer, but instead asked, "Would anybody do it another way?"

"What other way? There is only *one* way . . . unless you do it backwards."

"Backwards?" A weak feeling stirred low in the ranger's stomach. He swallowed. "Who would do it backwards?"

"No one would make the sign of the cross backwards"— he raised a finger for emphasis—"no one but a madman or a fool." Ernesto shook his head, dismissing such an idea. "The old ones used to say that to do such a thing as this, even by mistake . . . one would have just been touched by the devil."

Seeing the look on the ranger's face, JC and Ernesto shot each other a glance. JC felt a sudden urge to reach out and snatch the big pistol from the ranger's holster. Something told him that right then he could do it . . . he could get away with it. He bit his lip and ran his hand back and forth on his dirty trousers, tensing up—ready to make his play.

"What is it you want to know, ranger?" Ernesto's voice seemed to bring the ranger back from some distant place; and seeing it, JC eased down and cursed under his breath.

"Nothing," the ranger said in a flat tone. Samuel Burns stepped back with his rifle cradled in his arm and watched the ranger walk away a few feet and gaze off through the wavering heat, back across layer upon layer of rolling, jagged badlands, in the direction of San Paulo.

Part 4

Part 4

Chapter 19

Timing was everything. Time and place, Crazy Gravy thought, looking all around, leading his tired horse up through the tangled brush to the top of a rock shelf where Maria had already stopped and turned around. She looked back down at him. "Are you all right, Padre?" He only nodded and waved a hand, looking up at her with a tired smile. *Oh, yes, fine. Couldn't be better . . .*

He could have done whatever he wanted to do with her at any time last night as they'd searched the moonlight darkness for the two prisoners. But something had told him to wait . . . and so he had. Now he knew why as he moved up and looked around at the broad shelf of rock that reached back into the hillside twenty or more feet. The outreaching ceiling of rock above it swept upward and out, forming a natural shelter—a cathedral of sorts, he thought. *How appropriate . . .*

Evening shadows lay long across the valley and rock below them; and as he led his horse back beneath the overhang of rock, Maria said in a tired voice, "We will make camp here for the night." She shook her head, turning to him. "I cannot understand how they have managed to elude us for this long." She was more tired than she could remember being in a long, long time.

Crazy Gravy watched as she gazed out across the valley below and up along the narrow path winding farther upward to the top of the rock overhang. He was not tired. His energy was fueled by anticipation. His blood coursed high and fast in his veins. He reached over and took her reins from her hand. "Here, let me tend to the horses and strike us a fire," he said. "You go sit down and rest . . . rest is important." He almost reached a hand up to stroke her long black hair. But he stopped himself—*Patience, my son*—turned, and led the tired horses beneath the overhang.

Rance Plum slapped his hat at the flies spinning around his sour-smelling boot and trouser leg. They'd dogged the riders hard, keeping them under heavy rifle fire ever since picking up their trail above San Paulo. When Homer and his men had swung east and stayed in the cover of rough rock land, Plum was more than just a little surprised. Had the Mexicans made a run for it either to the north or the west, they could have outrun Plum and the Spider across miles of flatlands. Yet they hadn't.

"What's wrong with Ernesto?" the Spider asked as the two of them gazed from the cover of a rock ledge down on the scattered group of men below.

"I won't venture a guess," Plum said, putting his hat back on his head and fanning the flies away with his hand. "I've certainly never known him to be so concerned for the lives of his men. If they made a run for the flatlands, he might lose a couple of them. But, my goodness! He and the others would get away." Plum shook his head. "No, this isn't like Caslado at all."

A rifle shot rang out below them. Jack the Spider ducked back as it sliced across the rock and spun away. "Suppose they think there's a whole army of us up here? They can't be this worried about two rifles."

"I don't know, Mr. Spider." Plum looked behind, up and around at the rugged rock land they'd crossed. "But whatever they think, let's hope they keep thinking it, until we can get a shot at Caslado." He looked back at the Spider. "After all, that's the only person we're interested in."

Jack the Spider levered another round into his rifle chamber, peeped up over the edge, and fired down among the rocks toward the spot where the last shot had come from. "Missed! Damn it!" He pushed up his hat brim, levered up another round, then before firing, sniffed toward Plum and shook his head. "Can't you do something about that god-awful smell?"

Plum fumed. "If I could, Mr. Spider, don't you suppose I already would have?"

"Well, it's making me sick," the Spider said. He rose up, fired another round, and dropped down as three rounds fired back in reply. "I've never smelled anything so rancid and bad in my whole life."

"Shut up, Spider! It's not as if I've had an opportunity to do anything about it. We're shot on water." Rance Plum took his rifle, levered up a round, rose, and fired.

Down in the rocky valley at the farthest end of the trail, Homer Corona sat his horse behind a huge split boulder and watched as two of his men moved down on foot from among a steep up-slope of rock. Beside him, Roedor sat his horse with his rifle propped on his leg. "We must soon make a break for the flatlands," Roedor said to Homer Corona. "We cannot keep on this way."

"Wait until we hear what these men have to tell us," Homer replied, waving the two young Mexicans to him. "I will not risk the lives of our men. Not for what has turned out to be nothing more than Ernesto Caslado's personal reasons." He spit and cursed under his breath.

The two men came across the trail and slid to a halt behind the split boulder. They stood winded for a second, until Homer asked them, "Well, what did you see?"

"There are only two of them, Homer," one said. "We

could not get into range, or else we would have finished them ourselves."

Homer looked surprised. "What of the big rifle? Do they have it set up so they can pick us off?"

Both men shook their dusty heads. "No," one answered, "we did not see the big rifle . . . but then, we did not get a full look at them. They are partly hidden by rock."

"But we did see something more," the other man said. "There are *Americano* soldiers coming . . . moving up from the trail out of San Paulo. They ride quickly."

Homer glanced at Roedor, then out across the flatlands to the east, then back down at the two men. "You did good. Now go, take shelter behind the rocks. Pass the word along to all the others. Roedor and I are riding out to the far edge of the flatlands. Tell all the men to be ready to move out when one of us gives you the signal."

"*Sí,* we will tell them." The two men looked from Homer to one another, then turned and slipped away.

"American soldiers?" Roedor stared at Homer, a worried look in his eyes. "Then we must make a run for it. There is no longer a question."

"I know," Homer said. "You are right. We can wait no longer. You and I will get out front and bring the men forward."

"But the big rifle," Roedor said. "If they have it, they will kill us with it when we get to the flatlands."

"Not both of us, they won't." Homer fixed a serious gaze at Roedor's eyes. "If the rifle is there, they will use it when we are out from behind cover. But they can't shoot us both at once. When one of us falls, we will know they have the big rifle. But the other will come back and take the men away through the rock land."

Roedor rubbed his sweaty face. "I do not want to die just finding out whether or not they have the big rifle. We can send another. Are you and I not more important—as leaders?"

"If we are to lead these men home, what we fight for is more important than either of us. The one who lives will know the respect of these men from now on . . . because they will see that we place their lives as important as our own. It is the only way. Be with me on this, *mi compadre*." Homer collected his horse with a snap of his reins, and the big animal stepped back and forth in place and swished its tail. "Are you ready?"

"Sante Madre," Roedor said, crossing himself and turning his eyes upward for a second. "Yes, I am ready."

When the two of them gigged their horses out from behind cover and onto the thin rocky trail, Jack the Spider rose for another shot. "They're making a move!" he said to Rance Plum. "Two of them, like bats out of hell!"

"*What?* Is it Ernesto?" Plum rose with him, his rifle going to the shoulder.

"Can't tell for all the dust," the Spider said, taking aim and pulling off a round. Beside him, Plum's rifle fired in unison.

Down on the rocky trail, Homer and Roedor kicked their horses along hard, ducking low at the sound of the rifles. Behind them, along the trail, the Mexicans rose up and returned fire, causing Plum and the Spider to drop back for a second, then rise and fire again. Homer heard the firing back and forth as they raced forward for the edge of the flatlands, two hundred yards ahead.

At the flatlands, where there was no cover near and none in sight for well over a mile, Homer stopped his horse and swung it back, facing the rocky trail. "Here is where we find out. Be brave, Roedor . . . the day will belong to one of us."

Roedor swallowed against the tightness in his throat, swinging his horse around with Homer's. He braced himself for the impact of the big rifle that would tear through him at any second. Their dust settled along the trail. Their horses stepped back and forth on nervous hooves. From the trail, the firing had lulled. Homer stood in his stirrups, his eyes dark and tense, watching, waiting.

Seconds passed. Still no fire from the big rifle. He looked at Roedor, knowing they were well out of range from any ordinary saddle rifles. "We are alive, *mi amigo*," he said, his voice low, almost reverent. "We gambled . . . and won!" From the trail, rifle fire erupted again. Roedor flinched, then realizing it was only the same rifles as before, he gave a tense smile and wiped a hand across his face. "Now, if we can get our men out without losing any of them, we will make a run to the old Spanish ruins. From there we will find Ramon Caslado's *rancho* and take shelter."

Roedor sat watching as Homer raised his large sombrero and waved it back and forth slowly in the air toward the men along the trail. "I will tell my grandchildren someday," Roedor said, "of how I once rode with you . . . a wise, bold soldier."

"We are not home yet, my friend," Homer said, still waving for the men to make their move. "But I think maybe God is with us this day, eh?"

"*Sí*, I think so," Roedor said in a low tone.

From the edge of the ridge, Plum fired once more, then glanced at the Spider as he levered another round. "That's not Ernesto Caslado, is it? The one waving?"

"I don't know, but he's too far away to shoot from here." Spider dropped back as three rifle shots spit near them and kicked bits of rock and sand.

"Well, it certainly must be," said Plum. "Who else would be giving orders?" He rose enough to see the distant rider wave his sombrero back and forth. The Spider started to fire again, down onto the fleeing men who'd mounted and began moving out from behind their rock cover. But Plum raised a gloved hand toward him, stopping him.

"Save your bullets," Plum said. "These are only Caslado's flunkies. They're worth nothing to us."

The Spider glared at him with his one good eye. "We'll have to go through them to get to him!"

"We won't get anyone, you imbecile . . . if we run out of ammunition." Plum let out a breath. "I'm wondering if perhaps we've been misled by that blasted ranger."

The Spider gave him a bemused look. "What? You mean that ole ranger that we outlasted? The one we're going to outshine? The one I said we should stick close to?" He tightened his hand around the rifle stock and drew it back. "For two cents, Plum, I'd bend this barrel over your pompous, stupid—!" The Spider's words cut short as a bullet cracked against the rock at their feet.

"Jesus!" Plum threw an arm up over his head and scooted across the rock toward the back edge as bullets popped against rock and rifle fire exploded behind them. Jack the Spider dove in alongside him. Beside them their horses pulled against their tied reins and jumped back and forth.

"They've circled us!" Plum shouted, jerking his pistol from his holster.

"They couldn't have!" Jack the Spider raced along the bank of sandy soil to where it was low enough for him to return fire. He sprang up—rifle fire spitting past him—got off three quick shots with his pistol, then dropped back down, a bewildered look on his face. "It's the damned army! They're trying to kill us!"

"What?" Plum stared back at him, wide-eyed, shaken. "For God's sake, man! Are you insane?"

At the edge of the flatlands, Homer Corona and Roedor waved the last of the men past them as Homer stood in his stirrups and looked back at the distant melee.

"What is it, Homer? What is going on?" Roedor asked, his horse stepping high-hoofed back and forth beneath him.

"I don't know," Homer said. "Can it be, the American

army is now shooting at the posse?" He turned and shook his head as if to clear it. "These are strange, unpredictable people, these gringos."

The men gathered close, their horses stepping in place in a stir of dust. "You two have saved us," a voice said. "We will never forget what you did!"

Homer turned and looked at them, gigging his horse forward among them, forming them into a line as he rode past, Roedor beside him, the two of them taking the lead. "Move out quickly," Homer said, spinning an arm and pointing out toward the east.

Back on the ridge, Plum called out at the top of his lungs above the hail of rifle fire, "Hold, your fire, please!"

"They can't hear you," the Spider shouted; and he rose and fired three more rounds at the line of soldiers spread out behind the rocks above them.

What the—? "Spider! Don't shoot back at them! For God's sake, man!"

"What?" The Spider shook his head. "I can't hear you!" He rose and fired again. Above them the rocky hillside erupted once more.

Rance Plum slumped and shook his head. In a moment the firing lulled. A young, shaky voice called down to them, "We have you outnumbered."

"We know that," the Spider yelled. "Come and get us!" He started to rise and fire.

"Spider! Don't shoot! Quit provoking them! *Please!*" Plum's voice sounded shaky, almost out of control.

"They shot at me . . . I'm shooting back," said the Spider, his one eye wide and angry. "That's just how it is."

Again the young voice called out, "Step into sight with your hands raised."

"Uh-uh," Jack the Spider said. "You step in sight with your hands raised."

"He doesn't mean that," Rance Plum shouted up to the

soldiers. He snapped his eyes over to the Spider, his pistol pointing at him. "If you don't shut up, Spider, I'll be forced to put a bullet in you! Can't you see this is all a mistake? We've got to surrender to straighten it out!"

"Then *you* surrender, Plum. I ain't going to. There's no telling what they've got in mind for us." He shook his head and tensed his gun hand, ready to reach up and fire again.

"Waaaait, Spiiider!" Plum screamed at him, his voice high and raging, nearly hysterical. The Spider stopped and stared at him. Plum calmed himself, then called out to the soldiers, "My friend is a complete idiot. May I please surrender? By myself? Before he gets us killed!"

A silence passed. "All right then," the young voice said. "Step up into sight with your hands raised."

"Gladly, sir." Plum glared at the Spider, stood up, stepped above the bank, and kept his hands high.

"Come forward now," the voice called out from behind a dead-standing cottonwood tree. Beside the tree stood a horse with an army saddle. It looked down at Plum and blew and stomped a hoof.

He moved forward, and as he did, soldiers stood up from their rock cover and swung their rifles toward him. A young freckle-faced lieutenant stepped from behind the tree with his army revolver raised. "State your name, and what your business is here, sir," he said in a military tone.

"My name?" Plum kept his hands raised. "For heaven sakes, Ernesto Caslado and his men are getting away, and you want *my* name?"

The young lieutenant took a step forward. From behind the tree, the old goat tender stepped out, saw Plum's face, and let out a short, little laugh. "Lord have mercy, looky here." He moved around and up beside the lieutenant. "Don't worry. I know this feller. He's a bounty hunter . . . same as me."

"There, you see," Plum said to the lieutenant, starting to

move back. "Now, if you don't mind, I'll be on my way." He gestured off toward the trail. "I happen to be in hot pursuit—"

"As you were, sir," the young lieutenant snapped, cocking his revolver toward Plum. Plum stopped cold. The lieutenant added in a firm tone, "This is now a military matter. I'm in charge from here on."

"Well, you've certainly gained my confidence," Plum said. "Coming up here and attacking us. Didn't anyone in San Paulo tell you we were in pursuit?"

The lieutenant looked embarrassed, started to speak, but the goat tender chuckled and cut in, "Don't get your drawers in a knot, Mr. Plum. This is the young man's first command. He thought you mighta been more escaped convicts." The goat tender shrugged. "How would he know? We just caught the two who escaped from San Paulo."

"Indeed." Plum lowered his hands, turned slightly, and waved Jack the Spider in. "See, Mr. Spider—safe to come out now. They're not going to shoot us." Then he turned back to the goat tender and said as the Spider moved forward in a cautious manner, "Did you say the two convicts from San Paulo? You mean the two *we* captured there? The ranger let them escape?"

"The ranger wasn't there. Don't know who mighta let them escape, but I caught them. I'm claiming the reward." He beamed. "I seem to have a knack for this bounty hunting. Looks like you ain't done so well yourself."

"What's he saying?" Jack the Spider asked, stepping up beside Plum and looking around at the soldiers.

"He's saying that once again we've gotten screwed out of our money. That's what he's saying!" He looked back at the goat tender. "If the ranger isn't there, where is he?"

"Miss Fannie said he lit out, searching for Ramon Caslado's place. Said he found tracks headed east. Seems to think that's where he'll find Ernesto."

"Con-*found* it!" Plum stamped the ground. He has us out here fighting these flunkies while Ernesto headed *east*? "If he and that woman think they can get away with this, they are very mistaken, sir. Very mistaken!"

"The woman's got nothing to do with it," the young lieutenant said in his schoolboy voice. "She's missing now."

Plum cocked his head to the side. "Oh? She's not with the ranger?"

"No. She left with a priest, searching for those two up in the rocks." He thumbed back toward Al Kreeger and Levon Hawkins, who'd stepped from behind a rock in shackles. A guard stood behind them with a rifle at port arms. Their clothes were tattered rags, their faces bruised and swollen. "We haven't found a trace of her."

The goat tender cut in. "Not only that—turns out the priest she's traveling with ain't a priest at all. They found one of the priests' body back near the prison. His clothes and hat were gone—his body had been mauled like some critter got a hold of him." The goat tender shook his head.

Plum looked at the Spider with a stunned expression. "You don't suppose . . . ?"

His words trailed. The Spider said, "Crazy Gravy?" Then he rubbed his forehead and added, "Lord, surely she ain't got hooked up with that monster. I knew there was something wrong about that priest. I just couldn't put my finger on it."

"Indeed, and so did I for some reason." Plum looked back at the goat tender. "Do you think that's who it is?" He pictured the priest riding across the sand flats, always there, no one challenging him.

"I can't say." The old man looked away to the east across the flatlands in the distance. "But if ya see that priest, you better shoot first and ask questions later."

"Be that as it may." Plum stepped toward the young lieutenant, an excited tone coming into his voice. "Do you have fresh horses, Lieutenant? My partner and I have to be on our way at once."

"You and your partner are riding with us," the lieutenant said. "There's too many things getting out of hand here. It's time I organize this expedition."

"Organi—?" Plum's eyebrows shot up. "We were doing fine, Lieutenant. We don't need the army down our shirts! Everybody is headed east. There must be a meeting place there. Let us go on and maybe we can salvage this mess— perhaps save that woman, if she's not already dead!"

"Easy, Plum," the old goat tender said. "We're all on the same side here. But we're gonna have to stick together."

"Stick together! Ah-ha!" Plum's gloved finger shot out at the goat tender. "I see what you're up to, old man! You think you can take Ernesto back and claim the remainder of the reward!"

"I ain't gave it no thought," the goat tender said with a crafty smile. "But since ya mentioned it, I reckon the reward is open to all comers."

"Rest assured, I plan on protesting this to the department of the army," Plum said to the lieutenant. Then he added, "Have you any experience whatsoever in this kind of work?"

"No, I do not," the lieutenant said in a high, crisp voice. "But we all start somewhere. And you're riding with us. So I trust we'll do just fine, sir."

Chapter 20

Something was out of hand, and Maria knew it. She wasn't thinking straight—or was she? Perhaps she was just tired and letting her imagination get the better of her. But ever since she'd taken up with this priest, things seemed to be on a downhill slide. Her own horse was back in San Paulo, lame, for no apparent reason. Now, after a string of events that seemed determined to separate her from the ranger, she found herself in the roughest part of the badlands, on a tired horse, making no headway at all.

What about this priest?

Throughout the night and day, she'd noticed that the farther they got from San Paulo, the more this man had changed. His demeanor, although outwardly still timid and retiring, had taken on a subtle aggressiveness that seemed to lie just beneath the surface of his every move and mannerism.

At first she thought he simply saw her tiring and that he wanted to step in to be of more help; yet she wasn't feeling that way now. He wanted to control her, or the situation . . . or perhaps both, she thought.

Easy now . . . She ran a hand over her forehead, trying to dismiss her doubts—perhaps she was seeing things that weren't there. He'd struck a low fire beneath the rock shelf overhang, and prepared tea and heated some jerked beef. When the food was prepared and they began to eat, she'd noticed something was amiss—some little thing—but she couldn't put her finger on it. Then when they'd finished eating and she'd lain down bone-tired and thrown the blanket over herself, weary though she was, she kept running it through her mind.

What had been wrong? There'd been the boiling tea. He'd handed her a cup. The jerked beef had been heated . . . And they ate . . . But what had been missing?

She let out a long breath, feeling the strain of the hard day close her eyes and send her adrift. *Yes, she was tired . . .* That had something to do with her thoughts—those strange, wary thoughts toward this holy man.

Crazy Gravy watched her in the soft glow of firelight, and to make sure she was sound asleep, he moved over to her with a short twig of mesquite and touched it lightly to her lip. She did not stir. He smiled, feeling his breath quickening. His impulse was to move in on her, swiftly with the butcher knife. But he'd waited so long, watching her, feeling her near him. It would be a shame for this to be over so quickly.

He bent down, slipped his fingers beneath the blanket into the warmth surrounding her, and moved them upward along her side, searching for the pistol she'd taken from her holster and placed there somewhere near her breast. *There now . . .* He found it and slipped it out. *Smooth as silk . . .* He smiled, looked at her, running a hand along her cheek—not quite touching her—unloaded the pistol, and slipped it back beneath the blanket. *Wasn't that easy . . . ?*

Crazy Gravy stood up and looked around the campsite, the low, dancing flames reflecting on the rock shelf above them. A peaceful place. Too peaceful, he thought. As long as he had waited to have this woman, he wanted the night to rage around them. No, this would never do. He took the butcher knife from inside his frock, looked down at her again, then hurried silently over to the path running upward around the edge of the overhang, to where he knew there would be more mesquite brush and kindling.

He recalled seeing the long, stiff branches of a downed tree lying there when he'd brought back brush for the fire. Yes, that would do just fine. A nice roaring, raging fire . . . her there in the dancing glow of it, him standing over her when she awakened. His breath quickened once more.

It took two trips up and down the foot path. On his first trip he'd brought back an armload of short, stiff branches he'd taken from the tree, chopping and slicing them off as quietly as possible in the darkness of the full moon. He stacked them near the fire and hurried back up the path. On the second trip he brought a large armful of mesquite and pitched it near the fire.

Then he waited and watched her sleep, and he breathed deep, calming his blood. After all, he had all night.

Moments later, Maria lifted her eyelids slightly at the sound of crackling mesquite brush in the raging fire. Its heat reached her beneath the blanket, yet she lay still and listened, feeling perspiration trickle down her stomach. She saw his hands come down into sight, picking up the tree limbs one and two at a time and feeding them into the already leaping flames. Then she closed her eyes. *Yes* . . . Now she knew . . . she knew.

When another moment had passed, she opened her eyes again, this time to him saying to her from close beside the fire, "Maria, wake up, Maria." The sound of his voice, low, dark, and breathless would have sent a chill through her had she not been preparing for it while the fire crackled and grew behind her.

When she turned to face him, he stood naked before tall, licking flames, the firelight streaking along the steel blade hanging from his hand. She heard a low growl, like that of a mountain cat, come from deep in his chest, his face and chest darkened by the shadow of night, while up his side the silver-orange sharpness of the firelight defined him.

"Time to wake up, Maria," he purred, low and rasping. And as he turned his face slightly and the firelight glowed upward, his eyes flashed red from within dark shadowed hollows. She gasped in spite of herself.

"You're him . . . Crazy Gravy," she said in a breathless voice.

Again, the low, rasping purr. "I've waited so long for this," he said.

"To kill me. You have done all of this in order to kill me."

A dark strange chuckle from within the shadowed face. "It's what I do, Maria."

"Oh," she said, staring up at him from beneath the blanket.

He cocked his head slightly, bemused. *Oh? Was that it? Just Oh?* Was that all she had to say? Would she just lie there? There was a resolved, almost submissive sound in her voice. It unsettled him for a second.

"You don't seem surprised, frightened? Aren't you going to fight me, Maria?" He so hoped she would, there by the raging fire. That would make it complete for him.

"I am not surprised," she said, her voice almost matter-of-fact.

What was this . . . ? He stared at her. She seemed so unmoved by him.

"I knew something was wrong when we ate," she said.

"You did?" He cocked his head a bit more, the knife blade coming up from his side and patting against his palm.

"*Sí.* You did not bless the food before we ate. What priest would fail to do this? It was stupid of you. Perhaps you are not quite the crafty, intelligent monster everybody thinks you are." She summoned all her strength into forming a calm smile. "Maybe you are nothing but a pitiful, stupid man, Crazy Gravy."

Pitiful? Stupid? Her words stung him. "Get up," he said, the knife tightening in his tense, quaking hand.

"No. I will lie here. How can I fight you? If I am to die, it will be on my own terms. I will not perform for you or show any fear."

"You have a pistol," he said, feeling the mood he had set starting to get away from him.

"*Sí*." Her hand moved beneath the blanket, then came out with the pistol hanging on her finger. He noticed her arm was bare as she pitched the pistol to the side.

"There, now it is useless for me to fight you. I have nothing; you have a knife. Are you still afraid of me? You ridiculous little murderer, you."

Afraid? Ridiculous? His head pounded with rage. He flung the knife away. "I wanted this to be different! But now . . . I'll tear you apart with my bare hands!"

"Come then," she said, rising beneath the blanket. And he did, his arms spreading wide, his fingers drawn like claws. He squalled out like a panther and sprang forward. She threw the blanket off herself, and he gasped, stunned at the sight of her, naked, her body glistening with sweat. He wanted to stop, to see her like this, but he'd come forward too quick. No stopping now . . . He'd left the ground, leaping, pouncing down at her, wanting to stop midair, unable to. His body twisted, trying to stop.

She saw his face as he hurled himself toward her, and in the glistening wild flicker of firelight, for one brief second, she could have sworn that what she saw descending to take her life was not a man at all, but some snarling creature come to devour her, some terrible predator from within her darkest nightmare.

The horses bolted sideways against their tied reins at the sound of the long scream. Then silence loomed above the licking flames. Farther beneath the rock overhang, the horses' eyes fired red and wide in the darkness. They cowered close together, hugging the rock wall, and blew and nickered and shied away.

In the middle of the moonlit night, as the ranger gazed ahead watching Samuel Burns lead the party forward across the flatlands, he was stricken by a dark and sudden sense of dread. Maria had been on his mind ever since they'd stopped to rest the horses and wait out the heat of the day. When this dark feeling struck him, he recognized it right away as a message from a long way off. Maria was back there, and she was in trouble. He knew it.

Somehow he knew she was no longer in San Paulo. It was clear to him that she was at the mercy of a madman. He was powerless to help her. If he were to turn his horse now, leave Burns and the other two, and ride flat-out back to her, it wouldn't help. Besides, other lives would be at risk if he let these two go. There was also the matter of the person who'd committed murder at Cold Creek.

His heart pleaded with him to forget all else and race back to her. *Back to where . . . ?* Yet, his duty compelled him to hold firm and move forward. *Sacrifices . . .* He had made many of them over the course of his life for the sake of duty. But, God, would she be one of them? It sickened him to think it, but whatever had happened, or was about to happen to Maria—she was on her own back there.

At the lead Samuel Burns turned in his saddle and looked back past Ernesto Caslado and JC McLawry, at the ranger who'd sat his horse still, crosswise on the trail, holding the lead rope to the extra horses in his gloved hand. In the light of a full moon, Burns saw the ranger gazing back across the badlands in the direction of San Paulo. Caslado and JC looked back too, then turned, facing Burns again as their horses moved ahead at a walk.

"Looks like our ole ranger is losing his grip," JC said in a whisper.

Burns fell back beside them and looked once more at the ranger as they stopped in the trail. JC and Ernesto still rode double, their cuffs in place, only now JC sat in front. He looked at Burns, a foot from him, and added in the same low whisper, "Won't be long, Sammy-boy. We'll all three be rolling in cash."

Burns watched the ranger for a second longer, noticing how different he'd acted since they'd rested last evening. Was JC right? Was the ranger losing his grip? Something sure bothered him. *What is it . . . ?*

"You thinking what I'm thinking, Sammy-boy?" Again JC whispered, leaning a bit closer from his saddle. "Thinking, why wait till we get to the money? Just bust a cap on him right here?"

"No." Burns gave a guarded smile. "But I'm thinking maybe it's time we do something a little extra just to make this look good . . . don't you think?"

"Like what?" JC cut a glance to the ranger twenty feet behind them. When he turned back to Burns, he heard the swipe of the pistol barrel through the air. JC had time to flinch, but not to duck; the barrel cracked across his jaw, sending him off the saddle and taking Ernesto down with him to the ground.

"Try something like that again and I'll shoot you, JC!" Burns spun his horse around, jumped down, and grabbed JC by the shoulder as the two men thrashed in the dirt. "That goes for you too!" he yelled, sinking a hard kick into Ernesto's ribs.

"Hold it!" The ranger gigged his horse forward, bringing the string of horses with him. "What's going on here?" He had the big pistol out and cocked. Dust swirled purple and fine in the moonlight.

"He made a grab for my pistol," Burns said, excited.

As Ernesto gagged and rolled into a ball, JC groaned and threw up an arm. "I didn't do—"

"Lying dog!" Burns cracked his head again and kicked him in the face before the ranger could drop from his saddle and stop him. JC lay across Caslado, blood running from the swelling cut on his forehead.

"Settle down, Sam," the ranger said, catching Burns's arm before he hit JC again. "It's over . . . let it go."

Panting, Burns staggered back a step, running his sleeve across his face. "He almost got away with it," he said in a shaky voice. "I'd just stopped beside them to look back for you, and . . . and—"

"It's all right now," the ranger said. He reached down and snatched JC by his shoulder, pulling them both to their feet. Caslado stayed bowed at the waist, a string of saliva swinging from his lips, JC staggering, half conscious. "Help me get them mounted. I think that oughta keep them settled for a while."

"These lousy buzzards," Burns hissed, holstering his pistol, reaching out, and helping the ranger shove the two men back up into the saddle. "The most sorry day in my life was when I listened to them. Look what it's gotten me. Look what it's brought me to."

The battered men slumped in the saddle. The ranger picked up the reins and wrapped them around the saddle horn in front of JC. "But you didn't have to listen to them, Sam," he said to Burns.

"I know." Burns let out a breath. "I'm not blaming them. I did it myself. It just makes me sick looking at them, knowing how I let them make a fool of me."

The ranger stepped back up into his saddle. "Don't let it break you, Sam. Some men go their whole lives, being made fools of a little at a time. In your case you just happen to catch the whole load all at once." He settled and ran a gloved hand along the scar on his cheek. "However this turns out for you, be a man about it . . . do what's right from now on." Then he tipped back his sombrero and looked in the direction of San Paulo.

Burns had stepped up into his saddle. He settled and let out a breath. "Just how bad do you suppose it will go for me once we get back?"

"Now ain't the time to think about it." The ranger narrowed a gaze at him in the moonlight. "It might make you come to some wrong decisions." He reached out, slapped the prisoners' horse on the rump, and fell in behind it, leading the string. Burns sat still for a second, then gigged his horse forward. And they rode on another hour, to the end of the flatlands, where the land turned rough and steep, up into the maze of jagged rock.

Before daylight, when they had stopped long enough to switch saddles onto fresh horses, Burns stood before the two prisoners with his rifle across his chest, while the ranger stood fifteen feet away, checking his white barb. To Ernesto, Burns whispered, "It's time you let him know where we're headed. It'll be quicker than tracking them across rock."

Ernesto nodded, but before Burns turned away, JC whispered through his swollen jaw, "Not so fast, Sammy-boy. You've beat the living hell out of me, you know."

Burns looked into his eyes. "That's right, and it looked real good to him." He gestured a nod toward the ranger. "You've got to trust me—think about the money. We're *amigos* here, aren't we?"

"He is right," Ernesto whispered, "so shut up, and let him handle this." He gigged JC in his ribs before he could any more.

The ranger heard the three of them whispering, although he couldn't make out the words. When he rose from checking the white barb's hooves, he turned, facing them. "Caslado says he wants to make a deal with you," Burns said. "It might be worth listening to."

"Oh? A deal?" The ranger looked a bit surprised, past

Burns and at Ernesto Caslado. "I thought you had nothing more to tell me, Ernie." He looked back and forth among the three of them, then said to Ernesto, "Whatever you've got to say, get it said. We've got a long morning ahead of us."

"All right," Caslado said, "here is the deal. If you will find a way to uncuff me from this stinking pig, I will tell you where my brother is headed. It will save you much time." He jutted his chin and fell silent, waiting for an answer.

The ranger looked from one to the other of them. What had they been whispering about? What was going on here? Was Burns up to something? He rubbed his chin, then asked, "What do you think, Sam? Think we can trust these two without keeping them chained together?"

Burns hedged a bit. "It's your decision. I don't trust either of them as far as I can spit." He shot the two men a look of disdain. "Cuffed or not, though, if they make a wrong move, you can trust me to put a bullet in them . . . you've got my word on that."

His word? Trust . . . The ranger had heard too many people give their word lately . . . usually right before they stabbed one another in the back. His mind flashed on the madman, Crazy Gravy, in the guise of a priest. *Trust? Oh, Maria. What now . . . ?* He started to think once more of her back there somewhere on the badlands . . . in the grasp of a madman, and what the man was capable of doing to her. He shook his head to clear the dark picture. This was not the time to think of her. He couldn't allow it.

Eyeing Burns, the ranger reached into his pocket and drew out the key to the shackles. Ernesto stifled a slight smile. This kid—Sammy-boy Burns—was setting things up just fine, Ernesto thought.

"He's had that key on him all along," JC grumbled.

"Drop their cuffs, Sam," the ranger said, his eyes going deep into Burns's as he pitched him the key. Burns's gaze did not waver. He caught the key, stepped over, and unlocked the cuffs. He stepped back with his rifle on the two men as they rubbed their wrists.

"Now then, Ernie," the ranger said, "where are they headed?"

Ernesto glanced across their faces, still rubbing his wrists, taking note of how tense and ready Burns stood with the rifle pointed at them. "They are going to the old Spanish ruins. There, now I have told you." He spit, as if to cleanse a bitterness from his mouth.

Burns spoke over his shoulder to the ranger. "Do you know where it's at?"

"Yep, I know where it's at," the ranger said, still chasing the dark picture of Maria and Crazy Gravy from his mind. "And I know a shortcut from here. Maybe we'll wrap this up sooner than I expected."

Facing Caslado and JC without the ranger seeing him, Burns smiled at them. "That will suit me fine," he said. "The sooner we wrap this up, the better." His finger slipped away from the trigger. He stepped back, motioning them to the horses. "Come on, let's go."

The ranger noticed that for just a second, as they moved away, Burns had let down his guard and almost turned his back on them. Was that a simple mistake on Burns's part? Or, was there nothing for him to fear of these men anymore. What was going on inside Burns's head. *One more deal with the devil?* He hoped not, but he'd have to wait and see. The ranger finished with his horse, stepped up into the saddle, put the thoughts of Maria out of his mind, and moved forward onto the narrow trail.

Chapter 21

When they had come to a fork in the rock trail, the ranger took the lead and pointed them upward through a deep rock canyon until the land fell away. Before them lay a slim natural rock bridge, one horse wide, with a drop of over two hundred feet into a valley of brush and stone. Daylight seeped over the peaks of jagged rock in a silver mist and swirled before them. "This . . . this is the shortcut?" Burns swallowed the dryness in his throat, staring down at the pointed tops of juniper trees below them.

"It's not a good place for a skittish horse," the ranger said. "But it gets us to the Spanish ruins an hour quicker than the way we were going." He looked at Burns. "Are you up to it, Sam?"

Burns lifted his concerned gaze from the deep drop of thin air and looked out across the seventy- or eighty-foot stretch of trail. He nodded. "How about these two? How do we handle them?"

"I cover you while you cross with one. You cover me while I bring the other." The ranger looked at Ernesto and JC. "They ain't likely to get feisty out there. Are you, boys?"

Ernesto just looked away without answering, but JC had been staring wide-eyed down into the deep valley. "You're gonna kill us all, is what you're gonna do! I'm not going! You can shoot me right here." The two of them were no longer cuffed together, but still riding double, JC in front.

The ranger nodded, then said in a calm voice, "All right then. Go ahead and shoot him, Sam."

"What?" Burns's eyes widened a bit.

"Yeah," the ranger said, "just put one bullet through his head, about here." He tapped a gloved finger on his forehead and watched Burns for a reaction.

Burns hesitated for a second, then lifted his pistol from his holster. "Well . . ."

"Now hold on! Damn it!" JC fidgeted in his saddle. "You can't shoot me like a dog."

"Sure we can," the ranger said. "Where'd you ever get the notion that we can't?" He looked back at Burns and nodded, "Go ahead, shoot him, Sam. Let's get moving."

"Wait," Ernesto cut in, sitting behind JC. "Let me move first. I don't want to get shot over this idiot."

"I'll go! I'll go!" JC raised a shaky hand toward Burns, whose pistol pointed at his belly from six feet away.

The ranger nodded again. "Then get off the horse and start walking. Burns, take him across. I've got you covered. If he acts up, bump him off the edge."

The ranger drew his big pistol and stepped down, motioning Caslado over beside him. "Have a seat, Ernie," he said, gesturing his pistol barrel toward the ground. He stood behind him, holding the reins to their two horses and the lead rope to the four-horse string; and with his pistol half pointed down at the top of Ernesto's head in front of him, they watched as JC stepped out, his legs a bit shaky on the narrow rock bridge.

Burns walked slowly behind him, leading his horse by its reins, speaking over his shoulder to it in a soothing voice. The horse grumbled under its breath, nickered low and snorted, moving forward one slow hoof at a time, the sound of its steel shoes clopping against the rock in the silence of breaking dawn. The ranger watched them move away.

As soon as JC's feet stepped onto wider ground, he

turned, his hands slightly raised, and whispered quickly to
Burns, "Listen to me, Sammy-boy, while Ernesto can't hear
us. As soon as we get the money? As soon as you kill that
ranger? If you're smart, you'll kill Caslado too." He looked
past Burns to the other side of the bridge, where the ranger
stood loosening the lead rope from the four-horse string.
Caslado still sat on the ground.

"I hear you," Burns said with a slight smile, pushing him
back a step, his pistol pointed at JC's stomach. "A two-way
split beats a three any day."

"Yeeeah!" JC said, grinning, his voice low. "You're thinking more like me every day."

"I know," Burns said. He shot a glance across the rock
bridge toward the ranger, then back to JC. "Now I got to
rough you up a little more, just to look good."

"No wait—" He threw his hands out to protect himself.
But too late.

Burns had already dropped back a step and snapped a
hard kick into JC's groin. JC jackknifed forward. Burns
brought the pistol down from a high arc and cracked him
across his back. JC crumpled to the ground.

"What's the problem over there?" the ranger called out,
turning from the horses, his pistol up and cocked.

"No problem. He can't seem to keep his hands to himself," Burns called out, his voice ringing along the deep
canyon. He stood a boot on JC's back, JC groaning beneath
him. Then he lowered his voice down to JC. "How'd that
look, you think?"

JC's staggered words sounded as if they'd been squeezed
through a straw. "That's . . . good, kid. Real good."

Caslado sat watching from the other side. Now that his
hands weren't cuffed, he had to figure a way to get free from
all of them. He thought about the money and—more important now—how good he would feel once he lifted Ramon up

on the blade of a knife and watched his eyes go blank on him.

He turned toward the ranger and looked him up and down. He could handle the ranger, guns, knives, or bare-handed. But he wouldn't think about that. That would be Burns's job when the time came. Then he would kill Burns and that double-crossing pig, JC. And flee this country a wealthy man, never looking back. Yes, that was what he would do.

"Put it out of your mind, Ernie," the ranger said, as if reading his thoughts. "You're not going anywhere but back to prison." He'd loosened the lead rope from each of the four spare horses. Now with a slap of a gloved hand on their dusty rumps, he set them free back along the thin trail.

The horse JC and Caslado rode started to turn and bolt away with the others, but the ranger caught its reins and held it. With it and his white barb, he turned to Caslado. "I'm going to trust you to lead your horse across. Get stupid on me, and I'll kill you."

"I will not get stupid on you." Caslado stood up, grinning, and dusted the seat of his trousers. "It is worth waiting around here just to see how badly you die, old man."

"Fair enough," the ranger said. Then he reached into his vest pocket and took out the broken spur rowel. "While you're in a good mood, here's something for you to think about till we get to the ruins." He flipped the rowel to him. Ernest caught it, stared at it, and squeezed it tight in his hand.

"Oh? And what is this supposed to do, make me feel grateful to you?" He shook his closed fist at the ranger. "This changes nothing. You are still a pig of a gringo law-man. For this and this alone . . . I would kill you without a second thought."

"I know. Just thought you ought to hold onto it. A man

needs to know what it is he lives for . . . or dies for, in case he has to make a quick decision. Don't you think so, Ernie?"

"I see what you do," Caslado said. "You play with a person's mind. But not mine, you don't." Ernesto snatched the reins the ranger held out for him, turned, and walked the horse out across the narrow bridge.

Once they reached the other side, Burns took his boot off JC's back and stepped back with his pistol on Caslado. Then he said to the ranger, "You turned the extra horses loose?"

"Yep. They did what we wanted them to do. They got us here in a hurry. It would have been a risky business crossing them. We're only an hour's ride from the Spanish ruins now. The way I figure, we've gotten a jump on Ramon and his men. They'll be getting there about the same time we do. From here on we'll have to ride quiet and keep our heads low."

He reached down, took JC by the shoulders, and raised him to his feet. "You better quit testing Sam here, or he'll have you beat to death before you get back to prison."

"I . . . I will," JC said, his breath and voice still strained. "You'll get no more problems from me . . . that's a promise." He shot Burns a glance. The ranger caught it, but turned as if he hadn't seen a look of some sort pass between them.

"How are we going to play it, once we get to the ruins?" Burns asked.

The ranger looked at him for a second, then said, "Let's just wait and see what we've got." He looked from one to the other of them, then stepped up on his horse. "See what the smell of big money does to everybody's attitude." He backed his white barb back a step and stared down at the three of them.

Behind them, at the eastern edge of the flatlands, Rance Plum turned his tired horse and waited as Jack the Spider and the old goat tender came sliding to a halt beside him. They'd ridden hard, straight east through the night, the Mexicans' tracks never breaking off in any other direction.

"They knew exactly where they were going," Plum said, looking all around. "They're headed up to the old Spanish ruins. I'd bet on it. They're worried about their horses—they need to hole up and rest them, or come up with some fresh ones somehow."

Behind them, three hundred yards, the army patrol trailed. The goat tender stood in his stirrups and waved his hat back and forth to them. Plum shook his head. "We'll never get anywhere waiting for those children." He snapped his gaze back to the old goat tender. "It's time you made up your mind. Do you want to be a bounty hunter? Or do you want to stay back here and nursemaid a bunch of greenhorn soldiers?"

The goat tender sucked air through his teeth. "I can't just leave them high and dry." Throughout the night he'd seen that the soldiers were only slowing them down. He rubbed his jaw, looking back at them. A wide-brimmed cavalry hat lifted up and spun away in their rise of dust.

"Nor can you continue to hold us back and allow Ernesto Caslado to get away!" Plum raised a finger. "And for all we know, that poor woman could be right around the next turn—Crazy Gravy ready to have her for breakfast any moment, sir!"

"Dang it. I sure had my heart set on more reward money," the goat tender said, shaking his head.

Plum looked at the Spider, then said to the goat tender, "If the money is all you're worried about . . . let the two of us slip ahead and shake loose of these soldiers. They can't surprise anyone—you can see their dust for five miles! Once we get Caslado, we'll share the reward with you."

The goat tender squinted and scratched his head up under his hat brim. "How do I know you will?"

"How do you know? My goodness, man"—Plum shrugged his shoulders with his gloved hands spread—"you have my word on it! What more can you ask?"

"Well . . . I don't know."

"Listen to him, old man," the Spider said. "What chance you think them kids has got at taking Caslado? Once we get where they're going, we're going to have to sneak up and catch them by surprise. Think that shave-tailed lieutenant has enough sense to do it?"

"What makes you think you two can handle all of Caslado's men?" the old goat tender asked, then looked back and forth between them.

"Because, sir," Plum cut in, his gloved finger in the air, "we are professionals."

"So what's it going to be?" the Spider asked. "You want a part of the money or not?"

The goat tender let out a breath. "All right, get on up in the rocks and head left at the fork in the trail. It'll shortcut ya by a few miles. I'll lead these boys on, the long way . . . down through the canyon."

"Wise decision, sir," Plum said. Then he snapped his horse around and headed deeper up onto the rock trail, the Spider close behind him. When they'd moved out of sight among the rocks, the Spider said as they climbed upward, "I don't like the idea of your cutting him in on the reward without asking me."

"Please, Mr. Spider. Use your head for once! Do you suppose we're actually going to cut him in? After all the trouble we've been through?"

"But you gave him your word, Plum."

"Oh yes, *that* . . ." Plum smiled and pushed his horse forward.

Chapter 22

"What do you think of my shortcut now, Sam?" the ranger asked Burns in a quiet voice, the two of them lying at the edge of the cliff less than fifty yards above the old Spanish ruins. "Looks like they beat us here by minutes." Below them, Ramon and his men stood around a large rock in the open, sand-swept remains of a crumbled adobe courtyard. Short, broken adobe walls encircled them.

The ranger scooted back a couple of feet and began loading the big rifle he'd taken from his saddle scabbard. He looked up, judging the sun that now shone in bright golden streaks from the eastern horizon. Behind them a few feet, Ernesto Caslado and JC stood shackled once more, the chain between them looped over the branch of a scrub oak. Either one could have climbed up and over the limb, but for now, the ranger had a close eye on them. Either of them could have called out to Ramon and his men, but the ranger knew they wouldn't. Not yet anyway.

"You're going to use the big rifle? This close?" Burns looked at the ranger as the ranger ran his bandanna along the barrel and across the scope.

"No. This is just in case Ramon makes a run for it while his men put up a fight. Otherwise, we'll do this job with pistols."

"But there's so many of them," Burns said, swallowing, gazing down at the men. They stood there, some mounted and some on foot, all of them gathered around and staring at the large rock as if it were some holy object.

"Yeah, but we'll change all that if they give us any trouble. The only one I want is Ramon Caslado. If they give him up, they're free to go."

Burns shook his head. "I don't think they'll give him up."

"Neither do I. But you can always hope, can't you?"

Burns just looked at him.

Below them in the ruins, Ramon turned to the man beside him and said, "There's a foot of sand around it. We will never turn it over until we first free it up." He snapped his fingers at the men. "Quickly . . . dig the sand away."

"Maybe we shoulda brought Ernesto with us," said Earl Jaffe. "In case he was lying."

"He was not lying. My brother is not that smart. He trusted me when he told me." Ramon shook his head, a faint, tight smile on his lips, and added, "He is a fool, my brother, Ernesto. I almost feel sorry for him." He watched as most of the men fell to their knees and scraped away at the sand in a flurry of dust.

Earl Jaffe grinned, running a finger beneath his long, dirty nose. "I always did say, it's a dog-eat-dog world. A man ain't got a taste for dog . . . he's gonna starve to death."

Ramon looked at him with disdain and had started to say something when a voice from the cliff behind them called out. "Ramon Caslado, you're under arrest for murder—two counts of it."

Ramon spun and looked up toward the voice, squinting at the wavering figure in the glitter of sunlight. Beside him, Earl Jaffe did the same, stepping away to the side, visoring his hand at the brim of his hat. Behind them the men stopped scraping the sand and stood up. Ramon took a step forward, trying to get a clear view before drawing one of his crossed pistols from the holster on his stomach. "What? Who is there? The ranger? The one I've heard so much about?"

"It's me all right," the ranger shouted. "Now lift them pistols, pitch them in the dirt, and give yourself up. It'll save your men's lives."

On the ground beside the ranger, Samuel Burns grimaced and lay closer to the ground. Behind them, at the scrub oak, Ernesto looked at JC with a stunned expression. "The ranger has lost his mind! He is loco!"

Ramon shot a glance over his shoulder. "Keep digging," he said to the men. As he spoke, he stepped sideways, closer toward the low, crumbling adobe walls for cover if he could make a jump to it. "The murders at Cold Creek? Is this the ones you speak of?"

"Good guess, Ramon," the ranger called down to him. "You got to answer for that young woman and her father."

"But I did not kill them, ranger." He moved a step closer to the crumbled wall. "That was one of my men . . . and he is dead now."

"Take another step toward cover, and I'll put a bullet in your leg," the ranger said.

Ramon stopped short, feeling sweat gather at his hat brim and across his forehead. Again he glanced back and said to the men, some of them already moving for cover themselves, "Keep digging as I told you to do, you fools! There is only one of him. What can he do against all of us?" Yet even as he said it, he felt dryness tighten in his throat.

"Wrong, Ramon. I got a deputy with me . . . got your brother, Ernesto too. Found him chained in your barn. He's real unhappy with you. Says he wants to cut your heart out. Best give up now. Keep me from killing off your men."

Behind Ramon the men looked back and forth at one another. "Is he serious?" one whispered.

"Sounds like it," another replied.

"My men will do as I tell them," Ramon called out. "And my brother can go to hell." None of the men were digging now . . . all of them shying away, a step at a time, looking for cover. Earl Jaffe had managed to get closer to the large rock. He'd leap behind it any second.

Ernesto laughed long and loud from beneath the limb of the scrub oak. "Don't listen to this *loco* ranger, Ramon," he yelled. "Be an *hombre*! Take the money! With my blessing, you pig! Go, get it! Now!"

"Ernesto," Ramon called out, "you make me sorry I did not cut your throat!" As he spoke, his hand went up to the butt of one of his crossed pistols. He took a step sideways.

"Big mistake, Ramon," the ranger called down.

Even as he heard the shot from the ranger's big pistol, Earl Jaffe made his move, jumping behind the large rock as Ramon flipped backward and landed in a flurry of dust. *Damn all this!* Let 'em all kill each other as far as he was concerned. Earl Jaffe flattened for a second behind the rock, then crawled up against it, shots from the men around him exploding up toward the cliff where the ranger stood crouched, firing back. Ramon rolled back and forth in the sand, blood spurting from the hole in his leg.

On his fifth shot, the ranger dropped down, thumbing cartridges from his belt and reloading, then glancing back at Ernesto and JC still chained to the scrub oak. Burns started up, but the ranger held him down as shots whistled past the edge of the cliff. "Stay put," the ranger said. "Keep an eye on the prisoners."

Down in the courtyard behind the rock, Earl Jaffe turned his back against the rock, braced down, and shoved with all his weight against it. While they shot hell out of one another, why couldn't he just tip the rock, get the money, and light out of here? Well, he could. He strained and grunted and felt the rock shift forward. He squatted deeper and pushed harder. *Damn right, he'd get it!*

Ramon had crawled across the sand to cover behind the stub of a broken adobe wall. He saw the ranger getting back up and drew a bead on him. The ranger had risen to fire, but seeing the rock tip forward, a quick glance at Ernesto showed him grinning, a strange glint in his eyes. Burns had started up beside him, but the ranger felt a chill down his back and dropped flat, grabbing Burns on his way. "Cover up!" he yelled.

Pushing the rock, feeling it ready to fall forward this time, Earl Jaffe heard the sound of a sharp, metallic click from the gap beneath it. *What the—?* He caught a glimpse of a short metal plunger attached to a dusty bundle of dynamite sticks. The plunger stuck for a second, then sprang up against the cap. *Oh, God!*

The explosion ripped high and wide.

Samuel Burns felt the flat earth beneath his chest rumble and jar, as it seemed to rise for a moment, then crash down hard. He saw parts of Earl Jaffe and large pieces of rock and earth swirl upward in the air and fall toward him. Burns covered his head with his forearms.

Even in the cloud of dust and debris as the explosion still resounded, Ernesto called out, "When I set a trap, it lasts forever!"

The ranger coughed and fanned the dust with his sombrero; when he looked back at the scrub oak, Ernesto and JC had disappeared. Now this, he hadn't counted on. He looked to where the horses were tied, twenty feet away. "Come on, Sam, let's get moving."

They ran to the horses, scanning the brush for JC and Ernesto. "They can't be far," Burns said. Behind them the smoke and dust from the explosion hung in the air.

"Let's get down there," the ranger said. "If the money's down there somewhere . . . Ernesto won't be far from it."

At the edge of what was left of the crumbling adobe walls, the ranger and Burns stood ten feet apart with their reins and their pistols in their hands. Dust still hung and drifted in the air, and the ranger coughed a bit and fanned his sombrero before him. The dead lay tossed about like rag dolls thrown from an angry heaven. Somewhere farther back inside the sprawling maze of roofless adobe walls, the ranger and Burns heard a scraping sound.

"Ernesto, you and JC get on out here," the ranger said. "This little explosion doesn't change a thing. I'm still taking you back." The scraping sound stopped for a second, then started again.

A weak voice came from behind a low wall covered with loose dirt and rock. "My brother, Ernesto, is still alive . . . ?"

The ranger and Burns swung toward the voice with their pistols pointed. The ranger called over the wall, fifteen feet away. "Ramon, is that you?"

"*Sí* . . . I am alive. Where is my brother?"

"He's here somewhere," the ranger said into the dust.

"Then he . . . is not dead?"

"No, he's escaped . . . but not for long." The ranger's voice turned louder as his eyes searched the drifting dust. "Hear me, Ernesto? JC? Now's a good time for us to settle accounts. Come on out."

"If he . . . is alive, he will kill me." A pause, then, "I want to surrender," Ramon called out. "See, here is my gun." A pistol dropped out from behind the wall.

"Sorry, Ramon," the ranger said. "You had your chance. You should have surrendered when I asked you to. Now I've completely changed my mind about it."

Burns looked at the ranger with a curious expression on his dust-streaked face. He whispered, "Aren't you gonna let him give himself up?"

"In a minute," the ranger said.

"No, please. I am coming out now," Ramon said. "I am bleeding, bad." His dirty, bloody face peeped around the edge of the wall, low to the ground, one dirty hand raised above his head.

"I said *no*." The ranger's big pistol bucked in his hand. A chunk of adobe block flew into the air. Ramon ducked back out of sight. "I don't care if you bleed to death. You're not surrendering to me, Ramon. Not unless you tell me you killed those people at Cold Creek."

"I told you, ranger . . . the man who killed them is dead! He died shortly afterward!" Ramon's voice grew stronger for a second. "Now take me prisoner. Charge me with it. Take me before the judge. You must! It is my right!" He started to scoot out again, his boot venturing out first. The ranger took note of the fancy silver spurs on his boot, then drove him back with another shot, this one kicking dirt up around his boot toe. His boot jerked back.

"You hearing any of this, Ernesto," the ranger called out through the dust. "Ramon has decided to throw himself on the mercy of the court. Claims he didn't kill those people . . . that poor young woman, that little unborn baby. You believe him? Because I don't. Now come on out here. Maybe you'll have better luck getting him to answer for them." The scraping sound stopped again. "Get him to tell you where he got these fancy silver spurs he's wearing."

Back in the maze of adobe walls, Ernesto had heard the ranger's words, and he'd stopped scraping the sandy earth from beneath the old remains of a stone hearth. "What?" JC looked at him, then over his shoulder toward the sound of voices. "Forget about them, Ernesto . . . dig up the money!"

"Shut up and listen," Ernesto said. In one hand he held a piece of rock he'd picked up. His plan had been to crack JC's skull with it, get the money, and go, dragging JC with him until he could free himself of the cuffs.

With their hands still shackled together, JC couldn't dig unless they worked together. He shook the chain between them. "Come on, *amigo*! Dig!" Inside his shirt JC had a large knife he'd snatched from one of the dead men as they'd scrambled through the dust. Once the money was in his hands, his intent was to plunge the big knife into Ernesto's chest, cut his hand off at the wrist, and leave him.

From the front courtyard, Ernesto heard his brother, Ramon, say to the ranger, "I don't know what you are talking about! I won these in a card game from one of my men . . . a long time ago! Long before Cold Creek. Now let me surrender, please! I have lost too much blood!"

"I don't think so," the ranger said. As Ramon slipped forward again, the big pistol bucked once more, sending up a spray of dirt and shattered rock. "I know you killed those people, and you broke your rowel off into that poor woman's face. Admit it, Ramon! Admit it loud and clear to me. Then we'll patch you up and take you back for a nice clean trial."

Burns stood stunned, his pistol hanging in his hand, staring at the ranger. *What was this?*

"The man I won these spurs from," Ramon said. "He . . . he did it. I swear to you—"

"No, Ramon, not good enough!" the ranger raged. "Spill it now. It wasn't somebody else. It wasn't even somebody acting under your orders. It was you, Ramon, you personally! We both know it!" The ranger fired another round, this one spinning off above Ramon's head, where he'd come close to the edge of the wall.

Back in the ruins, JC tugged the chain again. "Come on, Ernesto, help me here!" But Ernesto stood staring toward the sound of the voices, a glazed look on his face. The rock fell from his hand. He yanked the chain so hard, JC almost fell to the ground. *Damn this!* JC stared up at him, wiping a hand across his mouth. He'd had it with Ernesto Caslado!

"All right, all right," Ramon sobbed from the front of the ruins. "You know I did it! What do you want from me?"

Ernesto jerked JC along and started toward the sound of their voices like a man in a trance. "Wait, Ernesto! The money!" JC pleaded one last time.

"Just needed to hear you say it, Ramon," the ranger's voice resounded back along the adobe walls.

"Damn the money. I will kill Ramon even as the ranger blows us to pieces." Caslado dragged JC along.

What? Blows us to pieces! Us!!! JC shot his hand inside his shirt and around the knife handle . . .

"Now crawl out here, Ramon," the ranger said, "and stand real quiet." He raised his voice and added, "Did you hear that, Ernesto? Brother Ramon, making a little confession here. Come on out and hear it for yourself." Back in the ruins, he heard the sound of a struggle, a muffled yell, followed by silence. Ramon stood before him now, five feet away, stooping slightly on his wounded leg, his hands raised.

The ranger listened for a second, staring into the thick standing dust farther back in the ruins. He raised a cautious hand and fanned Burns farther to the side. "Be ready," he whispered. He waited with his big pistol poised, cocked, and pointed.

"You . . . have brought me . . . to this, ranger," Ernesto Caslado said, moving forward out of the swirl of dust. The handle of the big knife rode high on his chest, rising and falling with heaving breath, blood pumping with each beat of his heart. His right hand had been severed off at the wrist and blood poured steady and dark into the dirt at his feet. In his left hand he carried a one-shot derringer he'd lifted from one of the bodies, and he raised it slowly toward the ranger.

"Decision time, Ernie," the ranger said. He took no regard of the derringer pointed at him as he uncocked the big pistol, broke it down, thumbed four bullets from his belt, and began replacing the spent cartridges. "I figure that single bullet will be the last one you ever fire. Better make it meaningful."

Back in the ruins, JC scrambled through the dirt, searching among the dead for a pistol, a rifle, a knife, anything. *Damn it!* He turned, swinging the chain still on his wrist, Ernesto's severed fist somehow still dangling in the steel cuff. *All right now, steady here . . . still some time left . . . get the money!* He scrambled back to the stone hearth, scratching the dirt away with his fingertips.

Out front Ernesto rocked on his heels, then caught himself, and said in a failing voice, "I do not know . . . how much of this you planned . . . or how much is happenstance, ranger. Perhaps, it is all . . . just luck."

"Ernesto," Ramon sobbed, "don't kill me, not your own brother. I only did what I did for the money . . . don't you see? But now it is yours again, as it should be. I want you to have it, all of it." As he spoke, Ernesto moved close to him, the pistol turning from the ranger now and pointing at Ramon's head.

"For the . . . money, eh?" Ernesto tried to smile, but it wouldn't work for him. The ranger stood still, watching. With the derringer in his palm, Ernesto reached up, wrapped his hand around the handle of the knife, and, letting out a short grunt, yanked it from his chest. He glanced at the ranger. "*Sí*. My last shot must be meaningful." And as he turned back to Ramon, the blade came around in the palm of Ernesto's hand. He opened Ramon's throat and watched him sink to his knees, trying to stay the flow of blood with his dirty hands.

The ranger winced and tensed, his pistol ready to come up cocked. There was still that one bullet in the derringer. But Ernesto opened his mouth wide—"Meaningful, eh?"—turned the tip of the barrel into it, and pulled the trigger. His cheeks puffed for a second, orange flame and powder smoke streaming through the cracks between his teeth. Then he collapsed straight and toppled over against his dead brother, the two of them bleeding into the sandy earth.

The ranger's voice was low and quiet as he turned to Burns, who stood stunned, staring at the bodies, his pistol hanging from his fingertips. "Ernesto knew all along it was Ramon who killed his woman and child. He just couldn't

abide it—had to hear it from his brother's lips." He gestured
his big pistol over the ruins—the dead, the dust, and the silence. "It took all this to set it straight. Life's strange, ain't
it, Sam?"

Life's strange? Burns shook his head, batting his eyes. He
swallowed, coughed on dust, then said, "What did Ernesto
mean, about whether you planned this?"

"What?" The ranger cocked his head to the side.

"You know . . . about, was it happenstance, or luck?"
Burns seemed to need an answer right then and there for
some reason.

"Luck? Happenstance? Ain't they the same?" The ranger
shrugged and whispered in a soft tone, "I wouldn't know.
I'm not a superstitious man." He stepped forward and motioned Burns along with him. "Now let's go get JC. He's
back there right now, driving himself nuts . . . looking for
that money. He still thinks he's got an ace in the hole. I almost hate to disappoint him."

Burns stepped forward behind him, his pistol righting itself in his hand, his mind still a-spin with what had happened. "How do you know what he's thinking? How do you
know stuff like this?" He looked once more at the two bodies. "Did you know about the rock being a trap? I mean, you
told me to cover up before it even went off."

The ranger glanced back at him, lying to him with a
straight face. "Sure, I knew it. Think I'd come all this way
without an idea of how things were going to go?" They
moved on through the swirling dust, deeper into the ruins.
The ranger stooped a bit with his pistol half raised before
him, Burns right behind with his gun up now, the barrel hov-
ering close to the ranger's back.

Chapter 23

"What on earth was that?" Rance Plum and Jack the Spider heard the explosion and jerked their horses to a halt. They sat staring at the rise of smoke a mile ahead. Plum's horse shied back a step, but he checked it down. Flies circled his foul-smelling trouser leg, and he kicked at them to shoo them away.

"I'm not sure," the Spider said, looking a bit in awe, "but it sounded like dynamite." His one good eye followed the smoke upward and to the side as it began its slow drift on an upper breeze. "Looks like it mighta come from the old Spanish ruins."

"Dynamite . . . ?" Plum studied the smoke for a second as if dumbfounded, then his eyebrows rose as if stricken by a sudden realization. "It's that blasted ranger. I'd bet on it!" He gigged his horse forward. "If he's gotten there and blown Ernesto Caslado to pieces somehow, I swear I'll kill him! I will not be beaten out of that reward money!"

"Take it easy, Plum," the Spider cautioned. "Don't get all stoked up. Let's not go charging in till we see what we're charging into." He heeled his horse forward beside Plum, and they moved on through the last narrow pass toward the ruins. Smoke drifted high and black along the rim of the canyon.

"Don't tell me to take it easy!" Plum shot the Spider a hateful glare. "I think I'm more than capable of seeing what we're charging into! That ranger has played us both like a couple of fine-tuned fiddles—and I'm sick of it! I utterly loathe and despise him!"

"See what I mean about you?" The Spider returned the hateful glare. "Don't go acting like a damn fool."

"Acting a damn fool, am I?" Plum raised a dusty gloved finger. "Unlike yourself, it so happens that I am one of those rare individuals who has a keen inner sense of danger—a nose for it, you might say." He raised his chin a bit, riding on. "Damn fool indeed!" he huffed.

"*Shiiiit.*" Jack the Spider glanced down at Plum's fly-circled boot and trouser. "All you've got is a nose for sour mule guts."

"Oh? Do you think so? Well, let me tell you something, Mr. Spider . . ."

Above them on their left, up in the rocks and crevices, Homer Corona's men lay in wait. In perfect ambush position, they had weapons ready, watching, tensed, some of them already sighting their rifles down on the two riders. They switched their glance back and forth from the riders below to Homer and Roedor, who sat higher up, partly hidden by a large split boulder.

"Give the signal," Roedor whispered, "Stop these two gringo fools once and for all."

Homer crouched with an arm raised, ready to drop it, but for now keeping his riflemen at bay. "No," he replied in a whisper. "Only if they spot us and fire on us. Otherwise, we let them pass through. If the army hears our gunfire, they will know where we are."

Three miles back Homer and his men had looked down from a rock perch and seen the army patrol moving along the canyon floor. They'd seen the old goat tender fall back, then turn around, leaving the patrol and heading in the opposite direction. Any moment now he would be coming through this same pass.

Roedor let go a tense breath, watching Plum and the Spider near the other end of the deep canyon. He noted how they hadn't even looked up, but instead seemed to be arguing back and forth about something. "I think you are right, Homer. Perhaps these two are too stupid to waste our bullets on. They did not have the sense to look up here!"

"*Sí*. They are too busy quarreling to notice us." Homer remained poised until the riders left the canyon, then he lowered his hand slowly. The men relaxed with their rifles. "We do not want to kill anyone unless we have to. These people are not our enemies, whether they know it or not. We only want to get our men home safely. They do not deserve to die for a dirty pig like Ernesto Caslado."

"Again you are right. No good will come of us fighting these gringos unless it is forced upon us," Roedor said, looking around at the tired, ragged, dirty men scattered into position among the rocks. He shook his head, adding, "No good has come out of this whole business."

"But have hope. God is still with us," Homer said, making the sign of the cross on his chest. "At least fate has seen fit to give four fresh horses." As they'd come down the trail toward the stone bridge, the four horses the ranger had cut loose came trotting down into their midst. The horses were tired, but not nearly as much as their own.

"It is so," Roedor said. "The horses were a sign, I think. A sign that we must keep faith, and not give up, no matter what the odds."

Homer only nodded and looked away for a moment, then said, "We are learning these things together, you and I. It is a test—at the end of it we will be much wiser, eh?"

"I hope so," Roedor said, offering a tired smile, "I certainly hope so."

They stayed hidden up in the rocks, and in a few minutes the old goat tender came riding through the canyon at a fast trot, holding his floppy hat down on his head. Then, in another moment, Homer waved his hand, signaling the men to move out. They eased slow and silent from their positions, back up to the rim of the canyon, where one of the men had stayed, guarding their tired horses.

"Once again you have brought us through," one of the men said. The others nodded and commented among themselves. More and more Homer Corona had proved himself a good leader.

"We still are not out of danger," Homer said. His eyes moved up, following the drifting smoke above the ruins. "Soon the army will circle up from the canyon and come back to investigate the explosion. We must move farther up where we can see them, but they cannot see us." He pointed to an upthrust of jagged rock that looked impossible to climb. "We go up there."

The men looked at the steep climb before them, their eyes tired but willing; with their reins hanging from their hands, they trudged on across the narrow width of flat rock shelf and struggled upward, Homer and Roedor in the lead. Halfway up they stopped and looked down at the two riders on the winding trail. Behind the two riders, they saw the old goat tender, farther back but gaining on them, leaving a wake of dust, his hand still clamped down on his hat.

In the deep canyon northwest of them, they saw the army patrol struggling across rock, brush, and downed juniper and pinyon trees, their broken ranks scattered out in a long, straggling line. Homer shook his head. "If there were riflemen along the canyon walls, those soldiers would be sitting ducks. What kind of leader would put his men in such danger?"

Roedor shrugged and said in a quiet tone, "I do not know. But we would never do something so foolish, eh?"

Down in the canyon the freckled-face lieutenant stopped at the head of the strewn-out column and looked back. His face was streaked with dirt and scratched by stiff branches of downed juniper. He turned to a young corporal behind him and said, "Can't we keep this line a little tighter? Think of what would happen to us if we got ambushed, strewn out this way."

"I know . . . but heck, sir," the corporal said, "these men are plumb worn out." He looked around the rocky canyon floor and up at the drift of smoke that had passed unseen above the canyon walls until it drifted across, ahead of them. "Whatever that sound was, I'm thinking it might have been back that way." He thumbed back over his shoulder.

"It's difficult to tell from down here," the lieutenant said. "But we must stay down here until we come to some kind of trail. It only stands to reason that the kind of men we're chasing would be down here . . . where it's extremely difficult to track them. Don't you suppose?" He gazed at the corporal, a little uncertain himself.

"To be honest, sir, I have no idea what men like these are apt to do," the young corporal said, rubbing a gloved hand across his brow. "All I know is, the more I see of these danged badlands, the more I wish I'd joined the navy."

In the ruins JC McLawry leaned forward on his knees, digging hand over hand, throwing the dirt back like a dog. A long string of saliva swung from his gaping lips. He mumbled and cursed under his breath. His fingers struck something hard, and he gasped, running his hands back and forth in a frenzy, brushing dirt aside. *There it was!* The metal buckle on one of the saddlebags. His heart leaped.

JC hurried, no longer realizing that the ranger was out front somewhere this very minute . . . that a shot had rang out. *Who had died out there? Hell! Who cared?* He had the money!

He laughed, an insane wheezing and coughing sound beneath his labored breath. With both hands he wrenched and pulled upward on the leather saddlebags, straining, grunting, until at last they came loose from the earth all at once and pitched him backward. He scrambled back onto his knees, the chain with Ernesto's severed fist in it still swinging back and forth with his every move.

He paused for a second, trying to catch his breath. Noticing the severed fist for the first time, he slung it back and forth until it flew from the cuff, hit the wall, and flopped onto the stone mantel above the old hearth. *Ayii! Son of a bitch* . . . Then he snatched the bags up, hefted them onto his shoulders, stood up, and started to duck out through the rear of the ruins when he heard the ranger call out to him from fifteen feet away.

"JC," the ranger said, "don't you think it's time you stopped all this foolishness? What good's that money going to do you where you're going?" He wagged his pistol barrel toward the dirt. "Now pitch it down. Let's get started back to prison. I got more important things to do."

JC staggered in place, the saddlebags feeling heavy on his shoulders, sweat running down his dirt-streaked face. He stared at the ranger for a second, at the big pistol pointed at him. His breath pounded in and out of his lungs. A strange look came over his face as he moved his gaze past the ranger and saw Samuel Burns behind him and three feet to the side, his pistol also raised and cocked.

"*Ha*— Prison? Me?" JC chuckled.

"That's right, JC," the ranger said. "Pitch it down, or I'm going to shoot you right here and now."

"Uh-uh." JC shook his head. "I don't think so, old man. Not today! There's one thing you haven't seen coming." He gazed past the ranger again, at Samuel Burns, Burns wearing a strange smile, the pistol tight in his hand, casting a glance toward the ranger's back, then over to JC.

The ranger noted the look in JC's eyes, but didn't seem bothered by it. "I see everything coming," he said; he sighted the pistol on JC's chest.

JC jiggled the saddlebags on his shoulder, staring past the ranger at Samuel Burns. "Here it is! All ours, Sammy-boy! Send this fool to hell, where he belongs! Pull that trigger, pull it *now*!"

Samuel Burns's smile widened, his eyes dark and gleaming. "Sure thing, *amigo* . . . don't mind if I do." Before the ranger could turn, Burns squeezed the trigger and felt the pistol buck in his steady hand.

The ranger braced tight at the sound of Burns's pistol shot behind him and stared straight ahead at JC McLawry. "Umm-um," he said, shaking his head slowly, watching JC's leg flip backward out from under him, then going down with a loud scream until the sound of it muffled short when his mouth hit the sandy dirt. He stepped forward to JC, shooting Burns a glance over his shoulder, and saying, "Sam, we're going to have a talk about the way you handle prisoners."

"Lord-God!" JC writhed and rolled in the dirt, the saddlebags coming off his shoulders, his hands going to the deep bullet hole in his leg—the same leg Burns had grazed before. Blood spurted.

"Come on now, JC," the ranger said, lifting him by his shoulder, "it won't hut no worse, whether you're lying or standing." He chuckled a little. "I told you before, you better quit aggravating this man. Burns has had a bellyful of you and your *desperado* ways."

"Damn you, Burns!" JC sobbed and screamed. "You lied! You tricked me! We had it all! Was supposed to be *amigos*! You dirty little—"

"Now now . . . calm down, JC," the ranger said, shaking him back and forth by his shoulders. "There's no need in resorting to rude talk here." He looked over at Burns, who had holstered his pistol and bent down beside the saddlebags. "Sam, did you mislead this poor man in any way? Make some sort of promise that might have gotten his hopes up?"

Burns looked up at the ranger, smiled, and turned back

down to the saddlebags. "Well, I might have, just a little. I figured if Caslado would tell us where his brother was headed, it would get us here quicker. And it did." He jerked back and forth on the metal strap buckle, freeing it of packed dirt. "I also wanted a good reason to beat the hell out of JC every now and then on the way here." He opened the strap, glaring at JC, and jiggled the dirty saddlebags. "How does it feel, JC . . . being lied to by somebody who's supposed to be your friend?"

JC stood sobbing, blood running down his leg. "But this time I wasn't lying, Sammy-boy! Couldn't you tell? This time I was being honest."

"We'll never know now, will we?" He held the bags upside down and shook them. Sand and loose rock poured out in a long, steady stream. Burns let it run through his fingers, looking up at JC with the same dark gleam in his eyes.

"And there's your train robbery money," the ranger said, giving JC a tight smile. He shook his head. "It's enough to make you bitter, ain't it."

"That dirty bastard, Ernesto!" JC slumped, shaking his dusty, sweaty head. "I never should have trusted that rotten, lying crook."

"If you ever get out of prison and decide to be a *desperado* again," the ranger said, "the first thing you better learn is that you can't trust another *desperado*. Come on now, let me help you," he added, pulling him forward, then looping one of JC's arms across his shoulder. "I can't waste any more time here. Gotta patch your leg wound up and get moving." He thought about Maria, back there somewhere, not wanting to wonder whether she was dead or alive.

Chapter 24

"Whoever is in there, come out with your hands high!" Rance Plum called out into the ruins, as Burns and the ranger helped JC limp through the settling dust. Burns almost stopped at the sound of the voice, but the ranger kept moving forward. JC hung between them, his arms spread across their shoulders. He sobbed under his breath, and blood ran down into his boot and squeezed out through the sole with each halting step.

"Come on," the ranger said. "I know that voice. It's Plum. He won't shoot us. He's lucky he hasn't shot himself by now."

As they neared the front of the ruins, a shriek of delight resounded along the walls, followed by a peal of laughter. "It's Ernesto's body!" Plum hooted. "He wasn't blown up!"

The ranger smiled over at Burns, and as they moved forward, he said, "See? Plum's a happy man now. He'll collect his reward, and head for New Orleans, I expect."

"You never claim the reward for yourself?" Burns asked, looking across JC at the ranger.

"Naw. I get paid by the month, not by the job. That much cash all at once can cause a man to do stupid things. Right, JC?" He smiled, moving along. JC only groaned, his sweaty head lowered.

"There you are, you wonderful ole rascal you!" Plum spread his arms and stepped toward the ranger. Behind

Plum, Jack the Spider stooped over Ernesto's body and rolled his face to one side with the toe of his boot.

The ranger raised his free hand toward Plum, keeping him at bay as Plum tried to throw his arms around him. "If you want to show your appreciation, Plum, just help Sam here get JC's leg bandaged. I've got to get a move on."

"Oh? Going right after the rest of those Mexicans, I suppose?" Plum smiled at him with a look of newfound admiration, now that he had Ernesto's body.

"No. Those boys aren't going to cause any more trouble unless it's forced on them. Caslado used them, bad, and they know it now."

He thumbed toward the trail leading back to San Paulo. "Maria's back there somewhere. I think she might be in danger."

Plum settled as they sat JC down on a pile of crumbled adobe blocks. "I fear you may be too late, sir," he said, a grim look coming into his eyes. The old goat tender had caught up to Plum and Spider as they entered the ruins. Now he'd stepped down from his winded horse and came over to the ranger.

"I'm afraid he's right," the old goat tender said, nodding at Plum as he spoke to the ranger. "I think that priest she'd been riding with might be Crazy Gravy, the madman."

"I know," the ranger said. "I figured it out on the way up here."

Standing over at Ernesto's body Jack the Spider called out, "How'd you manage to shoot this man in his mouth? Was he yawning?"

They all turned and saw the Spider holding Ernesto's head up off the ground. "I didn't shoot him," the ranger said. "He shot himself, after cutting his brother's throat."

"My goodness." The goat tender scratched his beard. "That's the second one . . ."

The ranger started to ask him what he meant, but Plum cut

in before he got the chance. "Cut his own brother's throat? See?" Plum spread his hands. "People like these simply kill one another for no reason at all."

"You have no idea what the reasons were, Plum." The ranger thought of the killings at Cold Creek, the dead woman with the baby inside her, and remembered the look in Ernesto's eyes after he'd killed Ramon and put the barrel of the derringer in his mouth.

"Nevertheless," Plum huffed, nodding toward Samuel Burns, who attended to JC's leg wound, "that's why I've been telling you not to trust this young man."

"I've trusted Sam Burns with my life more than once since this all started," the ranger said. "You better be careful what you say to him from now on, Plum. He's developed quite a knack for shooting people in the leg."

"Well . . . be that as it may . . ." Plum looked around at the carnage, wanting to say no more about Burns, as Burns looked over at him with a dark gleam in his eyes. "What was the explosion we heard? It sounded like dynamite."

"Yep." The ranger looked around. "Evidently, Ernesto set a trap for whoever might come here looking for the money. Pretty clever if you think about it. I believe he might have told me where it was . . . if I had pressed him about it . . . the night I talked to him in his cell. Good thing I wasn't a greedy man."

Plum's eyes widened slightly as some dark possibility ran across his mind. "I . . . I almost visited him myself, to ask where the money was hidden," he said, swallowing hard, glancing again at the dead and all the upturned earth and rock. One of Earl Jaffe's boots lay twisted and smoking on the ground. "But I just assumed he wouldn't tell me."

The ranger smiled. "As it turns out, I'm sure he would have."

The goat tender looked at the pale color on Plum's face and chuckled. "Speaking of money, looks like we'll all three be taking Ernesto's body back to the warden." He rubbed his hands together. "Can't wait to get my hands on that one thousand dollars. Figure on getting me some ammunition, a couple of good firearms . . . go into this bounty-hunting business full time."

"Oh? Indeed?" Plum stood tapping his gloved fingers on his pistol belt.

"Yep," the goat tender said. "I already seen it don't take no genius to make a good living at it."

"You don't honestly expect us to share that remaining three thousand dollars with you, do you?"

"Damn bet I do." The goat tender nodded. "You gave your word, and that's good enough for me."

"See. Plum, you idiot!" The Spider called over from beside Ernesto's body. "I said you shouldn't have told him that!"

The ranger looked at Plum. "Is that true? You promised this man a share in the reward?"

Plum shrugged. "Perhaps I may have mentioned something to that affect . . . but if so, it was only some trivial reference, made during the heat of the chase . . . certainly nothing I actually intended on doing, of course."

"Bullshit!" The goat tender stepped toward Plum, but the ranger stepped between them.

"I have no time to waste here," the ranger said. "If you promised this man a third, then he gets it. If not, I'll take Ernesto's body back myself and keep the whole thing. Is that clear, Plum?"

Plum seethed, but his hand dropped away from his gunbelt.

"Now, hold on," the old goat tender said, his voice softening a bit. "I don't want to keep you from searching for Maria." He turned to Plum and added, "And I don't want no hard feelings with you and Mr. Spider, especially since we'll be in the same business from now on. If you're willing to take Ernesto's body back by yourselves, maybe I can come down a little on my share of the reward." He cocked his head to one side and waited for Plum to respond.

Plum eased a bit, thinking about the five hundred dollars in his sour-smelling boot. "What kind of figure are we talking about here?"

The old man rubbed his chin whiskers. "Let's say, just to clear accounts, instead of one thousand, I'll take eight hundred cash, in hand, right now—with the ranger as a witness that it's all on the up and up? How does that sound to you?"

"Not a chance," Plum said, feeling crafty all of a sudden. "I'd say, for no more than you've done, *four* hundred should be more than adequate." He arched his brow and waited.

"I'm not much at dickering, and the ranger here needs to get on his way," the goat tender said. "I asked for eight, you offered four. Let's just split the difference. And that comes to?"—he counted back and forth on his rough thumb and fingers for a few seconds—"five hundred dollars." He nodded. "Yep, five hundred dollars, and Ernesto's all yours."

"Wait a minute," the ranger said, shaking his head, "the split between four and eight doesn't come to—"

"Then five hundred it is," Plum said, cutting the ranger off, seeing a way to beat the old man out of a hundred dollars. He reached out and shook the goat tender's hand in a hurry. "Five hundred and you're out of the picture."

The ranger looked from one to the other, then said to the goat tender, "Are you sure this is agreeable to you? I don't have all day to stand around here—"

"Of course, it's agreeable to him," Plum snapped, cutting him off again. He'd already dropped to the ground and started taking off his sour-smelling boot. "We shook on it. A deal's a deal!" He swatted a fly away, rolled down his dirty sock, and took out the folded dollar bills from against his ankle. When he stood up and handed the goat tender the money, Plum smiled over at Jack the Spider and said, "I'm sure you have no objections, do you, Mr. Spider?"

The Spider only grumbled, spit, ran his hand across his mouth, and looked away.

Nearly an hour had passed before Rance Plum and Jack the Spider had thrown Ernesto Caslado's body over his horse, made themselves ready for their journey, and moved away onto the thin dusty trail back toward the stone bridge. No sooner were they out of sight when the goat tender chuckled under his breath and shook his head as he stepped up into his saddle.

"You realize what you did, on splitting the difference with them, don't you?" the ranger asked, helping Burns push JC up onto his horse. Four horses that hadn't been killed by the blast milled close by. The ranger had stripped their saddles and bridles and slapped their rumps, but they'd moved away only a few yards and grazed on clumps of grass.

"Yep," the goat tender said, "I know that the difference between four and eight is six, not five. My arithmetic ain't all that bad."

"Then why'd you do it?" The ranger stepped up into his stirrups and looked at the old man. Beside him Burns had stepped up, sat down into his saddle, and had the reins to JC's horse in his hand.

The goat tender grinned across stained, broken teeth. "Because I figured five hundred in hand is worth more than what they're apt to get back at the prison." He pushed up his floppy hat brim. "Once I took the other prisoners back and got paid, I told the warden what you said about keeping Burns here with you for some questioning . . . and danged if he didn't go back behind the wall a few minutes later and blow his brains out too, no different from Caslado."

"You mean . . . ?" The ranger's words trailed.

"Yep. It'll take Plum at least six months to get their money, if they're lucky enough to get it at all." He chuckled.

The ranger stared at him for a second, thinking about the warden. Then he shook his head and said, "Guess he couldn't face what would come down once the truth was known that he'd been in on the prison break."

Burns looked stunned. "You mean the warden was *in* on the prison break? Had a hand in the whole thing?"

"I knew it as soon as you told me he gave you the key, Sam," the ranger said. "You were being played by everybody involved." He turned slightly, looked at JC, then back to Burns as JC hung his head. "That's the only reason I didn't send you back with the other prisoners to begin with . . . figured the warden would find a way to kill you before you had a chance to tell how everything happened."

"Jesus. What a fool I've been." Burns rubbed his forehead with his free hand.

"Don't feel too stupid, Sam," the ranger said. "In a case like this everybody's out to use everybody else." He gazed away for a second, out across the rugged land, then back. "Just call it staying alive in a land where everyone has to feed on one another."

"If you know so much, ranger," JC said, "where's Caslado's hidden money? That's all I was after to begin with."

"Oh, it's here somewhere. Ernesto wasn't about to give it up. But you could hunt for it a hundred years and never find it. Someday, somebody'll happen onto it . . . somebody who wasn't even looking for it in the first place. That's usually the way it goes."

"Ain't that the danged truth," the goat tender chuckled. "A man would be *loco* to search a land this large for one little spot with money in it. It'd take a miracle."

The ranger looked at the goat tender as if an idea had just

come to him. "Are you really going into the bounty-hunting profession?"

"I sure am . . . already made arrangements back at the prison settlement for a man and his wife to pick up my goats and keep them." He paused, then added, "I'll miss them goats. But a man has to go where his living takes him, I reckon. I'm getting old, but I've still some miles left in me."

"Are you interested in taking on a partner?" the ranger asked.

The goat tender's eyes lit up. "Why, sure! Between the two of us, we could make—"

"Not me," the ranger said, cutting him off. He nodded at Samuel Burns. "Sam's a good man . . . he's got a lot more miles left in him than you and me put together."

The goat tender looked puzzled. "But ain't you going to take him back to . . . ?"

"Naw." The ranger gazed across the badlands. "He don't belong in prison. Anybody can come up wrong once. I can't see where it serves anything to send him back to that kind of life. Let a few years out here be his rehabilitation if he needs any." Without facing Burns, he asked, "How's that sound to you, Sam?"

Burns couldn't answer right away, but JC cut in, saying, "What about me? Why don't I get another chance? I ain't all that bad once you get to know me. I could straighten right up, if somebody would just trust—"

"Shut up, JC," the ranger said. He reached over and took JC's reins from Samuel Burns's hand. "If you hadn't led this young man astray, he wouldn't been here to start with. You and I are headed back to prison. You can think about what you've done for the next ten or so years . . . if they don't hang you."

"Hell, this ain't fair," JC whined.

"I never said it was," the ranger replied. He nudged his

white barb forward, leading JC behind him, JC's hands cuffed to the saddle horn.

"If you don't let me go too, I'll tell them Burns was involved," JC said. "I swear I will! I'll tell them everything!"

"Go ahead," said the ranger. "It'll give you something to do to pass them long days and nights. Far as I'm concerned, Samuel Burns went out looking for escaped prisoners and never returned." He moved his horse farther away, over to the trail winding down into the rock land.

"Ranger, wait," Samuel Burns called out. But the ranger knew there was nothing more to say. Without turning or stopping, he raised a gloved hand for just a second and rode away from the ruins.

Chapter 25

In the hottest part of the afternoon, the goat tender and Samuel Burns rode off in a drifting wake of dust toward the stone bridge. It was no more than right, Burns had told him, that they should go down into the valley, find the army patrol, and lead them back to some sort of trail. With JC in custody and Caslado dead, there was nothing left for the soldiers to do out there. Besides, the army patrol had food and water. Leading them back to San Paulo would be a lot easier than traveling alone. After considering it, the goat tender chuckled and said, "I think we're going to get along fine, you and me . . . partner."

No sooner had their dust settled and quiet once more surrounded the old Spanish ruins, when Homer Corona stood up from the rocks above, looked back higher up at his men, and waved them down. The dusty, ragged men stood up slowly, and after looking around, they led their tired horses down from the wavering heat and into the dark slanted shadows of the crumbling adobe walls. On their way two men broke off from the others, gathered the four loose horses where they stood grazing, and brought them in on a lead rope.

"By the saints," Roedor whispered as they all gathered and looked around at the bodies lying about in the courtyard. For a moment no one said a word. Their reins hung from their hands, and their horses blew and stood with their tired legs spread, froth streaking their haunches.

Finally, Homer took a deep breath, gazed up at the circling buzzards that had swooped in overhead, and said to the others, "Get these bodies moved out of here and cover them with rocks somewhere. Someone might see the buzzards and come to investigate." No one recognized Ramon Caslado's face, lying covered with dark blood and dirt.

Roedor bend down and picked up a piece of shattered rock from the explosion. "Do you think Ernesto had anything to do with this? It looks like some of his handiwork."

"I do not know what has gone on here," Homer said, still looking around. "But I think we must stay here and rest our horses for a full day—maybe more. Then we will forget about finding Ramon Caslado's rancho and slip back to *Mejico*. With all these extra horses we have found, we will be all right. The soldiers will soon tire of chasing their own tails. They cannot track us through the high rocks."

"*Sí*," Roedor nodded. "I will send a man out to search for water. Perhaps he will find something for us to eat as well."

They made camp in the ruins and rested. By evening a small fire had been struck. Above it large chunks of rattlesnake roasted on knife blades and sharpened sticks. A small pool of run-off water had been found less than two miles away, and a detail of men took the horses, two and three at a time, to let them draw water and graze on pale clumps of grass.

Homer and Roedor walked back deeper into the ruins, into the room where Ernesto Caslado's clenched fist lay black and shiny on the stone mantel above the hearth. With his pistol barrel, Roedor raked the fist off onto the dirt floor and looked at it. He saw only a sliver of the shiny broken spur rowel showing between the tightened fingers. After a moment his interest in the severed fist waned, and, not wanting to touch it, he kicked it away and looked at the empty saddlebags lying in a pile of sand and loose rock.

"It would be interesting to know what has gone on here," he said as Homer sat down in the cool darkness and leaned back against the stone hearth. The explosion had loosened some of the stonework on the hearth, and he felt it crunch into place with his weight against it.

"I am only interested in getting everybody back to *Mejico* in one piece," Homer said. He closed his eyes for the first time in what felt like days and let himself drift for a moment. Roedor stole away quietly to let him rest. But as Homer felt himself fade into sleep, he heard the sound of fluttering wings in the hearth above him. Bats no doubt, the explosion having stirred them. Yet as he settled, he heard one of them drop from inside the hearth and land with a soft plop near his leg.

He opened his eyes in the grainy darkness, saw it lying there, and brushed it away with his tired hand. Then he closed his eyes and slept . . . for about thirty seconds. Then his eyes snapped open, stunned; he looked at the body of the bat in the gray light. *"Holy Mother!"* He rubbed his eyes, then cried out through the ruins. "Roedor! Come quickly! All of you! Hurry!"

Even as the men arrived with their pistols drawn and cocked, Homer had stuffed himself up the dirty chimney and hung there with his boots kicking back and forth for a moment. The men froze, their mouths gaping, their eyes wide.

"Turn him loose!" one of them yelled, pointing his pistol at the chimney as if it were a living thing attempting to swallow their new leader whole; and as if the big chimney obeyed and set Homer free, he fell to the stonework and rolled back in a shower of dust and fluttering dollar bills. Some of the bills were bundled, and they fell and bounced off Homer's chest with a soft thud; others were loose and floated down in the looming dust like large green months.

A sound came from Roedor's throat, a tight shrill that squeezed itself from deep within his broad chest. His pistol dropped from his hand, and he sprang forward, lifting Homer to his feet with one hand, while tossing money into the air with the other. The men looked at one another in awe. They stepped forward with caution until they fingered some of the dollar bills and saw that it was not something to be frightened of. Then they fell as one, laughing and yelling, and rolled in the dirt with the money, until at length Homer settled them and himself and asked, "Is someone on guard out front?"

"No," Roedor said, his breath flat and strained, "all of us came running to see what was wrong." Then he pointed to two men and without a word sent them scurrying toward the front courtyard with their rifles across their chests.

Homer rose to his feet and moved back and forth, his hands to his temples. One of the men asked, "We are rich now, eh?"

"No." Homer stopped and looked back and forth among them. "None of us are rich because of this. What we do, we do in the name of freedom for our people. This money belongs to them." He looked around again. The men nodded, but some of them seemed hesitant. "Once we provide for our people, we will use much of this money to arm ourselves and our villages."

"But perhaps we could use some of it . . . just a little?" One of the men pinched his thumb and finger together to show just how little he meant. "Just enough to drink for a day or two . . . to celebrate our good fortune?"

Homer shot him a stern glance, and the man shied back. But in a second Homer's expression lightened, then a smile spread easy and wide across his face. "Once we are safely out of this dangerous country, I don't think our good people would mind if we celebrate." He too pinched his dirty thumb and finger together. "Just a teeny bit, eh?"

When they'd settled down, they divided the money into several small bundles for each man to carry until they returned home. Afterward, as Homer and Roedor sat alone in the rear of the ruins, Roedor asked why he had not kept the whole amount of money together, and one man be appointed to carry it. Homer said, "Then what happens if we run into trouble and something happens to that man? We lose all the money."

"I see," Roedor said, nodding. "But what if we cannot trust some of these men with the money? What if they desert us?"

"If we have men like that among us, it is worth an amount of money to know it. How can we later trust one another with our lives, if we cannot first trust one another with money?"

"Ahhh, *sí*, Roedor said, tapping a finger to his head, "you have already done much thinking about this."

"No. This is only common decency . . . if a man has to give much thought to such a thing as this in order to understand it, then perhaps something was missing inside him the day he was born." He smiled at Roedor. "You understood it as soon as it was said to you, *sí*?"

Roedor thought about it for a second, then chuckled, "*Sí*, but I did not know it until you brought it to my attention."

Homer sat back again against the stone hearth. "Perhaps that is what all our lives must be about," he said, "each of us understanding common decency and bringing it to one another's attention." He relaxed, looking about the ruins and thinking of all that had happened since he'd crossed the border into America. "Do you think everybody here lives this way? Always so unpredictable?"

"I have heard that they do," Roedor said with a slight shrug.

"Well, then I will be happy when we get back to our beloved *Mejico*. This America is a wild and beautiful place to come and see, but I do not think I would want to live here." He sighed and closed his tired eyes.

Fifteen miles from the ruins, in the fading light, the ranger sat his white barb at the crest of a high, rocky bluff and gazed down at the thin stream of dust on the flatlands below him. JC sat in silence behind him, atop his horse with his head lowered, his horse's head lowered as well. The ranger squinted at the stream of dust for another second, then drew the big rifle from its scabbard, wiped the scope, and gazed through it. What he saw caused him to bolt upright in his saddle.

"Sit tight, JC," he said, and he slipped down from his saddle, put a cartridge in the big rifle, steadied it across the top of a rock, and sighted down again. He took his time, scanning the horse in front, making sure it was the one the priest had ridden into San Paulo, then back to the second horse and the blanket-wrapped body lying across it. His heart sank.

He fought back the sickness and rage in his chest and lined the scope up onto the low crown of the priest's wide-brimmed hat. Beneath it the faded brown frock lapped back in the onrush of wind. *Time to pay up, Crazy Gravy* . . . He leveled down, tight and steady, taking a breath and holding it, as his finger touched back on the trigger.

In the second that the ranger made the shot, JC kicked his horse forward, spinning it and bolting away. And in the same second, the ranger felt himself flinch, saw the shot go wide and kick up a spray of sand near the horse's hooves. He turned, already reaching into his vest pocket for another round, and saw JC disappear around a turn in the trail. He reloaded the rifle, turning back toward the target below him, and saw the rider sway as the lead horse shied away from the kick of sand. JC was gone, but this couldn't wait. *I've got you this time* . . .

Now he hurried, seeing the low-crowned hat turn back

and forth, searching the badlands. The ranger settled tight and quick, steadying down with the rifle stock to his cheek, his crooked thumb locking his cheek in place. He took a breath and held it, seeing the bead stop and fix on the target. His finger touched back on the trigger.

But then he stopped, seeing the hand come up and peel the hat away. As Maria shook out her long hair and glanced once more across the land and up toward him, the ranger felt his knees go weak. "Oh, God," he whispered, letting the rifle slump against the rock, as if he lacked the strength to hold it.

On the flatlands Maria stepped her horse back and forth, pulling the other horse with her. Both horses stirred up a low swirl of sand, and she fanned it away, searching upward among the rocks to a dark line along the high bluff. She let out a tense breath, seeing the small figure standing there at the crest, the rifle waving back and forth above his head.

"You could have shot me, you know," Maria said after they'd met halfway along the trail. He turned her loose from against his chest and looked at her, arm's length from him. After a moment she said in a quiet tone, "So now you have lost a prisoner. What will people say when they hear about this?" A slight smile moved across her lips.

"Don't start on me," he said, returning the smile. "He'll show up before long—we haven't seen the last of that blue star tattoo. I hate to think what would have happened if he hadn't caused me to flinch and miss my shot. What in the world are you doing wearing that frock and hat anyway?" he asked as they walked to the blanket-wrapped corpse across the horse's back.

"My clothes were covered with his blood, so I wore his." She shrugged.

"Even your hat?" He spoke over his shoulder, unwrapping the blanket and flipping it open. Flies lifted in a black swirl.

"Yes, even my hat. I had my clothes and hat beneath the blanket when he lunged at me."

The ranger winced at the sight of the blue corpse with the stub of a sharp tree branch stuck through its chest. "Couldn't just shoot him, huh?"

"He unloaded my pistol while I slept. Somehow I think he was around earlier and cut a strand of my hair." Her hand went to the back of her head. "I found a braided length of hair in his pocket." She patted the side of the faded brown frock. Dust stirred.

He shook his head. "What bothers me is that neither of us saw it coming . . . never had a notion that he might be Crazy Gravy. He made the sign of the cross backward, you know. That's what made me wonder about him."

"That means nothing," she said.

"Ernesto said it meant he was marked by the devil," the ranger said.

"Ah—" She tossed a hand. "That is only foolish superstition, something the old folks talk about on winter nights when they have nothing else to do."

"I know," he said, "but still I should have caught on sooner. It was Crayton Gravely's way of thumbing his nose at us, I think."

"Perhaps," she said, "but we will never know."

The ranger flipped the blanket back over the hollow-eyed blank face of the madman and looked off across the long black shadows of late evening. "Maybe I'm starting to slip," he said. "Maybe I'm getting too old for this kind of work."

"*Sí*," she said with her slight smile, laying her head over against his shoulder. "I think that is it. A younger man would have never been tricked by something like this . . . and he would have cleaned up these badlands in half the time."

"Don't start on me," he said again, drawing her closer

against his side. "To tell the truth, I was worried sick about you. Wasn't nothing I could do but stay my course and ride things out."

"I know," she said. "I expected no less of you. As you can see, I did well on my own."

"Yep. And I expected no less of you. But I like it better when we work as a team."

They gathered their horses, and on the way to a thin stream he'd spotted earlier from atop the bluff, she told about what had happened with Crazy Gravy, about how he thought he was a panther, and about how once she'd seen that he had unloaded her pistol and what he was about to do, she slipped one of the tree branches beneath her blanket. When he lunged at her like a cat, she simply raised the sharp end of the branch, held the other end firmly under her arm, braced it against the ground, and let his own weight impale him on it.

She did not tell the ranger that she had lain there naked before him, because while she'd only done it to distract the madman, she knew the ranger would consider it immodest. So why mention it?

"As it turned out," she said when she'd finished her story, "in the end he was only one more small monster in a world of so many." She shrugged. "When you've seen one monster, you've seen them all."

"Yep," he said, seeming to like her bold fearlessness. He nodded and told her of all that happened with him and Samuel Burns since last she'd seen him. When he finished telling her about all the twists and turns, the double-crosses and betrayals, he stopped his horse beside her and let out a breath.

"Strange, ain't it?" He wagged a gloved thumb back toward the body on the horse behind them. "One man destroyed himself by thinking he was an animal when he wasn't . . . and back there, more men met their ruin by think-

ing they weren't animals, when their every act only proved
that they were."

She did not answer, but only nodded. They rode on in silence until they came to where the land dropped to the low
banks of a thin stream. The ranger stopped his white barb
again and said to her in the grainy light, "Go on ahead. I'll
catch up in a minute." Beneath him the white barb with its
black-circled eye stepped high-hoofed in place beneath him.
She gazed back at the harsh land blackened by night for a
second, then with a nod of understanding, she turned and
rode ahead.

When she was nearly out of sight, the ranger turned toward the badlands and sat listening to the silence before
him, feeling for something out there in the black holes in the
distant sky, where a whole lesser world than man's would
now come forward and take from one another the stuff on
which it fed. A violent place—the badlands where the rules
of living remained forever simple and harsh.

*Yet, how peaceful now, the ringing silence of this stark
and rugged place* . . . No unrest there, now that man and
man's trouble had come and gone.

He understood this land and what it said to him; he felt
akin to it somehow—its motion, its thinking, its pulse beat,
its blood. Its voice and his were one and the same.

"Let's head for home, Black-eye," he whispered. He
turned the white barb and put it forward on the thin trail with
a touch of his heels . . . the land having said its piece.

Read on for a sneak peek at

HARD JUSTICE

the Ranger's newest adventure,

coming from Signet in Spring, 1999

Once the doctor at Bannet had cleaned and dressed the bullet graze on the ranger's side to Maria's satisfaction, the two of them headed out onto the upward slope of flatland north of town. For three hours that evening they followed the tracks of the Bannet stagecoach until the shadows of night grew long across the trail. They made camp alongside the wagon tracks, spent the night, and at first light the next morning set out again, the tracks leading them ever upward into the rocky badlands.

It was afternoon when they rounded a turn between two large boulders and the ranger spotted a big, dusty stagecoach horse grazing on a clump of grass alongside the trail. This was the safety horse that the stage always brought with it over the rough stretch of rocky terrain between Bannet and Circle Wells, in case one of their regular horses faltered on them, pitched a shoe, or picked up a sharp stone in its hoof.

From the looks of things, this extra horse was all that had survived whatever deadly game had played itself out here on the high switchbacks of the badlands hills.

With its broken lead rope pulled down sidewise and dangling in the dirt, the safety horse raised its head and sniffed toward the ranger and Maria as they rode closer. Past the safety horse, the wheel tracks they'd been following snaked forward another forty feet, then took a sharp turn off the trail and over the edge of the canyon. Found it . . . The ranger let out a breath, stilled himself, and prepared his mind for what would come next.

He knew what to expect at the end of those wheel tracks. Indeed, this *wasn't* his *first* missing stagecoach. Somewhere below on the canyon floor would lie the broken, splintered remains of man's toil and handiwork. Whatever care and craftsmanship had gone into creating the old high-spring Studebaker comfort coach would now be reduced to twisted steel and shattered rubble—these elements to succumb at length and wed themselves into the greater element of earth around them.

Now its handiwork from hell, he thought, looking around, trying to picture the dark scene the way it had happened. His mind caught the sound of gunfire and screams; he saw the frightened horses plunging out into clear, thin air, their bodies writhing, their hooves struggling to take purchase beneath them but finding none. Nothing lay below them but a long drop into endless death as they whinnied loud and long to a silent sunlit sky.

As his dark thoughts and darker images settled, above the canyon buzzards circled and dipped down out of sight. Beyond them in the far distance, a thin gray cloud streaked on the southern horizon. Weather coming from a long ways off.

The horse he rode was a hard-boned white Spanish barb with a black circle around one eye. He stopped his horse on the trail, and turned back to Maria as she looked past him at the safety horse and shook her head. She heeled her bay gelding and rode forward to him.

"Looks like a rough one." He ran a gloved hand along the white barb's damp withers, patting it, settling it. The white barb stepped high-hoofed in place, feeling edgy, wanting to move on. The ranger stiffened the reins and checked it down.

Maria lifted the brim of her Stetson, let air under it, then adjusted it back onto her head. "This is all so ugly, so sense-

less. If they only wanted money, why didn't they just take it
and go?" She gestured a hand along the trail behind them.
"Why all this?"

Envelopes from a spilled mail bag fluttered in the hot
breeze. Pillaged baggage lay scattered along the trail. A hundred yards farther back, they'd found the opened strong box,
where in a last desperate attempt to save themselves, someone, most likely the shotgun rider, had hurled it from atop
the stage.

The ranger did not answer her, but instead only looked at
her for a second before turning away. He heeled the white
barb forward to a small dust-covered object lying in the
middle of the trail where the stagecoach had taken its sharp
turn. He stepped down as Maria moved her horse closer, and
when he'd picked up the crumpled rag doll and shook it free
of dust, he almost wished he'd kicked it to the side—hidden
it from her somehow.

She had asked him why. But to him the why was not important. She knew why . . . so did he. The men who'd forced
that stagecoach off the edge of the canyon were not sea-
soned professionals. He pictured the faces of the three
drunken cowboys he'd killed back in Bannet—how the one
had bragged about robbing the stagecoach. *Stupid, violent . . .* This Half Moon Gang. Whoever they were, they
were newcomers to crime, still learning their trade. *Sloppy
at their work . . .*

Instead of why he thought about who, and he tried to get
an image of the kind of men who would do such a thing.
These were all young men, he figured, young and wild and
not very smart—like the ones back in Bannet. No doubt
they'd fueled themselves on hard liquor first, something to
raise their courage and at the same time keep them from seeing themselves for what they really were. These men would
be snakes and cowards of the lowest order. He'd bet on it.
They hadn't been at this gruesome business long—but

they'd been at it long enough that money alone no longer mattered to them, if it ever had in the first place. These men hadn't been hurting for money . . . he'd bet on that too.

How did he come to see all this about them, from one lone safety horse and a set of stage tracks? He had no idea, gazing down at the dusty rag doll in his gloved hand, turning it, pressing it slightly, feeling its soft body give beneath his thumb. But this was the picture he conjured up from his instincts, and he wouldn't second-guess it. His instincts seldom steered him wrong. These men were strictly out for blood sport. Money had been only the twisted justification for their deed, merely the kindling that sparked the fire inside them.

Dangerous young men . . .

Now that their fire had spilled out and touched the world around them, it would feed on, raging out of control until someone dropped a hammer on them. Well, that would be his job—his role in this streak of madness. And he had no qualms about it as he studied the rag doll in his gloved hands, its flat stitched smile, its blank button eyes. Somewhere below, over the edge and down on the canyon floor, lay the cold tiny hands that had nurtured this doll. He gazed away and swallowed hard, and made what outward expression he needed before turning back to Maria.

Maria had been been with him only a short time. While she'd seen her share of outlaws and hardcases, she was still stunned by senseless brutality of this sort. But the ranger had long lived close at hand to men like these. In a dark world of bloodshed and violence, he had long come to reconcile within himself, as all lawmen must, that there were no boundaries—no bottom to the lower depths of man's depravation.

He no longer asked himself why, and now he no longer wondered who. All he cared about now was when. When could he get these men in his gun sights. The when part couldn't come soon enough to suit him.

Early on, as a younger man, when he'd taken on the mantle and calling of the law, he'd made up his mind that man's action and deeds would not shock or surprise him, and it hadn't yet. Perhaps this resolve was all that had kept him alive many times throughout his life, up on the high badlands. To be shocked or surprised by the action of man left him at a disadvantage of sorts, he'd always thought. In his business he could not afford to be at a disadvantage.

He acknowledged that man at his best was by far God's most noble creature, yet he accepted that at his worst man was the true incarnation of all demons the imagination could conjure up from its darkest depth. Man was still the only species he'd ever encountered who killed simply for the sake of killing. There lurked in man a taste for blood and carnage that went far beyond mere survival.

Somehow in man's twisted thinking, taking life bacame a means of righting wrongs done to him—wrongs both real and imagined. When fate, or luck, or circumstance acted in ill favor toward man, there lay a terrible dark force beneath man's outward personage that compelled him toward violence. What other animal possessed such a perverse nature as that? None that he knew of.

Only the devil . . . The devil in skin, he thought, and he ran a gloved hand along the deep scar on his weathered cheek and gazed over to the edge of the canyon. Always, in confronting a gang of men such as these, he found that one stood out foremost in his evil and brutality. Sometimes it was the leader. But not always. With a young upstart gang like this, it could be someone that even the others least expected. Which one would it be? he wondered, already anticipating their capture, already trying to fashion an image of these men in his mind. But why they did it wasn't important. Not now, not ever.

Asking why was merely Maria's first step in accepting the reality of man's latest cruelty to his own kind. He had accepted that reality two days earlier when the stage lines had wired Bannet and reported the stage missing. Any stage could be a fews hours late, maybe even a day. But four days? No, not likely. Four days meant more than a broken wheel or a downed animal, or even a rock slide or a closed trail. He'd known what they would find out here before they'd ever left town.

"You can stay back here and hold the horses." He handed the rag doll up to her.

She held the doll for a second, staring at it with a hollow expression. The she shook her head slowly. "No." And she stepped down from her saddle and let out a breath. "I will see whatever there is to see here, and I will take that picture with me when we hunt these animals down."

"Suit yourself, then." The ranger spoke under his breath, knowing that it would do no good to try to dissuade her.

They led their horses off the trail, following the wheel tracks right to the edge, where the weight of the stagecoach as it shot out into thin air had caused a break in a short pile of loose rocks. Overhead, the buzzards squawked and scolded and batted upward and hovered as if in protest— how dare they disturb what man's dark nature had provided?

"Watch your step," the ranger cautioned, when they'd left their horses back up the steep slope and moved down on foot to the next lower edge. Leaning forward, they looked farther down and saw the strewn wreckage: a dead horse here, another there; the glistening, swollen body of a man whose clothes had been shredded, ripped away, and slung aside by scavengers. The body of another man lay facedown, this one broken and twisted backward at the waist, a length of his raw white spine glistening in sunlight. A black swirl of flies droned above him.

At the next drop to the deep canyon, half of the crushed

stagecoach lay on its side, teetering on the edge of the cliff. A woman's naked arm hung out and over the passenger step. The arm was blood-streaked and bruised, but not swollen like the bodies of the others. The ranger noticed it. "I better get a rope and get down there. From the looks of her, she could still be alive."

Maria stood beside him staring, shaking her head slowly. "But—but how could she be?"

"Hey." He nudged her arm to get her started. "I don't know *how*. That's God's business. It's his game, we're just the players."

"*Sí*," she said, as if snapping out of a trance. "Perhaps if the woman is alive, so is the child."

They hurried, scurrying over loose rock and brush, back up to the horses. "Maybe, but let's not get our hopes up." The ranger glanced back down at the stage, seeing it seem to slip forward an inch or more closer to the edge of the canyon.

At the horses, the ranger took down the rope from his saddle, tied one end of it around an upthrust of rock, made two turns around his saddle horn across the back of his white barb, and pitched out the rest of the coils. With the rope from Maria's saddle tied to the end of it, doubling the length, he stepped down to the next level of the canyon. There he took up the slack, threw the rope around his waist, and stepped down backward feeding the rope hand to hand around him.

Above him, Maria steadied the white barb with one hand on his bridle and her other on the taut rope as if gauging its strength through the tightness of it. Down the steeper slope the ranger moved, through loose rock, through the cloud of flies and the strong smell of death beneath him, until he reached the battered half of the stagecoach.

"I'm there," he called out to Maria, his voice echoing across the open canyon, his boots back-stepping beneath him as loose rocks trickled down off the edge.

At the sound of the ranger's voice, the woman's hand moved. It was only a slight flicker, But that was enough. Hope surged in his chest. "She's alive!" he yelled, quickly taking up the ten or so feet of loose rope beneath him, throwing another turn around his waist and back-hitching it.

Glancing up behind him, he saw where the wreckage had slid forty of more feet, perhaps all at once, perhaps over the course of time since the wreck.

"Hang on, ma'am, I'm coming." He scooted closer to the wreckage, and had just reached up toward the hand, when he saw the coach bob up and down, an inch, just slightly up off the steep ground, suspended, held there only by its weight against a boulder at the canyon's edge. He heard a low groan from inside the wreckage and saw the woman's arm move, the hand trembling as it forced itself to reach out to him.

"Don't move, ma'am!" he yelled. The wreckage raised higher with a creaking sound, then settled an inch. Loose rock spilled from beneath it. *My God!* He dared not touch her yet, lest the shift of her weight send her tumbling over the edge.

He scooted forward, snatching up the broken brake handle from the ground—something to shore up the wreckage long enough to get her out—down to where the front of the coach lay tightly against the boulder. He looked down over the edge. His breath stopped in his chest. *How in the world . . . ?*

The body of one of the team horses lay swaying against the canyon wall, wrapped in a tangle of traces, and harness, impaled on the broken wagon tongue, the narrow strip of steel along the wooden tongue badly bent, some of its rivets gone, but still holding the tongue together. He shot a quick glance to where the back of the tongue and the front of the wrecked coach lay held together by a steel pin. The thick wooden plate on the bottom of the coach was separating farther from its nails and bolts with each bob and sway of the wreckage.

"Ma'am! Lay real still! I'll get you out!" He scooted back up from the edge to the rear of the wreckage where the side of the coach lay crushed, no more than two feet high. He lay flat and looked in, across the splintered remains of a broken seat. And there he saw her lying sidelong and upward, her arm over the edge, still waiting for his hand. "I'm back here, ma'am! Don't move yet. It'll make the stage slide! Lie still!"

He started to ease himself into the crushed wreckage. But at the touch of his hand, it creaked upward and settled forward another inch. He jerked back. "What is going on down there?" Maria called out from above him.

He didn't answer—there wasn't time! He tied a short loop in the end of the rope, lay back down, and pitched it inside toward the woman. "Ma'am, put your hand through the loop! Hurry! You've got to help me!"

Her voice was barely more then a whisper. "My—my daughter."

"What? Is the child in there? Is she alive?" The wreckage creaked up and down, and forward another inch. "Loop it around her!" Again the wreckage creaked and groaned. "Ma'am, hurry! Help me!"

He saw her arm rise, then fall, then reach over the broken seat toward the rope. The wreckage slipped forward an inch, then another. *No time!* He shot a glance up behind him toward the edge. "Hold tight, Maria! I'm going in!"